THE
COMING
OF
THE
KID

Also by Oakley Hall

SO MANY DOORS

CORPUS OF JOE BAILEY

MARDIOS BEACH

WARLOCK

THE DOWNHILL RACERS

THE PLEASURE GARDEN

A GAME FOR EAGLES

REPORT FROM BEAU HARBOR

THE ADELITA

THE BAD LANDS

LULLABY

THE CHILDREN OF THE SUN

as O. M. Hall

MURDER CITY

as Jason Manor

TOO DEAD TO RUN

THE RED JAGUAR

THE PAWNS OF FEAR

THE TRAMPLERS

THE
COMING
OF
THE
KID

A NOVEL BY
OAKLEY HALL

**HARPER & ROW,
PUBLISHERS,
New York**

1817

Cambridge, Philadelphia, San Francisco,
London, Mexico City,
São Paulo, Singapore, Sydney

A portion of the Preface was originally published under the title "The Kid Meets Big Mac" in the anthology *Wonders: Writings and Drawings for the Child in All of Us,* edited by Jonathan Cott and Mary Gimbel, published 1980 by Rolling Stone Press/Summit Books.

"The Coming of the Kid" was originally published in somewhat different form in *TriQuarterly* as "The Kid."

Chapter 1 was originally published in somewhat different form in *TriQuarterly.*

"J. D. Dockerty" was originally published in somewhat different form as "Horseman," and "Lieutenant Grace" was originally published in somewhat different form as "Blindman" in *The Antioch Review.*

FIRST EDITION

Designed by Ruth Bornschlegel

Library of Congress Cataloging-in-Publication Data

Hall, Oakley M.
     The coming of the kid.

     I. Title.
PS3558.A373C58   1985   813'.54   85-42568
ISBN 0-06-015465-9

THIS BOOK IS FOR MY GRANDSON,
OAKLEY HALL IV

THE
COMING
OF
THE
KID

Preface

My name is Frank Pearl, and first off I will say something about myself. I am a man that knows being small has disadvantages, that's for certain. Looking another man always in the placket instead of the eye does not give the best impression of human nature, but a small fellow will sometimes notice things that might be beneath a regular-size person. For instance, once when I was making water and eating an apple at the same time, I noticed that the odor of piddle made the smell of that apple stand out, a fine smell that I'd never noticed before. Now a fellow whose nose is further away from his private parts might not have noticed that. Since then I have made experiments with many other varieties of fruit, and I have discovered that it is the peach that smells the most satisfying in this context. I am a born experimenter, with an interest in all natural phenomena (and unnatural too), especially in herbs and medicines. Famous for it in the Territory.

For instance, it was my gunshot salve that saved the Kid's life the time he was shot. It smells bad but it does the work. I did a favor for an old witch doctor up on Shingles Creek, and he showed me some Kimanche herb cures. For gunshot wounds there is a plant of the spurge family you find in warm places in the middle altitudes of the Bucksaws. You wrap leaves mixed with fat inside some larger leaves and cook the whole business, burying it in hot ashes. Then you pound this into a mash with boiled water and apply. I saw this witch doctor operate on five 'manches that had been shot up in a scrape with the cavalry, using just a Barlow knife and his gunshot salves. Two of those fellows survived. It was lucky for the Kid I was by when he was shot up by Big Mac's fellows.

It did seem like the Kid was a long time coming to the Territory, and things had got to a pretty poor pass. You'd see more and more of those black riders, bigger and bigger packs of them galloping with their horses all close-jammed like they all rode with a boot in each other's stirrup, and every day from over beyond Helix Hill the dust and smoke climbing higher and spreading wider so the sun would look like a gone-bad egg through it, some days so thick you would have to beat what we called smust off your clothes with your hat. Every day it was like there was more heat from the mills and machinery so that even streams that were still running ran hot water, and it hadn't rained in the Territory for so long it was like that was a curse Big Mac had put on us too.

You will ask how did we know he was the True Kid, for there had been a couple of likely ones before him that I will not name here, that turned out wrong. Well, Doc Balthazar said of course there would be the Signs; but mostly we would just know. I did not believe him when he told me I was to be one of the Right Bowers the Kid could not do his job without. A little fellow gets used to others funning him. But I was one of them!

In that waiting time I would see the Doc paging worried through his ledgers and histories in that place he had in the back of the wagon, and he would say to me that we must keep faith in our hearts. And that is what we tried to do when things looked dark.

He had different versions of the Kid's birth and kin that he'd collected there. One was that the Kid was treated so cruel by a stepfather that he ran away to join the gypsies, or else was sold to them for fourteen dollars. That was where he learned the crafts and tricks that served him well later on. These gypsies traveled up and down putting on shows in mining camps—knife-throwing exhibitions and roping, which the Kid was especially good at, fortune-telling, monte games, bull-and-bear fights, and such. If the

Kid had an especial friend among the band it was a big grizzly named the Duke of Cumberland. The Kid tended to him, and it was said he could all but talk with that big bear, who later on would turn up to the Kid's advantage when the Kid got into a fix.

Those were times when miners were hard set against foreigners. Fellows with the wrong-color skin or slant of eye were run out of the district, some of them tar-and-feathered, or worse. In one place a mob came against the Kid's band of gypsies, with ropes, and it looked like stiff trouble. But they reckoned without the Kid. He sneaked through that crowd, told the Duke what was wanted, and let him out of his cage. Well, wasn't that a fine show, with the grizzly chasing miners every which way. The Kid was just a lad when he first showed what he was made of, and got his friends out of trouble slick as you please.

The Doc had another story of the Kid's beginnings that gives me the laugh every time I hear it. This one has him floating down the river in a tiny coffin, which a mineowner's wife sees and brings to shore, and she adopts the child. It seems the mineowner's wife already had a daughter, a beautiful fair-haired girl named Flora, and the Kid and Flora were brought up as brother and sister. But the mineowner lost his holdings, he and his wife died of the influenza; and the Kid and Flora were orphaned. They were taken in by a man named Paddleford, who ran an orphanage in that place, and was a kind man, though strict.

The reason that gives me the laugh is because I was the one that delivered Flora, which was recorded by Doc Balthazar in the books he keeps on all things to do with Territorial history: and so I know who Flora's people were, and it was not any busted mineowner and his wife, that is for certain. Still, it is a fact that during the second time Flora was lost for so long, she was at Paddleford's school with the Kid.

There was also a Kimanche chief's son at the school. One day, the river being in flood, he slipped in and was just managing to hold on to a branch to keep from being swept down and drowned in the falls, when the Kid happened by, though on the wrong side of the river. It did look like Jimmy Tenponies was a goner, but the Kid was equal to the occasion, as always.

He was carrying a hank of rope with which he'd been practicing roping tricks, and, quick as lightning, he slung a loop over a high branch of a cottonwood there, and started running around and around the tree, winding the rope up on it. When it was all wound he began running the other way with the rope unwinding and swinging him off the ground and spiraling farther and farther out over the river until he was flying over the far bank, where he let go. He staggered around half drunk for a bit, from all that go-round, but just in time he got hold of Jimmy Tenponies' collar and pulled him to safety. You can believe that lad was grateful, and became the Kid's faithful sidekick until he was carried off by Big Mac.

Though the Kid was not a hardcase-looking fellow, slight of frame and mostly pleasant-tempered, and apt to win the trick by quick thinking instead of violence, he would swell up like a poison pup when he fell into a rage. Those rages would come on him even when he was a little chap. It was like he would be burning with a fever. They would have to pop him into a barrel of stream water they kept under a tree there, along with two other barrels. The water in the first barrel would come to a boil and spurt up. Then they would plunge him into the second barrel, where the water wouldn't boil, though it would turn hot enough to make a man yell if he stuck a hand in it. The third barrel would only come warm enough for bath water.

A fellow would not scoff at this if he had seen the Kid in a rage one time.

The Kid would rage especially if Flora was being fussed. Once at the school an older boy was scaring her, and the Kid went after him. The bully, who was twice the Kid's size, lit out of there for his life. He was halfway across the river before he realized he was running on water, and so he was another one the Kid had to save from the falls downstream.

*   *   *

4

When the Kid was older he was chief boy at Paddle-ford's school, and a great help to the schoolmaster. Once when the orphanage had gone for an outing on the train, he saved the other children from Big Mac's clutches. It was his first meeting with the outlaw chief.

Big Mac's crew had jammed a log across the rails so the coaches were cut off from the locomotive and dumped over on their sides. When those passengers and the orphans from the school climbed out through the windows, they found they were captives of the outlaw band.

Big Mac was sitting on his big black looking over the scene, with half a dozen riders ranged around him. He slumped in the saddle with his eyes sleepy like he'd seen everything there was to see and here it all came past again. His chins ran down to his neck, his belly hung out before him, and his black hat was turned down all around to keep the sun off his face, which was scabby with sun sores and bristling with beard.

People were already so affrighted of Big Mac it was like a sickness on them, and even strong men armed could do no more than herd like a bunch of sheep, women crying out, insulted and worse by those desperadoes, and Mr. Paddleford and the Kid trying to keep the orphans from the school together and their spirits up. Jimmy Tenponies was especially downcast because he had lost the medicine bow and quiver of vermilion-painted arrows his father had given him.

Everyone was set to marching north, very smart, those that couldn't keep up helped along with a slash from a blacksnake whip, and the men and older boys, like the Kid, with their hands tied behind them. That march was pure hell, and that night, which they spent herded into an old corral, the same. But in the dark the Kid slipped over to sit close to Flora, and she managed to help him untie his hands. He ducked out of that place quiet as a shadow. There were a few from the school that thought he had run out on them.

Come daybreak they started on again, and that day there was terrible suffering, everybody whipped along by those blacksnakes, and some of the older folks left behind to perish of thirst in that desert country. It was clear that Mr. Paddleford's orphans would begin dropping soon, but just when everything looked hopeless there was a shout, and coming hard toward them was a cloud of dust, so big, and rising so tall, that it must be cavalry, or a posse at least. Everybody began pointing and rejoicing, though not too loud for fear of those riders of Big Mac's. The dust came closer, and the riders began conferring, the whole bunch gathering around Big Mac, and all at once they all lit out together.

The big dust cloud came on, and the smaller cloud of Big Mac's crew faded off. Then weren't those passengers from the train, who had been captives bound for who knows what abominations, running and cheering to meet their saviors? But it wasn't cavalry, or a posse, it was a herd of longhorns with branches tied on them to scrape up a great dust. And all over the place, waving his hat to hurry along his blown pony and bulldoze those steers into a staggering run, was no one else but the Kid!

It seemed that every woman in that bunch, whether she was a schoolgirl or a grandmother, had to kiss that boy with his shock of fair hair, and those eyes so blue it was said you could chin yourself on a glance from them; though it was Flora that kissed him the longest. And every man had to shake his hand, though it was Jimmy Tenponies who shook it hardest, and slapped him on the shoulder time and again. But the Kid told them there was no time to be lost. They must hurry back to the railroad to the relief train in case Big Mac decided to circle around on them. So they turned back in as great a hurry as they had come this far, the Kid chasing back and forth on one side of the column and the other, hustling them along waving his hat.

And they were not finished yet with Big Mac, treacherous as a rattlesnake that will slip roundabout for another strike. Just in sight of the backing engine and crane that had been sent out to right the cars and repair the track, when that raggedy, cheering bunch of men, women, and children broke into a run, all of them afoot except one sickly girl up on that scarecrow pony of the Kid's, women scampering with their skirts hoisted, and Flora and Jimmy Tenponies holding the hands of the youngest children— just then down off a hill came a pack of riders yelling and quirting, and it was a near thing whether Big Mac's men would cut those poor refugees off from the relief train.

There'd been a couple of sheriff's deputies sent out along, and though they hadn't much enthusiasm for getting into a shooting scrape with Big Mac, they did let off a shot or two, upon which, to everyone's amazement, that unholy dozen turned tail. Meanwhile they all came to safety on the relief train, where there were rifles to pass out. Jimmy Tenponies scouted through the upset car until he found his bow and arrows.

There was a shout, and out in front of the wrecked coaches rode Big Mac on his seventeen-hand gelding, black-hatted and wearing those fringed buckskins that made him look rippling with motion, like pine needles in a good breeze.

He bellowed out that he would like to see the fellow who had tricked him.

There was a good deal of palaver about this. Paddleford and one of the deputies warned the Kid, who was inclined to show himself, that there was no trusting Big Mac and never had been.

But Big Mac yelled that he was unarmed; they had his bond he had no iron about him. The Kid mounted up on the scarecrow horse, and shambled out to meet Big Mac. You could almost hear every last breath sucked in and held at the same instant, while the two horses faced nose to nose, the big black and the pinto that could hardly hold his muzzle up from weariness. And mounted on them that barrel of a scab-faced, whiskered horror, and the handsome lad who couldn't have weighed a hundred pounds dripping wet.

Big Mac said, "You mean you are the one that contrived it? Or is this another trick on me, which is one too many?"

The Kid said he had contrived it.

Big Mac asked him his name, and the Kid told him. Big Mac nodded like he was not apt to forget it, and said, "Well, you have beat me this time."

"Oh, I was pretty lucky," the Kid said, respectful enough.

"I wouldn't lean on my luck again," Big Mac told him.

To which the Kid replied that probably Big Mac wouldn't see him again until he had got his growth. Big Mac could rest easy until that time.

Big Mac made a noise like the air going out of a balloon. He raised in his stirrups so that he towered over the Kid, and all of a sudden there was a blacksnake whip in his hand that he had jerked out of his coat sleeve. The whip snapped around so fast no one could make out what had happened. The Kid didn't flinch and it seemed by some miracle Big Mac had missed him. He sat his pony very straight watching the big fellow spurring away in a flurry of sniping shots from his men hidden behind the ridge. Jimmy, alongside one of the upset cars, had a vermilion-shanked arrow nocked to the head, swearing under his breath in Kimanche for not knowing whether to loose it or not.

When the Kid came back behind the relief train there were some that noticed his face was white as a fish's belly. Paddleford and one of the deputies got him into the cab of the locomotive and away from the people clamoring over him.

He sat down on a wood crate beside the firebox and they helped him off with his shirt. There was a welt around his chest the size of two fingers, like a red snake coiled there, that fine young fellow marked by Big Mac's treachery. The deputy stroked some salve on while Paddleford waved his hands and fluttered like a mother hen. The boy never let out a whimper, staring straight ahead of him into the future with that blue gaze of his, and smiling just a little.

"Well, I guess that is one apiece," he said.

8

While they were tending to the Kid there was a scream, and shouting. Three of those riders of Big Mac's had run in behind the cars, swept Flora up and carried her off.

The Kid leaped off the wood crate with his fists clenched and his face scarlet. You could almost see the steam coming off him. He snatched up a rifle and was aboard the blown pony in an instant. Yelling like a crazy man, he spurred after the desperadoes who had borne the girl away.

He rushed over the ridge and down into a clearing behind it, where he reined up so hard the pony was pulled to his haunches, for he had ridden into an ambush. Big Mac sat his big black with his revolver drawn, and with him were the three others, Flora white-faced up before one of them on his saddle; all of them with guns trained on the Kid. Big Mac's buckskin fringes shivered as he chuckled. It was said he avoided gunshot keeping himself always blurred with those fringes moving like that, so no one could take aim for his vitals because of the blurry motion.

"Drop your piece, if you please," Big Mac said, and the Kid had no choice but to throw down his rifle.

Just then the rider furthest over on the left side disappeared off his horse, which nobody noticed because of their concern elsewhere.

"I believe I can still show you a trick or two," Big Mac said. "Maybe even after you have got your growth."

The Kid did not respond to this, and something that might have been a bird settled on the neck of the next-to-the-end rider, who went down with a horrid gurgle.

Next there was a twang, and an arrow with a vermilion shaft stood out on the neck of the rider who had Flora up before him, both his hands grabbing on to it while he made a noise like a turkey gobbling. Lightning quick, Big Mac spurred forward to clap the muzzle of his revolver to the Kid's temple, his pig eyes twitching this way and that as he shouted, "Call off your dogs or you are a dead man!"

Meanwhile Flora's captor toppled and fell, bearing her

down with him, where she sprawled beside the dead road agent not quite as ladylike as she usually took care to be seen. And just then, with a growl, swarming out of the brush, came a bear bounding like a great, hairy ball, to rise to his hind legs and make one swipe, with a pawful of claws like knives, at the haunch of the black gelding. The horse screamed like a woman, rearing, and bore Big Mac from that place at a dead run, while the grizzly disappeared into the brush and the Kid lit out after Big Mac, jerking his lariat loose from his saddle horn, and swinging a loop.

The loop settled over the outlaw, and the Kid pulled the pony to its haunches to take the shock. Big Mac came out of the saddle with his fringes all a flutter to hang in the air for what seemed like half a minute before he smacked down with a jar to shake his grandmother.

As Big Mac staggered to his feet, groaning and cursing, the Kid was running around him, winding the lariat around him and cinching it tight. Then he mounted again, and with Flora up on her captor's horse, Big Mac at the rope-end lurching behind, and Jimmy Tenponies with his bow coming up to trot alongside, led that little procession back to turn Big Mac over to the deputies at the relief train, who were about as pleased to take him into custody as they would a timber wolf on a short leash. They promised the Kid they would lock him up where the walls were high enough and thick enough, and the iron bars strong enough to hold him once and for all.

And that was the run-in the Kid had with Big Mac before he got his growth.

Doc Balthazar keeps his smutty tales in a separate book, and I will just set one down here that is supposed to explain why Flora was kidnapped so often. You can be certain this story was never told in the Kid's presence. It seemed that as a young girl Flora would bathe in a creek in gold country so heavy-freighted with gold dust washing down from the diggings that she acquired a golden fleece, so to speak. Some men could never deflect their minds from this, once they had heard of it, and especially men who were old, or impotent for one reason or another, for the golden fleece was held to be a certain cure for disabilities of those kinds. Though I have a cure for that which I got from a gypsy woman that sells for three dollars and is worth every penny of it.

The Chinee cook we had then, Wong his name was, but we called him McQueue, did love to hear the tales from that book of the Doc's. McQueue was a fine cook, and clever at cards, and he knew a bit about herbs and natural medicines. He'd catch rattlers and hang them from a hook squirming and throwing themselves this way and that to give you fits. He'd cut open their belly with two slits, take out a little black gland, one from each side, and slup these down like oysters, claimed it kept the eyes sharp. You never saw a Chinaman with eyeglasses, did you? Though he said these glands, maybe they were spleens, were a good deal better from a cobra than a rattlesnake.

McQueue's weakness was smutty tales, which would get him looking sideways and turning red and giggling. The Doc did love to tease him. He'd talk about the Chinee girls he'd known in a special house of them back East, skin like mother-of-pearl, black snapping eyes, hair shiny like it'd been lacquered, etc. These beautiful girls sat around sipping tea just as demure as you please except they didn't have a stitch on them. It had been pure heaven, Doc said, lying around smoking a pipe of opium and these girls giggling and tickling each other if they felt merry, but regular little princesses the rest of the time.

When the Doc said a man could buy one of those girls, trained from a baby in her arts of serving tea and tricks that would nail a man's hat to the ceiling, for just fourteen dollars, that was too much for McQueue, and he almost yelled to inquire where he could get himself a fourteen-dollar girl. That was the rub, the Doc said, travel being so costly. The Shanghai girls were the best. Hong Kong ones just weren't as good, they didn't train them up as well there, though as far as he was concerned you had to be experienced to tell the difference. Of course you had to pay pretty high for the really special ones. These came from a place called Ching Kung. He'd never met one himself, only heard tell of them. McQueue had got to be the color of a brick by now, and he cleared his throat to ask what was special about the really special ones?

The Doc showed him his pressed-together fingers laid sideways. There'd been a tribe of them built that way, he said, almost extinct now, but they'd managed to keep a breed of them going. Most of them had crossed eyes, something to do with the breeding process, though cross-eyes were highly favored in Ching Kung, and in the rest of China too, by those that *knew*. But these ones were rare, and probably cost a man upward of a hundred dollars.

You can imagine McQueue's eyes were crossing by this time, and I was swallowing my tongue to keep from laughing. One day the cook just up and left, and that was the last we saw of him for some time. But if Lieutenant Grace had stayed the course with that rattlesnake-gland cure of McQueue's, I believe he would have had his sight back.

Well, there were no walls high enough or thick enough, nor bars strong enough, to hold the big fellow. It was not long before he was on the loose again, and Jimmy Tenponies was the first to suffer for his part in that humiliation of Big Mac. And so it all came around again, but where was the Kid this time? I confess that I doubted what the Doc had worked out about the Kid coming again, and my part in it. Those were bad times, waiting and fearful and despairing sometimes, trailing around the Territory with the medicine show. Sometimes I would fall into black gloom, and I knew Doc Balthazar would come close to it. We would sit by the campfire of an evening, and, like McQueue and the Chinee girls, I would ask to hear again of the Kid coming, and how I was to be one of the Right Bowers. It was to be my medicines that would cure him up when he got hurt. And it was the Doc who was to be the historian of it all.

And, when time finally passed, and the Kid came back, and his people found him, or him them, then all of it including the Lost Dutchman came to happen just as the Doc had said it would.

ONE

■■■■■■■

Henry Plummer

It is my intention to tell my tale truthfully as I am able, now that the fellow who will kill me is known to be headed for Bright City. And so now I know how Jack Dale felt when he heard I was coming. This one, that they call "the Kid," is thought to be the True and Real thing at last, but I believe that was thought of me also, in my time.

There have been many lies told of me, but a man of consequence enough to have lies told of him ought to be flattered by it. Moreover, any man that has taken pleasure in fine things said of him that were not altogether so has no call to fuss when things turn the other way round. In this respect I was pleased in my young days to be called "Holdfast," and sometimes "the Holdfast Kid," which had some true cause. But now there is a different meaning to it, and people do not call me that to my face. I am a bitter man for what they call me behind my back, tired as I am and my welcome here long ago worn out.

I know it is said that my mother was a whore, and that I was one of her bedmates. The fact of the matter is that I was taken into the bed of the woman who called herself my mother as early as I can remember, and learned between her legs that my whole purpose and reason was to kill the man that murdered my father. Throughout my boyhood time, and even now that I am a man grown and young no longer, that was a perplexing stew, what was so and what my mother's fancies, who was not my mother at all, and whose husband might have been my father or might again have been the fellow who murdered him, so that, as I say, my boyhood time was spent planning vengeance against one man, only, when the desperate moment came, to find I was not sure that he was the right one. This same perplexity has been the ruin of my life. Once it seemed the thing that all men wanted was that I drive Jack Dale out of Bright City, and later on to protect this place from Big Mac's outlaw gang from Putaw Crossing, only to find that that was not sufficient, and in my turn I have become a man they hate and fear and must rid themselves of, like Jack Dale before me, and I have become Holdfast in the other sense of it.

Well, then, what I know is this: my adoptive mother's husband was an older man than she was by many years. His name was Frank Plummer, and hers Clytie. They had no child of their own, and I was acquired as a foundling from some traveling people. Clytie, when she was not pleased with me, would rail that they had paid too much for me. As a boy, when I might have inquired more into all this, I was not much interested in it, or maybe it was an orphan boy's fears that what he will learn will destroy his safe haven. Moreover, when I did question Clytie on certain matters, she was apt to tell the first story that popped into her mind, for she was a born liar and any man was ill-advised to believe her report on anything where there was room for embroidery.

I was brought up to love my foster father and foster mother as my own parents. Though I could not remember Frank Plummer at all, I was sworn and bound to hunt for his murderer, a man named Eubanks, and shoot him down like a dog. Clytie would grieve for her husband most dreadfully sometimes, especially when she had no other man on hand to comfort her loneliness. He had been the most beautiful fellow alive, she would say, with skin on his fundament as fine as suède. Though on other occasions she spoke of him as a mean old man with bad breath who beat her in his jealousy every time she went into town to buy food for supper. This, however, did not alter my responsibility in the matter of his murderer.

I did come to suspect that Eubanks had been Clytie's

lover, who shot Frank Plummer in a quarrel over her favors, which were not worth anyone's quarrels as they were always either for sale or freely given, depending upon the financial situation of the moment. Still, it is a powerful business to imbibe revenge with your food and drink and absorb vengeance in passion's height. They say that a man's character is formed by his early influences, and so mine has become what it is; I am considered to be a natural-born pimp and whorehouse gunman, who marshals the peace in this town I hate and that hates me.

For an angel gone bad will come to look worse than a devil to ignorant fools, and so I know there are many here who would be pleased if Big Mac would come in with his riders all together, to shoot me down and annex Bright City to Putaw Crossing, so to speak. Then these fools would see hell at first hand, and look back on me to say there had been some worth in Henry Plummer after all, who had kept that crew out of Bright City because they were afraid of him.

When I was ten years of age Clytie and I lived in a town called Goldville in the southern foothills. Clytie had a little place slung together out of boards and canvas where she served meals. Little by little it all turned into planking when a sawmill opened up and Clytie became acquainted with the sawyers. Goldville was a place where people didn't have money in the way of ready coin, and transactions went mostly by barter. Those were not bad years for me, with plenty to eat and a warm place to sleep. There was a young schoolteacher in that town, Mr. Paddleford, a tall stoop-shouldered fellow, who spoke so well I knew I would never be satisfied until I could talk half so bookish and high-tone as he did. Clytie made a trade to furnish Mr. Paddleford his dinners so I could attend his school, instead of spending my days throwing my knife at a target painted on a tree. I had been doing this in the knowledge that I must set out to find the man Eubanks when I came of age, and we could not afford to buy cartridges for Frank Plummer's cranky old revolver for me to practice with. Which is also the way the branch was sprung, and it has always been interesting to me that men are scareder of cold steel than of hot lead.

Well, one day in the spring I was along the river with another boy from the school named Bill Mackie, whose father was a miner, and the river was running high with melting snow in the mountains. We boys were chunking rocks in a competition to see which one could throw the furthest, and Billy Mackie flung one too hard for his balance and slipped on the mud bank, and the river sucked him in. I ran along beside him where he was screaming and fighting arms and head above water till I got to a willow tree that hung a branch over the river, and skinned out on that and caught hold of Billy's collar as he came by. I hung there on that limb holding Billy Mackie from drowning for what seemed like an hour, shouting for help, until some men came running. The first one of these was a big fellow named Ted. He is a man I will have more to say about later on. Anyhow, because of that time I came to be called Holdfast.

It was a help to Clytie. Miners began coming to her place to eat because of it. So she got herself a bigger establishment, and there was money to buy cartridges for the old hogleg. I'd go out back of town and blow bottles to smithereens, or keep tin cans jumping, though I always did favor my bowie knife, since I had teethed on it, so to speak. But, although the miners were friendly with Clytie and me, there is a thing I have observed many times in my life, which is that a person you have done a favor for is not always grateful for it, or anyway is resentful because he is supposed to be grateful. So Billy Mackie turned against me. At first he would show this in little ways, but later on it got clearer, until I became his chiefest enemy in the world, and he mine.

As I have said, I had been bedding in with Clytie as long as I could remember, anyway since the time Frank Plummer was killed. I don't remember when the change came. No doubt it was a gradual business, as such things usually are. Clytie would always pretend there was nothing happening, as though that down there was two different people entirely, until at the end she would be grunting in her pleasure, and afterward explaining that this was my great reward for having sworn to shoot Eubanks down in the dirt. As time passed I did come to understand that this was not a proper state of affairs between mother and son, and there would be many nights when I would pretend I had a bellyache and then lie awake on my pallet beside the big bed with its jingling springs until she would inquire if my bellyache was better, and then say why didn't I come in bed anyway to keep her warm, for she had taken a chill walking by the river, or washing dishes after supper, etc. I would get into the big bed to warm her, and nature would take its course. Afterward, I would suffer in my mind. It kept me a skinny boy, small for my age and apt to go to sleep in school, to the displeasure of Mr. Paddleford, who once gave me a lecture on self-abuse, though that was not a vice I ever fell into.

There were times when she would take to drinking whiskey, and often then she would bring a lover home with her. Then I would have to sleep in a kind of lean-to from where I could hear them wrestling, and fierce whispers. Commonly she would have to do with men at her eating place, after it closed and before she came home, and these times if I was called to warm her chills I could always tell if she had had help washing up. She would make fun of me as such a little manny, and say I rattled around like a jellybean in a stewpot.

Once I said that it was a relief to me she was not my mother, really, for otherwise I'd've been upset when fellows said my mother was a bad woman. Though what they said in fact was that she was a whore.

"Who says that?" she demanded, fierce in her indignation. I was lying between her plump legs with my head on her bosom for a pillow.

"Boys at school," I said. "Bill Mackie for one."

"That overgrown ungrateful little bastard. I could tell you a thing or three about his daddy, couldn't I now!" Whatever this was it cheered her up to think of it, and she giggled, shaking like soupstock in a pan. But then she said, "You ought to kill a boy that says nasty things about your mother."

I said I'd thought of it, but he was almost a man grown, a head taller than I was and weighing half again as much; so it was a relief she was not really my mother.

She cussed a little, and then began to sigh and push her breast into my face, stretching. Later on she smoothed down my hair and whispered, "Poor little manny. But I done it all for you. Otherwise we'd've starved, with me a poor widow woman. And never you forget you are honor bound to shoot down that pox-faced T. P. Eubanks that murdered your father, the finest man that ever lived."

I bided my time and took from Bill Mackie and the other school bullies what I had to take, hoping I would soon get my growth and maybe more rest at night so I would be stronger. Clytie took up with a frizzy-haired, wild-eyed stringbean of a fellow called Frenchie, and I was sent to sleep in the lean-to. I must admit I was gnawed at by jealousy at first, but relieved to be shed of my duties too.

Frenchie sometimes gave Clytie beatings when the liquor was on him, and beat me once or twice too. I have never been one to blame a man for what he does when he's in drink. I myself have never taken more than a glass of whiskey at a sitting, but I know many a man drinks to ease his mind of knowing what will be his end, which is carrion buried in the earth for the worms. Even then I forgave Frenchie his drinking, the knocks he gave me, and Clytie's blacked eyes. She was a woman to drive a man to drink with her ways anyhow.

Frenchie had been sold a map of the Lost Dutchman mine, but had found only "rattlesnakes, cactus, and turkey buzzards" as he said, though still sometimes he would pore over the map by lamplight. He also had some property in another mining camp, including a bull-fighting grizzly that could make him a deal of money, he said, if he could just get it back, the difficulty being that he had had to leave that camp in a hurry for his health. He'd left his daughter there with some friends, and he thought of her often, wondering if she was happy and safe. He took to fretting more and more, and, after a week of drunk every night stewing and bragging up his courage, he left town. Just when I'd begun to worry about being called in from my lean-to, Frenchie came back again. He didn't have the bear, but he had brought his daughter.

Well, Florrie was as pretty a thing as you'd ever want to see, just my size, but blonde instead of dark, with golden hair that rippled down to her shoulders and tied with a blue ribbon at the back. She wore crisp, starched dresses, and on her feet tiny black patent leather shoes. Seeing Florrie all pretty and clean and neat and sweet-smelling, with her round blue eyes that seemed as though they ought never to have to look on anything bad, made all those years in Clytie's bed bear on my conscience hard.

Frenchie had returned with a considerable bundle of money, too. He bought the house of a miner who'd been killed in a rock slide, and Florrie came along with me to Mr. Paddleford's school.

Well, right off she was the most popular girl at school, at least among the younger boys. A great pack of them would walk home with Florrie and me after school, poking and pushing each other and giggling, until I was heartily sick of it. Frenchie said it had always been that way with Florrie.

The boys would hang around our house in a languishing kind of way, and I considered Florrie more hospitable to them than she need've been. She would sit on the porch with them clustered around her, maybe holding hands with two at once, and the one she had to pull her hand away from, say to scratch her nose, would fall into despair because of it. Of course it was just a matter of time before the older boys thought of some devilment to do with her.

One day after school was out there was a hullabaloo down by the river. Bill Mackie had opened his pants in front of Florrie. She sat on a log with her eyes big and round and her mouth sucked into a line a quarter of an inch long. And of all those boys who walked to and from school with us, and hung around the house every day, not one had the spunk to try to make Bill Mackie stop pulling on himself in front of Florrie.

I took my bowie knife out of my lunch pail and shoved my way through the boys there. I showed the knife to Bill Mackie and told him he was to stop what he was doing and button his placket or he wasn't going to have anything to show another time. He blustered, and he and some of his friends called me and Clytie some names, but they made themselves scarce pretty quick. And that was the start of the stories about Holdfast and his knife, which were wild and fanciful but I must admit were true at the bottom. All the bigger boys were a good deal carefuler around me after that, and respectful of Florrie.

That was a pleasant time for Florrie and me as "brother" and "sister." Frenchie and Clytie were settled in Frenchie's house, like husband and wife, and the eating place was making good money. Frenchie spent evenings poring over a new map he had bought somewhere, with a compass and ruler and logarithmic tables.

But Frenchie never did like me much. Whenever he looked at me his face under all that wild crimped hair would cloud and muscles bunch under his eyes, so he'd seem to be trying to remember something forgotten a long time ago. When I began to get my growth he did not beat me anymore, but always was to speak to me short and hard of voice. He never touched Florrie in his anger either, or I don't know what I would have done. Always he treated her as his little princess, who was indeed a princess to me too.

Now at this time boys like Bill Mackie and Bobby Mangan had left school to go to work in the new mines that were being drifted in, and I had become the chiefest boy at Mr. Paddleford's school, athough I was not the oldest nor the biggest either. But I was quick in my studies and always quiet and attentive to Mr. Paddleford, and respected by the other boys, for the story passed on from year to year how when I was just a little fellow I had taken a knife to the school bully. So it is that a man's acts will stay with him all his life, and I have gone from protecting my sister from dirty-minded boys to keeping order in a whorehouse, and peace in town.

Well, come that April Frenchie became dissatisfied, grousing and drinking again, and saying he was sick of wasting his life away in such a place as Goldville. And all at once he sold the eatery for a good stake, bought a team and wagon and some supplies, and headed out of town. He was bound to make one more prospecting expedition before he settled down for good.

By summer there'd been not a word from him, there was no more money, and Clytie had to take in boarders. Soon we had only one downstairs bedroom and the kitchen to ourselves. Clytie and Florrie slept together in the big old bed, and I had a cot in the kitchen that was folded up and stored away during the day. Those were trying nights for me because the cot was hard and narrow, and I could hear Florrie and Clytie giggling in the bed, and the familiar chinking of springs when one or the other of them turned over. They were always hugging and kissing in that way women will do, which is trying to men to witness, though I suppose that the snuggling and bussing that women take pleasure in is the plan of nature and women's function. For my own part I am repelled by physical contact with others, even disliking shaking hands, and I will not have men slapping my back or laying an arm over my shoulders in excessive friendliness. And the same with women, in their characteristic lollying upon men or tickling them about the neck as they are so ready to do.

Yet, in that time when it appeared that Frenchie had either deserted us or was dead in his prospecting for the Lost Dutchman mine, there were enjoyable occasions. I was the man of the house or anyway the kitchen, with two women to fuss over me like an Oriental potentate. I remember lying in my cot in the kitchen by first light hearing the whisper of Clytie's slippers and the iron scrape of the lids lifted from the stove, the chunking in of kindling, and the match struck with its whiff of phosphorus. In the gray light I would watch Clytie's fat arms shaking as she

23

sifted flour through a screen, and the herky-jerky motion as she sliced the bacon. Soon fat would be spitting in the long-handled skillet while she broke eggs into the pan, tossing the shells aside. Florrie would have been setting the dining-room table, coming in and out, slim and fair against Clytie's heft, the two of them going about their morning chores with no word spoken, Florrie carrying out laden trays while Clytie turned the eggs in the skillet, and I breathing deep of that smell, the finest in the world, of frying eggs and pork smoke and coffee on the boil. The first word spoken would be one or the other of them calling out that it was time I got up for breakfast.

For a while the issue of Clytie taking up with other men did not raise itself, but I knew that this would not continue if Frenchie remained away for long. And, sure enough, little by little this one or that one would begin making up to her, or the other way round, though each time trouble passed by. I knew that if trouble did come it was apt to be of my making, for I considered myself a man now and did not intend to be treated as a boy and of no account by one of the roomers, or some other who had taken a strong fancy to Clytie. I had wanted to wear Frank Plummer's old revolver and cartridge belt, so as to give myself more authority around the house, but Clytie would not let me have my way in this, and Florrie joined her, very passionate, saying that if guns were where men could lay their hands on them they were bound to go off, and she neither wanted her dear brother shot down nor hanged for a shooting either. So I had to be content with carrying my bowie in a sheath that a crippled fellow living with us fashioned for me, which I hung from a cord around my neck so it lay beneath my left armpit. I put in considerable practice snatching it from this place, so that Clytie grumbled about the shirt buttons I had burst loose. But it was a good thing I kept my knife to hand, for a time came when I must use it.

Evenings Florrie and I would study our homework at the kitchen table under the pull-down lamp. She would help me parse sentences and I her with her algebra. Clytie would gossip with the roomers on the porch, and more often now return tipsy and coarse-mouthed from the saloons. It was clear she had her eye out for a man again.

Now Florrie, who was high-spirited and mischievous, liked to play tricks on Clytie when she came home fuddled. Several times we hid from her, squeezed close together and breathless in the closet or behind the bed, from where we would hop out to give her a scare.

On this occasion on which so much of the direction of my life was to depend, when Florrie heard Clytie's footsteps, she grasped my hand and pulled me into the dark bedroom, where we slid together behind the bed, waiting to spring out and surprise Clytie. But right away it was clear there was a man with her.

We could hear them arguing in the kitchen, Clytie in a whining voice and the other rough and low. Clytie called out my name, and Florrie's, but Florrie only whispered in my ear, "Oh, Henry, it is Bill Mackie that I am so afraid of!"

Bill Mackie was a mucker at the Isabella mine now and he and a bunch of other toughs were town bullies of a Saturday night. When I started to climb out of our hiding place to do my duty as the man of the house, Florrie restrained me, and clutched me, shivering in fright. There were two men with Clytie.

She whined that they must go away now. She couldn't have them here, with children in the house, by which she meant Florrie and me. It was bad of them to follow her in this way, she went on, first begging them to leave her alone and next trying to strike a bargain. They laughed and cursed, barging around in the kitchen there, and finally Clytie said they could have turns but it would be three dollars for the two of them. There was a good deal of palaver about that and no way I could stop Florrie's ears from it. And next they were all lumbering into the bedroom with Clytie still protesting the arrangements, and Florrie clinging to me as though she were drowning.

We edged under the bed just as there was a crash and spring jangle, and the mattress came down on us hard, mashing us together. The bed got into regular motion, heavier, then lighter, and heavy again. In the light from the kitchen I could see boots just beside the bed, and trousers down around the second fellow's ankles. The bed creaked faster, with Florrie pressed hard against me making a small humming sound in my ear, and, situated as we were, I could not help but become inflamed. Then all of a sudden my foot was caught and I was dragged out from under the bed. Florrie screamed as she was laid hands on too. It was Bill Mackie standing over us with only his shirt on and what he had tried to show Florrie once before laid up against his belly like a tree branch. Bobby Mangan was on the bed between Clytie's knees. Her mouth was spread all over her face screaming.

Bill Mackie jerked Florrie to her feet, at the same time shooting a kick at me as best he could with his boots trouser-hobbled. I managed to scramble to my feet, snatching out my knife. I swung it on Bill Mackie as I had told him before I would do if he troubled Florrie. I missed my mark that time, though he shouted with pain. But when I swung again he shrieked like a gelded hog and fell back against the wall, shaking the whole house. He had his hands jammed to his crotch as if trying to stuff himself back together again.

Bobby Mangan sprang off Clytie, and with a great racket he and Bill Mackie tried to crowd out the door at the same time, wedged together and hitting at each other in their frenzy. Bobby broke free in the kitchen, shouting at me to keep away. He had his forty-four in hand. Bill had fallen huddled up on the kitchen floor and I stepped past him as Bobby tore outside looking back at me as though I was the devil himself. In the yard in the dark he looked like a piece of marble statuary in a graveyard, only running and shouting. Then he swung around and I saw light gleam off the barrel of his revolver. He banged away at me, fanning the hammer, glass smashing all around, and the roomers upstairs yelling. I stepped out of the lighted doorway. I had not that first time, nor any other time since, any fear, only determination to do my part, which was to hit my man and put him down. Especially there is no use worrying about a gun fanner who is more than six feet off, for if he has not ventilated you with his first shot it is little likely he is going to, with every shot jerking the muzzle up another six inches until he has finished shooting at the moon.

I flung my bowie. I didn't see where it took him, but he staggered back, to fall in a heap of shadows near the alley. While I waited to see if he was frauding, Bill Mackie came out past me, bent over himself and grunting, and, while the fellows upstairs yelled to know what was happening, was war broke out?—scuttled out of sight in the dark. I trotted on over to Bobby Mangan, stretched out like a barrel of moonlit white flesh, jerked my bowie from his neck, wiped the blade off on his hair, slipped it back into its sheath, and collected his forty-four where he had dropped it. Back inside the kitchen Florrie and Clytie were clinging to each other and blood was puddled on the floor.

I told them they had better throw their things together as quick as they could, for it was already past time for us to be leaving town. Bill Mackie had his cronies, and probably a bunch of miners could get here faster from the saloons on Main Street than the deputy could from the jail by the bridge, and the deputy might not be in a hurry anyway with a bunch of drunken muckers on a tear to worry him.

While I loaded up Bobby Mangan's forty-four and Frank Plummer's old piece, and slung cartridge belts on, there was a great noise of the roomers banging on the door and wanting to know if we were all killed. I sent a couple of them out to saddle horses for us in the horse barn, and quick as I could got the women mounted and started down the alley behind the house, but not quick enough, for already there was a roar of shouting coming out of Main Street, and torches lighting the sky. At the end of the alley we almost ran into a bunch of them. Others were coming up faster than I'd counted on. The torches made an orange light over everything and the church bell was tolling. I remember well enough feeling a sight more irritated than scared, because there was such a racketing I couldn't make myself heard above it. I was determined to see Florrie and Clytie safe out of there if I had to shoot every miner in Goldville, and it would have been useful to announce the fact.

Just then a fellow on horseback spurred toward us. He had no trouble making himself heard, shouting as loud as the lot of them together, and silencing them enough so I could hear Clytie cry out, "Oh, it is *you!*"

Now, he was the man named Ted I mentioned earlier in this narrative. He would show up in Goldville now and again and was the kind of man that treats a boy like something near equal and not like a halfwit servant or a pet dog. Once he had shown me some tricks of knife throwing when he came on me practicing with my bowie, and afterward sat and talked to me. I told him I practiced so regular because I was sworn to kill the cur that had murdered my father, to which he nodded his big, pockmarked face in a judicious sort of way, saying that was a likely commission for a young chap. And it was this same man that had showed up when I was holding Bill Mackie from drowning in the river. It goes without saying that I was mighty glad to find him on hand at this juncture, with his shotgun held up and the torchlight flickering up and down the barrels like heat lightning.

Standing in his stirrups he hectored those miners bunched around us, and others running up, saying that Henry Plummer had only cut down the man that was trying to violate his sister, and killed the one that had raped his mother, etc.—though how he could have known all that so soon was a puzzle. He announced to that rabid crew that what I had done was justified in the eyes of heaven, and they would do well to head on home and leave us alone.

He slowed them down at least, though there was noisy calling back and forth to the effect that I had castrated poor Bill Mackie and slaughtered Bobby Mangan in cold blood. And that raping Clytie Plummer was a damned lie, for once a whore always a whore. But there was arguing and qualifying among them, which kept steam from building again. There were fellows surging this way and that and occasionally yelling for a hanging, but not in a concentrated way anymore, Ted facing them down with his shotgun slanting over his arm. Clytie looked half dead with fright, moaning whenever the yelling built up again, but Florrie sat very straight and tight-mouthed in her saddle.

Finally Ted said to me, "You and these ladies just get along now, and don't stop till you are out of range of here. And I'll be seeing you again, I don't doubt, son." Before I could thank him he was spurring his big stallion into rearing this way and that so the miners nearest us had to keep shoving back. In a minute we had clear track. I reached for Florrie's bridle, set my spurs, and we lit out. Behind us there was a great cheated shout.

We rode all that night, never stopping till we were on the other side of the mountains. Coming into a little town where two creeks joined, with big cottonwoods along the creeks, what should we chance upon but a medicine show with signs announcing the world's greatest bull-killing bear, the world's longest rattlesnake, and Teeth Pulled $3. It was Frenchie's medicine show.

Frenchie told us he had been cheated out of every cent of money, and his map proved a fraud again, but by a stroke of luck he had got his property back that he had thought was lost forever, and he was just heading for Goldville. He was so glad to see us it was hard to hold against him that he had neglected to write or send any message; he was hugging Florrie and Clytie to him and looking me straight in the eye to tell me I was a hero. So it was we all came to be part of the medicine show, and what we had joined was this:

There were two bears, one the old grizzly named Duke, a shambling big fellow with pig eyes you couldn't see anything special about until you saw him climbing a bull, for they would put on a bull-and-bear fight whenever they struck a likely town for it. The other bear was a half-grown female named Betsy. They'd acquired her for Duke's pleasure, but he wouldn't have anything to do with her, seeming to hold himself above that sort of truck, they said. She was a likable bear with a snouty black face that always had a smile on it. A greaser was teaching her to dance so she could earn her victuals, since there'd been no call on her for what she'd been acquired for. The greaser would beat on a tambourine and Betsy shuffle this way and that with her paws held up in a comical way, but always pretty quick she would fall back on all fours, and just twist her head from side to side. It would have been a fine thing if she could ever keep interested, but it just wasn't in her. The "world's longest rattlesnake" was a fraud, a dead snake coiled up in some cloudy liquid so you couldn't make out how long it was at all, in a kind of museum with a stuffed owl and a stuffed hawk near where Frenchie had a desk. He was forever studying maps and old papers, and writing in a book he kept there.

The greaser could play the mouth organ to make you cry, and there was a gypsy fortuneteller who wore an orange cloth on her head with two knots over her eyes, and rings on all her fingers. Carmen would spit whenever she caught sight of Clytie, and when she quarreled with Frenchie, which was most of the time, she talked so fast you couldn't make out what language she was haranguing him in, English, gyp, or greaser. She walked in a queer, backward-leaning way with skirts that trailed on the ground while she took long, dipping steps, twisting around to peer over her shoulder to see who was watching, and often jerking a hand with forked fingers up before her face if she caught somebody at it. Florrie took to her right away, and said she was all bark and no bite, but it was some time before I felt easy with her. She had a booth in one of the wagons with a phrenology chart on the wall and a crystal ball she kept wrapped in cloths—so it wouldn't take a chill, she told Florrie. She would bring the ball out and hunch over it, making motions with her hands and muttering to herself, and sometimes jerking up the forked fingers, which meant she had seen some evil in the ball. She could trace the lines in your hand so softly it was like spiders crawling there, and you could feel the ghosts of her fingers for a long time after. Mostly, though, she told fortunes from a pack of cards.

Florrie and I decided on our own act for Frenchie's medicine show. At first I would throw knives at a target while Florrie came walking by, pretty as cake icing with her white dress, and hat, and lacy parasol. She stopped to watch me admiringly, after which she sang a song, for she had a sweet voice. While she sang I would retrieve my knives, and, for a finale, throw them at the target so fast as to get three in the air at once. Later on the act became more complicated, but at first this was what it was.

I also helped the greaser and Frenchie with the bull-and-bear fights. For all his lazy ways the Duke was as smart a bear as a man would ever want to see. First Frenchie would buy a likely-looking bull and we'd saw the tips off his horns so he'd be less apt to get at the Duke's vitals if he hooked him. Then we'd put out broadsides announcing the fight, for those miners dearly loved a show where something was sure to get killed. Sometimes there was betting, but it was well known the Duke had never lost a fight yet, and so mostly money was to be made charging a dollar a head to watch the fight.

We'd enclose a square, about a hundred foot on a side, using whatever we could find in the way of wagons, bales, or down-timber to do it. Then we'd tackle the main business of collecting money from the miners. The Duke was let out into the corral to wander around in his slow, nearsighted way, while the miners, that he paid no attention to, jeered and flung pebbles at him. There were always miners to say they wouldn't pay, it was a free country, and they had a right to stand there, but we wouldn't turn the bull loose until they'd settled up, and after a while the fellows that had paid would get after those that hadn't so the fight could start before nightfall.

Meanwhile the Duke had had plenty of time to dig his hole. He'd lazily scoop dirt with his claws till he had a bathtub big enough to scrunch down in with about half of him showing, when the bull tore into the corral, horns and tail up and eye-rolling mad from being prodded. The Duke would lie there not moving a muscle, just one pig eye showing in a hairy heap on the ground, while the bull pranced around snorting and pawing, and the miners cheered and waved their hats, and pointed toward the Duke. While the bull barged around the lot, you could see the Duke's eyes moving to keep on him, and all this time it was very suspenseful waiting for the bull to spot the bear, or else wander too close where the Duke could spring out at him. The miners would fall silent then, though sometimes they'd set up a great noise of warning to the bull.

If the Duke caught the bull by surprise the fight was over in a hurry, with the miners yelling with disappointment, but even if the bull did charge the Duke he couldn't do much damage, being unable to hook his horns under the part of the bear that was in the hole. Though the Duke might get banged pretty hard sometimes, he never was torn up.

For, just as soon as the bull had smacked him and so lost his momentum, the Duke would be out of his hole. You never saw anything move so fast. While the miners were bellowing and clamoring for the bull to "git 'im, hook 'im," the Duke would go straight for the bull's tongue and tear it out of his head. Right there the bull lost interest in the proceedings and the Duke could take his time clawing the insides out of the poor beast, which he did very slow and cruel. You could see he was punishing those miners for jeering and tossing pebbles. The Duke clearly hated those wool-hat miners that paid a dollar to watch two animals kill each other, for always cheering the bull and not seeing he was the class of the fight, and soon enough I came to hate them too. They were a pretty poor specimen of mankind, which is a pretty poor specimen already.

When it was all over the greaser would come into the corral calling to the Duke, who shambled off after him and back into his cage as tame as you please. Then he'd pace in the cage while the greaser told him how fine he was and how proud of him we were, talking and talking until the Duke calmed down and slumped in a corner scratching his belly and his eyes half-closed, for all the world like a fat man sleeping off a drunk.

Well, we moved from camp to camp, and those months were pleasant enough. Then in one place, I can't remember its name, Bill Mackie came riding in on a tired old splay-footed plug just as we were starting to set up. I will say it was no pleasure for me to see him, though right off he announced to Florrie that he was a different fellow from what she had known in Goldville, having renounced his previous ways for which he had suffered heavily, etc. He was a good deal plumper now, which was natural, especially fat about the face, so his eyes seemed to have got smaller, though he was soft-spoken and easy-seeming, with a quick smile to him. He had a way of laughing very sudden and spitting some through his teeth, which had wide spaces between. He said he had left Goldville because fellows there made fun of him, and swore he bore me no ill will for what had been done to him, for I had only done what I must. Florrie, who had the softest heart in the world, took his side and nothing would do but that Frenchie hire him to help the greaser with the stock. And soon she had contrived a way to use him in our act besides.

First he just carried out a chair and a placard to prop on it, which said:

HOLDFAST THE KNIFE ARTIST
With Miss Flora

Next Florrie came out in front of a wooden backstop painted to look like the corner of a building. She put her parasol up and down, in a pretty way she had of doing, and sang her song. Then Bill Mackie appeared again. He would be holding a whiskey bottle, which he brandished tipsily, and, when she tried to run from him, he seized her and tried to kiss her. Whereupon she screamed, and I appeared, dressed in black and with a flat-crowned black hat, and my bowie knives concealed all about me, not one in evidence. Bill released Florrie to back up against the wall and produce his own knife, which he threatened me with. Swiftly then, in a manner I had devised and practiced to perfection, my knives leaped to my hand from their concealment, and I hurled one after another so that they surrounded him, vibrating and glistening in a very brave way, with their tips embedded in the backstop. Bill would drop his own knife to stand terrified among the knives I had thrown. Then he fled off the stage and I advanced to kiss Florrie's hand to applause, and we bowed and curtsied to the audience. And I suppose that, besides my skill, they were applauding because we were young and good-looking, for Florrie was just then changing from a pretty girl to a beautiful young woman.

Our act was well-attended always, but soon I tired of it. My life seemed at a standstill, and there was an urge in me that is hard to describe, an impatience for that young part of my history to be over and the real business to begin. And I could never bring myself to like Bill Mackie, eager and friendly though he seemed to be. There was a grossness about him that seemed a reproach, and I could never trust him. If he had turned against me long ago because I had saved his life, what must he feel toward me now, who had damaged him so terribly?

Little by little our act changed as I became more accomplished with my knives. Now I was handling nine of them, and Florrie had become so beautiful sometimes it would seem that the crowds were struck dumb by her. And Bill began to see his part differently. I suppose it is natural for a fellow not to want to regard himself always as a low masher and a coward, and the villain of the piece where another is the hero. He began to strike postures and make faces, first as a clown, though later that changed, too, as though he had convinced himself he was as important as Florrie or even I was. Nothing would do but we add his name to the placard. I'm not sure he did not finally come to see himself as the hero and I the villain, and indeed our audiences responded to his antics in a disgusting manner. The greater the prowess with the knives I would display the more they favored Bill, in that same way they favored the bull over the Duke.

But just about this time something happened to raise

my spirits considerably. The gypsy had a jackdaw that for a dollar would come out of his cage, cross over to a pigeon-hole box stuffed with tiny rolls of paper, and choose one with his beak. When you untied a bit of string, and unrolled the paper, there was a message that was meant just for you. One day, sitting with Carmen in her booth lined with red and purple hangings and her phrenology, I gave her a dollar for the jackdaw to do his trick for me, and the message in the little roll was:

YOU WILL BE FAMOUS IN THE TERRITORY

Carmen jerked her forked fingers up before her face, and, much flustered, unwrapped her crystal ball and held her hands over it to warm it while she mumbled with her eyes closed. Then she looked into it with a squinted eye as you would aim a rifle. I told her what I had almost forgotten, in my negligence, that I was sworn to kill the man who had murdered my father but didn't know how I was to begin this task. It seemed to me my life was passing with nothing to it but being a knife artist in a medicine show for muckers and bumpkins, and I was heartily sick of it.

Carmen squinted into her ball, finally saying, "Yes, you will find this man you seek." Then, after a spell of muttering, she came out with: "You will have many ene-mies, many. The enemies of a brave and famous man in the Territory. There are many women, with white shoul-ders." I begged her to go on, and she said: "There is one who is your greatest enemy and greatest danger, and there is another who is to be a greater man."

I said I did not feel bad about that for I did not have a jealous nature. But I had an impatient one, and when was it to start?

She said it had already started: "As a leaf in a pond seems not to be moving, but already is in the grip of the current that will carry it into the cataract!"

I lay awake that night so excited my limbs felt light enough to fly, racking my brains for some evidence that my destiny was already in motion. All I could think of was that Frenchie, who ran a little gambling layout along with the medicine show, had got himself accused of cheating, and we'd been warned out of town by the Regulators. It did not seem enough of a thing for the leaf in the current Carmen had spoken of.

There was a considerable agitation in the mines just then to drive out the greasers, Chinamen, and white foreigners, too. This was what the Regulators were about, who were bullies by nature. We had already been hurrahed in one of the camps, and had to move on in a hurry, and everywhere the miners were turning mean and troublesome. The Holdfast knife-throwing act was poorly received these days, and the bear fights turned into riots. The miners railed against the Duke, calling him a yellow-belly for digging himself a hole, and as a result the Duke had become grouchier and slower, so that the greaser had to talk to him for a long time before every fight as well as after. And I know now just how the Duke was feeling.

The final time he didn't even bother to dig his hole. He scuffed at the ground and gave it up and just sat down. We all knew there'd be a riot if we called off the fight, for we'd taken in the money already, but the greaser went running out toward the Duke waving his arms. The bull took after him and the greaser had to run for the fence, with miners screeching and laughing and pegging rocks at the Duke, who was sitting out in the center of the corral exactly like a fat, narrow-shouldered old man except that he had knives stuck on his hands instead of fingers. When the bull started for him he got up on his hind legs. He looked ten feet tall. The bull slowed down some, but got going again as the miners set up a roar you could've heard three counties away, and he hit the Duke full clip. That was the end of the Duke. He died there in the dirt, though he pulled out that bull's insides before he died. It was a sad day for us all, and it wasn't over yet.

During our act that evening Bill Mackie was like a crazy man, jumping around like a flea on a griddle, the worst he'd ever been. Florrie kept whispering to him to try to steady him down. The audience was the worst we'd had, too, blood up from seeing the old bear killed, jeering and shouting at us the same way they'd done at him. And that was the night my hand failed me, though it was Bill's fault as much as my own. He had to be rushed off in the spring wagon to a nearby camp where there was a doctor, to see if he could be put back together again. Some of those people did think I'd done it on purpose, and there was a move to lynch me right there, till I showed them the knife I'd held back, which quieted them down.

Afterward I sat in Carmen's booth having a cup of tea with Carmen, Florrie, and Clytie, all of them mopping their eyes and carrying on in a way I found tiresome. What with the women's noise and the miners racketing outside my skin felt like somebody had taken a rasp to it. Behind Carmen the jackdaw was sidling in his cage, and Betsy was pacing in hers. It must be she knew the Duke was dead and was mourning for him, though he had never paid her a bit of attention in his life. She paced in a rapid, foot-lifting way the three or four steps the cage allowed, then swung around with her head banging the bars, to pace three or four hotfoot steps the other way.

Florrie said once again what it didn't seem to me needed to be said anymore: "Oh, surely poor Bill will be all right!"

I watched my hand take up my teacup that was full to the brim, and not one drop spilled. Clytie said what had been said before too, that if there'd been money I could've bought cartridges to practice with Frank Plummer's re-volver instead of always a knife. This time I said it looked like I had not practiced enough.

"There is a curse on knives," she said. "And knives will be the destruction of you, Henry Plummer." But she softened what she had said by smiling sweetly at me. She was not a young woman but she had a sideways way of looking at a man that was very taking. Her shape was still fine enough if she was laced into her stays, as she was for tending the tables in the saloon tent. With the proper ad-justments, and maybe it was her state of mind also, her bosom would swell like that of a great lady and her waist seem made for putting an arm around. When she was laced and primed, with her cheeks pink and her eyes sparkling, and hair fresh combed, men were apt to be more taken with her than with Florrie, in the dim light of the saloon tent.

It seems to me that I have spent more time in my life with women than with men, sitting with those three that night and so many other times with Florrie and Clytie, and with my present position in this place. In general I hold women in contempt, whores and servants by nature they seem to me to be, except for a few real ladies I have known, such as Florrie and another who has not yet appeared in this narrative. Still I will hold that I think as highly of women as I do of the opposite sex, for I have never met a one of those worthy of the name of man. They say the Kid is a rare one, but I will believe it when I see it.

Clytie said, "Well, it was Bill's own fault. Bouncing around like he had scorpions in his pants. Getting too big for his boots. Attentive to Florrie lately, I've noticed. Calling her 'sister dear' and such."

Florrie cried out, "Oh, no, no, no! You don't understand!"

"Well, I say it was unnatural and wrong that he ever come here in the first place, and I told him so!" Clytie said, folding her arms.

Carmen hunched over her teacup with her different-colored skirts tucked between her legs. Under her yellow headcloth, with its two peaked knots, her brown, wrinkled face was squinted anxiously as she studied the tea leaves in her cup. She held up a hand for silence. "Yes, he is to live!" she said.

"What do you see about me here?" Clytie said, pushing her cup toward Carmen.

"It remains the same. The future does not change every day." Carmen inspected Florrie's cup, and said, "Many children, many," pushed it away, and took mine from me.

"You will make your journey soon, Henry Plummer!"

She poked at the leaves. "You will kill a black man," she said.

"T. P. Eubanks is no nigger!" Clytie cried out.

Carmen shrugged elaborately. "I see a dark man dead." She continued to poke. "Many dark men fearful of Henry Plummer, but which are the true enemies, and which the false? It is very confuse!"

Clytie was always bored when the subject of conversation was not herself, and she said she'd better go, things seemed noisy outside and Frenchie might need her. Carmen left soon after, saying she must have a walk to quiet her nerves, and Florrie and I were alone together with the jackdaw turning his head to watch us with one eye and then the other, and Betsy pacing in her cage.

"I'm feeling very nervous tonight, too, brother dear," Florrie said.

"I'm not your brother," I said to her. "And you are not my sister."

She sat looking down at her hands in her lap. "It is a game we have played."

I said I was weary of games, we had grown too old for such games. It was time for my journey into the Territory.

"Do you think that what Carmen sees in her crystal ball is the only future there is for you?"

"I know there is no future for me here!"

"There is a present here," Florrie said. "Though it is a noisy one just now," she added, to make light of this conversation. "Do you know the future Carmen sees for me? It is like yours."

"Many children, she said just now."

"She has also said I am to make a dangerous journey. That I will become a famous lady and marry a famous man. Like a king and queen, Carmen said."

I didn't know what to say to that. Florrie's fingers plucked at her hair, which was braided thick and fair into a rope and hung in front of her shoulder. "I don't believe it," she said. "And I don't want to be a queen, anyway."

"Maybe you have to believe it for it to happen," I said.

"That's why I think I must start west to find this man Eubanks."

"Why?" Florrie asked.

"To kill him."

"*Why?*" she cried out.

"It is all I know of my destiny," I said. "And I must follow it or I have nothing."

She put her face in her hands. "Because Clytie has told you you must do that!" she said in a muffled voice. "And because Carmen—"

"No," I said. "It is just that I know I am meant to be something. Someone. I have always known that. I am good with my hand, and my head, and I am cool in trouble. I have some greatness in me that must get out."

"It will make you angry to hear it," she whispered. "But Bill Mackie feels the same way you do."

It made me so angry I could not speak, while behind us Betsy paced with three quick pads of steps and brushing sound, then three more steps. I said to Florrie then that if I was angry it was because I could not ask her to marry me, for I must take my leave of her to do what I must with my life. I was not meant to be a knife-throwing artist in a medicine show, even if that was a pleasant present, which it was not much anymore. I had to go to my destiny, whatever it was to be.

With her face turned aside Florrie said, yes, I must do that if that was the way I felt. The lamplight shone like a halo on her hair.

And just when I raised up to catch her into my arms, intending to kiss her on the lips for the first time in my life, there was another great racketing outside, and Clytie burst in upon us crying that I must arm myself because the Regulators had made Frenchie a prisoner.

There was nothing to be done then but strap on Frank Plummer's old revolver, and Bobby Mangan's on the other hip, and sheathe a bowie between the crossed cartridge belts at the small of my back. It had happened a time or two before that I was called for a peacemaker. Although

Holdfast the Knife Artist was not as popular as he had once been, my reputation with a bowie was usually enough to quiet rowdy men just by my walking past them.

I have noticed many a time that as women will look brighter of eye and firmer of flesh by candlelight, so do men see themselves as stronger, nobler, and more fearless by torchlight. In truth, men who are not cowards are rare, and fewer still have the spirit and intelligence to be of consequence. The very few, who are what they are by mathematical accidents of breeding, birth, and raising, will have, as well as calmness and courage, the knowledge from the beginning what their end is ordained to be. The end that is the same for all men is different for these few in that they knew it well all their lives: dead in the dust at last, and carrion buried under six feet of earth for worms to gorge upon. And they see too that most likely it will be some mistake of their own to ruin them, that missing the proper course by so much as a hairsbreadth will turn their lives to failure. So it is that this True Fellow, who is reputed to be now upon his way here, will no doubt, in the end, turn out either a fraud or a failure like those who have gone before him. For each of them was thought to be the Real Thing in his turn but took a wrong fork in the path, which ruined him. Looking back upon it now I can see my own missteps, where I blundered in the Kimanche camp, and maybe even in the fight with Jack Dale, which I have never questioned before now, and above all in not following the general's counsel that I rid the Territory of the Putaw Gang before it was too late. But how is a man never to fall into error out of ignorance or pride unless Heaven itself guides him foot and hand, head and heart?

I think these men I have spoken of before know when their end is near. I can feel it close upon me now, a kind of dirty tiredness blowing up like a dust devil inside me. I must say now that I do not care much what happens. In this place I hate, among townfolk whom at best I disrespect, though I have saved them from a slavery they will not understand until I am gone, I have long lost the certainty which once I had, that I was the True One; and which the Kid must now feel strong in him on his journey across the Territory to Bright City.

Moreover, my mind turns always to the great bear, the Duke, in his death. For in the end he found that he had been a fool, and like myself had not known his true enemies. He had believed these were the bulls, and had fought them with courage and intelligence. Later he came to think that his enemies were the miners, jeering him, pelting him with pebbles, and encouraging his antagonist. But at last he must have had to realize that he had wasted his hate even on the miners, for it was Frenchie who had contrived it all, with the greaser and me and later Bill Mackie to assist in his deception. And perhaps before he died he was able to trace that tortuous track to one more remove still, for life itself was the prime betrayer. Again and again I come to think of the Duke at his end, for it is like my own, but unfortunately by the time a man has gained the wisdom and experience to manage his existence, the very heart has gone out of him.

Now I see that as once I dealt with the Regulators, who were such an evil growth back in those dreary hills where the mining camps were scattered, so I might once and for all have dealt with the evildoers over on Putaw Creek, who now have come to see themselves in an exalted and heroic light as though by torchlight. I have chosen to keep them out of Bright City merely, otherwise allowing them to go their way as I go mine, thinking that their depredations outside my jurisdiction are not my business. And that was where I missed my True Course.

In that earlier time, when I was a different and more optimistic man, summoned to deal with all hell brewing up, I had no doubts about me. There was a great head of miners milling around the medicine show, many of them with torches. It was like that other time in Goldville, though a bigger crowd. Smoky light and shadows swung and swayed as they marched and shouted amongst the tents and wagons. They were singing a song I couldn't make out the words of, the music furnished by the bearkeeper greaser cranking the barrel organ like his life depended on it. There was a smoky smell of hot tar, and, on the little stage with its backstop for my knives, Regulators with their red sashes were strutting around a tub of tar tipped at a slant over a fire. Up on the stage were Frenchie, Carmen, and a bunch of greasers from the camp, all with their clothes off and arms crossed over their crotches and shoulders hunched down in shame, except for Carmen that they hadn't bothered in that way. Before the stage was a crowd of miners and their women, in poke bonnets, all of them guffawing and shouting back at something the chief of Regulators, a plump fellow named Moon, was haranguing them about. A screech of laughter went up as one of the Regulators slung a shiny sheet of tar from a bucket over the first greaser. The tar covered him from his head down to his knees, steaming and glistening in the cool night air.

Another Regulator emptied a pillowcase of feathers over the tar. I had never seen that done before. Frenchie stood among the other naked fellows, a head taller, with his frizzy hair standing up around his head like a comic drawing of a man in a fright.

The man they had tarred and feathered didn't even look like a human being anymore, except from the knees down. The Regulators, with a lot of cussing, pushed another poor fellow up to the front. They slopped tar on him, at which he yelped. Moon gave him a hard kick and then made an act of wiping tar off his boot, pulling faces and rolling his eyes like Bill Mackie clowning. And all the miners and their poke-bonnet wives thought this was a howl of fun.

I started forward through that crowd watching the show, saying, "Pardon me, boys," and "With your permission, ma'am." The Regulator crew had emptied feathers on the second greaser, with eddies of loose feathers blowing away. The two of them were stood side by side for everybody to laugh at, the stuck-on feathers ruffling in the breeze. With their hands tied behind them they looked like two great chickens but with no chicken heads, only their mouths with white teeth showing open. The crew started poking another one toward the tar tub and I plowed my way toward the stage faster, for Frenchie was being pushed forward too. Behind him Carmen in her orange bandana was giving the evil-eye sign.

Some other Regulators had hustled the first poor fellow off to one side, and all of a sudden he was shot up on a rail, struggling for balance with his hands tied back the way they were. Then the second one was up, jerking and straining in that smoky light. The men that had boosted them up on the rails started away through the crowd with them with a lot of cheering and catcalls.

They were pushing Frenchie up to the smoking tub when I stepped onto the stage. Moon and his bunch didn't look much pleased to see me. There were about eight of them, with their red sashes on, and that many more fellows set for tarring and feathering. Frenchie was trying to cover his face with one hand and his crotch with the other.

"Well, here is Holdfast," Moon said, with his hands on his hips.

"You have got some tar on yourself, Mr. Moon," I said.

He laughed and stuck out his boot to show where some had slopped, and said it was too bad, but part of a necessary business. The men with the rails were running now, yipping as they ran, and the two white birds disappeared into the dark.

I said I wondered what was necessary about it.

Moon drew himself up, sucking in his belly, and explained that Frenchie was a Frenchman or anyway a Jew, and Carmen a gyp, and the others greasers. The Regulation Committee had decided there were to be no more foreigners in the district. They were all to be run out. He was only carrying out the committee's orders.

I said why not let them go then, what was all this dirty business with tar and feathers?

Moon didn't reply to that, and the crowd had grown pretty quiet. I told Frenchie to go get his clothes on and start packing the show; it appeared we were not welcome in this camp. And I told Carmen to hurry along, and maybe the greasers wouldn't mind helping us pack up. Frenchie tripped and stumbled and hopped around trying to pull his trousers on while Carmen made herself scarce with the greasers a step behind her. None of the Regulators there made any move toward stopping this, though there was a good deal of muttering, and finally Moon said, "You have got no call to interfere here, Mr. Holdfast!"

I walked to the edge of the stage beside that stinking tar tub and stood looking out at the crowd. I announced that most of them had probably seen me in this place before. I was part of an act where I pretended to save a young girl from a masher. So I felt pretty natural here, trying to help people out against bullies.

Moon looked like he was about to choke. Some of the red-sash fellows were sidling to get behind me. Just then the saloon tent where Frenchie had his gambling layout came down like a burst balloon, which caused considerable stir toward the back of that crowd. We had moved the show so many times it could be done in a great hurry, and faster packing than setting up.

One of the fellows behind me was close enough to make my back itch, so I spun around, jerking out my bowie, and before he knew it his sash was on the floor. He gawked and pressed his hands to his belly, and that was the end of anybody trying to sneak up behind me. Sticking my knife back between the two belts I moved closer to Moon. Now there was a rise of voices shouting at me for cutting the fellow's belly, and the idea of someone out there aiming a rifle passed through my head. But there is no use worrying something like that, which either is or isn't, and nothing to be done about it.

However, it was a chancy moment, with that Regulator making such a show of holding his belly and then examining his hands for blood on them, and the yelling building up because there was something righteous now to raise a yell about. The whole pack surged forward. Just then there was a scream, and a choked-up voice yelled, "Rodge! Rodge Moon! Somebody has set that bear loose, Rodge!" And there was another scream.

Well, it closed down that moment when things looked out of control. I never did see Betsy, but there was no mistake where she was because of people jumping this way, and surging that, and women screaming. A part of the crowd would come apart like cloth tearing, and then heave back together when it tore open somewhere else. It kept up awhile. Meantime I saw a mule backing into harness out by the wagons, and lanterns going out so there were only torches for light now. Finally, when there were no more disturbances, it appeared that Betsy had gone on her way.

I motioned the Regulators to come around Moon and me, and they moved to do it quick enough. I said we ought to sing a song to entertain the folks, and I asked the one that had lost his sash what his favorite song was. He stared back at me with the muscles showing along his jaw like carpet tacks, but finally he said it was "Tenting Tonight."

So I began to sing that. I sang it alone, staring straight at him until he looked fit to burst, and at last in a voice like a rusty gate began singing along. Then I stared at another one, and right away he chimed in. One by one I got them all going except Moon, who stood with his arms folded over his chest and one eye squinted hard back at me to show I couldn't scare him. We sang "Tenting Tonight" a good many times, and then I asked another Regulator for a song, and we all sang "Do You Remember Sweet Alice, Ben Bolt?" with Moon abstaining still. There were catcalls and yipping all the while, but nothing much getting together, and I thought I might have won out by making myself ridiculous along with the Regulators. Now there was a wagon moving, I knew which one by the screeching of that back wheel, and I could hear the jingle of harness above our singing, which had got pretty ragged. I saw mule haunches shining brown by torchlight, and I had one glimpse of Florrie, up on the seat with the hostler. Our eyes touched across the space of miners. She was going off to the life Carmen had seen for her, or she wasn't; and I was going my own way. We would never see each other again as we were now, and we both knew that. And all of a sudden it came on me like vitriol eating my spirit that I was a fool to try to entertain folks so they would not harm themselves and others. They would not understand that I was trying to save them from that, but would only hate me for a bully. I was feeling what the Duke had felt at his end, and what I am feeling now at mine.

It had come around for Moon to select a song for us to sing. He only stuck out his jaw at me and slitted his eyes. What was I going to do about it? I remembered Florrie telling me that Bill Mackie thought he had a high destiny too, and I knew that Moon considered himself a hero holding out to the bitter end. At that time I did not know the danger you are in when you are up against a half-brave man.

"If you please, Mr. Moon," I said.

He only clamped his mouth tighter, and his fat arms over his chest. I drew out Frank Plummer's old revolver and showed it to him. His eyes squinted the more, and his jaw turned white with pressure in the silence all around. I smacked the barrel of the revolver against his head, bulldozing him, which is a course I have often pursued in my calling, for it beats shooting a man down. He is quick to lose interest in what he is doing and thoughtful not to take it up another time.

Moon staggered, and I caught hold of his collar with my left hand, ran with him a step, and then shoved him headfirst into the tar tub. Now it was his turn to scream, bubbling and hollow, his legs kicking. One of the Regulators jumped to help pull him out, keeping his eyes on me like a coon getting at the garbage. Moon slumped face down on the stage in a great pudding of shining tar, and I knew then I had gone too far from what my proper course should have been. There had been those coming around to my side during the singing, but now they could look on me as the bully, to the relief of their consciences.

I stepped down off the stage. A way opened before me, not in the sudden and comical way of Betsy running loose, but sullenly like cattle on a track parting before the cowcatcher of a locomotive. I could feel the hate pushing on me, and taste it on my lips almost, as I moved along saying,

"Pardon me, boys," and "With your permission, ma'am." I thought that at least in their hating they would never forget Henry Plummer.

I felt an itch on my back, and swung around to see Moon kneeling on the stage with the tar swiped from his eyes and a revolver held in both hands pointing at me. I shot him before he took his aim. He was jerked back and up, yelling, and dropped, with his legs kicking again, but stopping soon enough. Somebody close by me said, *"Murderer!"* biting it off sharp when I turned my head.

I passed on through the rest of them. The same voice, or maybe it was another, called out the same word again. Others took it up, and after I had moved on along they became a good deal braver yelling after me. The pinto was saddled up with a rifle in a scabbard, and a packhorse loaded with my gear, all waiting where I had known it would be. I swung into the saddle and sat awhile looking down at those buttery faces raised to me. On the stage a couple of Regulators were kneeling by Moon, who was stretched out in his death. There was a good deal of noise that quieted as I looked from face to face.

I had thought I would make a speech to them, at least tell them to remember me all their poor lives, but I knew there was no point in it. After a while, I swung the pinto away, and, with the pack animal trailing, rode on out of the light of their torches. They started up yelling again, but not as though they had much heart in it. At the crossroads I headed west toward the Territory, not south where I knew Frenchie would have taken the wagons.

The next day about noon, I saw a big dapple-gray grazing under a tree, and a fire with something cooking there. A fellow squatted by the fire, looking as though he was just waiting for me to pass by. He had a red kerchief tied at his neck, and wore a white sugarloaf hat, which he took off to wipe sweat from his pockmarked face. It was Ted, who had got us out of the pickle in Goldville. He had a voice that sounded like he was calling out of a well.

"Well, Henry Plummer," he said. "I understand you got yourself out of a fix without me."

I didn't see how he could've known that. I reined up in the shade of the tree, while he hunkered by the fire with his hat back on. He had a head too big for the features in it, so that toward the bottom of his face was a little trout mouth, and above that a good way and not centered very well, a jut of nose that looked small in all the sunburnt meat. Over on the right of the nose was one small eye, and in the other direction like an independent part of the landscape, another. Now all these pieces and bits convulsed in a grin.

I asked him who he was, anyway, always showing up like this.

"Sometimes I have been called T. P. Eubanks," he said, grinning.

I drew Frank Plummer's revolver and leveled it at the man who had murdered him, and Ted stopped grinning and inquired what this was in aid of.

I said I had sworn to my mother to kill the man that had shot my father, and that he should prepare to meet his end.

He rose up to his feet carefully, pushing his hat back on his head.

"First of all," he said, "it is a lie. That woman *isn't,* and Frank Plummer *wasn't,* which you already know. And I *didn't,* which you know now. There is no truth in Clytie Plummer and you know that. What's more, if you was to burn me down over such a fraud, who would conduct you to Bright City? Where you are due, son."

I slipped my piece back into its holster in confusion. And T. P. Eubanks said, "Now, why don't you climb down off that pony and have a bite of bread and bacon with me? And then you and me'll head on into the Territory together."

2

So Ted Eubanks and I crossed over into the Territory, brown and yellow country; in drought for more years than

49

anybody could remember, Ted said. Beyond were spiky mountains. The sun burned down all day to fry us in our saddles, until it was snuffed out in the evening by the cold wind. We didn't meet another soul in that torn-up land dry as jerked beef, nor anything living at all except lizards and once a rattlesnake big around as my leg. I shot his head off. Hot or cold I was still in one long shiver of excitement to get where we were going, and do what I was to do there, but Ted was not a man to gossip, and short-answered when I asked too many questions, which was anything more than one.

In camp he would cook and clean up after both of us as though he were a servant to me, and never let me help him. After supper he lounged by the fire smoking his corncob pipe. He would grumble that a man was crazy to take this route across the mountains, what with Kimanche, flash floods, heat to bake your brains and cold to freeze your privates, outlaws and the Livereater lying in wait, not to speak of the feverwater. It was far better to take the cars as far as they ran, and then follow the wagon road up from San Hedrin; but orders were orders.

Sometimes he would talk about the old Kimanche chief Stonepecker and his white-woman captives, which stories sounded like those the older boys at school told to tease the younger ones. He talked, too, about the gang that galloped around the Territory kidnapping white women to sell to the Indians and the whorehouses, the Putaw Gang they were called. I was learning that Ted's mind was a good deal on the white-woman captives and what was done to them, but I ought to've been listening to what he was saying about that Putaw Gang, a plague of dust and filth, of boils and stinging flies, spreading through the Territory.

Dirty snow was packed in the shady hollows in the first pass of the Bucksaws, and we led our animals slipping and stumbling in snow and loose shale on the western descent. In the valley below there were mosquitoes in the woods to eat you alive, and water running clear and cold in half a dozen creeks. Then up again to the next pass, where the snow was a foot deep, and winding down through pine and cedar with the sun dodging in and out of the treetops like a game of hide and seek.

That night we took supper in a lean-to amongst some boulders Ted had known to find. The mosquitoes were bad, even with the fire smoking to drive them off. Ted offered me his spare pipe, which he said was a help, but I have never taken to smoking except a cheroot after supper when I have been well satisfied with the meal. It is my opinion that a man has enough natural bad habits without going out of his way to collect more.

The next day I was having the shivers of a fever coming on, but I did not speak of it. In the afternoon we came down off a ridge and there was the Kimanche camp, six lodges looking very white and pretty in the green meadow, tall, with black tops and lodgepoles sticking through like the pictures in the schoolbooks. When we came out of the woods boys were playing in the grass, and women watched us out of the lodges, some with papooses strapped to boards on their backs. Horses in a woven-branches corral threw their heads around to whicker at our animals. Finally, a single brave trotted toward us on a whiteface pony. He had a feathered shield, a lance, and a buffalo-horn headdress. He was the ugliest man I'd ever seen, with a nose like a stepped-on potato, and eyes so close together they looked one on top of the other. He held up a hand, calling out, "How! Wapto!"

Ted called back, "How!" and the brave jerked his lance up and down some more, and said, "Wapto come!" He led us through the lodges to the biggest one, that had painted on it a yellow sun and black moon. Three branches were sunk into the ground in front of it. Dogs collected to bark at us. We dismounted, gave our reins to some half-grown boys to hold, and followed inside the big lodge.

My eyes took a while to get used to the dark, besides watering with smoke and fever. I made out that there was a considerable bunch of people standing in the lodge, which seemed as big as a church somehow with the edges lost out in the shadows, and a smoky fire in the center. My legs were feeling peculiar as I stood looking around. There were women in two or three bunches, some sitting on rolls of buffalo hides stacked like sofas, and children among them. On a pallet by the fire, a store blanket over him, bare feet sticking out one end and head, like a turtle's, out the other, was the oldest man in the world, with a face like a dried-up fig. Close beside him were four women all in white buckskin, with braided black hair. These were all young girls, while the other bunches looked not so young, and those off in the shadows old.

One of the girls propped the chief's head on a cushion, while the others fussed around him in that smoky murk. A plump one combed his white hair and crooned to him.

Finally he spoke up in a creaky voice: "Welcome, big soldier. And welcome to your young friend."

One of the chief's young women who had been standing with her face turned away from me now shifted a little so that I saw that, though her hair was black and done in braids, the line of the part showed white, and the curve of her cheek was milk white in that smoky teepee.

It was a shock to me to think those tall stories Ted had told me about the woman captives in the Kimanche camp were true, for I had disbelieved him.

The braves had gone on a long hunt, the chief was telling Ted in his creaky voice, for meat was scarce. I couldn't keep my eyes from that poor girl, who was afraid and ashamed to look back at me.

The chief asked about his friend Two-Star, and Ted said the general was feeling some better these days. And how was the great chief's health?

The old man pulled his blanket tighter around him with his black claws, while the girls bent, clucking, to help him. He patted the white girl's cheek, and said, "As you see, big soldier. Only very young women can keep the spark of heat in these bones as old as mountains."

He mumbled something to his wives in Kimanche, and they giggled and poked one another. And then the chief asked Ted, "Who is the young wapto? He is not comfortable here."

"He is a son of Two-Star," Ted said. "His father has sent for him from far away."

"You are welcome here, young son of Two-Star. Do not be frightened in this place of peace."

My head was whirling from the smoke, as the chief spoke in Kimanche again, and one of the young women went off to return with a stovepipe hat on a pillow. They managed to set the hat on the chief's head, which was propped up. All this time the white girl contrived to stand with her face averted from me.

The chief said. "We will smoke. Morning Sun, pretty one, you will prepare the pipe." Morning Sun was the white girl.

We seated ourselves on buffalo hides that stunk to make my stomach jump. The chief was joking with the young women, evidently, for there was a good deal of giggling. I clenched my fists until my hands ached, watching Morning Sun prepare the pipe, all the time keeping herself turned from me. Finally she lit the tobacco with a coal from the fire, and presented the pipe to the chief, who had trouble accepting it, lying as he was with his head propped up and the hat on. He sucked smoke, and gave it back to her to present to Ted. Finally she brought it to me, and her poor scared eyes met mine for the first time. I caught her wrist and leaped to my feet with my revolver in my other hand.

Women screamed, and the brave raised his lance at me, but I laid in my revolver on the old chief, at which the brave let the point of his lance drop.

Morning Sun looked as though she had been drugged in some opium hell. Her eyes were closed, and her mouth opening and closing without sound. I said to her that she was young, no one need know what had been done to her, she must not be frightened of her own people. And Ted said, "You durn *fool!*"

I showed him Frank Plummer's revolver again and said we were leaving with the girl, and if he interfered I'd just as soon ventilate him as maybe I should have done before.

The old chief had taken the pipe from Morning Sun's hand. He said, "But you must not steal what belongs to another, young wapto."

I pulled her away from him, pointing the revolver around that smoky tent, while Ted rose to his feet. Morning Sun still looked about to faint.

The chief said, "This is no son of Two-Star, big soldier. He is a fool and an impostor, and you have been tricked.

"I am very old," he went on. "I have no time to waste with blind fools who cannot see what is of importance and what is not, nor understand that they will remain as dust on the ground without a great chief's blessing." He held out a hand to Morning Sun, but I pulled her toward the open flap of the lodge, with my eyes streaming tears from the smoke.

The girl was sobbing as though her heart would break when I got her up behind me on my horse. Ted was cursing, his face as dark as a Kimanche's in his anger, as we left the Indian camp. No one tried to stop us, though the dogs trotted alongside yapping and snarling at each other. The girl sobbed piteously, whispering, "No! No! No—" between times, while she clung to my waist. I thought surely she would be grateful to me soon.

But that night when we made camp she would not stop her weeping, and Ted wouldn't speak to me. When I tried to discover the girl's name she only maintained that it was Morning Sun, and complained several times of luck being against her. Indeed, she was quite the opposite of grateful, and so unhappy that I laid off trying to talk to her at all, shivering with my fever and bitter that on every occasion when I sought to act to the benefit of others my motives were misconstrued.

That night, in the darkest, coldest time, shivering with a blanket around me as I sat by the fire with the trees whispering above me, I listened to Ted snoring like a man working hard, and listened in irritation to Morning Sun sobbing in her sleep. Sometimes I got up to pace up and down like Betsy in her cage, panting from the effort, for I felt very weak, and, seating myself again, shivered and spat into the fire. One of the horses whickered, and I could hear them moving nervously and stamping. Off in the dark there was a hoot owl, and another that set my nerves to jangling, for there is nothing to corrupt a man's grit like the thought of someone sneaking up on him in the dark. Finally I waked Ted to tell him something was out there, the horses were scary, but just then it was dead quiet. Ted grunted as though to say we wouldn't be in a fix of worrying if I'd not acted the fool, but he sat up with me, firelight gleaming on his rifle barrel. There was another horse whicker.

Ted's rifle jerked up and cracked once and a second time before they were on us. I couldn't make out how many there were or even which direction they'd come from; just all of a sudden a great bunch of shouting men and trampling horses were on top of us. I had both revolvers out trying to see something to shoot in the confusion, with my head whirling and my legs giving way under me. Morning Sun's screaming was the last thing I heard.

I came to my senses in full light with Ted squatting beside me patting a damp rag to my forehead, his big face worried as a man could look. Even trying to roll my eyes to see Morning Sun, my head hurt like I'd been poleaxed. But of course she was gone.

"Kimanche," I said. It sounded like somebody else talking, and it came to me to be thankful I was alive and still had my hair on.

"Might've been that hunting party at that," Ted said, but not as though he thought so.

"You mean it was somebody else?"

"Might've been the Putaw bunch from the way she was screeching."

"They took her off?"

He nodded and shrugged at the same time, trickling water from his rag onto my forehead. "Got yourself a fever you could fry eggs on," he said.

I carefully rolled my head to see that the animals were gone. It looked like we were afoot, though Ted said he'd scout around and see if they'd only got scattered, if I was content to rest alone awhile. So I dozed, and sometime later he came back with the packhorse. I asked if he'd found the trail, and he jerked his thumb west, away from the Kimanche camp, and that was all that was said about that.

When we started out, with me aboard the packhorse and Ted leading, I had to hang on fore and aft and my head felt like it would pull loose and float away. Ted was following hoof marks, or broken twigs and horse turds where the ground was stony. We headed into the setting sun, and the next day continued due west over ridge after ridge, each one a little lower than the last, which was at least an encouragement. At last the track we were following joined wheeltracks, which Ted said was the wagon road from San Hedrin, and now there was a mess of tracks running straight ahead or veering off this way or that. Most of the time I just jolted along with my eyes closed, hanging on as best I could.

Once Ted stooped to pluck up a sun-faded bit of blue cloth, which was so like a blue scarf Florrie had had that when he relinquished it to me I wore it wound around my hand, where I could bring it to my nose, though I could get no scent from it, and press it to my brow as though to cure myself with it. I knew I was far gone with fever.

It was all I could do to hold on to the pack saddle while Ted stumped on ahead through dry brush and brown grass over hummocks running down into flat land stretching west. My head floated off and floated back, and I hung on with fingers like sticks.

And all at once like a dream Ted and the packhorse were stopped in the midst of the strangest crowd of people. The most beautiful woman I'd ever seen sat sidesaddle on a gray horse with his mane cropped military style. She wore a kind of black cavalry blouse with a high-cut collar and a stock of lace at the throat. The gray danced sideways with his neck curving back as though he meant to nibble her little boot, and she laughed and cut him with her riding crop. She wore a velvet hat with a sweep of plume that nodded this way and that when she turned her head. She slashed again with her whip, this time at a gray wolfhound that leaped up by her stirrup. All this time she was talking to Ted. I heard the word "feverwater," and they both looked at me. There were others sitting their horses around us, most of them cavalry officers in blue with rows of gold buttons, but a civilian or two among them. They were all fidgeting with their mounts.

Then I saw what frighted the horses so that the men had to keep sawing at their reins: a big dead panther stretched out on the ground with yellow eyes open so that he looked alive still. From time to time the wolfhound would tear over toward it, jumping comically, like a puppy, to growl and worry at an ear, which would set the horses to spinning and curvetting, the men laughing and the women crying out in gay voices. It all seemed as beautiful as a fairy tale, as though my head had finally floated off to some other world entirely. And then I was falling, with Ted swift to catch me, and the last thing I heard was the beautiful lady saying we would certainly not continue on to Bright City, this young man was to be taken straightaway to the Castle.

That was how I arrived at the Castle. It was on Helix Hill above the dry riverbed of the old Sweetwater River, which had gone underground in an earthquake, some said, or else just turned to sand in the Dry-ups, when the gramma grass died, and the stock, and all the big ranches failed. On the other side of the hill was a place called Putaw Crossing, which had been the end of a spur railroad in the old days, where buffalo bones were piled as high as buildings. The side of the hill was riddled with old mine shafts drifted-in by prospectors searching for the Lost Dutchman mine.

I was there at the Castle for a month, for I was close to dying when the beautiful woman who was called Milady took me in, in delirium off and on for a long time and hardly able to feed myself for longer still. I will always be in her debt.

When I was better I would lie in bed on fine, cool linen in one of the outbuildings, where, if I propped my head over onto one side of the pillow, there was a view of the Castle through a corner of the window. It was many stories in height, all laid up out of natural stone, with blocks of shiny dressed stone running up the corners, and high windows cut in on the lower stories, and narrower ones in the turrets, which rose to conical roofs. Above all was a high cupola with a flag streaming in the breeze.

Nights in my bed I would watch those windows pouring out their light, with the silhouettes of people moving there, and faint music that seemed a part of all that light that filled the place. Almost every night there were levees, ladies with bare white shoulders dancing with fine officers from the fort, and gentlemen from Bright City.

In fact, however, Helix Castle was a great deal rundown from its best days, when the property had been a hundred miles square. Milady was having trouble keeping the place at all, and it was thought she must marry a rich man, maybe General Peach himself, though it would be difficult for her to give herself in marriage to any man in the Territory, where she had been almost a queen for so long, etc. All this gossip I had from the housekeeper, Bridey, and Thomas, the butler, a very old nigger with cotton balls of white hair clumped over his shiny skull. Bridey was as big and strong as Ted Eubanks, who had ridden on to Bright City, leaving me to the care of Milady and the servants. Bridey's face was round and red, and she had an accent like hot potatoes in her mouth. She would pick me up and hold me like a child in her arms while Thomas put clean linen on the bed, scurrying around it fussy as a chipmunk. It was Bridey who told me stories of the grand old days before the Dry-ups, when the river was so wide the officers would have contests for who could throw a dollar across, and so sweet the stock would bellow their pleasure to drink of it. And such goings-on at the Castle when Milady had been just a girl, the private trains coming in on the spur for the great hunts they had in those days; there had been elopements, and duels fought, and scandals, and great balls with three bands of music and a thousand candles, and cases of fine wines and champagne brought in. There was no real gentry in the Territory any more, Bridey said, and the officers of the fort were riff-raff compared with what used to be.

I have found in my life that people tend to think the old days more considerable than they really were, and see them in brighter colors, with no misery and all happiness and content, when in truth these very days of our dissatisfaction now will be the olden time of days to come. Yet it may be that the old days take their coloration from a person's own young optimism and good spirits, and it is the corruption of age and experience that makes those times seem so much brighter than these drab ones. Later I was to learn that Bridey was as easy a liar as Clytie, and had not even been at Helix Castle in those fine old times. She had all the stories from Thomas, whose account of things was never to be trusted, either.

Every day or so, about nightfall, Milady herself would come to pay a call on me, "her poor sick waif," as she called me, with her gloved hand patting mine, and her bright smile, which was, I came to see, always a little tired, as though like Bridey and Thomas she was forever remembering back to the grand time. Often a Captain Larkin would accompany her, with his wispy mustache and superior smile, and I liked him no more than he liked me. He was always overready to capture Milady's hand when she might be laying it on mine, and altogether too attentive to her, like a tongue-out dog.

When I was well enough to trust my legs I would walk about on short trips, and I saw for myself that what Bridey had told me of the decay of the place was true enough. Things were pretty worn out, and in need of painting and fixing. One day I went into one of the barns, which had a sprung door. There was dusty hay in bins, and broken harness hanging from nails, and spider webs, and the rustle of rats overhead. In the dim light through dusty panes of glass, I practiced throwing the bowies I had brought with me in their leather case, to see if I still had a good hand. I slung the knives in a straight line up a post at twenty paces, and then up two boards of diagonal bracing as though at Bill Mackie standing there with his arms out, before those days when he had turned into a jumping-jack clown. I felt a darkening of light of someone passing before the window. It was Milady in her black riding habit, the lace at her throat setting off her dark eyes.

She stood holding her riding crop between her hands and looking at the eight knives in their T with slanted-up arms, regular as though machine-set except for one that had sagged a bit. The big gray dog trotted in to plump himself at her feet.

"Why, Henry Plummer, you are an artist!"

She came closer, to stand beside a post where there was a horse collar hanging. The hound pounced off after a rat, growling and shaking his head to worry a mouthful of hay, which was all he had caught. Milady asked if she might watch me at my practice, as though she was not the owner of this barn along with everything else on Helix Hill, and I the "poor sick waif" she had nursed back from death's door, who owed her anything she asked of me.

So I jerked the blades out of the post and, ranging them up my arm, turned to face a section of plank wall. I flung them rapidly, three in the air at once, and this time not one so much as sagged, all standing erect and quivering in the dusty light from the window.

Milady said it was a marvel, and asked how I had come to this skill. She stood close to me, and her perfume, which was like violets mixed with musk and honey, seemed to fill my head.

I said it had been my trade in a medicine show.

"Oh, dear!" she cried. "I have never asked you anything of yourself! It does not show much hospitality, I fear!"

I said I had been shown more hospitality and kindness than I had seen in my life before this time, and, indeed, I owed my life to her. She looked pleased, but thoughtful too, and there was silence with the only sound the flies buzzing against the windowglass. But finally Milady said she must excuse herself not to hear more of my story now, for she was late for an appointment. She would have more time in days to come, as some of her guests would be leaving soon. And would I throw the knives once more for her?

I threw them once more, while she watched me with her little white hands with their cuffs of lace clasped like knots on her riding crop, and droplets of perspiration glistening on her short upper lip. When she saw that I had thrown an M for Milady, color flushed into her cheeks, and she whispered, "Thank you, Henry!" and was gone, the train of her habit flicking out the door, and the big gray dog loping after her.

That night, I slipped out of my room, hearing the sawing of a fiddle and the tinselly notes of the piano, to stand in the darkness outside one of the windows that gave onto the great central room with its sweep of stairs. On a little platform the piano gleamed, a skinny fellow with a high white collar leaning one way and the other as he banged away at it, and a sweaty-faced fiddler sweeping his bow back and forth in grand style. There must have been fifty candles burning in that place, where Bridey had claimed there had been a thousand once, though it was hard to make out where that many had stood. My eyes found Milady right away among the dancing couples, swinging in great circles around the margin of the room in the arms of one of the blue uniforms, her dark hair alive in the reflected candle flames that seemed always to bow toward her and her partner in the swiftness of their circling.

There were a dozen other dancers, men in uniforms or clawhammer coats and women like bright birds. The pounding and scraping of the musicians was faint through the glass, and the ballroom, whose top I couldn't even see from here, gleamed with light like Christmas. The music stopped and everyone moved to one end, where Thomas, in a cutaway and striped vest, was serving punch from a bowl. When the dancing began again Milady was swept away by a laughing major, and I drifted back to my room and tried to sleep with the music teasing at my hearing.

Then Thomas came knocking at my door to say Milady asked that I come, with my knives, to show her guests my skill. I hastened to dress myself and tie a white kerchief around my neck, looking at the face in the mirror that was still pale, and hollow in the cheeks. I left off my revolvers, but carried my case of knives toward the windows that carelessly threw their light out into the dark.

In the ballroom they were all standing at the punch-bowl again, the fiddler and the piano professor among them. It is an uncomfortable business to walk across a stretch of floor toward people you don't know but do know have been talking of you, but Milady hurried out to greet me and bring me up to the bunch of them, the officers giving me severe looks. There were painted smiles from the ladies, and one plump civilian-dressed fellow with mutton-chop whiskers was cordial. Captain Larkin was the tallest there, with his sleeked-sideways hair and wispy mustache, and arms folded on his chest so he wouldn't have to shake my hand. One of the ladies made over me to my embarrassment, and I heard another of them say behind her fan, "Why, he is just a boy, this marvel!" The laughing major said I looked considerably more fit than the first time he'd seen me, which was hanging on to a packsaddle like a life preserver in high seas. Thomas brought me a cup of the punch.

Two of the hostlers carried in one of the barn doors, shuffling and balancing and calling to each other to look sharp, finally bracing it against the piano to hold it upright, which displeased the little professor. All this while I stood with some officers who had nothing to say to me, nor I to them, though one said to another that he'd heard there was a new virgin at Mrs. Watson's, which ought to rouse the general though nothing else seemed to. There was coarse laughter at this. Another said he didn't expect many of those got by Jack Dale, which was the first I had heard of Jack Dale.

After I'd taken a second cup of punch, and finished

that, Milady inquired if I wouldn't consent to show these people what I could do, which would please them very much. So I took the knives from my case and hurled them swift enough so they crack-cracked into the rough whip-sawed wood of the old door, forming a cross there. The ladies cried out with admiration, and clapped their hands, and most of the men joined in.

I collected my knives and hurled them a second time, to split a long sliver of wood along the edge of one of the battens by driving in the blades along the grain of the wood. The wood split away as I had planned, but a knife dropped to the floor with a clatter, which caused one of the ladies, who had a beauty mark like a tiny black butterfly affixed to her cheek, to give a little scream.

Next I put four knives in the air at once, and then another four, to form another cross. The truth is that there are only so many tricks that can be done knife throwing, and I felt the lack of Bill Mackie for interest.

The laughing major asked if I was as swift with a side-arm, and I said I had had some practice with a forty-four, at which he raised an eyebrow and said sideways to another of the officers, "Maybe Jack's nemesis has arrived!"

Captain Larkin said in his sneering drawl that an armed man facing you was a different thing from a barn door. And Milady said, "Well, let's see if it is different with a woman facing him!" She hurried across the gleaming parquet, holding her skirt up from the floor, and arranged herself before the barn door with her arms held straight out to her sides, chin up and red mouth smiling.

"All right, Henry Plummer!" she cried out gaily.

"Now, see here!" the plump civilian cried. "This is too foolish, Vinnie!" The ladies all shrieked that she shouldn't do it, it was too dangerous, and Captain Larkin caught at my arm, commanding me to hold off. This caused me to drop two of my knives, and him to cut his hand. He jerked back, sucking on his cut.

"Please proceed, Henry!" Milady called. "It is a tiring position."

So I hurled the first blade into the planking above her

right hand, and saw her flinch at the solid chunk of the blade into the wood there.

The major leaned toward me to whisper that I was to be damned careful and not strike too close. Captain Larkin had taken his hand from his mouth to shake it, grimacing.

The second knife spun into the wood just below Milady's fingers. I could feel the force of her dark eyes fixed on mine, while her white neck was bent gracefully so her face was tipped to one side.

I flung the third knife into the door above her left hand, and the next below it, so now she looked as Bill Mackie had admired to stand, as though crucified against the backstop. Toward the end he had taken to jerking back and forth, making faces as Captain Larkin was doing now, and calling out as though to jigger me, and had done it one too many times. Milady stood still as a stone. The next blade I drove into the wood close to the juncture of her neck and shoulder, and I heard the suck of her breath. Quickly I threw the last three knives so her ordeal would be over, and raised my hands to show I was finished.

She stepped very quick away from the backstop, and halted to look back to the knives quivering in the wood. There was hearty clapping and bravos from everyone except Captain Larkin, who was making a fuss of tying a handkerchief over his wounded hand. Milady came smiling to me. "Very well done, Henry. I am glad it is over, however!"

The plump townsman called out, "You are a gritty little thing, Vinnie!"

She went over, then, to sympathize with Captain Larkin, who showed her his hand and pouted like a baby. I understood that I was excused now. Thomas pulled the knives from the wood and brought them to me, and I fitted them into their case, and bowed to the ladies and gentlemen, and was applauded one more time, though all was spoiling for me, with that bitterness like acid dripping in my veins; that I was a clown entertaining fools, who knew me for what I was but not themselves.

But just then another of the town gentlemen, this one skinny, with gray hair and a serious face, said, "You must be careful in Bright City, young man. For news of your prowess will precede you, and there's a very jealous fellow there named Jack Dale."

I thanked him, and said I'd been taking care of myself for all my life so far. I walked across the ballroom then, with my case under my arm, and heard a ripple of laughter behind me that I thought would be Captain Larkin having a joke at my expense.

Back in my bed I could still hear the faint, sweet music like bits of glass falling into a tin box. There was still no sleep for me as the past filled my head while I tried to strain my eyes to see the future, and so the two were mixed with each other, the blue scarf I had found that was so like Florrie's scarf, which had disappeared during my illness, and Milady's blue dress shimmering in the candlelight. I knew the night was passing in my sleeplessness and after a while there was no music in my head, but a quiet creaking of my door that might be part of the dream I had sunk into at last, and a sense of someone standing over me, and Milady whispering:

"Would you do something for me, Henry?"

Sitting up quickly, I said, "Anything, ma'am; you know that already!"

There was a shawl over her head against the night chill, and drawn over the lower part of her face.

"There is a man who frightens me very much—" she started.

And I broke in to ask if it was Captain Larkin that she meant.

She said that it was not in such a voice of disappointment that I can blush for my stupidity still. She left me then, as though she had changed her mind about asking the favor of me. I came to think it was Jack Dale she had meant, and later on to wonder if it was some other still. Or else it had all been the dream I had first thought it.

In the morning I woke to bright sun on blue cloth, gold

65

buttons, and gold Vs and half circles on a sleeve. It was Ted in army uniform, with his cap under his arm and a sweated circle dented in his short-cut hair.

"Boots and saddles, sonny. You have lazed long enough."

I asked him who Jack Dale was.

"Why, he is the pimp at a whorehouse and gambling establishment in town. What about him?"

I didn't answer, but slid out of bed. Before we set out for Bright City we drew up our horses in front of the steps that led to the great double doors to the Castle, and sent Thomas to find Milady. She came to the top of the steps in a riding habit so freshly pressed that not a wrinkle showed. She had on the cap with the white ostrich plume and carried her riding crop. The wolfhound hunched down beside her.

She nodded impatiently when I thanked her for her hospitality and for saving my life, but not so impatiently when I said, "I will hope to repay my debt to you, ma'am."

I saw she had a small white envelope in one hand. "Perhaps you will take this note to the general for me."

"Certainly, ma'am," Ted said, with a finger tipped to his hat brim. Thomas teetered down the steps to give me the envelope, which I tucked into my shirt pocket. Milady turned without another word and went back inside, snapping her fingers at the dog to follow her.

So, with Ted leading and the packhorse following, we rode on out the arched gate, and along the rutted track that led down the hill, with the sun warm on our backs. We crossed the dry river bed and began to climb again, instead of taking the wagon road around the mountain. The trail wound through clumps of stiff, dry brush, between granite boulders. Whenever I looked back the Castle on its hill was smaller.

The settlement on the other side of Helix Hill came into view, a cluster of shacks, a few set higher than the others; the rusted lines of the railroad spur, the ruined station with its stove-in roof, and thick walls of gray, heaped, tangled stuff. Ted told me these were buffalo bones. Putaw Crossing had been one of the chiefest stations for the old-time buffalo hunters shipping hides and bones east. The bones had been stacked waiting for a better market, which had never come but collapsed instead, and then the railroad had gone bankrupt in the Dry-ups.

Helix Castle was very small behind us now, red dust rising from beyond it to form a high red veil. Off in the east gray and white thunderheads were piled over the Bucksaws, the sun slashing through them gold as glory. Ted and I sat a bit watching the play of lightning inside one of the clouds. Plenty of rain and snow in the Bucksaws, he said, but what water ran off the western slopes of the Bucksaws disappeared underground.

Three horsemen watched us from a jut of rock a hundred feet higher than the trail, all of them black-dressed and black-hatted. At first I didn't know if Ted had seen them or not, but then he made a kind of offhand saluting gesture, hardly glancing up at them, and, after we had plodded on a ways, one on a black horse made a flipped-hand gesture back, not friendly nor unfriendly either. So we went on, the trail climbing no longer, but running sidehill now. When I ventured to glance behind me the three had disappeared from that high rock.

"Who were those preacher-looking fellows?" I asked.

"Some of that Putaw Gang," Ted said, and a way further along added, "Come to look you over, most likely."

"Most likely why?" I said.

He only short-answered, "See what you look like," as he would do when he intended to answer no more questions. We had started downhill now, and soon there was a prospect where he halted and only pointed, saying nothing. My mouth went dry and my heart pounded in my chest, for there was Bright City. In the clear air of this side of the mountain you could see the wagons rolling in the street, and horsemen. The sun lay on the plank-and-batten, false-fronted buildings, and, surrounding them, blocks of low adobes, with a glaze like honey. This side of town was the fort, a squared-off O of adobe walls, with a flagpole with a bit of red dropping from it. We started down a steep trail toward the fort.

Turkey buzzards planed in spirals so slow it seemed magical they could hover like that, ten or a dozen of them sweeping over the ground. Beneath their drifting shadows were papers scattered and bottles glinting, the town dump; beyond was a scraggly growth of wooden crosses and white-painted boards and whitewashed rocks, the cemetery.

At the fort a soldier passed us on inside. There was a parade ground with the flagpole in the center of it, and no soldiers in evidence, but a couple of washerwomen at some tubs down at the far end, and horses in a corral. To the left a sign hanging from a slant of roof said, MILITARY GOVERNOR, with two gold stars beneath it. Ted and I dismounted and tied our horses to the rail, and entered a door there. Inside it was dim and cool, and a sergeant passed us along a hall that was dimmer still, to the laughing major I had met at Milady's. He and Ted saluted each other; Ted gave a rap on a door, and a high voice called out to come in.

With our hats in our hands we went into a room where there was no light, and a stink of camphor. Ted flourished his right hand to his brow, though I couldn't distinguish anybody on the other side of the salute. I took the envelope out of my pocket to present to the general, when I could make him out. I was feeling nervy, for the general was a great man, a hero from all the wars, though very old now. The high, irritated voice told Ted to make a light.

A match whispered, a flame caught and climbed in a glass chimney, and there was the general sitting behind a desk with a bandage around his forehead. White hair stuck up in points above the bandage, below it a white-whiskery face with a shadow like a road agent's mask under the eyes.

Just then I caught sight of a coffin sitting on two saw-horses behind the door, the wood gleaming with polish. Other paraphernalia was stacked around to jerk at eyes: a bunch of flags with bullet holes in them braced in a kind of umbrella stand, stuffed animals snarling, marble statuary, and books in stacks everywhere. The general lowered at me from under his stinking head bandage as I stepped forward to hand him the letter. He inspected it front and back before he stuck a finger inside to pop the flap. Ted had lit another lamp.

The general fitted steel-rimmed glasses on his nose to read the note from Milady, and I ventured another glance around the room. The coffin had dovetailed edges and brass corners. Lamp flames were reflected in glass-covered photographs hanging on the walls. There were glass cases with stuffed bobcats, a coyote with yellow teeth, and a rattlesnake coiled to strike, natural to make you flinch. In the corner was a full-size white plaster grouping of a blown horse with a sagging Indian aboard, lance pointed down. Behind the desk was a painting showing cavalry riding hell-for-leather through a bunch of Indians, Kimanche maybe, toward some teepees that looked like Stonepecker's camp, only larger.

Last of all I swung a look behind me. On the wall opposite the general's desk was a painting almost as big as the cavalry charge. This one was a naked lady reclining on some red cloth. Her skin was so white it seemed to leap off the canvas. A hank of black hair was draped to cover her breast, and one knee raised and bent in. Her face was so like Milady's that I gasped out loud.

The general scowled up at me and said in his high-pitched voice, "So you are a young man to be reckoned with."

"Oh, he is one," Ted said. He stood rigid with boots set six inches apart, hands locked together before his crotch.

The general was sitting sideways-to, with a leg propped on a cushion. His gold-buttoned tunic hung over the back of a chair like a clothes horse, and in his shirt sleeves he looked frail enough to blow away in wind.

He asked me politely enough my name and age, my parents and the circumstances of my birth, and if I had any distinguishing birthmarks. He prodded me to relate my history, nodding the while and watching me with light glistening off his steel-rimmed spectacles.

Ted seemed impatient that I did not brag of my accomplishments, and broke in to say I was the wonder of the western world knife throwing, and a swift hand with a revolver besides.

"And is he lucky?" the general asked.

"Lucky so far, sir, and cool in a scrape."

"Holdfast," the general said, nodding. "It's got a plucky sound to it." He sat squinting at me in silence that seemed to squash me.

I asked what was wanted of me.

"But has the sergeant-major not spoken of it?"

"Not my place, sir!" Ted said, with another salute.

"To deal with the macquereaus!" the general cried out, which is a word I have learned since is French for pimp. Short for it is "mac," which I have been called myself, though not to my face. He went on talking fast and violent, but as I'd missed that first word his spiel got away from me. At first I thought he was talking about Jack Dale, and then "that Putaw crew," or maybe both at the same time, going on about "authority and jurisdiction," "liberty and license," and "freedom and order." Instructions or information that had to do with my destiny was coming to me in a high-pitched, complaining garble that I couldn't understand. I was feeling sick from the camphor stench, and I couldn't keep my mind from wandering off. I sneaked a couple of glances at the painting of the woman behind me, deciding that it couldn't be Milady. There was something petulant and mean in her face, and the way her knee was bent was not graceful.

The general rambled on, and it came to me that he wasn't right in the head, from his sickness or plain old age, but I saw that Ted was listening with close attention.

"For I am governor in name only!" the general went on. "Abandoned here without money even to meet one payroll after the next. With expenses I can get no one to heed. Transportation so I might as well be on the moon, and communication that is never anything but guesswork and error. And those damned savages arming again— *where* do they get those rifles?" He began laughing crazily and poking at his bandages with a finger. Then he slammed both hands down on his desk and cried out in a voice embarrassing in its passion:

"What have I done that even God has deserted me? To see these rainstorms beating themselves out on the Bucksaws while not one drop— And the river snatched away like His favor withdrawn! While I rail on helplessly here, unable to convince either God or the Republic of the danger—"

He stopped, and pointed his face at Ted like a blind man almost, while the silence bore heavy again. Finally in a low voice he said to Ted that I was to be seen to for the night, we would continue our conversation another time, he was very tired and taken poorly, etc. Ted hurried me outside.

He wouldn't talk about the general as we rode into town, and he seemed even more sour and silent than I was used to. The sun was hanging just over the peaks, splitting in two in the dust there, and rays of light spreading down the mountain and cutting sharp black shadows in the first buildings as we approached them. There was a bugle call behind us, and, as though that was the signal, the sun went down and everything turned to shadow but those bright clouds over the Bucksaws.

We came in along blocks of buildings with raised-up boardwalks in front of them, and wooden sunshades. A storekeeper in his shirt sleeves stood gazing west where the sun had gone down, and a little further along three or four men sat in chairs tipped back gossiping, one whittling.

Down a side street two soldiers were riding toward us on cropped-mane, bobbed-tail grays, like Milady's gelding; the men wore light-blue blouses, shiny black boots, and sharp-brimmed caps like Ted's cap.

Ted ignored them as we angled toward the main square, where there were taller buildings on three sides, boardwalks all around, and rails with horses hitched in twos and threes. Except for the church, the tallest building was a wooden cupolaed place that was the whorehouse, no doubt of it, where Jack Dale was pimp and badman. And just then I saw, tucked off in a corner of the square with a high white hoop of canvas cover, a wagon so like one from Frenchie's medicine show that I felt homesick like a kick in the belly.

There were people in the square, men in store suits and two of them with tall hats, cowboys leaning on rails and ladies in bonnets hurrying, though I noticed the proper ones kept away from the whorehouse side of the square, where three sporting women were parading to some whistling from the cowboys and soldiers lounging there. One of them, wearing a black straw hat and just turning in at the door, might have been Clytie. A man came out, passing her as she entered, and he caught my eye like nothing else yet as he stood just outside the door watching Ted and me riding across the square. I had a feeling almost of seeing my own self in a mirror. He was all in black clothing that was not rusty and preacher-looking like the three who had watched us on the mountain, but the same kind of fine-tailored black shirt and trousers I liked to wear myself, with revolvers on either hip, and a hand resting on his cartridge belt. The other raised a cheroot to his lip. He had on a low-crowned derby hat and what I could see of his face wasn't a young fellow's face nor old either, but like a young face very tired and hard at the edges, lined and dark-complected. He and I watched each other all the way across the square, where there was an eating place, for Ted said the first thing was to get outside a steak.

The man I knew must be Jack Dale watched us dismount and hitch and go on into the Dandy Café, with his arms crossed on his chest and the unlit cheroot in his jaw. I noticed that people gave him a wide berth passing.

We ate steak with potatoes and gravy, and afterward sat longer over black coffee than I cared to, though I was careful not to show Ted my impatience. But next, it seemed, we must stroll around the square in the evening. We passed close by the wagon I had seen earlier. Lights showed through the canvas walls of a tent set up beside it, and people were gathering. It was a medicine show, no doubt about it. As we circled around to the whorehouse, where there was a blue lamp burning now, a drum began to beat and a voice to shout like Frenchie touting our own show.

"Well," Ted said. "Let's us try a glass of whiskey at the parlorhouse yonder, and maybe a woman to chase it down." If I was so inclined, he said; and maybe to meet Jack Dale, too. I was inclined that way, anyhow.

Inside the piano was playing, its notes mixed up with the drumbeat outside, and a heavy rumble of talk and laughter and general racketing. We were in a room tall as the great ballroom at the Castle, with a chandelier that spread splashes of jeweled light everywhere, a balcony with a railing, and a higher balcony, with stairs sweeping up and around, very grand. Over to the right men's faces peered at us out of the mirrors of the back bar. Two barkeeps were working there, and between were tables with bottles on them. The professor, the same one who had played at the Castle, was throwing his hands into the air and sweeping them down in very florid style.

Jack Dale sat in a high chair under the chandelier between the faro layouts. He had his chin resting on his hand, his shotgun laid in slots across the chair arms, and his derby hat on. He looked sad and absent like he was thinking of something a long way off as he gazed down on the card players. One of the faro dealers was a fierce-looking little fellow in a green eyeshade, with arms so short he could hardly reach out to the box. There were whores among the men at the tables, all dressed in finery.

Once Jack Dale had seen me he never looked anywhere else, though his expression was amiable enough.

Fellows we met coming in said, "Howdy, Maje," and soldiers, "Evenin', Sergeant-Major," others just nodding to us as we passed them looking for an empty table. A barkeep hurried to bring us whiskey, and one of the whores came past swinging her hips in time to the piano music, as women will do. Maje gave her a smack on the rump, and she spun around to spit like a cat, then smiled at me to show it was all in fun, a painted young woman with bunches of rings on her fingers like shiny bugs. When she had gone on I saw Jack Dale moving toward us in a slow-sauntering, easy way I had to admire.

I stood up to make his acquaintance. He was more polite than friendly, but those deep lines in his dark face gave me some sympathy for the hard times he must have seen. He had yellowish eyeballs and dark pupils I could see myself reflected in.

"You are welcome here, young fellow," he said, and I thanked him, and said I was pleased to meet him, and wished it was Captain Larkin I had to deal with instead. He had a way of resting his hand on his cartridge belt that I know I have copied to this day, and his way of walking as well.

He inquired if we were interested in female company, and Ted said he had heard there was a new girl upstairs, which Jack Dale replied was true, and a spitfire. Ted said he would like a word with Clytie.

Well, I was knocked out of shape by that, and there was Clytie headed in our direction, wearing a black dress and white apron, but with strings of jet beads around her neck that swung as she came on, and her color up and her hair piled so that she looked younger, and prettier too. My heart was beating like the drumbeat from the square for I thought now she would berate me for my promise to kill T. P. Eubanks, but she only swarmed up to take me in her arms and kiss my cheek with a great popping sound, and then stand with her hands on her hips and her good teeth shot out grinning, and all the fine smooth flesh of her bosom jiggling. "Well, Henry, here you are!"

And to my amazement and confusion she grabbed Ted's arm and put it around her, holding me at the same time so the three of us must've looked like we were having a tintype made. Then Clytie pulled us down so we were all three seated at the table.

"Well, if this doesn't do my heart good! You two!"

Ted said, very coarse, that it did his pecker good to see her, and both of them laughed and slapped their legs at this, while I tossed off my whiskey. I swung around, hearing a yip at the door, where a young cowboy had come in, raising his hat and shaking it about as though greeting one and all, full of whiskey and jollity. Jack Dale was approaching him at his easy saunter. He spoke a quiet word to the cowboy, who made as though to come on past him. Something happened so quick I didn't catch it, and the cowboy staggered back outside the door with Jack Dale following him close, in a silence that had fallen on the place like a mattress. I had seen a man bulldozed by a master at it.

Well, then, the racket started up again, and Clytie must know what had been happening to me since we parted, etc. I answered her, talking fast so she would not get a word in edgeways and I'd learn something I didn't want to know. I didn't want to ask about Florrie, and I was ashamed of that, and feeling sick to my stomach as I had with the general and his camphor stink. Things seemed to be moving too fast. Just then the professor laid off his piano playing and the drum could be heard more clearly outside, and a little thin tootling as though they had a dancing bear.

Ted said to Clytie, how about a little trot upstairs for old time's sake? The two of them went up the steps with their arms around each other and his big hand kneading her bottom. There had got to be too many things spinning in my head, and I knew I had to get some fresh air, so I went on out, trying to saunter but not making much of a job of it.

I stood just outside the blue glow of the lantern taking deep breaths, and after a while headed across the square toward the lights showing through the canvas, where the drum was still beating. Sure enough, there was a dancing bear shuffling and turning with paws folded on her chest. Beating the drum and at the same time blowing on a kind of tin whistle was an old man with stiff white hair and tobacco-juice stains in his beard. From time to time he gave a jerk on the bear's chain, while a boy in a checked cloth cap passed a pan for coins. When the act was done the old man rasped out in a barbed-wire voice that Holdfast would start in five minutes more.

Well, if I had got my senses back in the cool air, that knocked them out of me again. Indeed, there was a painted backdrop of boards exactly the same as in my show with Florrie, and rows of benches before it and a good crowd of Bright City people. A girl came out twirling a parasol. It was not Florrie, but a girl with flat, dark features, maybe part greaser. She sang in a voice that grated in my ears while she beat her eyelashes up and down in a manner I found unbearable. Then Bill Mackie, in a derby hat, came on at a rapid, comical pace. He raised his hat to the audience, and bowed, and seemed to be a great favorite from the applause.

When it was silent again, the girl with the parasol turned, and screamed to see Bill. Right away a fellow all in black appeared, wearing two revolvers, exactly as I used to show up. He had a red face with a slash of mustache across it, and he drew his two guns while Bill staggered back against the backstop as he had always done, the girl twirling her parasol and simpering. All this was painful in the extreme for me to watch.

However, at this time Bill pulled from his clothing a bunch of roses exactly as I had once produced my bowie knives. He handed the bouquet to the gunman, who had to holster his starboard revolver in order to accept it. All smiles, Bill produced fruit of various kinds from his pockets, followed by vegetables, even a cabbage, and the gunman had to holster his other revolver to manage all these groceries. He had a particularly difficult time with the cabbage, to the great amusement of the people seated near me.

While the gunman staggered about balancing his load, Bill dropped down on his knees before the girl, folded hands raised imploring her. She simpered and postured some more, forgiving him, and the two of them started off-stage, arm in arm. The gunman, leaning against the back-stop, had managed to unship one of his revolvers, and Bill halted to slip a knife from his clothing and fling it into the backstop beside the gunman, then another on the other side, which seemed to pin the gunman's arms to his sides. With which he dropped all the groceries and ran offstage one way, while Bill strutted off with the girl the other, to great applause and laughter.

I chose this moment to take my leave, though behind me I could still hear the clapping and whistling. I think I have never felt so low in my life as I did heading back from there to the whorehouse, with no heart in me for anything.

But a voice said out of the dark, "Well, you look like a hardcase to me."

A cowboy was lounging against the rail with his face black shadow under his hat brim and his hands hooked onto his belt. I stopped by him, but he didn't seem to be looking for trouble.

"Anyways," he went on, sounding like a boy, with his voice cracking, "you are the only fellow in this town with nerve enough to *look* like a hardcase that I have seen, except for that clown in the medicine show over there."

I wasn't sure I wasn't being joked still, until he moved his head so that his face caught some light. His cheek was slashed with blood that had run down to his chin, dried and crusted now; he was the cowboy Jack Dale had bull-dozed.

I said I had seen him smacked, but not what he had done to warrant it.

He said a man didn't need to do anything but look a certain way to warrant a thing, what this town had come to. It was enough to make a fellow head out for Putaw Crossing to throw his duffel in with those fellows.

I leaned against the rail beside him to hear what else he had to say, which was that the general owned the whorehouse and half the town besides, and Jack Dale kept the peace for him except that all he did was run honest men out to join the desperadoes. It was about come to it that there were more good fellows on Putaw Creek than left in town, so everything had got turned around.

Others had sidled up to listen to him in his bitterness. One of these was the dwarf who dealt faro, who said, "Well, sonny, if you think those are fine, honest fellows over at the Crossing, you are going to find you are mistaken."

"I suppose you will tell Jack Dale I have been blowing against him out here," the cowboy said.

"Tell him the same thing you've been saying, myself; some of it," the dwarf said. He was in his shirt sleeves, and his cigar sparked as he gesticulated with it. He had a scratchy, sarcastic voice. "Told him he is taking too much on himself. People starting to turn against him. Oh, he don't scare me."

There were mutterings from the other men gathered around us. The cowboy was picking at the scab on his chin. "Hear they're paying good money out there," he said.

"Ha!" the dwarf said. "You think he takes things strict, you just go out there and see. They'll badger the soul right out of you, *that* bunch."

"Well, I don't know about that," another said. "I just see things are run for the bigwigs in this town. And Jack Dale does the running."

A white-bearded old man in a low-brimmed hat said, "He come over and laid down the law to us first thing. How the drum was too loud and disturbing the customers over here, and we'd better keep the bear on a chain—" I saw it was the old fellow that had introduced the knife-throwing act.

"Lucky he lets your show go at all," another told him. "Lot of fellows think you are making a joke of him over there."

The dwarf stuck his cigar out at me. "Just who are you, mister? He has had an eye on you pretty good all evening, am I right?"

I told the dwarf my name was Henry Plummer, but where I came from I was called Holdfast. It pleased me to hear the old-timer from the medicine show suck in his breath at that.

The cowboy put in that I was the only man he'd seen with spunk enough to walk around heeled and a knife in his belt, and another asked me what was my intention when Jack Dale told me to shed iron, as he was bound to do. I saw fit to make no reply to that, for it is easy to slip into cheap brag.

"I was about to choose him tonight myself," the cowboy said. "I had drunk me some courage, and I had a speech I was going to make for everyone to hear. How if a decent man has got to choose between suck eggs in Bright City, or gone to Putaw Crossing, why, we are in a bad way. And Jack Dale is the cause of it."

"That is a speech it is just as well you didn't deliver, sonny," the dwarf said contemptuously.

"Nothing's going to change around here so long as he stands in with the cavalry the way he do," a man in a white hat said. "Officers getting first crack at the new girls. I hear they have got a real pretty one up there now, too."

These fellows seemed to me a poor-spirited lot. I did not doubt that most of them would toady to a man's face and jump him when he was down. I said if they would excuse me I would be about my business. Various of them muttered one thing and another, very respectful, one of them whispering behind me, "Plummer, eh?" and another, "Quite a young fellow, ain't he?"

When I went back inside Ted and Clytie were sitting where we'd been, their hands all over each other. I said I wanted to see that new girl upstairs, and Clytie rose and I followed her over to the stairs and up them, like any fellow with a whore in a whorehouse, only this was the woman that called herself my mother, and I was going upstairs to see my "sister." I felt as though in this one day I had changed from flesh and blood to case-hard iron. When I glanced back no one seemed to be paying attention to us, except Ted Eubanks sitting there with a bottle of whiskey before him, and the dwarf with his green eyeshade on, back at the faro layout. Jack Dale wasn't in sight.

Off the balcony Clytie tapped at a door and a voice answered, very low. And we went in.

A girl was sitting at a dressing table in a long white gown, brushing her hair, which was black. I leaned in the doorway behind Clytie staring at her hair, and her hand running the brush through it, and a bit of white cheek that showed in the glass.

The room gleamed with candles like the ballroom of Milady's castle, colors flicking through the crystals of a chandelier and reflected like diamonds in tiny mirrors cunningly set into the wallpaper. Candle flames seemed to be dancing and flashing everywhere in the room, and the girl turned suddenly from her mirror. It was Morning Sun.

"It is you again!" she cried out.

"Where is Florrie?" I said, catching Clytie by her plump arm.

"Why— Why, she is schoolteachering—" She pried my grip from her flesh, and said, "Why, aren't you *ashamed*, Henry Plummer!"

"Henry Plummer!" the girl cried in a rabbity voice. "Haven't you done enough to me, Henry Plummer?"

I could only say I saw I had made a mistake when I had sought to save her from a vile slavery, for that seemed to be what she preferred. At which she screamed curses at me, jerking to a standing position with her bosom heaving in her white gown and her fists clenched at her sides. And I heard quick steps coming up the stairs.

Jake Dale pushed into the room past me and Clytie. He was without his derby hat, and his graying, crinkly hair grew low on his forehead. Standing between Morning Sun and me he said, politely enough, that I had made a mistake, Clytie had made a mistake evidently, this part of the house was reserved.

Morning Sun's face cleared of its fury like icing had been smoothed over it. Clytie said we two were old friends from a previous time we had met, that was all.

I said she had just wanted to thank me for rescuing her from a different kind of hell than this one, but there was nothing more to keep me here.

"Then just get along now, friend," Jack Dale said. "There doesn't have to be trouble."

I said the only thing that would keep me here was the feeling I was being leaned on to leave. I was not one to make trouble over a whore, but a pimp ordering me around was offensive. And Clytie clapped her hand to her mouth, her eyes bugging at me.

All at once Jack Dale and I seemed to be standing very close together and I was looking at myself in his dark eyeballs that had lids drooped half closed over them. A little cluster of veins beat in his temple.

He brought his revolver barrel up swift to cold-cock me as he had done the young cowboy, but I had my knife out just as fast, so he had to stop his stroke or cut his wrist. We held like that for a minute, his revolver barrel standing straight up and my blade alongside his wrist, with the only sound Clytie gasping. Morning Sun was leaning against her dressing table with a round spot of color in either cheek. Jack Dale sighed.

I brought out my own revolver when he did not holster his own, though I slid my knife back in its scabbard. There is a naked thing about a knife blade that does not want to stay bare for very long. Jack Dale said in a cold voice that there was to be no shooting in places where others stood to be hurt.

I said that sounded fair enough if it worked both ways, but neither one of us moved to put his revolver away, like a pair of locked-horn elks. But finally he holstered his piece, and I did the same. I said there was nothing to hold me here in this company except that I did not intend to go on his say-so, and after some jockeying he and I went out the door onto the balcony together, where there was the great glitter of the chandelier straight ahead of us, and beneath us the heads of the men at the gambling layouts, with their hair parted and Macassar-oil greased.

Jack Dale and I walked downstairs side by side and in

step, though he had managed to place himself on my right side. We came down into a silence that could've been cut into bricks and sold for building a library, with faces staring up through a haze of cigar smoke like from under water. The lookout was frozen in his high chair, and the barkeeps behind the bar. Ted was sitting at his table rubbing his face with his hands.

We stepped down together to the main floor, and, when I glanced back up, there were Clytie's and Morning Sun's faces showing pale in the dimness of the first balcony. Jack Dale pushed close to me on the right so I could not draw my revolver, but did not pull his own, either.

"Get out," he said. It was clear this was said for the benefit of those around us. "And don't come back here heeled again."

All at once Ted came barging through the men around us to grab me by the arm, saying, "Let's leave well enough be!"

I saw the dwarf staring at me, with a gone-out cigar in his jaw and his ugly face worried, and the cowboy with his eyes bright as green stones. I shook Ted's hand off.

"Boy," he said in his down-a-well voice. "You are about to go off half-cocked again, and it is one time too many."

I guess I knew it even then, but the day had been too much for me, with Bill Mackie and his knife act, with Clytie and Ted, and my thoughts of Florrie that shamed me still like a fox gnawing at my liver, and that pure hate in Morning Sun's face, and most of all maybe that young cowboy thinking I was some kind of hero for courage.

So I flipped open the buckle of my cartridge belt, dropping it and my holstered piece to the floor at my feet with a thump that made people start, and in the same motion caught my bowie out again with a naked blade, saying I didn't mind checking my forty-four, but I wouldn't consider visiting a whorehouse without my knife, the people a fellow was apt to run onto there. If he didn't mind; or if he did.

"Throw it all up then," Ted said in a voice that

sounded like he was strangling, and just then somebody cried out, I never did see who:

"Lot of folks' hopes riding on you, Henry Plummer!"

Jack Dale looked around for who had said it, very swift, his face dark, and a shine of sweat just above the eyes. There was a line of whores' faces up along the balcony railing, and the professor slammed down a great chord on the piano as Jack Dale unbuckled his own cartridge belt and let it fall, and stepped out of it.

He looked to be almost smiling at some joke that was just between the two of us, the long creases in his face looking cut deeper. His fingers crawled over the buttons of his shirt, and he stretched out his arms to unfasten the cufflinks, then stripped it off to show his sallow dark chest with a star tip of hair growing up his belly, clusters of hairs around the paps, and the breath of his life showing between. He wound his shirt around his left hand and let a droop of it hang down. That was to catch my blade with. I was reminded that he might know more of knife fighting than I did, who had had no practice handling a bowie in this close way, but I thought I would not take off my shirt as he had done, all the same.

Then he reached behind him, and there was a gasp from all around as he brought out a knife of his own.

He came at me strongly with a stroke of his knife for my belly that I sucked back from, and thrust out with my own blade, which he stepped away from graceful as a Spanish dancer. When he came at me again I caught his wrist and backhanded at him, to find my blade caught in his shirt. We held like that for a minute, me feeling the strength in his wrist and not even trying to free my knife, while all around us the faces with those bits of colored light dancing on them pushed closer to us. I saw his muddy eyes flick toward the stairs, and there were two officers standing there in their dress uniforms and gold buttons glittering. It was the general on the lower step, his hand on the haft of his sword, watching with a fierce scowl on his gray face, and on the step above him the major.

They stood without moving, and when Jack Dale's eyes came back to mine I saw in them he knew he was a goner.

We jerked apart and came at one another again, though I knew his strength would not last long from what I had felt in his wrist, and seen in his eyes. Toward the end he began panting as though he'd never get his breath again. I had slashed his hand so it was running blood, which was slippery beneath our feet. And at last I drove straight in to him, and stepped back knowing it was done.

Holding his belly and trying to walk upright he started outside through the men and whores pushing back to make a way for him. A couple of women were sobbing, and some of the men followed him outside. On the stairs the major remained watching, but the general had disappeared. As though everyone was frozen and it took some time to thaw out, it was a while before men began crowding around to congratulate me, quiet about it at first, but noisier and noisier, reaching out to touch me, some of them, or slap my back, and many to blow the spit of their enthusiasm into my face, until I looked back from eye to eye so cold that they began to draw away, and their noise quieted.

Those who had gone outside with Jack Dale began coming back inside. There was something strange about them, dark stains on their hats and shoulders. I realized it was damp, it must be raining, and in the silence then I could hear it splatting outside, the first rain since I'd come into the Territory with its terrible drought.

And that was how I replaced Jack Dale and came into the position of town marshal as well, which went along with it.

Two days later when there'd been time for the news to get abroad, a bunch of those black riders I'd seen three of with Ted Eubanks on the mountain rode in to hurrah the town. I stopped them, breaking the arm of one with a lucky shot, and getting the drop on the others, and told them they were posted out of Bright City by me the same as they had been by Jack Dale. A rat-jawed fellow with a sneer built into his face told me that one of these days

Putaw Crossing was just plain going to come in and squash Bright City flat, and all the Henry Plummers and Jack Dales in the world couldn't stop it.

Well, they have not come in yet. I have seen to that.

So I replaced Jack Dale, and what has become of the great destiny I had felt in myself and that was prophesied for me, that I have been content to pimp in a whorehouse and keep the peace in a broken-down town out in the Territory? It was like when I got rid of Jack Dale I was bound to become Jack Dale, and I can say I was not the first man to go to the bad because his hat was nailed to a lady's bedroom ceiling, but I will not plead that in whatever court it is that will sit upon my case.

Nor plead either that I made no pact with Bic Mac that he stay out of Bright City and I stay out of his business, as is said of me—for that has been the effect. And I should have known that with someone like Big Mac there is no such thing as his jurisdiction and mine, for every man's welfare is every other man's jurisdiction.

Bright City lost population to Putaw as men began moving out there every day for the money and flash of the place, and women too—some women, once they hear of it, there is no heading them off. They are bound to go there—born for it, so to speak.

The Castle was long ago deserted and gone to ruin, and Big Mac took it over when Putaw swelled up the back side and covered all of Helix Hill. And all of that part of the Territory has gone to ruin too, with the mill belching up that black smoke like hell on fire, and the copper-colored lakes of the slurry pits running out in every direction—between and beyond them the heaps of slag, waste, and chewed rock.The reek of sulfur smoke and rock dust is so strong that on certain days men can hardly breathe down there, but there is work for everyone and money paid.

It is said that Big Mac is bound to find the Lost Dutchman if he has to turn the earth inside out like a sucked-dry orange to do it.

In this life there are too many choices that have to be

made, each of a complexity multiplied by the last choice, and how is a man to determine when action is called for and when forbearance from action? How do you decide whether it is your destiny to become a parlorhouse pimp, a town marshal, general, or military governor in the do-or-die fight whose issues you don't even understand? How can a man ever discover who he is, his mere antecedents even, and what he is supposed to be?

I know one thing that will be held against me forever, for I will hold it against myself, which is that through those years when I was swallowing self-disgust with my morning coffee I never managed to get out of town to search for Florrie, schoolteachering somewhere in the Territory—maybe close by!—while she waited for the Right and True One. How did I know that that One was not me?

But, if it is too complicated for a man to know his own self, his jurisdiction, and his True Destiny, I know what the penalty for failure is, which is not complicated at all.

For the Kid is in the Territory now, they say, and I know a night will come when, stepping outside for a breath of fresh air, say, I will catch a glimpse of him where he has dismounted to head into the Dandy Café, halting to gaze down the boardwalk at me, slight of frame, bareheaded with his hat in his hands, and fair; and young and full of himself, as I once was.

TWO

Lieutenant Grace

On the third day we saw the great bear.

All day we had ridden across tumbled land toward mountains that must lie within the Territory, although the boundary was famous for its vagaries, a line drawn on a map merely—from this peak to those unreliable springs, to that disappearing river. My half-breed guide entertained me with the tales with which new-come junior officers are affrighted—the outlaw bands we might encounter en route to Bright City, the sudden fevers, the rattlers, grizzlers, and painters (as he called them), and the flash floods that burst down out of the Bucksaws like express trains, even when there had been no rain, and one must always listen for the mutterings of thunder that told of cloudbursts in these peaks that themselves loomed like thunderheads before us—although the Territory itself had been baking in drought for more than ten years.

The savages of these parts were notorious also, Kimanches sneaking in during the night to scalp, torture horridly, and take captives; and young braves who bound themselves in a mesh of rawhide tourniquets so they would not be brought down by loss of blood, while they hacked and counted coup in their murder-madness. I reached forward to pat the haft of my saber just to think of those fellows.

Our way led down an eroded gully, up a ridge and along it for some twenty yards, down again and up and along another ridge, in a series of tacks against the grain of the land. The mountains appeared no nearer. I rode in the lead, sweltering under the pitiless sun, flap of my kepi flicking at the back of my neck, rifle and saber scabbarded just forward of my right knee. Behind me came Josiah, shapeless as a sack of meal in the saddle, corner-knotted bandana covering his head, braided hair dangling down his back. Following him were the pack animals.

"Looky there!" he called out.

It might have been a locomotive speeding up the gully we had just climbed out of, the brush violently and progressively shaken by something huge tearing through it. A great, gray bounding ball was visible for an instant, crossing the ridge ahead of us.

"What was *that?*"

"Grizz," Jos said. He began making a keening sound, low at first but mounting in scale almost to a falsetto, some Indian incantation, apparently, that it seemed disrespectful to interrupt. I slid my carbine out of its boot.

"Looky there!" Jos said again. The grizzly had reappeared two ridges away, erect with front paws dangling, head raised attentively to inspect us. He might have been a fat, fur-coated man. I eased the carbine free.

Jos hissed. "What would you do, shoot your luck?"

"My luck?"

"Good sign," he said. "Some say she got away from a circus. Come visitin' like that sometimes. Good-luck sign."

The bear stood there motionless. Jos grunted. "Really lookin' you over." The bear vanished.

My guide had a habit of mysterious utterance that it was useless to pursue, but as we rode on I considered my luck. My orders to the 13th Cavalry of General Peach's command were wrapped in oiled silk in my kitbag. It was the most disreputable regiment in the army, Bright City the most godforsaken of posts. All the cadets of the Academy knew of General Peach as the hero of the Twenty Battles, and of surely twice that many Indian fights, but knew of him also as a renegade and disgraced old officer relegated to the governorship of a drought-ruined territory. There were as many tales of battles drunkenly lost, and of

cowardly retreats, as of victories gained by brilliant strata-
gems and thundering charges. There were also rumors of
the Territory run as a feudal fiefdom, harems, troops of
bastard get; an old man insane not only in the pursuit of
his lusts but of a fabulous lost mine, rich beyond imagina-
tion, that was known to lie somewhere within his domain.
It was said he was of such past reputation that he could
not be cashiered or even retired, that he had made a shaky
peace with the Kimanche but was locked into a war with a
giant outlaw known as Big Mac.

My orders were to report to the 13th Cavalry as adjutant, with a rank of lieutenant, and the general had asked
for me. It was thought that this was due to my high marks
in the study of hydraulics, for the lack of water in the Territory had stunted its progress, and, indeed, its civilizing.
My fellow cadets considered mine the worst possible posting in the Army, but it did not seem so to me.

At a range of half a mile, I saw, like some queer reflection of ourselves, two horsemen traversing a ridge on a
parallel course. When I drew my glass and tried to focus it
upon them, they dropped into a gully and did not immediately reappear.

"Make out if those beasts' tails was braided?" Jos inquired.

I said I didn't think so, removing my cap to fan my
face. "Kimanche?" I asked.

"Been talk of a gatherin' up on Greasy Grass," my
guide informed me. The two figures materialized further
off. I aimed my glass.

"Make out if they got themselves all strapped up like a
package?" Jos said.

I could only see that the horses and riders were gen-
erally brown in color before they were gone again.

"What's that Kimanche word for hide-tied-up-crazy-
man?"

"Hueycoha," Josiah said. "Now, you just follow up toward where those white stones is, Lieutenant. Spring and
some shade up there."

At the spring, where a trickle of water purled through rocks into a tiny glen of brushwood, we drank from the clear run and then turned the horses in to water.

"What did you mean, that bear was a good-luck sign?" I said, seating myself with my back propped against one of the white rocks.

Jos squinted at me with his beady eyes almost lost in wrinkled brown flesh. Bits of filthy ribbon were woven into his black braids. "Like she knows you might be what everybody's waitin' for."

"What's everybody waiting for?"

"Right man to come," Jos said, but when I asked him to elucidate on this, I had no satisfaction. I asked if the Kimanche gathering meant they were going on the warpath.

He hunked a chew of tobacco from his plug, his face working as though he was munching his upper lip, and I thought he was not going to respond to this, either. Beyond him the horses lowered their heads into the little pond.

"Use to be, they'd come to confabbin' like that, old general'd go after them," the guide said finally. "Then there'd be a fight, all right."

"Maybe I'll see some action then."

"Oh, you'll see some action, all right, Mr. Lieutenant Grace. But don't you be too sure it's going to be with Kimanche."

"Against the outlaw gang, you mean?"

"Hah!" he said, and pointed a filthy finger at my belt. "Action soon enough! You wear that shootin' iron on you from now on! Whatever you do, eat, piss, poontang—shooter on! This is *Territory,* you hear me!" And he was not satisfied until I had risen to search out my sidearm among my gear, and donned it.

While he busied himself building a fire in a blackened ring of stones, the sun extinguished itself beyond the peaks like a lamp blown out. Instantly a cool wind flowed down the slope, and I rose again to put my jacket on. Then I reclined against my rock watching the first pale stars reveal themselves, fingering the ring on its silver chain that hung around my neck inside my shirt.

One night in my bed at my aunt's, sobbing for my lost mother, it was as though the very intensity of my longing had produced old Ben Dandy, the groom from the old days, who had brought me the ring, saying my mother wanted me to have it. Before I could question him—where *was* she? why had she gone away?—he was gone. I turned the ring between my fingers, feeling the white cameo profile I had come to believe must be my mother's face, long patrician line of forehead and nose, and small, sweet mouth.

She had run away from my father. How could I blame her for that, who hated him also; except that she had left me behind. Run off with another officer, my dried-up, bitter, hater-of-my-mother Aunt Eliza told me. Never faithful to poor John in her heart, and only biding her time to be unfaithful outside it. My mother had gone "out West," where she lived like a queen among rough men. The memories of my aunt's poisonous utterances were as mysterious as my guide's.

I heard the distant rumble of thunder, and looked up into the star-studded night to see no clouds. Jos, squatting beside the fire, cocked his head to gaze upward also. The thunder grumbled again, more distantly, like someone muttering a message in unintelligible words.

And it came to me like wine in my veins that I would find my mother out here, for what was the Territory and Bright City but the epitome of "out West"?

The next day we surmounted a series of high passes, descending into hanging valleys like balconies, where dry creeks had been scoured as clean as brown granite gunbarrels. As we approached each of these, Jos would scout along the bank for the quickest crossing, and we would then scramble to the far side as though exposed to enemy fire. We continued to descend into a cloud that filled the broad valley like gray steaming liquid, denser and denser as we sank into it, although I could distinguish that we had encountered a well-beaten track. The Bright City wagon road, Jos said.

The fog thickened still more with evening, and Jos passed back an end of rope for me to guide on. I pulled on a rein of the lead pack animal behind me.

"Get a little fog in here sometimes," Jos said.

"Yes, I see," I said. I couldn't see much. The fog was cold and beaded my face with congealed droplets. I strained my eyes. The animals' hoofs clattered on stones. There was a yelp from Jos, and all at once figures loomed out of the fog. There was a shout and a shot. I drew and fired jagged flame, and in an instant the place was echoing with shots and yells. I tried to remember the name for hide-tied-up-crazy-men, firing at the moving dark bulges in the gray blankets. The clatter of hoofs surged again, receding, and then was gone. "Jos!" I panted. I had the exultant feeling of having acquitted myself well in my first action.

He appeared dimly, afoot, leading his horse, rifle in his hand. "Hueycoha!" I said.

Just then, sour and quavering, came a familiar shrilling: a trumpet sounding recall. I stared at Jos, stunned. Then I bellowed, "Soldiers! It is your new adjutant here! Soldiers!"

"Hush that noise!" Jos said.

The brass call continued to echo in my skull, as though repeated just out of earshot. I slid my revolver back into its holster. "Soldiers on the track of renegade Kimanche," I said.

"Maybe not," Jos said. "There's deserters gone over to Big Mac, that's for certain."

"The outlaw gang! Was that who they were?"

"Couldn't say," Jos said. "Whatever they was, gone now." The dim shape ascended into the saddle. I found the rope looped on my saddle horn, and it tightened against my hand. "Make camp soon," Jos said.

When we had scouted up some punky wood and made a fire, Jos was even more silent than usual, busying himself making supper, and grunting with ill-temper to my questions. For my part I was still shaky with excitement over the shooting scrape, hunkered down beside the bed of flames and pushing an oily wad through the barrel of my revolver. I had seen some action.

The next day dawned clear; we were in a grove of pines, and pine-spiked mountains rose on either side of us. Jos discovered that one of the pack animals was crippled by a bullet in the shoulder, and there was nothing to do but dispatch the poor beast and parcel out the load.

The Bright City road headed straight west along the valley floor. Jos dismounted to study hoof prints in a muddy depression. He only shrugged when I asked what he had found. Wagon tracks were visible now, even to my untrained eye.

A man in a tall white hat sat a buckskin horse watching us approach, rifle cradled in his arms. He raised a palm in greeting. He had a hard, beard-darkened face assembled around a hooked nose. His arms seemed disproportionately short, and his legs were so short they stuck out from his saddle like those of a child on a fat pony. A dwarf, I realized.

He crowded close beside me, too close for comfort, craning his neck to squint up into my face. "Army getting reinforcements, am I right?" He grasped rifle and reins in his left hand, and proffered his right. "Frank Pearl," he said.

I identified myself and shook the small hand.

"You and your breed better come eat with us. Best chink cook in the Territory. Right on ahead about a mile."

I accepted his offer of hospitality and we rode on together, with Jos trailing behind. "Some fog last night," he said.

I said we'd had a scrape with Kimanche or outlaws, we hadn't been able to make out which, and heard a bugle call also.

"Hard to say what's what out there," he said cheerfully. "Spooks as likely as anything. Didn't hear anything, ourself."

Presently he pointed out the high bow of a wagon cover pale against the trees at the edge of a meadow, where animals grazed in lush grass. "Maybe you're wondering who you'll be taking supper with," Pearl said. "Couple of sawbones, a red-head brat, and his mother that'll have you sitting up taking notice." He cackled.

On the side of the wagon, as we approached, I could read the words:

DOCTOR BALTHAZAR
DOCTOR PEARL
MEDICAL ASSISTANCE
MEDICINES
TEETH PULLED $5

A tall man and a red-headed boy came out to greet us, and a young woman.

2

Spreading his arms over the plank table beside the wagon where we sat at supper, Dr. Balthazar said, "We are very pleased to welcome a military man into our midst!"

"Thank you, sir!" I said. I couldn't keep my eyes from his niece, who sat opposite me, trim and dark-haired with a small hand laid to her cheek, as Balthazar continued to rattle on in his florid style. He had sharp eyes glinting behind eyeglasses, a dark little mouth tucked into his curly beard, and white hair like electrified wires. When I met the young woman's eyes she cast them down demurely.

At the far end of the table lounged the boy, with an aggressively freckled face and a gap-toothed sneering grin that turned on and off without apparent connection to the conversation. He stared at me steadily. Jos had retired to the shadows and the cook squatted by the fire. He wore a striped engineer's cap with his pigtail dangling behind. My eyes and the niece's encountered each other again. I did not like thinking of her as the mother of the ugly boy.

The doctor continued his flow of words, waving his big hands before him as though conducting an orchestra.

"Doc can go on talking like that," Frank Pearl said, "and fall in the creek because he was talking instead of watching his feet, and come out never stopped talking."

"One is reminded of Thales of Miletus and the Thracian maid," Balthazar said. "Do you know the story, Cora?"

"Who was she, Uncle?"

There was a gust of rich, steamy smells as the Chinaman brought a covered dish to the table. He popped off the cover dramatically and offered me the contents.

"Nice lice?"

I helped myself, and watched Cora's bosom as she spooned a portion onto her own plate. "Thank you, Mr. McQueue," she said. Next the cook brought a dish of curry, which he offered to each of us in turn. The boy watched me.

"Some feed, eh, Lieutenant?" Pearl said. Seated on a pillow, he was as tall as the boy beside him. He waved his cigar at me, winking. "Some hot, spicy dishes at this table, am I right?"

"Who was the Thracian maid?" Dr. Balthazar continued. "Well, she was a peasant girl who saw the stargazing Thales fall into a well because, in his scholarly ruminations, he was not watching his step. Her laughter rings down the centuries as hard-headed common sense ridiculing the flights of philosophy."

"Haw!" the boy said contemptuously.

I remembered my philosophy from the Academy. "Plato, I believe, sir."

The doctor looked pleased, his niece admiring. The boy heaped curry onto his rice. The Chinaman thrust a tray of condiments at me.

"You like, Mister?"

"Can't we hear the lieutenant's story, Uncle!" Cora said. She gazed at me with eyes that seemed preternaturally large and bright by the lantern light, her sleek little head cocked and laid against her palms-together hands. The others seemed to lean closer. I felt an excess of attention.

"Do we understand that you've come out to help the general with his troubles?" Cora asked.

"Haw!" the boy said.

"Just keep your yap shut, you can't say something pleasant," the dwarf said.

Balthazar waved his hands placatingly. "The boy is a crack shot," he said to me. "A talented knife thrower as well. Precocious! Perhaps he will demonstrate his prowess tomorrow. Meanwhile, it would be well not to keep staring at our guest, little fellow." He smiled benevolently down the table.

I explained that I would have mainly to do with office and paper work, a kind of chief aide to the general. But of course I hoped to have other responsibilities as well. At this there was again the sense of my hosts leaning closer.

"Just what responsibilities would those be, Lieutenant?"

I said I had had some special training in hydraulics. I found myself confiding to these strangers my dream. Means must be found for irrigating the drought-stricken Territory, methods devised for bringing the violent waters of the mountains to the plains beneath; rivers that now ran underground might be caused to surface.

Dr. Balthazar abruptly rose and mounted the steps to the wagon. A light glowed inside and was extinguished. He returned laden with a heavy volume with a gray-green canvas cover. Spectacles perched on his nose, he opened the book, turned pages, and ran a long forefinger down columns of script as curly as his beard. The boy was stabbing his spoon into his curry, jamming it into his face, chewing with his mouth open, revealing the mix, squinting at me with his green eyes in his speckled face.

Balthazar said, "It is written here that the waters will be freed by the blind."

"Written where?" I said, confused. Cora was leaning toward me.

"I wonder if, in your travels here, Lieutenant— Might you have seen a *bear?*"

I said I had, told them that my guide had seemed to feel this was very good luck, and laughed as though I considered the idea ridiculous. Balthazar closed the cover of his volume, and produced pencil and paper. As I described the encounter with the bear, the sighting of the two other horsemen, and last night's run-in with Kimanches or outlaws, he wrote steadily, nodding, his hand holding the pencil sliding across his sheet of paper like a spider.

"Huh, I seen that bear more'n once," the boy said in a scornful voice.

"Have you, little fellow?" Balthazar said, without looking up.

"One thing I can do is pee outten the wagon without standin' on a box," the boy said, and fled as the dwarf leaped up, jarring the table, and started after him. Both disappeared into the darkness. Cora gazed after them with her face a tragic mask. Her neck gleamed like ivory in the light, fine black hair growing to a delectable point at the nape.

"How I wish we could have one supper without this quarreling," she said.

Pearl stalked back, hands in pockets, and seated himself at the table. His face was murderous.

The boy shouted from the darkness, "He ain't him! He's just another fraud. He's just—"

"*Jimsie!*" Cora screamed, and there was silence.

Frowning, Balthazar consulted a fat gold watch. "Our celestial friend will be insisting upon his little game!" He smiled indulgently at the cook, who was clearing the table.

A bowl filled with small coins was produced, and a cube of metal with numbered sides. The game involved betting on the numbers and stacking the coins, which seemed to be Chinese, with square holes in the center, in different arrangements. I could not understand the play, for it was impossible to concentrate with Cora's hand guiding mine in the complicated betting. I quickly lost the little money I ventured.

"Shall we stroll out to view the moon over the peaks, Lieutenant?"

We left the table and moved out into the darkness where the boy had disappeared, blind at first outside the circle of lamplight, Cora's arm in mine. I could distinguish the dim oval of her face as we halted by one of the horses. She stroked his mane with long sweeps of her hand, murmuring to him. Her eyes and mouth were full of shadow. Along with the fresh scent of the pines and the warm smells of the animals was Cora's faint flowery perfume. Under the yellow lantern light the men were hunched over their game. I saw that the red-headed boy had joined them.

"Uncle is such a dear man," Cora said. "But he is so busy writing his great history."

I said it had seemed strange to me that the big ledger had said that a blind man would free the waters.

"Oh, but the prophecies are part of it, you see! We have to know that the Quest will succeed—"

"The Quest?"

She laughed tremulously. "It has made strange bedfellows, has it not, Lieutenant?"

I said what had been on my mind, that she was very young to have such a big son.

"Oh, he's not really my son. And Uncle's not really my *uncle*."

"I'm afraid I don't understand any of this. What Quest is it?"

"Why, the Lost Dutchman mine! Each of us must do his part, you see. And my part—" Her voice sank: "My part must be the general."

I had a sense of temptation and dishonor maneuvering close. I backed up a step and folded my arms.

"It is what I *am*," she continued. Her voice was almost inaudible. "Some men . . . find me attractive. And he is an old man, who—" The whisper trailed off.

I gasped. "Your uncle demands this of you?"

"We are all free agents, Lieutenant! But each knows he must do what he can do. The prophecies have it that a leader will come. But so much time has passed!" She swept an arm toward the men at the table. "See them gambling against the gold they have been told they will find! But I am the one who must make the sacrifice."

Then she was in my arms, her heart beating against my beating heart. Oxen lowed and stamped. The moon seemed to sway in its seat between two sharp peaks. Drawing away from me, Cora asked me what was the hard thing that had bruised her.

"A ring, " I said, and her fingers fumbled to unfasten the buttons of my shirt until she held the ring in her hand.

"Your sweetheart's!"

"My mother's."

"May I wear it just this one night?"

It was a temptation that in my excitement I could not resist, this night's earnest against its promises. Against my better judgment I permitted her to take the chain over my head and don it herself.

Her uncle was calling. She gripped my arm possessively as we started back to the lamplight. Balthazar was standing, beckoning.

"Mr. McQueue has cleaned us out again, my dear!"

"Trust a military man to come to attention," the dwarf said in his coarse voice. I glared at him. The boy glared at me.

When Cora excused herself to retire, he hurried after her. I grimaced to see him catch her hand as they walked to the wagon. Frank Pearl was grinning at me over his cigar. I excused myself also.

From my bedroll I could see Jos sitting on the other side of the fire with his blanket over his head so that he looked like a dark Buddha. I was irritated to know that he was watching over me. I was also irritated that I had let Cora take my mother's ring, and in a state of masculine discomfort as well. I wondered if she and the disagreeable boy who was or was not her son slept together in the wagon.

In the gray dawn I rose to heat a pan of water and shave, Jos and Mr. McQueue squatting on either side of the fire like a pair of bookends. After I had scraped my chin and combed my hair with a wetted comb, I donned my saber, cartridge belt, and sidearm and paced up and down before the wagon. I was determined to retrieve my mother's ring.

Cora appeared, parting the curtain at the rear of the wagon and holding her skirt as she stepped down the stairs. She did not look so young in the early light. Behind her was a concert of snoring. I was shaken to see Jos's face creased with hatred, watching her.

I invited her to a stroll before breakfast, and we walked out into the meadow, our boots leaving dark tracks in the dewy grass. She carried her hand against her chest, where the ring was concealed beneath her bodice. Out of sight of the wagon, we seated ourselves on a log rotting into the earth. She leaned against me.

When I put my arm around her she spun to fasten her mouth to mine. Suddenly my clothing seemed stifling. "Dear Lieutenant!" she gasped. "I have dreamed—" Then she was whispering both "No!" and "Yes!" and I had a glimpse of a thigh as white as heaven. She screamed.

The two Kimanche, eagle feathers in their hair, sat their spotted ponies just at the edge of the woods. Their dark flesh looked as though it had been quilted.

As I scrambled up they both dismounted. "Hoo *hey!*" one said, in a conversational tone. He carried a stick and a long-handled hatchet. So did the other. They began to trot toward us.

"Run!" I said to Cora. She swung away over the log, pulling her skirts over her legs. "Hoo *hey!*" the Kimanche cried. My revolver lay tangled in my cartridge belt in its heap around my boots. I jerked my saber from its sheath.

The Kimanche were running in the fantastic slowness of a dream. Their limbs were bound at close intervals with thongs that furrowed the flesh into fat bulges. I raised the saber with both hands and slammed it down on the head of the leading warrior. He dropped without a sound. When I jerked the saber loose blood shot up in a geyser. Behind me Cora was screaming.

As I swung to face the other, raising the saber high again, I heard too late the instructor's voice in the School of the Saber dinning into my head that a thrust always beat a cut. The Kimanche's hatchet descended a hair ahead of my own stroke. I could only tilt the haft to try to deflect the tomahawk, swinging halfway around for a glimpse of Cora running with her skirts caught up and beyond her Jos with his head bent over his aimed rifle, and a puff of smoke at the muzzle but no sound.

In the exploding hollow of my skull there was no fear, only acceptance of the boy's shouted taunt that *I was not the one.* Out of my arrogance, out of too much faith that my luck would sustain me, I had chosen to thrust instead of cut; out of a false certainty that whatever came to my hand was right, I had disregarded Josiah's imperative of my revolver. And so I had lost the great game whose existence I had suspected but not acknowledged until too late. I was conscious only of falling through fiery space like Lucifer cast out of heaven.

3

In an aching darkness of air sucked and spent I listened to a muttering of two voices, life and death as I took it, in argument over my every breath. I slept and dreamed. General Peach stood over me, stern and unforgiving; my mother pleaded: "Don't be too hard on the boy, John!"

But John had been my father's name! When he died Aunt Eliza held me to her starched meager bosom and called me her poor orphan; and when I protested that I was not, said, "There, there, my sad little boy, you will get over her, the world is full of women like *her.*" I hit out at the thin-lipped, dried-up sister of my father, who called my mother an evil woman; I waked panting with the memory. My open eyes saw nothing but a shadowed paleness, and I cried out in fear and lurched against hands that restrained me. *"I can't see!"*

"You are all right, Lieutenant." That was Josiah.

"I must get to Bright City, to report—"

"Time enough," Jos said. "You just don't exercise yourself now." It was the halfbreed grasping my wrists. Other hands held my ankles. There was a sense of light outside the darkness in my eyes.

"Givum summat!" a guttural voice said. My wrists were released and cautiously I raised a hand to my breast. The ring was missing. I had given it to Cora! I raised my hand farther to find bandages covering my eyes and head.

A metal rim was tipped to my lips; a strong hand raised my head. Hot, spicy fluid flowed into my mouth. I swallowed, gagged, coughed. My head throbbed. I slept.

When next I opened my eyes there was no obstruction to my vision, and shapes and colors shimmered tantalizingly. I was in a cave—rock walls, dusty moss, a light source I couldn't identify. An iron spike supported a side of red and yellow meat. Yellow jackets buzzed and crawled over the meat. Decorating the wall above this was an Indian shield painted in red, black, and white, and three headdresses of dusty eagle feathers. Flames flickered in charred wood against one wall, smoke drifting across the ceiling until it was sucked out through a crack. There was a strong, brown smell of cooking soup.

Turning first my eyes, then, carefully, my head, I saw a man in greasy buckskins seated whittling beyond the fire. Above a ridge of graying hair the top of his head appeared to be made of yellowed bone.

Later, wearing a wool hat pulled down to his ears, my host brought a bowl of soup and a spoon, grunting something unintelligible. Red-veined eyes in an unshaven face scowled down at me as I spooned the thick broth into my mouth. "Good," I said, letting my bandaged head sink back. "Good!" he said, nodding.

Josiah's face appeared. His eyes glittered anxiously out of the creased leather of his cheeks. I raised a hand to touch the cloth covering my forehead, beneath which was a vast tenderness. I managed a grin. "Almost went to meet my Maker."

The two nodded in concert. "One more like 'at," the

wool-hatted man said, and blocked his eyes ominously with a filthy hand.

"How long have I been here?"

"Nine days," Jos said.

Panic jerked me into trying to sit up. "I was to have reported yesterday!"

Jos pushed me back down, the other grunting disapproval. "Don't have to do anything with a head cracked like a egg," Jos said. "Old General don't need any busted-head adjutants reportin' in."

I rested, panting.

"This here's Smithy," Jos continued. "You can thank him for bein' alive."

Smith grunted ungraciously when I thanked him. Jos only shrugged when I thanked him for shooting the hueycoha who had brained me.

The next day when Smithy and Jos were out of the cave, I cautiously swung my legs aside, rose, and shuffled a step or two, to lean panting and light-headed against a rock wall. I was resting beside a plaited rope, from which were suspended, like a string of garlic flowers, rounds of dried leather attached to long black hair. Scalps, I realized. There must have been a dozen of them, and the bottom two had not dried to leather. My stomach heaved, and I staggered back to collapse upon my pallet again.

When I felt stronger I dug into my kit for my mirror and razor. In the little glass my bearded face and sunken eyes were domed by soiled cloth. The steady, dull ache in my forehead, which I knew to be a healing ache, pained sharply when I moved too fast. I was amused to think that practicing deliberation was one small advantage gained from the assault of the hueycoha. I couldn't find my saber among my gear. I didn't ask Jos about it.

A guilty fretting about my mother's ring occasionally obsessed me, like the yellow jackets buzzing on the side of meat. Bad luck had come from letting the ring be taken from me by what seemed to me now an unbalanced young woman, with her fictions of a Quest for a lost mine, and nameless obligations, which, however, fit in with certain gossip about General Peach's government of the Territory.

At last Smith removed the filthy cloths, peeled herbs from my scalp, and with gentle fingers washed my head with warm water. When I looked in the mirror at the red wealed scar curved like a centipede in a stubble of new hair, my stomach lurched, and I thanked Smithy once again.

He grinned at me with yellow teeth. "You get sun on head. Hour ever'day! Eat plenty soup." He slapped his hands together. "One week, go!"

The week passed, and one morning Josiah saddled the horses and strapped our gear upon the pack animals. I swung into Missy's saddle, and pulled leather for a moment, dizzy. The mountain man, in his wool hat, came out of the cave to lean on his rifle. Grinning, he said, "Now you go Kimanche camp."

"Greasy Grass by noon," Jos said.

I demanded to know why in the world we should go through the Kimanche encampment, where he had already told me Indians were gathering who might be on the warpath.

"Meet old chief," the halfbreed said.

Slapping his thighs as though at something hilarious, Smith cried, "Never fear Kimanche; *you* wapto!"

I was surprised that I seemed to know that "wapto" meant white man, but confused by this conversation. I promised Smith I would send money from Bright City to reward him for his services.

His teeth shot out in a bony grin. "No need money here!"

"Please tell me what you do need."

He jerked off the wool hat. Revealed was the shiny yellow and brown skull I had glimpsed once before.

"Need hair!" He cackled with laughter, but his face was savage. "Kimanche do this too!" He was tapping a finger on his skull when I jerked Missy's head away. I could smell the cooking soup even outside the cave, and I spurred to a smart trot, with Jos and the pack animals following.

After a time I reined Missy in until Jos came up beside me. "He's been scalped!"

Jos's braids jerked in a nod. "Twenty years ago. He takes Kimanche scalps to pay. You see 'em in cave?"

I had seen them. "Who *is* he?" I demanded

But I had already realized who he must be, as legendary as the general himself, as the old chief of the Kimanche whom we rode to meet. Livereating Smith! I swung down out of the saddle. My knees gave and I almost fell, bending over to vomit as though my stomach would turn inside out.

"You got a little somethin' to make gift to the old chief?" Jos inquired. "Old chief like finger rings."

I didn't answer, spurring ahead. It was infuriating that my mother's ring should be demanded as a gift for the infamous Kimanche chieftain. At the same time I felt a turn of the screw of dread that I no longer possessed it. It seemed to me that my luck, which had always changed as though miraculously from bad to good, was accumulating a negative that could never be overcome.

Presently Jos sang out, "Looky there! Greasy Grass!" Through treetops I could make out a narrow valley hazed with distance. Beyond it a slim mountain rose, a long banner of cloud floating from its peak.

We wound down through pines to a bald ridge, where there was a clear view of the Indian camp. I gasped at the number of lodges arrayed on the gleaming grass, smoke rising from many of them, pale cones smoke-stained at the peak with blackened lodgepoles protruding. There seemed hundreds of them, brown bodies moving among them, and the flash of a red blanket shaken like a signal. Far along among the teepees children were running, surging back and forth in some game, and I became aware of sounds, dogs barking, the whinny of horses. There were three herds of these. It occurred to me that I should be making a count of the lodges, and perhaps of the horseflesh as well.

As we continued our descent I unsnapped the cord on my revolver, and eased my carbine in its scabbard. Other horsemen were winding through the trees on a parallel course to ours, brown motion glimpsed past tree trunks. More and more became visible, on both sides. Within a group of a dozen Kimanche we came out into the meadow near the first teepees. The braves were armed with bows and spears, but more than half of them displayed repeating rifles. Three wore ragged cavalry blouses. Our party was surrounded by dogs of all sizes and colors, shrilling and snapping at fetlocks to make the horses buck and plunge. I had to rein Missy in sharply, furious under the eyes of the grinning savages who surrounded us.

One of these jerked his eagle-feathered braids at me and spoke to another. I was surprised that I could almost understand his words. "This young soldier has much medicine!" The second warrior nodded and reached out to touch my shoulder, jerking back his hand as I recoiled.

The brave who seemed to be in charge here said, "Come, let us take young wapto to Stonepecker!" But certainly he had spoken in gobbling, guttural Kimanche!

Six horsemen advanced to meet us. All of these bore carbines, and, to my horror, also wore campaign hats and cavalry blouses in fair condition, and bestrode gray cavalry geldings. There was an exchange between Josiah and the ugly, broken-nosed chief of this squad, in which I understood Jos to say that I was the son of Two-Star come to salute the great chief. The other replied that it was clear the wapto soldier had much medicine. Although I had been a good student of language at the Academy, I was stunned that I could understand their words.

The original escort now dropped behind, and the more soldierly guard accompanied us. Anticipating my questions, Josiah said, "Old general's lost some stores and no mistake. Goin' to see the great chief, now, son. You have your little gift by you; old chief makes a lot of luck!"

I inventoried my possessions for some trinket I might present to the chief of these warriors. It was a conscious effort to keep my hand from rising to touch my chest. More horsemen joined our procession as we headed for a teepee larger than the rest, with a corral to one side of it in which a white stallion was penned, tossing his long intelligent head over the top rail to gaze at me.

Sunk upright in the earth before the teepee were three straight branches with the bark stripped from them, which somehow I understood to be the mark of the chief's rank. The teepee was painted with three red stars, one above another, and a black sun. All was silent except for the jingle of trace chains and the pad of hoofs, as, hemmed in by horsemen, we approached the three posts. One of our escort reached out to lay fingers on my arm in a reverent way, and another jockeyed close to touch me also. It was as though I could understand their very thoughts! "It is the true son of Two-Star!" Other voices clamored in my skull as other hands reached out to me. Who was One-Star? Two-Star must be General Peach, One-Star a deputy sheriff or town marshal? Who was Gopherman? It was like madness closing in and the memory of Smith's terrible soup swept over me again. I pulled my képi lower over my eyes, my right hand curled on my thigh close to my revolver.

Beside me Jos slumped in the saddle, his dark, deeply-graven face unreadable. He had removed his bandana covering his graying hair. Women now packed the opening of the teepee before us, flat brown faces staring out.

A stovepipe hat appeared among the women, and made its way through their ranks, a man old as time, wearing creamy buckskins decorated with rainbow-colored porcupine quills. His hands were concealed each in the opposite sleeve, like a Chinaman's, and his features were eroded into a fantastic mesh of wrinkles.

Following the halfbreed's example, I dismounted. I saluted, and Stonepecker placed his fingers to the brim of his black stovepipe, raised it an inch, and lowered it again. In Kimanche Jos announced that he had brought the son of Two-Star from White-Father-City for the great chief's blessing.

"A son of Two-Star is always welcome, my son,"

Stonepecker said in slow, thick-accented English. "And perhaps you will answer a question that concerns us very much."

"If I can, sir." I felt a cool slick of sweat on my face.

He said it in Kimanche first, then in English: "How can one and two and three preserve the good earth, my son?"

My mind seemed to close in panic, but the voices in my head intruded. One seemed to state what I could not even understand. "The stars in their courses—" I said, and paused to get it right, "must combine together, one and two and three."

Something kindled in his old eyes, although he did not change expression. He repeated what I had said in Kimanche. There were mutterings behind me, approbation, the clamor echoing in my head. I crossed my arms, feeling confidence like a warm breath on my face. Jos jabbed his elbow into my side. The gift.

With a sweep of his arm, Stonepecker indicated his teepee. "If you enter, we will smoke and talk, son of Two-Star."

"Thank you for your hospitality, sir. But Two-Star will be impatient for me to join him in Bright City."

Nodding, the chief said, "A father is strong with his strong son at his side."

Two of the women had inched closer, one reaching out a hand to brush my arm. She whispered to the other, "He is very tall, very manly, the son of Two-Star."

"Why does he not produce the True Gift?" the other asked, just as Jos nudged me again, and I suddenly realized what my gift must be.

As a cadet I had practiced an elaborate, sweeping, and most irregular salute before a mirror, imagining myself posted to duty in foreign lands and presenting myself to the potentate there. I threw my hand out and away, then swept it to the bill of my képi, arching my back radically and cracking my heels together. "Sir!"

Stonepecker's face crumpled. It was a complicated expression, of profound disappointment mingled with patience. The voices in my head died for a moment; then resumed. I had made a mistake. I had treated this moment too lightly. I had not known its importance. I had failed.

The chief lifted his other hand to his hat brim this time. I saw that the fingers of the dark claw were thick with rings. "Go in peace, young wapto," he said mildly, turning away as though no longer interested. There was disappointment in the faces of the squaws as he passed through them back into the teepee.

As I swung back into the saddle I could feel Jos's disapproval like a cold wind on my back, compounding my despair, which was already turning to anger. I swung Missy's head away from the star-decorated teepee. The mounted braves gave way before me, but still they reached out to touch me as I rode past them. I led Jos and the pack animals at a brisk walk across the meadow, guiding on the teepee-shaped, snow-capped mountain. My face was burning with vexation.

At the treeline, where a creek wound into thickets of willows, I glanced back one last time, estimating a hundred ten, a hundred twenty lodges, and too many head of horse even to try to count. Sunlight caught on the white stallion's flank and gleamed like a star.

Jos came up beside me, his face bitter as a snapping turtle's.

"I understood you told him I was the general's son," I said.

He didn't reply, sucking on his teeth.

"I got his question right," I said. "Didn't I?"

He nodded once.

"Who is Gopherman?"

"What they call Big Mac."

"And One-Star is the Bright City marshal?"

He nodded.

"They kept saying I had big medicine and touching me."

"There's different kinds of medicine. A blind man's

got big medicine, but another blind man's one that won't see same as can't. What they call can't see his reflection in the water."

I tried to spur on ahead, but he kept up with me. "You should've give the old chief his True Gift!"

"I didn't choose to."

"Didn't choose to see your reflection in the water!"

"I wish I hadn't seen those cavalry carbines and blouses. I think the general'd better go after those savages before they get any stronger."

"Looking glass either," Jos muttered, dropping behind.

The horses jolted downhill through the cool shade of the pines that seemed to generate its own breezes. Hunger caused me to recall again the liver stench of Smithy's soup, with a churning of my belly. By an act of will I summoned up the memory of the bear raised to its haunches watching me, that good-luck sign. And the Kimanches had said I had strong medicine! I tried to recapture the surety of my destiny, my faith that everything turned out the best for me.

"Black-hair woman bad luck," Jos said gloomily.

4

We plodded along a wheel-scarred road under a brutal sun. Past the dark flank of a mountain dust clouds rose as from some savage wind there, although it was windless where we were. I had a sense of enormous activity in process, of the scale I had been thinking would be necessary for the system of dams and canals that would bring water down from the Bucksaws.

"What's all that dust?"

"Look for gold over there."

"But what can they be doing to raise such a dust?"

"Machines," Jos said.

Things connected: Gopherman, Big Mac, the Quest—
"You mean they are digging for the Lost Dutchman
mine?"

The guide sucked noisily on his teeth and did not seem
inclined to answer. We crossed a wide, sandy dry river
bottom, the hoofs of the animals kicking up dust. "Sweetwater," Jos advised me. "Ten years gone. One day—earthquake. Sweetwater no more."

"Gone underground," I said. "There are ways of finding where the water's gone. There are textbooks—"

"Huh!" Jos said, and spurred on ahead, up the rocky
bank. We surmounted a ridge, and he reined up to extend
an arm, hand, and finger in dramatic gesture. "Bright
City!"

In the dusty air our destination was visible, toy blocks
of buildings laid out in cruciform along a road junction, at
the base of a dun-colored range of hills. Nearer to us was
the mud fort with its shred of color hanging from a pole,
the flag of the Republic I was sworn to defend.

The wagon road led us above the fort and the town,
descending a long arroyo to come out among the first tarpaper shacks of the territorial capital. As we progressed,
more were of adobe, with some frame buildings, one a general store with a raised wooden boardwalk, tie rail, false-
front, and plank awning. The street angled, widening. Two
troopers stood in conversation with a townsman, and I sat
Missy a little straighter and trimmed the slant of my képi.
Neither looked my way. Farther along four blanket Indians were peering into a store window. We turned into
the town square.

Here there was a church with a respectable steeple,
and, catercornered from it, an imposing three-story building. The hotel, I thought first, until by some instinct I recognized it as the brothel. Gazing down at me from the
highest window was a pale face, hazed and glimmering in
my eyes as I squinted up against the sun. A slim, dark man
clad in black, revolvers slung low on either hip, eased like
a shadow out the door of the place, to lean there watching
us. He looked dangerous as a rattlesnake, and I felt hostil-

ity flicker between us like an electrical impulse. A five-pointed metal star was fastened to his jacket.

"One-Star," I said.

"Henry Plummer," Jos said.

I knew there were towns out West where the gunmen hired to keep peace in gambling, drinking, and whoring establishments were often called to serve as town marshals as well. Henry Plummer was as famous, or infamous, in his way, as were the old general, Livereating Smith, and the Kimanche chief.

A hostler in faded overalls in the doorway of the livery stable nodded affably to us as we passed. I saw another soldier through the window of a tonsorial parlor.

Past the town, on the road to the fort, was the town dump, where turkey buzzards picked among glinting bottles and heaps of tin cans. Boot Hill was on higher ground nearby, a cluster of crude crosses. Chocolate ridges lay across the horizon, and the high peaks sailed above the parched landscape like snow islands.

The fort hulked up. The open gate in the adobe wall was guarded by a lounging trooper, who saluted with some style. Through the gate, which was wide enough for heavy caissons, we debouched into a parade ground perhaps four hundred feet on a side, in its center a flagpole ringed with whitewashed rocks. Six troopers took their ease in the far shade, shirtless and sun-browned. Close by them horses leaned their heads over the fencing. I was as shocked as I had been at the stolen gray cavalry mounts in Stone-pecker's camp to see that at least half of these were gaudy-faced Indian ponies, as though this were some perverse turnabout of Greasy Grass, brown bodies and paint ponies here, and the military horseflesh, arms, and uniforms there; as though these two forces had been in conflict for so long their distinctions were blurring, until at last they became indistinguishable in the dust and heat of the Territory.

Under the gaze of the half-naked troopers Jos and I headed for a stoop with a wooden awning, where a red board bore two gold-painted stars. I dismounted and hitched Missy to an iron post, took my orders in their oiled silk from my kit, and followed Jos into the interior gloom.

"Who're you?" a voice demanded. An ugly fellow with hair swept sideways like a barkeep's and a sergeant-major's stripes glared at me from behind a cluttered desk. His shirt was unbuttoned to the waist, and his face gleamed with greasy sweat in this low-ceilinged oven of an anteroom.

I tossed the packet of orders onto his desk and identified myself. "And what's your name, Sergeant-Major?"

"Eubanks, sir. We haven't had any word on you, sir." He brushed at the lick of hair across his forehead.

Jos said, "General sent me to collect him. Due a good while back."

"Didn't say anything to me," Eubanks grumbled. "Well, I guess you are replacement for Captain Larkin. We haven't had an adjutant for so long I'd forgot it was in the tables even. There's a couple of non-commissions putting up in your quarters. I'll just go get them moved out—"

He rose, so tall he had to bend his head under the rafters, and barged toward the door.

"I'd like to report to the general," I said.

Eubanks swung around toward me. "Seeing nobody, sir. He is bad sick, though he will not admit it."

A voice called from beyond the door: "Who's that, Sergeant-Major?"

Eubanks stamped across to the door, opened it, braced to attention, and said, "Lieutenant Grace, General. And the breed guide."

"Send them in, send them in!"

Red-faced, Eubanks stood aside for Jos and me to enter a darkened room. Visible on a clotheshorse, like a dwarf general, was his dress uniform, reef of medals, golden epaulettes, plumed hat. Gleaming boots stood below it. Sitting up on a cot, braced against fat pillows, was an old man with close-cropped white hair and beard. I saluted with a more regulation flourish than I had mustered for the Indian chief.

"Ah, Jos!" he said, gazing past me with a casually raised hand. "Come in, my friend. Well!"

In the gloom I could make out a massive roll-top desk, beside it an elephant-leg umbrella stand from which sprouted a growth of swords, spears, cavalry pennons, and furled flags. Hung on the wall were bows, shields, rifles, and framed, glassed photographs of generals, chiefs, troops of cavalry, groups of Indians, and officers on horseback. On a shelf between the windows was an amateurish plaster casting of a statuary group I recognized as "The Wounded Scout," and, half-hidden by the open door, a box raised off the floor on sawhorse legs and covered by a flag. A scarf was draped over this, on which was a bowl filled with red roses.

"Well, how did you find your journey, Mister?" He squinted at me with a convulsion of half his face.

"Had a run-in with some hueycoha, sir. I'm afraid I've been a while convalescing." I touched the fat ridge of the scar on my forehead.

"No prejudice, no prejudice," the general said. "At ease, Mister."

In Kimanche Jos said, "Fair bunch of braves up on Greasy Grass."

"We saw between a hundred ten and a hundred twenty lodges, sir," I said, "and a good many gray horse and repeating rifles. There was a kind of honor guard got up very soldierly—" I stopped, for the general was staring at me intently, leaning forward with hands braced on his blanket-covered legs.

"Understand Kimanche, do you? How does that happen, Mister?"

I stammered that I'd always been quick with languages, but before I could finish he snapped, "Old Stoney didn't give you a silver horse, by any chance?"

"No, sir."

He doubled his hand into a fist and tapped his leg. His expression reminded me of Stonepecker's, disappointed, but angry instead of sad, impatient instead of patient. The gleaming box that supported the roses was a coffin. But of course many eccentrics had been known to keep their coffins by them, even sleep in them, as reminders of their ultimate end.

"Seen it all so many times," the general said suddenly, white head bowing forward. "Hope showing up out of sheer hopelessness to tantalize me. And then gone up in smoke! To see it over and over. The Flying Dutchman of this benighted place!" He aimed a jut-jawed face at me and Jos. "Injun gathering! I tell you I wish we were back in the old days with only Kimanche to fight. There is evil sprung loose here to sink the world! And one old man left with not much strength to thumb the dike!" He stopped, panting.

Of course he was insane, as rumors in the army had it. This was not a time to announce my plans for bringing water to the Territory. I blurted out, "You are the general the young officers look up to, sir!"

He straightened on his cot, and pulled in his chin for all the world like a plebe bracing. "Thank you, Mister!" He called to the sergeant-major, who still stood at the open door. "Here's the new adjutant, Eubanks. Log him in, get him settled, see he has himself a wash. How's the major?"

"Off his head again, sir. Raving and whining."

"Perhaps we can presume on the lieutenant to stand retreat this evening. A Troop, if you please. You will sup with me after, Mister."

"Sir!"

The general extended a hand and I stepped forward to shake it. I felt turned inside out by a gaze as cool and sane as any man could hope for. When I left the room past the sergeant-major, I heard my commanding officer say, "Have a seat, Jos, and tell us all about *this* one!"

5

When I stepped off the porch to march across the baked earth of the parade ground to the flagpole, A Troop was drawn up in their dark shirts and sky-blue breeches. My face burned under the inspection of those ranks of eyes.

The troop was greatly understrength, that was obvious, but the men appeared spruce enough, and came smartly to attention when Sergeant-Major Eubanks shouted, "Troop Aten—SHUN!" He saluted, I returned the salute, and he bawled, "Pre—sent—HARMS!" Sabers flashed up before brown faces. The bugler sounded "To the Colors," a young trooper unfastened the lanyard, and, as "Retreat" sounded, the colors descended against a darkening sky.

"Orderrrrrr—HARMS!" Eubanks commanded, and I saluted again, about-faced and marched back to headquarters.

"Well, Mister," the general said at supper. "How did A Troop strike you?"

"Very smart, sir!" I sat at table alone, with crisp napery, gleaming crystal, and heavy silver, while a corporal poured wine into my glass. The military governor was propped up by his pillows, a wineglass in his liver-spotted fist. He looked less hale this evening, his face transparently pale, dark smears beneath his eyes. I pretended not to see his shaky hand slop wine in a pink stain on the bedclothes.

"To the Cavalry!" General Peach said, in the customary first toast. We drank. I had never appreciated the sour, medicinal stuff.

"A bit understrength, I'm afraid," the general said.

"Quite a bit, sir."

"B and C Troops are no better off. B Troop's on patrol, out hunting outlaws. He tossed back a good swallow of wine. "They won't catch 'em. Don't want to, for one thing."

The corporal brought in bowls of stew, which he uncovered with a flourish and set before us. The smell was thick and brown.

"Slumgullion!" the general said heartily. "You'll find the rations here excellent, Mister. Cook hasn't deserted us yet, eh, Jones?"

"No, sir," the corporal said, and backed out of the room. The general dug into his stew, and I did the best I could with mine.

"Well, my boy, Josiah tells me you had some interesting adventures en route. Hueycoha! Mighty difficult to persuade those fellows they are dead. But you met the Livereater! A shy one, that."

"Yes, sir," I said, halting the bite of slumgullion en route to my mouth, and laying the fork down on my plate.

"And the big she-grizzly came around for a look. No doubt that was why Jos decided to take you through Greasy Grass."

"I'm afraid he introduced me as the son you'd sent East for, sir."

He laughed, hiccuped, and blotted his mouth with his napkin. "We must always trust Jos to know what's best in certain situations. And so you were quick with their gibble-gabble tongue, but chose not to give up your ring for the old nigger's collection! Might've been well rewarded, my boy. A lady love's ring, no doubt."

"My mother's, sir."

"Ah! May I see this precious object?"

Sweat felt like cold lace on my forehead. "I've mislaid it, sir."

His pale eyes glared at me ferociously. *"Mislaid* it! By God, Lieutenant Grace, I advise you to have a close look for that object. You will find that ring, Mister!"

"Yes, sir!"

I watched his shaking hand carry a lump of meat to his mouth. It bulged in his cheek as he chewed. He continued to glare at me as he sloshed down more wine. The corporal returned with a tureen of stew.

"No, thank you, Jones. Tell the cook very good! Another bottle of claret, if you please."

I could not think why a cameo ring given me when I was nine years old by the groom Ben Dandy should be so important. I knew I had sunk in my commander's estimation. I longed to assure him that I was a serious and destiny-marked officer, not merely lucky or unlucky. I had solved the Kimanche chief's riddle, which was that the townsmen under the marshal, the cavalry, and the Kimanche must combine to destroy the outlaws. With the

Territory pacified, rail service would be resumed and commerce flourish, and meanwhile my ideas for bringing water down from the mountains, and perhaps up from beneath the earth, would have been successful also. But it was presumptuous for a junior officer even to think of these things, much less give them voice.

Jones returned with the wine. The general held out his glass, and settled back against the pillows with a sigh, closing his eyes as though with exhaustion. "History is only repetition," he said. "But it is not dull, it is only terrible. Your time is different from my time. Your time runs in a straight line from Point A to Point J, N, or R; or Y if you are *lucky*. But my time spins like a great mill spinning, like the earth turning through the seasons. Past all the same points again and again. It is what damnation is, sir!" His reddened eyes snapped open.

The light was failing in the room and he made a pistol of his hand and aimed it at the unlit candle. The corporal flicked a fingernail at the head of a match and applied the flame to the wick. The flame trembled and steadied. The general gaped at me with baffled eyes, and I knew he had forgotten who I was.

"Lieutenant Grace, sir," I whispered.

"Ah!" He seemed to collect himself. "I have to depend on you, Grace."

"Sir?"

"Larkin's dead. Plummer shot him, quarrel over a woman— And the major's out of his mind. Heat stroke! And two captains I can't trust through that door. They'll go over to the enemy any day. Any day! Do you know how many men deserted last month? In a *month*, Mister!"

"How many, sir?"

He only shook his head, eyes closed again. "I need a strategist, Mister. Larkin was the strategist. Plummer shot him." He halted, panting. He mopped his mouth with his napkin. "Too damned old! I don't mend! Bedbound! By God, if I was twenty years younger we'd see some action. Timing is everything, of course, in any affair with allies."

He swung around to glare at the corporal. "Clear this damned truck away, Jones!"

The corporal hastened to comply, while I daubed at my forehead with my napkin. I said, "Stonepecker seemed concerned about how to stop Big Mac. They called him Gopherman, I presume because he is digging for the Lost Dutchman mine—"

The crazed eyes in the chalk-white face glared at me. *Presume!* Digging for the— By God, sir, he is endeavoring to destroy this very earth we walk on!"

There was a knock, and Eubanks entered with a square white envelope. The general studied the envelope; his passion forgotten, he almost simpered as he held it to his nose to sniff. Then he frowned as he opened it. "Well! It seems Henry Plummer is anxious to restore good relations!"

He winked at Eubanks with a convulsion of the left side of his face. "Sergeant-Major, I suspect Lieutenant Grace may be quite a ladies' man."

"Might be at that, sir."

"The fact is I need a volunteer for some special duty, Lieutenant."

"Count on me, sir," I said.

"Since you are my adjutant. Act for me in certain instances." His face convulsed as though he were masticating something very large and tough. "Since I am incapacitated. Well, sir, you will not find this duty onerous. A new girl's arrived at the French Palace in town, and there's a custom here I'd hate to see fall into neglect— And it's clear Plummer is mending fence. By God, we'd all better be mending fence!

"The governor is always offered first privilege, you see," he continued after a moment. "There's a pleasant little ceremony come down from old times in the Territory. Expect you to act for me. Since I'm . . . on sick call."

"Yes, sir!" I said, rising. Blood beat in my face like hot wings. Was this to be another test, like the bear, the encounter with the hueycohas, Livereating Smith, and the

Kimanche chief? And another test I might fail; for I was not "quite a ladies' man," but quite the opposite. I faced the fact that my mother's ring was mislaid because it had been proffered for my relief from a condition that might be a maiden's most precious possession, but was only an embarrassment in the male.

"Diplomacy, Mister," the general said, "is convincing the other fellow that what you want him to do is what he wants to do. Just don't make Larkin's mistake and meddle with any of Henry Plummer's women if you are not invited to. Your objective is this new dove, *only.*"

"Sir!"

"Eubanks, you ride along with Mr. Grace and introduce him. Plenipotentiary, and all that." He grinned mirthlessly, showing stumpy stained teeth. Now his eyes were sane, but very sad. "Dress uniform," he said to me. "It is a kind of wedding ceremony. Eubanks will provide the flowers; eh, Eubanks?"

"Yes, sir."

When I started for the door with the sergeant-major, the general said in a blurred voice, "Remember, Mister: a gentleman takes his weight on his knees and elbows!"

6

By moonlight the road into Bright City was white as pipe clay, my new guide fifty feet ahead of me on his gray cavalry gelding. I shivered continually, as much because the general considered me his strategist and one dependable officer, as because I was serving as his stand-in in a brothel adventure.

Rectangles of illumination bloomed in the darkness. The church spire spiked into the night sky; beyond it were the windows of the French Palace, a welcoming blue lamp glowing beside the door. Shadowy men lounged along the boardwalk as the sergeant-major and I secured our horses among the other animals tethered to the rail.

Carrying the newspaper-wrapped bouquet of roses

from the bowl on the general's coffin, Eubanks pushed open the heavy door. I entered a violence of reflected lights, from mirrors, chandeliers, polished bars and table-tops; clamor of voices, clatter of glassware, chips, dice, and counters. Men stood at the faro layouts, where there were dealers in green eyeshades, and a lookout with a meaty red face in his high chair. Men were drinking at tables and a mahogany bar backed by an opulent array of mirrors. A straight-backed little "professor" in a cloth cap toiled at a piano keyboard in a far corner, producing an occasional note audible over the general hubbub.

Women in richly colored dresses moved among the men, the light catching their polished hair and bare shoulders. Above the main part of the room was a balcony with a wooden balustrade. Stairs executed a half turn to this, and swept around to another, higher balcony lost in shadow. I remembered the pale face gazing down at me from that highest window.

There was a perceptible lessening of noise as we entered the room, and, with nudges and whispers, all eyes turned toward us. I returned each glance, looking particularly for the black-clad gunman I had seen this afternoon. One of the whores hooped her painted mouth at me suggestively. Another wore a short blue dress with a bow at the back, black patent-leather shoes, and long hair combed like a young girl's. I whispered to Eubanks to ask about her.

"Always find a 'schoolgirl' in a decent parlorhouse, Lieutenant," he said in a superior tone. "Special tastes. There's the 'jockey.'" He indicated a girl bending in conversation with the professor at the piano, revealing a neat bottom in tight pants, and high boots.

"Sometimes you'll see a Queen of Spades," Eubanks added. "All in black, black domino and such." He continued his lecture, but my attention was caught elsewhere.

Henry Plummer had appeared out of the crowd, black hair parted in the precise center of his head, a white neckerchief knotted at his throat, revolvers slung on either hip. I felt again that powerful aversion as he approached, the murderer of my predecessor in a quarrel over a woman.

Eubanks explained that the general was indisposed and had sent me to stand in his place. The marshal offered his hand. Although it lay lax in mine it seemed filled with a kind of static tension. His black eyes regarded me with a disinterested examination that made me grit my teeth. His badge of office gleamed dully on the breast of his jacket.

"A glass of whiskey, friends?" He led us to an empty table. The haft of a bowie knife showed at the small of his back, the blade secured between the crossed cartridge belts there. He snapped his fingers at the bartender, who hurried to us with a brown bottle and three glasses. Eubanks laid the bundle of flowers on the table.

The vibrato of many conversations picked up again, the piano notes filtering through. A cowboy and a woman with red, high-piled hair mounted the steps arm in arm. Plummer seated himself in the corner, where he could face the room with his flanks covered. His eyes flicked past mine to survey the scene behind me.

"Where's she at?" Eubanks asked.

"Roombound yet," Plummer said. "She's a shy one. Claims to be maiden still." I watched his glass rise in his slim hand, reputed to be one of the swiftest of the Out-West gunmen. Roses poked their dark red petals out of their covering paper.

Hunching forward over the table, Eubanks said, "General says there's been three for-sure ones he's knew."

"The percentage is not high," Plummer said. He had a precise, almost finicking way of speaking.

"And how's your score, Henry?"

"Not up to the general's," the marshal said. "I can't count any for-sures, but there's a hundred and eighteen possibles."

His eyes were focused on a spot in the center of my forehead, and I could feel the blood burning in my cheeks with dread that these questions would be asked of me.

"But, Henry," Eubanks said. "How many of them was greasers?"

A grape-stem cluster of veins in Plummer's temple

swelled and beat, but he smiled coolly. "That's not counting greasers, Ted."

The plinking of the piano sounded more loudly, different: the familiar notes of the wedding march. Two women stood at the top of the stairs, one in white, the other in purple lace, arm in arm. I gasped with shock, half rising. The bride was Cora.

But, after that first astonishment of seeing her in this situation, it was the other woman who captured my eye. Hers was the beautiful face I had glimpsed as I rode into town, pale, not young, sweet-mouthed, wreathed in a cloud of dark hair, dark eyes fixed on me as she and Cora descended the stairs in step to the wedding march, Cora gowned in white, white blossoms in her hair. Henry Plummer and Eubanks had also risen.

The people in the gambling room made an aisle, both moving aside and assembling, cowboys, miners, and townsmen, brightly-gowned whores, the jockey and the schoolgirl among them, while the little professor played with extravagant motions of his arms. Eubanks saluted and presented Cora with the bouquet, from which he had stripped the newspaper wrapping. She lowered her head as though to sink her face into the blossoms, eyes slanting white-rimmed toward me. Then she looked uncomprehendingly at Henry Plummer as he explained that I was standing in for the general, who was ailing.

The other woman smiled at me with pink lips and dark eyes that seemed to reach out to me. Henry Plummer stood possessively at her side, a hand on her arm. Her figure was both full and slender.

The big man from the lookout stand had donned a minister's dickey and reverse collar, and carried a fat black prayer book. We were shuffled into two groups, Cora with Henry Plummer and the woman in purple, Eubanks standing next to me as best man. It seemed almost another tactic to force me to produce my ring, and I was grimly amused that the bride had already appropriated it.

"Do you, Miss, take this man for your husband? Do you, Mister, take this lady for your wife tonight?"

Cora murmured something. I said, "I do!" Past Henry Plummer's dark profile I could see the madam's pale one. Cora and I were encouraged to kiss, to clapping, whistles, stamping of boots. "Honeymoon! Honeymoon!" Cora's hand on my arm, we ascended the stairs, I had earlier watched the cowboy and his doxy climb. The steps swung upward to the first balcony, then half a turn and more dimly seen to the second. The great chandelier glittered with lights.

"I thought you were—dead!" Cora whispered.

"Only out of action for a while."

On the balcony I glanced back and down, hating Henry Plummer the more now for his obvious possession of the woman in purple, whose dark eyes were raised to me, pink, parted lips smiling in some message or encouragement while his arm circled her back.

Cora directed me through a door, and, when I paused to close it behind us, continued across the room to place her bouquet in a vase. She took a considerable time to accomplish this, while I glanced around the room, which was large, with embossed red wallpaper in recurring patterns, each one centered upon a small mirror like an eye. These concentrated and reflected the light from the numerous lamps and sconces. The bed had scrolled head and foot of burnished walnut, with a white counterpane drawn tight upon it.

Cora moved back to me, to spin around again, presenting the pale nape of her neck. "A gentleman would unbutton me, I think."

My fingers fumbled with the stubborn cloth-covered buttons in their tiny loops. I said stiffly, "If you don't wish—"

"As well you as another," she said, in a sad little voice.

I retreated while she slipped off her white gown. Facing me in her petticoat, she folded her bare arms in a W over her breast. Tears gleamed like jewels on her cheeks, but they did not touch me. I remembered her professed part in the Quest, and I knew it was not as well I as another. Moreover, it seemed to me that somehow I had been

124

made to pay in advance for these embraces; and that I was being used in ways I did not understand.

"General Peach is indisposed. I'm sorry you are disappointed."

"Oh, I have no luck. I know that now."

It came to me that she was the kind of woman my Aunt Eliza had warned me against. I shouldered out of my jacket and hung it over the back of a chair while Cora relieved herself of her petticoat, and lowered her arms to stand bare-breasted and rather meager before me, bloomerlike undergarments swaddling her legs. Her flesh was milky white with a hint of blue running beneath the skin. I had thought she would be wearing the ring on its chain, which I would now reclaim.

"My ring!" I said.

"Oh! I don't have it!"

"Where is it?"

"Mrs. Watson has it. She— You'll have to come again!" She made a coy mouth I found distasteful. "Yes! When you come again!"

I said through my teeth that I must have the ring immediately.

Her face twisted into childlike dismay. Hand to her throat, she said, "I promise it! Next time." Then she said quickly, "Am I to leave my stockings on? I understand some gentlemen would have it so."

"As you wish." I sat down to remove my boots, while she stripped to long black stockings. It seemed time to extinguish the lights, but there were far too many. The little round mirrors winked their fire. Although I was angry at almost everything that I could think of, my flesh had proved to have a mind of its own. Cora lay back on the bed and whispered, "Please be gentle, Lieutenant."

I found myself envisioning a more beautiful face as I embraced my duty. The famous business seemed to me vastly overrated, and was over rather more quickly than I intended, while she stirred and sighed in her transports.

"Is Mrs. Watson the madam here?" I asked. "She's very beautiful."

"I wouldn't think of her if I were you. Henry Plummer is a very jealous man."

I thought Henry Plummer might be another matter that was overrated, as I put my clothing back on, stretching my arms through my braces, and buckled on my cartridge belt with its holstered revolver. Cora lay unmoving, staring up at the reflected light play on the ceiling. I was feeling a complex of frustrations that focused upon the marshal, with his fast hand like a bundle of wires, his hundred and eighteen possibles, and his possession of that beautiful woman with her drowning pools of eyes.

"I will have my ring tomorrow!" I said. Cora nodded and I passed from the room, no longer the young man who had entered it.

As I descended the curve of stair, my hand sliding on the polished rail, no one seemed to be paying me any attention, the gaudy women and the gambling and drinking men tending to their pleasures and business. Mrs. Watson was not in sight, and I halted to glance back and up to the high balcony past the vast glitter of the chandelier. A lamp glowed like a warm hole in the darkness there.

Henry Plummer glided toward me from the faro layout, darkly smiling with the contemptuous set to his lips, the arrogant set of his head, wrists flicking past his revolver butts. He seemed to me some principle that threatened my self-esteem, a threat I must deal with or fall into a limbo of defeat and contemptibility.

Eubanks sat at the same table we had occupied earlier, rising sweaty-faced as I took the chair opposite him. Plummer came to stand beside the table.

"You must be fast off the mark, Lieutenant," he said.

"Yes, fast," I said. Staring into his eyes I leaned forward as though to reach for the whiskey bottle, but instead slapped both hands down on the butts of the revolvers one whisker ahead of his hands. Sharp metal cut into my palms. I heard the explosive hiss of Eubanks's breath.

"Fast enough," I said, grinning into Henry Plummer's strained, expressionless face in the thickening silence. I could feel a queer warmth flowing down into my hands, and the concentration of eyes upon me. The marshal's pupils danced from side to side, never meeting mine exactly. Eubanks rose, his chair jarring back. Several men vacated their places along the bar.

Plummer's hands clawed down on mine, as I forced the cartridge belts down his hips. Trickles of sweat cooled my forehead and I watched the bright drops form on the face above me. His pupils continued their dance, and the little cluster of veins pulsed. I maintained the pressure, and the belts slipped to his knees, and fell with a heavy thump, encircling his boots. The knife clattered free. Out of the corner of my eyes I saw that the sergeant-major had drawn his service revolver, which he held low at his side. His face also gleamed with sweat.

The marshal straightened from his crouch. I straightened also, although remaining seated. He stepped out of the circle of leather but otherwise did not move, as though awaiting my command. His eyes were fixed on my forehead as though to bore a hole there.

I bent to scoop up the heavy belts with their holstered weapons, and dumped them upon the table before me. Henry Plummer turned away. With a small crack of his heels he moved toward the door. I saw a white-faced girl with spit curls at her temples cross herself as he passed her. The big lookout, still wearing his black dickey and minister's collar, crouched, half-erect, on the top step of his stand, holding his shotgun at a kind of port arms. I did not yet dare glance toward the high balcony.

Eubanks slipped back in his chair again. His revolver had vanished. "You have gone and done it!" he breathed. "You are a dead man like Captain Larkin, and you have broke the general's heart besides. Why didn't you kill him when you had the chance?"

"Pour me a glass of whiskey, if you please, Sergeant-Major."

He poured, making little popping sounds with his pursed lips. Sweat was dripping from his chin. There was still a frozen silence in the room, all eyes fixed upon me. Something dark had begun fretting the edges of my exultation. I tossed down the burning whiskey, rose on unsteady legs, and slung Henry Plummer's cartridge belts over my shoulder.

In the dead hush I started again up the curving staircase, where, on the first balcony, behind the second door, Cora plotted the moves of her Quest. On the second, past the myriad glitter of the chandelier, the single white flame of a wall lamp burned beside a doorway, within which the most beautiful woman I had ever seen waited, with my ring. I strode on up the steps.

From the darkness beyond the open door words were whispered, a welcome. I entered, closing the door behind me as a candle flame licked to life. It drifted from left to right like something in a dream, illuminating only a dark vertical pool, and drifted on, doubling—a mirror, a moving female shape in the mirror, its twin interposed between me and the reflection. Or was it the other way around? Two figures met, each with a candle, dark cloud of hair mingling with the darkness, pale flesh of face and dark pits of eyes, smiling pout of lips, breathtaking long curve of throat sloping to a breast, low laugh like a caress.

Both figures and one candle flame vanished as a hand touched my face, exploring my cheek, and sealing my mouth when I would have spoken to ask for my ring. I was trembling as though I would shatter like crystal. I let drop Henry Plummer's cartridge belts, and then unbuckled and dropped my own.

I grasped perfumed flesh in my arms and fell into softness. My trembling had become a throbbing insistence. She whispered, "No! You must not!" This time I stopped her mouth with mine. Her fingers scraped my back, first in resistance, then differently.

She cried out as the door burst open. I lurched to my feet and stumbled toward it, blinded by the blaze of lights so that I only glimpsed the silhouette with the raised arm that was the last thing I was to see in my life, for I was struck blind by the terrible blow that fell upon me there.

THREE

J. D. Dockerty

In my life I have been a fool with liquor and a wise man with horses. I was born on a horse, or just off one anyway, for my mother died in a fall a month before she was due to be light of me, and they cut me from her there. Which was the last time I was throwed, except by whiskey.

In those days before the Big Dry-up, I rode for the Castle Hundred and proud of it. That was when the squire's lands comprised a third of the Territory, who went to smash with the rest of the foreign owners when the country turned to desert.

I know that a man's memory will confuse him, and there is a true saying that the past has a rosier bottom than the present, but I can remember well the assemblies at the Castle, and the beautiful women, so fair-fleshed, with hair piled up to gleam like gem stones in the light of a thousand candles. You will ask if I remember the general at those affairs, and I will answer that he was only another youngster of an officer, though he had a powerful carriage even then. He was a hotheaded young fellow, and I am sure no better at fighting temptation than I have been in my life, and there was temptation and plenty amongst those ladies at the Castle.

The Hundred was green then, trees everywhere, and grassy meadows that would be a blanket of flowers in the spring. I remember the squire and his guests hunting through the woods and meadows with that pack of white-and-liver-spotty hounds, the fox flying hell-for-leather with the dogs bellowing, and after them the riders coming.

In those old times I remember the fat cattle, belly-down in grass like they were afloat in it. Cattle trailed down to the bottoms to drink at creeks that ran clear and fast and two yards wide. Those were prime days for man and beast.

The Dry-up came like a curse. The creeks went dry, and the Sweetwater turned to dry sand. Then you would see cattle baked into lumps of hide and horn in the dry bottoms, and all the fine foreign landowners, the squire among them, went back to where they had come from, and their foremen and cowboys turned into rustlers and desperadoes, and I will not deny I was among them.

Those were terrible times, with all men at their worst. Water was brought in in tank cars on the railroad until the railroad stopped running. Prospectors searching for the Lost Dutchman mine died of thirst and you would find dried lumps of hide and hair in the bottoms that were man and donkey. But others died besides prospectors, and of lead and scalping knives. For it seemed all men were turned into outlaws preying on each other, with Kimanches raiding out of the mountains to pick off stragglers, and not just stragglers. Many times the cavalry was too few to drive them off.

But little by little the general began beating them back. There would be a truce, then the hatchet dug up and more fighting, and another truce. In the main the general won the scraps, and that was a time when he was acquiring the little spreads that the Hundred had been cut up into. Putting it back together by hook and by crook; for there were some to say that, if a man didn't sell out cheap, that would be the next place Kimanches would come down on, and the cavalry slow to show.

I was riding with a bunch of turned-bad hands then, no better than the fellows next to me. But I saw that what the general was doing was right, putting things back together the way it used to be, and so I went to him and threw in with him.

So I became his horsebreaker, and trusted man besides. He confided in me secrets that will never pass my lips, and I came to be trusted with more than mustangs, as I will relate. And did betray my trust which I would not have done if the liquor hadn't turned me into no more than a beast.

Besides the Kimanche beat to where they scarcely troubled anymore, it even rained a time or two, as it had not done in a coon's age. The grass came back a little, and Putaw Creek even ran a trickle, though the Sweetwater never did, and Bright City, where the fort was, became a considerable town.

And then the general asked me to undertake a task for him. I was to travel East to bring back a lady, and I knew that lady from the old days. I promised I would bring her back safely to him.

For I thought I saw that it was all coming around again, the great days returning. First the Kimanche beat back, then the rains coming, and the fine ladies and gentlemen returning to the Castle. For I know it can come round again if the right man shows up with his good sense, courage, and strength.

When I came to the place where the general had sent me, it was as though I had walked up to a mirror, spit and image of the Castle in the old days. There was green river bottom, and forests sweeping down from the hills, so that it seemed any minute there would be a horn call, and a fox streaking out with the hounds and riders after it. A great stone mansion lay on the far side of a creek with a covered bridge over it, and a road spiraling tan against the green hillside.

A plump fellow in a uniform of red trousers and striped vest showed me up some stairs to where she was standing in a slant of sun from a window behind her, in a velvet gown with crisp ruching down the bosom and white lace at the sleeves. She didn't remember me at first, but then she did, her rosebud mouth puckering once as though to blow a feather, and then softening into the winningest of smiles. All around her head was black hair in long sweet waves.

I told her what I had come for, and she nodded as

though she knew it already. She said that we must hurry.

She went out of the room and came back with a carpet bag, which she tossed some clothing into. She put on a hat that had a feather on it, and swung a cape over her shoulders.

I followed her carrying the carpet bag, which was heavy to pull my arm from its socket. Outside I swung the team around with the tassels on their harness nodding, while she whispered, "Hurry! Please hurry!"

Glancing up at the windows above me, glistening red with the setting sun, I saw one of them open with a child's face in it, twisted up like he was screaming, and a hand reaching out, though I couldn't hear him for the scrape of wheels turning in gravel. Then we were flying down the road. She never looked back, only laying her little gloved hand on my arm to urge me faster.

She couldn't have said a dozen words to me on the long way to the station, where we booked seats on the train to San Hedrin and the Territory.

Jolting along the river and then through plains country in the cars, she watched out the window with her little chin braced on her hand like if she took her eyes off those mountains they would disappear.

For company we had a fat man and his fat wife in a poke bonnet, and a tall old drummer with hair like he'd been lightning-struck, and with him a pretty young woman with black hair, very demure most of the time, looking down at her hands in black net gloves, though once in a while her eye would catch mine sideways and smolder like a hot coal. The other men would snicker and nudge each other whenever the drummer called her "Niece."

There were two prospectors with skin like boot leather and those far-off-looking chips of eyes; a half-grown boy playing cards with his old lady aunt; and a blind man with black-lensed spectacles and a terrible scar twisted across his forehead at the hairline like a pink centipede. He sat his seat with a military bearing, both hands clasped on his long stick.

Once my lady took a sewing kit from her reticule to fasten a button back to her sleeve. When it was done she cut the thread with a tiny curved blade she sprung from her finger ring, like a cat's claw coming out. She showed it to me, a ring with a pale face in cameo on it. I couldn't make out where the shiny little blade had come from, which pleased her.

When a new conductor came on my heart sank, for it was Dan Slagle from the Castle Hundred crew that I knew well, stepping along the aisle with his eyes slitted at the fat couple, the drummer and his niece, and me and my lady, like tallying stock. He gave me a nod.

"Well, hello, Dan," I said, and he said, "Well, hello, J. D."

When he'd gone on I eased my piece in its leather and never rested easy for a moment, for if it was Dan Slagle, Big Mac was nearby.

And all of a sudden there was a jolt that flung everybody out of his seat. Another jolt tipped the coach up. It went over on its side with screeching metal, women squalling, and men shouting. My lady and I were tangled together from the wreck, and we extricated each other, moving a limb here and another there. The screaming had stopped and all through the car people were sorting themselves out. No one seemed much hurt. The coach being on its side, fellows climbed on the seats to try to open the windows. Just then glass was smashed with a boot kicking it in, and a man dropped through. It was Red Hoskins I had known all my life. As I reached for my revolver Jack Carew ducked in from the forward passage with a gun in either hand. My lady stood holding on to my arm as we faced these two fellows, and I was in a cold sweat over my task of bringing her safe back to the general.

We made our way outside with the rest, Jack relieving me of my revolver as I went by him, saying, "There's a good fellow, J. D." Outside, I saw they had broken the two coaches and the caboose off from the locomotive like wolves cutting a calf out of a herd.

Big Mac was sitting on a big black looking over the

scene, with a dozen riders in a half-circle with him. The coaches had been laid on their side by a log warped across the rails as I have seen done more times than I care to remember. All this while my lady kept her hand on my arm, not tight but reminding me I was responsible for her safety.

Big Mac slumped on that seventeen-hands black, the corners of his mouth turned down steep and his eyes sleepy. His chins ran down to his neck, his belly hung out before him, and his black hat was turned down all around to keep the sun off his face, which was scabby with sun sores and bristled with whiskers.

He didn't seem to take any notice of anything in particular, though some of his riders nudged each other to see me and my lady, and one or two nodded to me not unfriendly.

My lady leaned against me like she was taken faint, and whispered, "Who is that man?"

And I told her he was Big Mac.

Just then she cried out in a muffled way when Jack Carew came up behind her to stick his ugly face against her neck.

"Oh, this one do smell so *good,* J. D.!"

I hit him, but he bounced back with his revolver out and slashed me across the face so I thought I was blinded and sank to my knees. My lady helped me up and daubed at my bloody face with a handkerchief. Big Mac must have signaled Jack off, for he did no more.

They tied my hands behind my back then, with a chunk of sapling through the elbows, and tied hers too, though I noticed they were gentler with her than with the other women. Very nasty they were with the drummer's niece, sticking dirty hands down the neck of her dress until she flinched back, then Red coming up behind to make her scream and jump forward. They were vile men that rode for Big Mac out of Putaw Crossing.

They said he himself was not interested in women in a natural way but could only watch others in the exercise of their lusts, though I have also heard he could take his re-

134

volver barrel so cunning and skillful to those Putaw women they would beg him never to stop.

We set out with some of his riders alongside, up a stretch of dry creek, and then turned north through winding washes and big boulders. My lady looked elegant even with her hat gone, her hair loose, and her cheeks streaked with sweat. Her bosom stuck out proud from the way her hands were tied behind.

Big Mac rode drag, hulking along with the motion of his gelding. Once my lady whispered to ask where they were taking us, but I shook my head I didn't know. I thought she and the other women were headed for Putaw Crossing, with some stops along the way. The men would be lucky to get much further at all. Though I noticed they had left the blind man his stick.

My lady spoke up to ask Jack Carew where we were going, and with a wink at me said, "Oh, you'll find out soon enough, ma'am."

And she asked him who they were.

"Oh, just some fellows out rounding up the estrayed mares," he said, and grinned like he was the cleverest fellow alive.

The blind man had listened to this, and after it attached himself alongside us. I was able to help him step out faster by warning him what to watch for in the path.

But the old woman, aunt to the boy, plumped herself down on a little pile of rocks with the boy crying and trying to tug her to her feet. She announced that she would just as soon die here as further along. Red Hoskins drew his rifle from its boot and laid it across the saddlehorn aimed at her. She folded her arms and gazed back at him, while the boy ran a few steps away, and then ran back. I saw nothing pass between Red and Big Mac except that Red shrugged and put his piece away. We all marched on past where she sat straight-backed with her arms folded. The boy kept sobbing and looking back until Red told him to shut up, which he did.

At sundown we came to sheds and a big corral, with a low adobe wall on two sides, and, rising from that, posts with barb wire strung between, and branches woven through the wire. In the corral we all sat on bales and gunny bags that were scattered around, and waited for what was to happen next. And I waited with my heart in my boots.

Big Mac strolled by us, rolled by, I guess I should say, in his bulk. He wore a greasy cowhide jacket with fringes on it everywhere. Whenever he moved there was a haze of motion, so it seemed he moved swifter than another. He stood bellied out in front of us, scratching inside two buttons of his shirt and chewing on something like a cud, while he looked my lady over with his black-glass chips of eyes in his scabby, bristly face.

"You have brought us a rare one, fellow," he said, in his high voice.

I said I was bringing her to the general, whose guest she was to be, and who would not take it lightly that we had been interfered with.

"What'll he do about it, do you suppose?" Big Mac said, taking a gold toothpick from his pocket and jabbing between his jagged, stumpy teeth with it. He scratched a thumbnail through the scabs of his chin, and asked if my lady had been educated.

She said she had.

"You know men's preferences, then, ma'am?"

She blushed very hot and did not answer him.

"Sometimes we must send the ladies to school for their lessons," Big Mac said. "Other times it is unnecessary." There was loutish laughter, to which he closed his eyes as though offended. When it was quiet he said to my lady, very low, "I will give you your freedom if you can discover mine. And much besides."

"Your what?" she said.

"My preferences." He swung away with his fringes all in blurry motion, and minced over to where the drummer's niece was sitting, with men crowding around him as men will around a bully. My lady was looking at me with her hot black eyes.

"You will tell me who he is!" she said.

She pried at me until I told her he was in the business of seizing women and selling them into certain slavery, but I did not tell her that Putaw Crossing was the call station for every kind of rustler, deserter, miner, trapper, and every other hard, lonely, and desperate man, and every color of nigger, breed, greaser, and Chinaman too. Nor that it was said Big Mac sold women to the Kimanche, who paid well for white women.

All she said was, "I see."

The blind fellow, who was seated nearby, said, "He is a heartless man, but he may pretend to be a civilized one if it suits his purposes."

"Thank you," my lady said, as though she took comfort from that.

Dark came like a curtain let down. Big Mac's people had made a bonfire in the center of the corral, dragging in branches and pine knots, and my lady and I sat together on a pile of sacking as close to the adobe wall and fence as we could get, with the blind man next to us. On a post nearby, but high up, I could see the rusty handles of a pair of wire cutters, though there was no way I could reach them with my arms tied back, aching as they were.

My lady moved closer so she was doing something behind me. She had the knifeblade out of her ring and was sawing rope, stopping once to catch her breath from exertion. Below us Big Mac had climbed into a big high-chair affair, like a judge's stand at a rodeo, made of saplings rawhided together. He had a jug, which he lifted to his shoulder to suckle from, and, in the flickering of the bonfire, he cast a shadow over all that was a fearsome brooding thing.

When my lady sawed I could feel the heat of her breath on my ear. Then my hands were loosed, and in an instant I had the rope off, and her hands untied as well. Still, I could not reach the wire cutters until my lady whispered to the blind man and borrowed his stick, and carefully I pried the cutters loose from their nail, and caught them as they fell. Squeezed up close to my lady and the blind man on the pile of sacking, I managed to clip one of the wires behind me with what seemed the loudest snap in the world. I clipped another, and another, finally turning to push a hole in the brush and loose wire. I helped my lady crawl through, and she dropped to the ground outside. Then I whispered to the blind fellow that it was his turn.

His fingers touched my face, quick and soft as the ghosts of fingers, exploring my features. "Do not worry about me," he whispered, "for men like these take me for good luck and will not molest me."

I swung through the wire after my lady, and we waited there, hardly breathing, but it didn't seem we had been missed.

There was a whicker, a horse tied to a post nearby. I helped my lady up behind the saddle, and swung up myself. I reined the animal away, whispering to him how I was counting on him, for likely he was one I had broke and trained myself. He jerked his head like he understood, and we moved away from the big corral with my lady's arms locked around my waist. Then I touched my boot heel in and whispered again, and we made tracks away.

But as though Big Mac, in his cunning, had laid a trap for my downfall, looped on the saddlehorn by its thong was a leather-covered flask. And of course I must sample what was in it, and go on sampling. With whiskey heat in my belly, and my lady pressed up against me, before much of that night of riding was gone we had tumbled off the horse to rut like beasts on the bare ground.

In full light she cried out my name. I came to my feet still drunken. There were two of them not fifty yards away, Jack Carew and another, with his rifle slanted at us, a rat-jawed dirty face showing under his hat brim.

Jack said, "Well, J. D., I allus said you was one selfish son-a-bitch. Now!"

There wasn't a thing in the world I could do while my lady scrambled to cover her limbs, except to back on over to the paint horse that had carried us here, with my hands raised to satisfy Rat-Jaw, who kept his rifle trained on me. Just then Jack Carew started to swing out of his saddle.

Well, there are those who say I can talk to a horse and

know what the horse replies. I have had a hand in the gentling of most all the riding stock in the Territory, and if I don't know each one by name, I know most, and Jack Carew's mare was called Magpie for her thieving habits. A horse will remember me because I chose to train him with words and whistles instead of hitting him over the face with a rope end like some ham-handed busters will do. Once I could whistle to bring in a horse at a gallop from a mile off.

So I called "Magpie!" just as Jack started to swing down. She jerked toward me, and Jack yelped as he started to fall. I whistled, not loud, and Magpie began trotting in a big arc, Jack with his boot caught in the stirrup bumping on the ground and squalling. The other fellow took up the chase, yelling to Jack to hold on and let go all at the same time. I had the lariat off the saddlehorn in a second, swinging a loop while Rat-Jaw raced up beside Magpie, grabbing for her bridle. I settled a loop over him and with a yelp he came out of the saddle and hung in the air about a minute before he came down like a dropped pumpkin. I sprinted barefoot through thorns and sharp pebbles for his rifle, and laid it in on him, but his neck was broken where he sprawled there. His horse was high-tailing away, and Magpie had stopped to graze the dry grass. Jack Carew had managed to break his boot out of the stirrup. His face was scraped to raw bacon. I took his revolver away from him while he sat there groaning, "Jayd—Jayd—Jayd—"

I grabbed his hair and shook him hard, calling him an evil toad who had once been a decent man. "Jayd—" he kept saying, "Jayd—" until I blew his brains out.

I took Magpie's reins and, with the revolver and rifle, tender-footed back to where my lady, with her clothing all together, stood watching me with those great dark eyes I would drown in every time I looked into them.

I got my clothes on to cover my nakedness, with Magpie pulled between us like a curtain. She mounted the other pony while I tended to the horses, feeling their legs, lifting each foot to look at shoe and hoof, talking to them both the while so they would know how we were depending on them. Then I swung up on Magpie and we made ourselves scarce from there.

My lady and I never spoke a word of what had happened that night I got into the whiskey. We never spoke of that or much else either in those days of riding and nights with a little cookfire, she sleeping on one side of it and I pretending to on the other, staring at a red coal gleaming in the ashes and listening to the small sound of her breath. It was in small roundabout ways that we came to know each other, both of us, it seemed like, afraid of saying more than good morning, and good night, or how many days now?—and maybe a word or two when I had shot a little game for supper and we sat broiling bits of meat over the fire.

So I brought her safe to the Castle, which had been my charge. I had done the best I could, but failed in what the general might never come to know of, and I'll never know myself whether he did or didn't. He could see, on the outside of it anyway, that she was worn to a frazzle. He greeted her and me from the veranda of the Castle, very grateful to me, shaking my hand, and courtly with her, putting an arm around her and pecking at her cheek. And at that moment she looked past him at me, opening her eyes wide so I fell into them once and forever.

I had sworn off strong spirits and stuck with it for a long time after the flask was left on that pony's saddlehorn. I lived in the foreman's quarters back of the Castle, and often, despite myself, dreamed of those nights with my lady across the cookfire, a little red coal winking a warning.

And one night, when I was half asleep, half dreaming, I knew there was someone in the room with me. I jerked a hand for my revolver in its holster hanging from the bedpost, but did not touch it. There was a sniff of flower garden in the room.

In the morning it seemed to me it must have been one of those dreams a man will have when he has been long without a woman and cannot control himself, until I got up from my bed with the covers thrown back, and there was a white flower with its petals mashed brown, one of the kind that grew in pots in the solarium of the Castle and that I had seen my lady wear in her hair.

After that once, though I would lie awake at night shivering to jar to pieces, it never happened again. Sometimes I would almost weep in my disappointment, and in the end I all but forgot it, as though it had been the dream I had first thought it was.

As that year wore itself out my lady became plumper and plumper, until it was certain she was carrying child and near term. One day I was riding in from the corrals watching clouds boiling up black this side of the Bucksaws. These clouds had flashes of lightning in them, and their shadow came sweeping over just as I rode beneath my lady's window, where her white face showed, calling down to me: "It is coming!"

At first I thought she must mean the rain at last, but she cried, "The waters have broken and you will have to help me! There is no one here but Cook!"

Her eyes weighed down on me very heavy. She had sent for the general and Dr. Pipkin, she said, but there would not be time. Big splattery drops dashed against my face just then, and in seconds it was raining hard.

I ran up the stairs to where she was sitting on her bed, holding to the bedpost. I had helped mares with colts enough, but churning in my mind were all the things that could go wrong. The rain was battering on the roof and windows, and there would be floods if this kept up.

"We had better get you in your nightgown, ma'am," I said, trying to sound dead calm so she would take no nerves from me.

She fussed at bows and buttons, and I helped her. There was a mountain of her for certain, all buttermilk white with little blue veins. As quickly as could be managed, for her modesty, I had her in her nightgown and her bed. Right away she cried out with a cramp and hung on to the bedstead with a white fist.

There was a commotion downstairs that I thought

must be the general and Dr. Pipkin, by a miracle, come sooner than expected, but Cook called up very excited to say it was visitors.

Her pain had passed for a minute and she lay there gasping, so I hurried out to the landing just as two men came up the stairs, one of them a dwarf, tapping his hand to the brim of his stovepipe hat to see me, the other a tall old fellow with a thick mat of white hair. This one introduced himself as Dr. Balthazar, and said they'd heard from a fellow on the road that a doctor was needed.

"Lady come to her time, am I right?" the dwarf said. He had a doctor bag with him, Dr. Balthazar a big ledger book. They were strange-looking medical men, but I was pure glad to see them.

"Will you take us to the patient, sir?" Dr. Balthazar said, pouting his dark little mouth like a kitten's button. Just then she cried out, so I led them on into the room.

"Bring boiling water, lots of it!" the dwarf called, when Cook looked in the door. He took off his coat and rolled his sleeves on his short, hairy arms, frowning down at my lady groaning in her labors. Dr. Balthazar had seated himself at a writing desk and was calling out questions, how often were the pains now, and so forth, writing the answers in his book with a good deal of flourish. The dwarf held up a gold watch for her to see while she answered. He took a potion from a brown bottle in his doctor bag, poured it in a glass, and gave it to her, saying it would make her easier. Outside it was raining by the barrelful.

Cook came grunting upstairs with a pot of steaming water. He slopped some in a basin, and we all washed our hands. My lady was in heavier labor now, crying out in a muffled way and straining her mound of a body. The labor came so hard I must go and stand at the window with my back turned.

The black clouds had blown apart and a solid bar of sunshine slanted down, with rainbow stripes across it. In that light I saw three Kimanches on their paint ponies trotting around and up the hill. The sun shone like a lantern beam on their eagle-feather headdresses and vermilion-painted bodies, feather-rimmed shields, and spear-heads hidden in feathers like bouquets. I had never seen redskins done up so, and I knew it was not war paint they were wearing, for I had seen that a time or two that I would not forget. And just then, on a loop of road below them, there came in sight a squadron of cavalry at a brisk canter, pointy pennons flying and a bugler with a horn to his lips, though I could not hear him through the glass and my lady crying out behind me. The Kimanche devils held up just below me, glancing behind them as they waited, and raising hands in the peace sign as the troopers came up. All of them dismounted and disappeared together, and I could hear their commotion in the ballroom downstairs, and Cook calling up in Chinee jabber.

There was a wailing cry then, and I wheeled around. The dwarf doctor was holding up a pink-and-white baby, and my lady was smiling and pushing her hair back from her face while the other one scribbled away in his ledger.

With a great trampling on the stairs, in they came, Kimanches and troopers all mixed together, the soldiers with caps off and redskins in their bright paint, holding up their spears with the feathered tips. There was a clamor of grunts from the Kimanches and blurted speeches from the soldiers, and admiration from all, for it could be seen that the baby was the most beautiful ever to see the light of the world, with a fine mist of golden hair, and perfect-formed little arms and legs all rosy and pale at once. And, as the sun leaned further in the window to make the child glow golden, everyone drew a breath suck as though that had been a sign from Heaven, more and more crowding into the room with a choiring of sound. They formed a line to pass by the bed so each in turn could look on the child.

From where I was squeezed back against the window, I saw that the general had appeared, with his staff officers, to join the line, wearing his dress uniform with its chestful of ribbons and medals. He bent his head before the child, while my lady held the child to her breast, smiling and smiling in her great joy.

*　　*　　*

Before she was three Flora was sitting a mare fine as you please, a good seat on her, straight little back, and a commanding way of looking at you with her chin set and those eyes that seemed to gather in right away just what you were or weren't, but pink lips smiling as though to show she understood and forgave. She was her mother's very light and life when in her pinafore and a pink ribbon in her golden hair she ran to my lady, who would snatch her up to cover her with kisses. And the general's also, who often sat in the solarium when he was at the Castle, with his book and a blanket over his knees, and Flora standing beside his chair touching his medals and asking about each one.

When it came time for the child to learn the ways of horses, it was me that was turned to. First, in the little ring I had built, I would let her turn and turn at the end of a rope on the gentle mare Jessie, sidesaddle in her velvet riding habit like her mother's riding dress, and her black velvet cap with a feather in it. Then, with me beside her, we rode close around the Castle, and later down the hill and splashing through Putaw Creek, where water ran now.

I would only have to tell her once to hold the reins higher or tip her quirt a hair straighter, and she had done it and kept it that way, her mouth tight with concentration. Now that there was peace in the Territory, when we passed a band of Kimanche she would raise her quirt just so, while the young chief returned her greeting, raising his rifle or spear. The same with a squadron of cavalry, who would salute her very formal and as though she had been the general himself. Once we saw a pack of black riders off to the north that must be Big Mac's, a great rush of hoofs and dust and jammed-together men, too far off to make much out of, although I felt my blood turn to whey at the sight of them. But they showed no interest in us and came no closer, so that I thought we were safe from them here because of the general and cavalry at the fort.

But another time when we were out together we saw four riders trotting along a ridge line. At the distance we could make out that one of them was so small it might've been a monkey sitting his pinto horse, and another much bigger than the other two. Closer, they reined up to look us over, and I spurred Billy-Bub so as to get between them and Flora. For the big one was Big Mac, in a black slouch hat and about an acre of fringed buckskin; with him was one of the black riders, a boy a little older than Flora, with a mean, squinched face glowering down at us, and a woman seated sidesaddle, all in black velvet, with a cap of black feathers over a white face. It was the drummer's niece from the train. I didn't get my breath right until the four of them had swung away to disappear over the ridge, and we had got distance between us in the opposite direction.

Flora asked who they were, and I replied that they were from Putaw Crossing, which was on the other side of Helix Hill from the Castle, and was a place I hoped she would never see, for it was a filthy place.

"Are those bad people, J. D.?" she asked me.

"Yes. Bad."

"How can you tell?"

"For one, they have got different ways of looking at you, kind of sideways instead of straight on."

"But could you tell that from here?"

"So could you, which is why you asked about them."

The whiskey was after me again. It would gripe my insides like a half-hitch on the strain for one swallow of the stuff. I had sworn I would not drink in my room, and I did not, but I began to stash bottles here and there, one in a cairn of stones in a place Flora and I would pass when we rode out. I made sure we rode close by there, and with the excuse that I must relieve myself, which was true enough, walk down into the bottom and around a crag of rock, where I would take out my bottle and have a swig or two of whiskey.

And so I did this one day, taking the bottle from its hidey-hole with the glass blister-hot where the sun had got to it, and uncorked it, and knocked back a long pull, standing there panting and hating myself and everything else. I tipped the bottle up for another dose to wash out the fire, and a third to drown the ashes, when there was a heavy drumming I could feel through my boot soles, like a flash flood bearing down from a cloudburst in the mountains. It was hoofs, a herd of buffalo it seemed, so many, building and building but whatever it was invisible except for a rise of dust coming on. I began to run back to where I had left Flora, so slow-footed it was like running in quicksand, and my shouting drowned out by those beating hoofs. Then they passed and went on, and the dust cloud passed along. I ran on panting and knowing I was too late. She was gone, with only the tracks of a great bunch of horses heading off to the north where the dust was still moving.

I set off riding hard following those tracks. The dust faded away before me. There was stony ground, and then a place where some tracks swung off to the left while the others ran straight ahead, and further along another party veering to the right. I didn't know what to do but keep spurring after the main body, though what I would do if I caught up I didn't know. Then there was hard ground for a spell, and a tangle of rocky draws, and night coming, and that was the end of it.

I rode back to the Castle with a half moon sailing in scud cloud over me, slow and slower up the winding road toward the lights of the Castle windows. I dismounted there and climbed the steps with my hat in my hand.

Inside my lady came running toward me, with the general behind her, and two officers from the fort with them. *"Where is my child?"*

When I told her what had happened she didn't speak a word, and the officers made a great hubbub that they would ride out, they would find her and bring her back, though I saw the general only crossed his arms on his chest in that way they lay dead men out sometimes. My lady crouched back against the marble fireplace there. She said, *"It is a judgment on me!"*

The two officers stopped their foolish talk and turned to try to comfort her. But she burst past them with the poker raised high to brain me, her face as fierce as a tigress. I did not even put up my hands to protect myself.

But she did not bring that poker down to kill me for my sins, for just then the general fell. He fell like a tree falling, not even trying to ease it, just toppling straight over with a crash on the parquet, like a dead man.

In the months of my wandering I took the pledge and failed, and pledged again and failed again in drunken shame, and misused myself in many ways. Through an old acquaintance met by chance in a saloon in some trailhead town, I learned that my lady had never got over her grieving, that the Castle had been abandoned and was run down to ruin, and she and the general were moved into Bright City, where he never rested sending out cavalry troops to search for the band of renegade Kimanche that had stolen his daughter. But I knew it was not Kimanche that had taken Flora.

And so I returned to Bright City, coming in past the adobe fort, where a trooper with a rifle paced before the open gate and a bit of striped color hung from the flagpole as limp as I felt; and on along past the dump and Boot Hill, and into the town square with the dust from Blackie's hoofs itching on my face. A carriage drawn by a fine team of grays came at me swaying on its thoroughbraces, a big sergeant with yellow chevrons on his sleeve up on the box. Seeing the two gold stars on the door I brought a hand up to jerk down on my hat brim, for I knew the general was inside that carriage, though I could not see him through the window.

I sat Blackie with my hand still pulling on my hat brim as though saluting, dust settling over me as the carriage jounced on by—heading for the fort where my lady was.

I gave Blackie a low whistle to start him along. For I knew I had come back not to Bright City but to Putaw Crossing, where I must find Flora, and if Big Mac decided to put me under for shooting Jack Carew and Rat-Jaw that time when I snatched my lady free of him, why, that was all right; and if I had to go into harness like those other fellows I had known in the old days, in order to snatch Flora free, then that was as it must be too.

There was a smoky sunset fading as I rode along the railroad tracks, with their rusty flashes like old blood in the last of the sun, and night coming on as I passed those musty-smelling heaps of rotting bone left over from when the hide and bone markets collapsed, miles of those cliffs of rotten bone so that you couldn't believe there had been that many buffalo in the Territory once, not to speak of the killing that must have been done: queer twisted and flanged gray blades that it didn't seem could have come out of buffalo, but must be from some huger ancient beasts whose shapes you couldn't even imagine. There were flashes of phosphorescent light where the shadows were darkest, and scurryings and corner-of-the-eye flicks of motion, which must be the rats that lived in there. Blackie shied away from that moldering wall of bone time and again, and I was nervy of it myself, as though something in there might reach out to grab a person passing by, or the whole bank topple, or that queer keen stink smother you. It was a relief when the bone piles began to taper down to where I could see over them to the distant black of the mountains, and presently dwindled to nothing.

The air was fouler coming into Putaw Crossing, first that dry nose-prickling of the ash fields, and then dust and smoke, "smust" I'd heard it called, and stronger and stronger too the open-sewer stench that was a stink you would never forget. The black expanse of the pulver mill hulked up, the three stacks seeming to rise forever against the night sky, merging so you couldn't tell where they ended and black space began. Further along the red glow of banked fires was reflected in the slurry pits, with their stink of bitumens and naphtha. Beyond all that was the tortured land you could only imagine, with the heaps of chewed-up rock and gravel waste where the land dredges had plowed. In the sulfur, petroleum, and sewer stench I rode along by that black and invisible vast of destruction to Putaw Crossing.

At the crossroads the bridge sounded hollow as a coffin

beneath Blackie's hoofs. In black night we mounted a potholed road past a solid rank of storefronts. There was the creak of a shutter in the wind, and once a caterwauling with two toms tearing across the way in front of us. Blackie jumped pole-legged and then stood steady, shivering, while I patted and whispered to him.

There were sounds in the silence now, a voice raised somewhere, and laughter and a spate of tinny music shut off like a door had closed. I could remember when there'd been no more than a dozen adobe huts at the Crossing, and now the hill was thick with them.

Pretty soon I could make out dark forms of men, and lights showed where the road narrowed between two-story 'dobes, with lantern light inside. Women leaned out windows, some of them in their bare flesh, calling to the men below, me among them, sometimes sweetly but more often coarse to chill your belly.

There was a big horse barn at one of the turnings, there must have been a hundred horses stalled inside, and I left Blackie with a one-armed hostler there. Big Mac's "palace" was on up the narrow, curving way another half a mile, he told me.

More men crowded the track, some few in town clothing, most in rough dress, and many in leather jackets aping Big Mac's buckskin fringes. There were hardrock miners in their sashes, workingmen in heavy boots, skinners, drifters, ruffians, and hardcases of every shade of color. From a window above me a red-headed woman opened the blouse of her dress to scoop her breasts at me. " 'Ey, 'andsome, you come see me, eh? Further up they's all clappy." When I went on past she spat down at me.

I could not even look down the side streets of cribs, though I knew I might have to before I was through here.

The cobbled street led along a ridge where there was a breeze with the sewer stink blown away for a spell. Above the slot of a canyon a black peak towered, which, as I came up further, I saw was not a part of the hill but a tented, sprawling structure with lights piercing its sides. Just here three of the black riders leaned together like blackbirds watching me come past them. One of them was Jim Eggers, who chose not to recognize me, nor I him.

There was another cross street of cribs, with the whores hanging out the tops of the dutch doors, and as I hurried on past I wondered if each one of the black riders had come here in this same way, with a blight on his conscience and no decency left him, or on some hunt that put a good face on his coming to Putaw Crossing and Big Mac's service.

So at last I reached the top with the "palace" piled up before me in a confusion of lights and shadows. Nearer was a long building that had burned, with the roof timbers fallen in; all at once, like a kick in the belly, I understood that the "palace" was no less than the Castle, for Putaw Crossing had grown up and over Helix Hill. Coming up the back way I had not realized that until now.

I stood there trying to catch my breath, staring at the Castle which was so changed, with the outbuildings burned. On a broad veranda I could make out the pale glow of cheroots where men lounged on benches. Someone sent a butt spinning sparks out into the dark. Each of the steps up to the veranda seemed three feet high as I climbed them.

The first person I saw, sitting above the pack of people inside, was a big, wall-eyed shotgun, slumped on his lookout stand between the faro layouts. He nodded to me just as though he had been certain I would come in the door at that very moment. Beyond him stairs curved to a landing. Walls had been knocked out to make the ballroom bigger, while the height seemed lower, as though the Castle had slumped down somehow.

I was nervy as a spooked horse as I made my way through bunches of men who paid me no attention, and whores with their bogus smiles and winks, until I came to the bar, where first I ordered a whiskey, then changed my mind. I jumped half out of my skin when there was a slap on my back.

"Well, hello, J. D.!"

It was Bobby Kettle from the old Hundred, in the rusty

150

black the hands all seemed to wear here, scratchy little beard with a thin, dark mouth grinning out of it.

"Well, hello, Kett," I said.

"Whiskey with an old pard, J. D.?"

I said I had taken the pledge, and he shrugged and set about swinging his elbows to clear a space for us among the men ganged around the bar.

Those who weren't black-dressed were quick to make way for one who was, and the barkeep hurried to bring whiskey.

"Come out to join the boys, have you?" Bobby Kettle asked.

"Just thought I'd look in, Kett. How is everybody?"

"Oh, everybody is mighty healthy and prosperous," he said with a wink

All at once there was a shout that broke off in a snarling rousting. I switched around to see a man hurl himself out the door with a big black hound after him. The laughter all around sounded like a toadying laugh at the antics of a bully at another's expense. Then I saw Big Mac on the balcony, in his pale blue buckskins that made him look big as a grizzly, with a cigar in his jaw and hat brim pulled down. Two others were with him, a red-headed boy in a dickey shirt, with a squinched-up grinning face, that I had seen once before; and a thin woman in black wearing a black domino mask with pale eyeholes, who must be the drummer's niece from the train.

There was a stirring and quieting as the black hound trotted back inside, to bound up the steps and haunch down before the three on the landing.

The boy rubbed his ears and said in a voice that scratched like chalk on slate, "Good dog, sir!"

"That's a big dog," I said to Kett.

"He will just take out after a man for no reason sometimes," he said, and giggled.

"Bear-killing dog," said another black-dressed fellow who had drifted up.

The boy took a ball from his pocket and tossed it bouncing down the steps. The hound lit after it, down and across the floor, with people piling out of the way, some of them falling over each other and women squealing, until, with a scraping clatter, the dog caught the ball and trotted back up the steps to release it to the boy, who scratched his ears some more. All the while Big Mac stood there straddle-legged, slanting his eyes over the men and women below, so that I found myself sidling to get behind Kett.

I asked who the woman was.

"Ain't she just a Queen of Spades?" Kett said.

The other said, with a laugh, "Chief's still looking for his Queen of Hearts!"

I saw Big Mac flick away his cigar butt and snap his fingers. A butler-dressed fellow in a tail jacket and striped vest trotted up the steps holding a silver salver with a cigar on it. He lit the cigar for his master. The butler was an Indian fellow with short-cut black hair and a proud back like they have. I noticed he looked fearfully over his shoulder for the dog as he hurried back down the stairs.

Another one in rusty black clapped me on the shoulder and called me by name, though I couldn't recall his. Others came up to shake hands, and more whiskey was poured, though I still managed to refuse a potion. And, when I glanced back at the balcony, Big Mac, the boy, the Queen of Spades, and the hound were gone.

One of the fellows asked if I wasn't the one that was supposed to be able to talk to horses. "How about mules?" another wanted to know.

They were a hard-eyed, sharp-jawed bunch, dirty-faced like they hadn't washed this month. They were quick to nudge one another and have the laugh on someone else. Now they kept after me very scornful, who was the one supposed to be able to talk to horses, and I pretended to think it as funny as they did, though finally I said there might come a day and a reason for me to call in all the riding stock in the Territory, and then we'd see who was on foot.

This gave them a great laugh. They quieted down when a tall, bare-headed fellow came toward us. He had black spectacles on and swung a stick out before him, saying, "Pardon. Pardon, gentlemen." He was greeted very polite by those around me, and called Lute. He was the blind man from the train, with that twisted scar on his forehead.

He came close to me and asked me my name, and, when I told him, asked if I would mind his touching my face: "For I have other means of seeing than the sight of my eyes."

His fingers, that I remembered, chased over my features, light and quick, and like he was remembering me, too.

"Think you'll know him next time you see him, Lute?" Kett said, to snickers. And I heard another fellow whisper, "Damn-all how he knows when there's a stranger showed up."

"J. D. used to ride with the old Hundred bunch one time, Lute. Come back to join up again."

The blind man looked like a young fellow who had been struck old in an instant, a pulse ticking in his scar.

He said, "If you gentlemen would pardon us, I'd like to have a word with your friend. What I have felt in his features may be of value for him to know."

Kett said, "Lute can tell a man's fortune fine as any gypsy woman!"

"Do you see a table where we can have privacy?" the blind man said in a low voice. He took my arm, and I led him to a table in the corner. When we had seated ourselves he commanded me to put out my hand.

Leaning forward, he made to be tracing lines in my palm, whispering, "You must tell me why you are here!"

I told him that I had come to find a child who had been stolen, a girl I thought must be in this place; and that her mother, who was out of her senses with grief, was the woman who had been with me when Big Mac had derailed the train.

"And you are the father?"

I said that the general was the father.

He folded my fingers into my palm as though finished

reading what was there, and leaned back with the round black lenses of his spectacles fixed on me. He said, "The child is here. She is an influence for the good."

My heart began to bang my ribs. "It was my fault she was taken, you see," I said. He was silent, considering. "The mother—" I started, but did not go on, for he had nodded his decision.

"I can help you release her from here, but how will you escape from the Crossing? There would be two hundred riders in pursuit."

I said he could leave that part to me.

"Very well. Prepare yourself, for presently the butler will come for you. He will lead you to me, and I will lead you to the girl." He headed away across the room, stick flicking ahead of him as he called out, "Pardon, gentlemen, ladies!"

I wandered among the gambling layouts, watching a play then moving on. One of the fancy-dressed women attached herself to my arm, but I shook her off, saying, "Later." The young Indian butler marched toward me between the tables. He had a dark, sorrowful face, and a jut to his jaw as though he had his teeth set hard together.

"Come," he said quietly, as he passed me. I followed him, moving idly like I didn't have any real purpose. Outside, he headed along the veranda, past men smoking and taking the air there. At the far end he was lost in shadows. "In here," he said. When I moved toward the wall my arm was caught and I was pulled inside a door. A strip of leather was placed in my hand, which I realized was a belt end.

"Hold to that," Lute whispered. "I know these passages well."

He set off at a good clip, pulling me behind him. I brushed a wall of splintery wood, then one of dressed stone. We were in a long passageway of many turns, very narrow, and I remembered in the old days hearing of secret ways about the Castle.

"Steps," Lute said. It was a long flight up, making a right turn and then another. Once there were glimmers of dusty light from cracks in the wall, so that I had a glimpse of him climbing before me, holding the other end of the belt. Then there was another long passageway, and more stairs, until I had lost all sense of direction. At last he halted, so abruptly I banged into him from behind. He worked at something in the wall and became visible again in a dim square of light. It was a judas window. He pulled me to it.

In the exact center of a room Flora sat on the floor with her back to me. She was wearing a pinafore, and her long blond hair, caught in a blue bow, hung down her back. Squatting facing her was the red-headed boy. The big dog sat, tongue lolling, beside an open door in which the drummer's niece stood, sumptuously dressed in black velvet, with her domino mask pushed up on her forehead. Her lips were moving; she and Flora seemed to be conversing past the boy and the dog. I could make out voices, but not the words.

"Tell me what you see!" the blind man whispered in my ear.

I described the room and the people in it. Meanwhile the woman disappeared with a flick of her black skirt.

Flora gestured with her hand, and the boy rose and retreated across the room. A shelf there held dolls seated against the wall. He brought one of these back to Flora, who incorporated it in some game she was playing, which was invisible to me. He squatted before her again.

Tapping my arm, Lute demonstrated that the square of smoked glass could be slid to one side, and that we stood behind a secret door into the room, which was secured by bolts at the top and bottom.

Flora gestured again, I heard the distant voices again, there was considerable more back and forth talk, and the boy, hands in his pockets, stalked out of the room.

"The boy's gone," I whispered to Lute. "Now there is only the hound."

He nodded as though that was to be expected, and pressed something round into my hand. It was a red ball like the one the boy had tossed down the stairs. "You must be certain it goes out the far door," he whispered, and slid the glass aside.

I aimed the ball, flipped my wrist several times to limber it, and tossed the ball through the judas window. It flew over Flora's blond head, bounced past the hound and out the door. The dog leaped after it, skidding around the corner and out of sight. Lute had slid the bolts and I pushed the door open. Flora's astonished face swung toward me.

"J. D.!" She scrambled to her feet and ran to me. I caught her in my arms, pulled her back through the door while Lute swung it closed behind us and threw the bolts just as the hound slammed into the door. I pressed my finger to Flora's lips in the dust-smelling dark.

Now the boy's voice was audible: *"Florrie.* You come out from where you're hiding, you hear—" Then Lute slid the judas window closed.

We hurried blind along the dark passageway, me holding to Lute's belt end with one hand and pulling Flora along with the other. "Step!" Lute whispered to me, and I whispered, "Step down!" to Flora. We shuffled down the first stairs.

"Are you taking me to my mother and the general, J. D.?" Flora asked, and I said I was.

I touched dressed stone again, but Lute continued to descend, a ramp now instead of stairs, and raw rock walls, mossy and damp. Further along I heard water trickling, and there was a feel of other passages drifted off this one, with puffs of cooler air sometimes and once a swatch of starry sky giving light enough for me to see the blind man hurrying along in the lead, and Flora's pale face behind, her hand gripping mine. We had to pick our way over a rock fall.

"I knew you'd come, J. D.," Flora panted. "I'll be so happy to see my mother and the general again! Have they been worried?"

"Very worried," I said, and asked if those people had been bad to her.

"They were as nice as they knew how to be. But they

156

are a different kind of people, you see. They look at you out of the corners of their eyes the way you said, but then if you are straight with them they stop doing it."

"We must move swiftly," Lute said, and we hastened on. All at once we were under the stars again, all around us the feverish clamor of Putaw Crossing. I saw we were not a hundred steps from the big stable where I had left Blackie. The blind man remained behind the pile of rubble, where the tunnel had come out. When I said he must come with us, he only shook his head.

"Others may need me here. But you must hurry. There will be many men in pursuit."

"You can trust *me* now," I said, clasped his hand once, and hurried Flora down to the corral. There was no light, but I found Blackie quickly and boosted Flora up behind the saddle. I gave a low whistle, and heard the answering stirring and whickering of the other animals in that place.

I swung up and cautioned Flora to hold on tight. Her arms came around me, and I could feel her warm face pressed to my back. I jammed my knuckles to my lips and blew a blast.

Behind us in the corral a terrific racket began, and the one-armed hostler, hurrying up with a lantern, gawked open-mouthed at Flora and me and the open doors of the horse barn behind us. He backed away, swinging the lantern like a railroad switchman.

I pushed Blackie into a hard trot down the cobbled street, men jumping aside with yells and curses. I blew another whistle to rattle the windows. One of the rusty-black riders leaped out to try to catch Blackie's reins, and I jerked out my piece and cold-cocked him with the barrel. We rode rattling on downhill.

The whole stampede of us, Blackie in the lead and all the horseflesh of Putaw Crossing swarming after, surged on down the street between the dark shacks and storefronts, thundered across the bridge, and swung north on the road for Bright City. When I looked back over my shoulder it seemed that all the horses in the world were galloping after us in the starlight. Far back I saw a rider, but he had disappeared before I could unship my revolver. Her arms clasped around my waist, Flora spoke to me sometimes, but I couldn't make out what she said for the pounding of the hoofs. Horses had caught up on either side of us, a big bay named Lopey on the right, and on the left a pinto I couldn't recall the name of. Others were saddled and many trailed ropes. I gave a whistle from time to time to keep them coming.

When we reached the fort a white quarter-moon hung over the Bucksaws and the sky was paling for dawn. The trooper at the gate stood with his carbine at a half-ready, gaping out at Blackie and me with Flora pillion, and most of an acre of horses crowding around us. I swung out of the saddle to lift Flora down, so tired she could hardly stand.

"Take Miss Flora to the general, pronto!" I said, and the guard gasped. He clutched for her arm.

Flora said, "J. D., you just wait right there till my mother comes!"

"No," I said. I just wanted to secure these animals inside, for I'd bet the cavalry could use some remount. Then I'd be on my way.

The trooper rushed her inside the gate, with her little face turned back toward me and a hand raised up and waving me to wait.

It took me some time to herd those Putaw horses inside the fort, and swing the gate to, and mount up on Blackie again. My lady came running outside in her long wrapper, with her hair up in a cloth, to stop by me with her breast heaving and a hand held there, and those black disks of her eyes fixed on my face. The white knot of her hand sought mine where I held the reins. And she said, "You have brought me back my child!"

I said I had brought her back, who had lost her in the first place.

I drowned again in those black eyes, and she whispered the name of a place in Bright City. Just then the general trotted outside holding Flora by the hand. I raised up an arm in greeting to him, pulled Blackie to his haunches, whistled to make him jump, and lit out of there.

I found the place in town she had whispered to me, and lay there on the bed with my hands locked beneath my head staring up at the water stains on the ceiling. Then I went down the street to buy a glass of whiskey for my dry throat, and ended up bringing the bottle back to my room.

The next morning I woke up not even sober yet, to smell on the pillow beside my face the scent of a white blossom laid there by someone who had come, and gone.

FOUR

▰▰▰▰▰▰▰

Flora

The air had been dense all this hot, windless day, so that the heat waves seemed almost to congeal above the roof-tops of Bleeker, and Flora's face felt crusty with perspiration and dust. All day she had felt a gripe of irritation with the eighteen faces of her students, blank and blackened as the bottoms of so many skillets. Facing those wanting-something-from-her faces in the cramped classroom for the remaining hours of this day, tomorrow, the next day, next week, next month—the waiting; she dismissed them half an hour early.

The queer, stifling irritation persisted as she walked home along the boardwalk in the afternoon heat, little puffs of dust rising between the cracks of the boards with the pressure of her steps. Her emotions were familiar, and she realized others must be sharing them. So tonight they would come for her.

When she had bathed and donned the white gown with its high collar and lace insets and tied the belt beneath her breast, she halted once to inhale the faded flower scent from the glass bowl of her potpourri, which allayed a little the Territorial stench. She brushed her hair out long down her back, the brush crackling with electricity, the fair hair floating around her head and shoulders at each stroke, lighter, it seemed, than the foul air. When she had reddened her lips with rouge from the little pot, she seated herself in a straight chair to wait, ankles crossed, hands folded in her lap, gazing at the blank wall opposite her. Finally she sensed rather than heard the approaching creaking of the cart. The sound came louder, rounding the corner, and ceased. Boot heels rapped on the boardwalk, knuckles on her door.

Mr. Porter, the grocer, waited against the darkness outside, frock-coated, stovepipe hat tucked under his arm, in his hand the bridal chaplet of white silk blossoms. She bent her head to facilitate his setting this in place, and he murmured, "Might as well try her again, Miss Flora."

Patting his own hat onto his head, he took her arm, accompanying her to the cart where four other men waited. Toward the square she could see the smoky glow of torches.

In silence the aldermen jockeyed to help her to her seat beside Mr. Jencks, the proprietor of the livery stable, who greeted her with a stiff nod, and dipped his whip over his mule's back. The wheels creaked again, the cart turning. The aldermen walked alongside, two and two. She sat very straight, shivering a little, already feeling the pressure of the hopes and despairs of her escort and of those who awaited her with the torches.

The square was half-filled, the townspeople crowding together before the church. There was a low, concentrated sigh as the cart rounded the corner, shivering the flames of the torches the men held up—all in Sunday best, men in suits or clean shirts, women in gingham and bonnets, the children from the school clustered together. She saw not one smile of greeting as the crowd drifted apart to open a lane to the church steps. "Hup! Hup!" Mr. Jencks called as the mule hesitated. Reverend Holmes stood on the steps, his white collar gleaming in the torchlight. The cartwheels creaked as the cart rolled slowly through the silent crowd. She was shivering again, with all the eyes upon her.

When the cart halted the frock-coated men maneuvered to help hand her down. Mr. Porter presented her to the minister, who took her arm with a comforting pat. Inside the church massed candle flames trembled, and the altar was heaped with artificial flowers, in this place where there were no real ones. Reverend Holmes smelled of talcum and toilet water, and their shadows slanted before them down the aisle. At the altar he halted a step below her.

She stood waiting, glancing once toward the orange gleam outside the door. Each moment as it passed seemed to beat against her nerves, and she thought her legs would not support her much longer. She could sense the fraying away of hopes from the increase in rustling in the square, the coughs. And finally the minister sighed, and, when she turned to face him, shook his head once. He took her arm again and side by side they moved back along the aisle to where the aldermen were stationed, hulking large against the smoky light.

Outside the crowd was quietly dispersing, some of the torches already doused, others flaring toward the streets out of the square. Reverend Holmes turned her over to Mr. Porter, who handed her up to her seat beside Mr. Jencks. He dipped his whip, the cart turning, the aldermen, top-hatted, pacing the boardwalk beside it. Already the square was almost empty, only a few of her students standing together watching their teacher borne away.

"Hup! Hup!" Mr. Jencks muttered, and she closed her eyes, shivering, trying not to breathe the corrupted air, as the cart returned her to her little house.

FIVE

■■■■■■■

The Coming of the Kid

He was shoveling manure at the corral, stacking the dried cakes in the wheelbarrow, when a tickle of dust signified a horseman coming down the track from town. He straightened to lean on his pitchfork, batting flies away from his face.

The horseman appeared at the corral gate, Mr. Conroy, stout in his black suit. "Kid, there is a blind fellow up town looking for you."

"What's a blind fellow looking for me *with*?" he said.

Conroy frowned and scratched his nose. "Got a long stick he jabs around with," he said. "Maybe he'll take it to you if you smart-answer him like that."

The Kid laughed. "Well, no point changing clothes if he can't see."

"Ought to wash up, though," Conroy said. "Probably he can smell."

He washed and changed his clothes, and strode toward town through the fields so as to keep out of the dust of the road. Off to the west flat-bottomed gray clouds hung over the Bucksaws, and a little wind was turning the grass to shine in the sun. He took great breaths of the sweet air, and, as he tramped along the boardwalks of town, thumped his boot heels down cheerfully, even though it was clear some he passed were irritated by the noise. He grinned at the men and tipped his cap to the women. Eddie Davis called to him from the pharmacy doorway that there was a blind fellow and a halfbreed looking for him. Waiting in the Last Dollar right now.

He turned in through the batwing doors, out of the sunshine of the street into the murk and sour stink of the saloon. Next, it was Fred Masters to tell him that the fellow at the table in the corner, with the breed, was looking for him; whispering behind his hand, "He's *blind.*"

The blind man was sitting tall in the corner with a play of light from the louvers of the batwings catching in his hair, which was curly, fair, and graying, with the pink glaze of a fearful scar showing at the hairline. Beneath it a bandage covered his eyes, and a pair of spectacles with black lenses was propped on his nose, which seemed to the Kid a foolish piece of fixing. There was a glass of whiskey before him, and another before the breed, whose gray braids hung from beneath a round-crowned hat, framing a face as wizened as a last winter's apple.

The blind man seemed to know him when he came, for he rose from his seat saying, "Ah, they found you, did they?"

"They did, sir," he said.

"My name is Grace, and this is my guide, Josiah."

He shook hands with Mr. Grace. Josiah, who looked as though he might have died a while back, grunted. He sat down but the blind man remained standing, face pointed down and on the strain as though trying to make him out through the bandage and the black lenses. "Will you mind if I touch your face? It is my only means of knowing a person's features."

He said he did not mind, and sat stiffly while a light tattoo of fingertips explored his face. When Mr. Grace sat down he looked more at ease. "Will you partake of a glass of whiskey with us?" he asked.

He said he didn't drink whiskey, promise to his mother. At this the blind man pushed his own glass away from him. The breed cupped his in his hands. Sometimes little gleams of eyes showed in the dark wrinkles.

"Well, sir, I expect you know why we have come," Mr. Grace said.

"Can't say that I do," he said, hugging his arms to his chest as though he had taken a chill.

"It is time for your journey."

"Well, I thought I had a while longer."

Mr. Grace shook his head. "What's his coloring, Jos?" he said. The breed muttered something. They both sat looking at him with their mouths tucked flat.

He said, "Well, I guess I oughtn't to go off without giving Mr. Collins a couple of weeks' notice. A week, anyhow."

In a harsh voice, the breed said, "They have your friend."

"What friend is that?"

"Jimmy Tenponies."

"Who's got Jimmy?"

"Big Mac," the breed said, who could evidently make himself understood when he wished.

Lines of light broke and knit across the table as the batwings swung. The blind man passed a hand before his spectacles as though he had perceived the changing light. The Kid swiped at the cool beading of sweat on his own forehead.

"I've got to get some stuff from my place, at least."

The blind man rose, tall and military in his bearing. He took up a long stick, which he flicked from side to side before stepping boldly around the table. The breed had also risen, not much taller standing than he was seated.

"Let's go there, then," Mr. Grace said in a somber voice. "There is need for haste, you see."

"Jimmy," the Kid said, nodding.

"Your friend is only incidental," the blind man said. "You understand the issues, do you not?"

"Well, I guess I do," the Kid said.

At nightfall they hunkered around a campfire, the breed broiling chunks of meat on the end of a frogsticker and passing them to him or the blind man. The Kid squatted shivering. He had never stopped shivering since the meeting at the Last Dollar, even with his corduroy jacket on and the fire blazing. Mr. Grace leaned back against a tree trunk, chewing meat. "Feeling shaky?" he asked in a friendly voice.

"Well, I am!" the Kid confessed.

As though understanding that he might wonder how a blind man had perceived that, Mr. Grace said, "When one sense becomes useless others sharpen out of necessity. Do you know what fear smells like?"

The Kid chewed the gobbet of meat the breed passed him on the knife tip, juice running out the corners of his mouth. Shapes danced yellow in the flames as he considered. "Smells like something going bad, but kind of sour too."

Mr. Grace nodded gravely.

"All I had to do was take a good whiff of myself," the Kid added, and managed to laugh. The breed made a sound that might have been a chuckle.

"There is no need to ridicule yourself," Mr. Grace said. "There are not many capable of taking a whiff of themselves." Then the blind man asked if he knew what it was all about.

"Well, some of it." He raised a hand to touch the ring that lay inside his shirt on its chain.

"No one knows all of it, not even the general." Mr. Grace took the bit of meat the breed held out to him, chewing and wiping his fingers on his bandana. "There is great evil abroad in the Territory. It has multiplied faster than the general thought possible. Are you aware of the difference between an arithmetical and a geometrical progression?"

He said he hadn't got that far in math at school.

"Let us say it is like locusts multiplying," Mr. Grace said quickly, as though apologetic for having embarrassed him.

He nodded. Then he remembered to speak aloud. "I see, I guess. How'd they get hold of Jimmy?"

"I only know that he is a captive."

"How do you know that?"

"It is known he is at Putaw Crossing. We have friends there. Your companions are waiting for you," he continued. "With their individual qualities that are of no account without yours."

"Well, I guess I don't know what mine are."

In his somber voice, Mr. Grace said, "The ability to take a whiff of yourself. To shiver with your responsibilities, which you would doubtless be relieved to evade. To deflect forces that have been heading in one direction into another. Henry Plummer will present a problem. If he cannot be brought around you will have to kill him."

"I'm not killing anybody! No sir!"

They both sat looking at him while he shivered like a dog with the pip. He asked who Henry Plummer was.

"A man who was thought to have your qualities once," the blind man said in a tired voice. "But went wrong. As did others before him."

"Well, what if I go wrong too?"

"Then the last hope is gone," the blind man said.

There was a long silence. Off to the south coyotes were talking. He blew his breath out with a rubbery sound, squatting by the fire with his arms wrapped around his legs now. The guide was squinting toward the sound of the coyotes, his face jutted out like a hatchet. "Territory now!" he grunted loudly.

"What he means," the blind man said, "is that from now on every little thing may be of the very greatest consequence."

On the second morning he sat in his bedroll watching the night fade. The dark of the sky lightened, and all at once there were the jagged shapes of mountains so high above him he had not even thought to look that far up to see them. He gasped at their loftiness. Presently they moved closer, and all at once fierce light drove down their slopes from the sunrise behind him.

Woodsmoke tickled his nostrils. Mr. Grace was squatting beside the smoky ring of rocks teasing last night's fire back to life with a handful of twigs. This morning he wore a bandana tied over his eyes instead of the bandage and spectacles. In his long-handled underwear he looked bony and starved. Jos sat up, grunting and shielding his eyes from the sun.

"How many days to Bright City, Jos?" the blind man said.

"Five," the breed growled. "If we keep lucky."

"Don't you fellows worry your heads," the Kid put in. "I've always been a lucky one."

"Hah!" the breed said. They both watched him while he extricated himself from his bedroll and dressed in his striped store pants and boots. He tucked his soiled shirt in all around and armed into his corduroy jacket.

He strapped on his cartridge belt, drew his revolver, and flipped the cylinder out to check the loading, while the breed nodded approvingly.

"Something pretty big moving around in the night. Anybody else hear it?"

"Grizz," Jos said.

"Horses didn't scare."

"This particular bear doesn't seem to scare horses," the blind man said. The breed stumped off to look at the ground, finally squatting beside the big rock that leaned over the little encampment.

"Grizz come to take a look," Jos said.

The Kid joined the breed to inspect the cluster of scratches and indentations in a patch of damp ground. There were no tracks to be found except this one.

They set out with the breed in the lead, dumpy in the saddle, following him the blind man with his ramrod back and his free hand curled on his hipbone. The Kid brought up the rear, from time to time chirruping to the pack animals trailing behind. The breed wore a bandana tied over his head like a mammy, Mr. Grace the bandana over his eyes; chuckling, he tied his own bandana at his throat. Following their little party a tail of reddish dust drifted south.

Their way led down an eroded gully, up a ridge and along it for a way, down again, then along the next ridge. The runneled land climbed toward the soaring peaks with their scarf of clouds. Some of the gullies had been planed to bare rock by flash floods.

"Hsst! Grizz!" Jos called over his shoulder. There was

a figure on the third ridge over, like a fat, fur-coated man with hands held as though hovering above revolvers. It was a grizzly standing motionless, watching them. The Kid waved a hand in greeting, and without any apparent movement the bear vanished.

They rode on in silence, plodding down a gully and up and along the next ridge. The peaks never seemed any nearer. When the sun was overhead they halted in a glen of ferns and green brush, and drank from a run of cold water. They ate jerked beef and sweet pearly pear halves from a can. After lunch they continued to climb the more steeply tilting land with cold wind flowing into their faces like liquid. Sometimes Jos seemed to be singing in a minor key, like a long moaning, though it was not entirely sad in its tone.

"Hsst! Looky there!" Jos called again.

This time the Kid had already seen the bear behind them. It rushed along the gully out of which they had just climbed, the brush violently and progressively shaken. A great furry ball bounced over the ridge ahead of them, and vanished. Within minutes the grizzly reappeared as the fat fur-coated man standing a quarter of a mile away, fore-paws dangling. Jos began singing again.

Abruptly the peaks seemed nearer, full of rocky detail in the clear air, almost leaning toward them. There was a rumble of thunder. They climbed in shadow to a grassy saddle with outcrops of gray rock like bones protruding from the ground. Camp was made beneath one of these reefs, where there were the remains of old campfires. He helped Jos tend to the stock while Mr. Grace squatted, heaping twigs and dried moss into a little pyramid, to which he applied a match.

When they joined the blind man at the fire, the breed slapped his holstered revolver and said, "Best friend now. Watch every minute."

"For what, Jos?"

" 'manche. Soldier. Hubychoby. Everything."

"What's hubychoby?"

"That's 'manche for black riders come very fast, go

very fast, very bad." Jos's braids jerked in emphasis. "Maybe they watching like big grizz."

"Sure, I know," he said, grinning. "I got eyes in the back of my head, too. Two, three of them skulking back there, I believe."

"Maybe more," Jos said.

"Perhaps you would help me," Mr. Grace said. He had some loaf sugar wrapped in a cloth, and a brown half pint of liquor. Liquor was to be poured over the sugar. When this was done the blind man sucked the sugar greedily. Jos accepted one also. "Please help yourself," Mr. Grace said.

"I don't partake, thanks. Promise to my mum."

"As Jos says, we must be very careful from here on. We will all take turns on guard duty tonight."

"You mean they might—"

"Impossible to know what they will do," the blind man interrupted. "And one must never be certain what is to come, for then another thing may take place to one's surprise. And one must be only careful, never fearful."

"Jos and I can handle guard duty, I expect."

Mr. Grace drew himself up tall. "Perhaps I am better equipped than either of you for night watches."

The Kid hit his forehead with the palm of his hand. "Sorry. Didn't think."

"Apology accepted," the blind man said, smiling.

Jos stumped about with a pan and skillet, and the blind man warmed his hands over the fire and pressed the heated palms to the bandana covering his eyes. There were nervous whickerings from the stock.

Jos halted motionless and the blind man pointed the knife blade of his nose toward the sky. The Kid sniffed the air also. He heaved a sigh when the moment passed, and Jos returned to his chores.

But after supper, when the bedrolls had been laid out and watches for the night parceled, he ran a rope through a split in a rock outcrop and brought the other end into his bedroll. Jos, who had the first watch, squatted watching him from beside the dying fire.

The Kid was awakened by a clatter of metal and a cry

of warning. Hoofs pounded close. A rifle cracked and flashed furry red against the dark, and in the flash horsemen were bearing down on the blind man and Jos, who were both standing firing their revolvers. With a chorus of shouts the mounted black shapes raced toward them. He rolled over, taking the rope around his hip to pull it taut. As the span of riders thundered over them, he was jerked so hard he was brought to his feet. With a confused thrashing, and a long whinny of pain, the clattering hoofs diminished to silence.

Jos cut the throat of the horse with the broken leg, but they didn't find the rider until first light. He had crawled beneath a rock, with a revolver in either hand and a rifle across his knees, his face a mess of blood and white bone showing through, one of his legs twisted half around. He was snoring, asleep or fainted.

Skipping forward under the rock, the Kid snatched away the man's revolvers, and kicked the rifle out of reach. The man stretched after it, and cursed him, long and obscenely. He looked like an Indian, with black greasy hair hanging in short braids, dark-complected, filthy features, and a stubble of black beard. He kept poking his bloody, ugly face forward like a snake striking, sometimes groaning as he tried to hoist himself into a more comfortable position beneath the shelter of the rock. He wore a rusty black frock coat, like a preacher's coat, torn and stained with dirt and blood, cavalry breeches so old they were faded and almost white, and fine black boots.

"Who are you?" the blind man said, standing before him with his arms folded on his chest.

The other cursed him.

"Name's Cark," Jos said, to be cursed in turn.

"Who strung that rope?" Cark demanded.

"I did," the Kid said. "Went to school where the big kids liked to hurrah the little tads' beds at night, scare them sick. They didn't do it anymore after we started stringing ropes."

Cark examined him silently, with bloodshot eyes. "So you're the Kid. Wouldn't be in your boots."

"Better mine than yours."

Cark began to grunt and groan again, sliding himself forward and trying to reach down as though to straighten his twisted leg, reaching further and further until the blind man cried, "Watch out!" just as a Deringer appeared in the hubychoby's fingers.

The Kid shot the Deringer out of Cark's hand, ventilating him in the process. The hubychoby died hard, and the Kid had to go and sit by himself for a while. They heaped stones over the corpse to preserve it from the buzzards.

The stock had been scattered, but Jos recovered one of the pack animals, which they loaded. They started on afoot. The way led downhill, the blue wink of a lake showing in the forest below. Cloud shadows sailed over them as they clambered down the rocks. He noticed that the blind man, who had cut himself a long stick, made as good time as he and Jos.

All morning they descended the western slopes while clouds gathered. They kept to the ridges as much as they could, but more and more found themselves scrambling down the slick-sided gullies.

Thunder pealed. Once, looking back, he saw lightning split a black-bellied cloud. At noon they halted to eat bread and jerked beef, the pack animals cropping grass along the walls of the canyon. They had started on again when the first drops of rain fell, fat and chill.

Jos urged them out of the canyon, and they scrambled up its steep banks as a distant rush of sound grew louder. Jos shouted and beat the packhorse as though he had gone crazy. A tower of water shot up out of the top of the canyon, and toppled toward them.

The leaping, twisting, frothy face was filled with branches, raw chunks of wood, boulders, a drowned antlered deer revolving stiff-legged. The flood peaked, then slumped where the streambed widened, peaked again. It bore down on them with a roar so vast the Kid couldn't hear his own voice shouting.

Slamming down like a gigantic hand, the water

plucked up the pack animal like a toy horse. The Kid boosted the blind man over the lip of the bank. Just then he was smashed flat. He was borne whirling and gasping for breath on down the canyon at express-train speed. In the last of his consciousness he had a sensation of calmer water, and of being dragged to dry ground by someone grunting like an animal.

2

The Kid wakened in a cave. There was a heavy buzzing sound he could not identify, and a thick, rich cooking smell that made his stomach heave.

Turning his head he saw rifles supported on nails driven into cracks in the rock wall. Further along were painted shields, spears with fringes of eagle feathers, three long headdresses, a buffalo-robe bed. Two men were sitting over a wooden table, smacking cards down on it. One wore greasy buckskins and a wool hat pulled down to his ears. The other was Jos. The two of them muttered back and forth as they collected the cards again.

The blind man appeared from the direction in which the light came, his stick flicking right and left before him. He stood over the cardplayers, tall and stiff-backed, silver in his hair.

The smell of cooking meat filled the cave, too thick, too rich, and the buzzing of insects resounded in the Kid's ears. For a time he held his breath against that smell, but soon he slept again.

When he came to himself he was standing buck naked outside the cave. There was a small glade with sun filtering through green leaves, a corral in which half a dozen brown backs showed. Long heads thrown over a rail regarded him curiously. His stomach was empty. He whooped once, "Anybody home?"

No answer. He went inside to inspect the cave, which was a commodious one. Flies and yellow jackets crawled buzzing over long strips of red and yellow meat hung up to dry, and before a fire-blackened wall an iron cauldron simmered. The pot contained a soup as dark brown as its smell, which made his empty belly heave again. He went back outside.

A squirrel regarded him from a branch, tail twitching. Carefully he squatted to gather up three round pebbles. He knocked the squirrel off the branch with his second throw. Carrying it inside by its tail, he found a knife with which he gutted and skinned it. He spitted the carcass over the coals and ate it down to the bones. Then he lay down to sleep again.

This time he wakened to three giants standing over him, Jos, Mr. Grace with his bandaged face, and the wool-hatted man, who had yellow animal eyes. Smoke was drifting along the roof of the cave to sweep out through a crack in the roof.

"Hello there," he said.

"Finally come to," Jos said.

"We thought we had lost you," the blind man said, face pointed to the ceiling.

"Cook meat?" Wool-Hat asked. He talked as though he had a harelip, though he hadn't. "Don't like soup?"

"Smells pretty strong for my taste," he said. He sat up. "Well, I'm ready to go on," he said, though his head was spinning.

"Eat soup," the mountain man said. "Soup make strong."

"Afraid I couldn't keep it down. Always been delicate that way."

This displeased Wool-Hat, who stamped away to the wooden table, where Jos presently joined him. Mr. Grace still stood there.

"I thank you for saving my life," the blind man said.

"Did I do that?"

Mr. Grace nodded. "When we leave here we will pass by Greasy Grass, where you will meet Stonepecker, the old chief of the Kimanches. If he likes you he can be of the greatest assistance."

"We'll get out of here tomorrow, then." He squinted up at the blind man to see if that might be taken as an order. Mr. Grace nodded. Beyond him Jos and the other were slapping cards down again. He blew out his breath against the smell of the soup and lay back down.

In the morning he killed a chipmunk, and cooked and ate it under the fierce disapproval of the mountain man, whose name was Smith.

As they saddled up in the little corral, Smith stood watching them, wearing a trapper's fur hat, with a long rifle and cartridge belt, and a packsack slung over his shoulder.

"Smithy come," he said.

The Kid swung into the saddle. The blind man already sat his, bandaged eyes and rifle-sight nose pointed toward the sun. Jos had assumed a familiar expression of not understanding the language.

"I guess not," the Kid said firmly. "But I thank you for your hospitality."

The yellow eyeballs seemed to throb, and yellow incisors appeared in a stiff grin. "Need me."

The Kid shook his head. He swung his reins and clucked, taking the lead. "Wait!" Smith cried in his harelip voice. He jerked off his fur hat to reveal what at first appeared to be a yellow-brown, curiously shiny skullcap. It was his skull. There was a hairy ridge where the flesh stopped and the bone began. He tipped his head forward and pointed. " 'ware 'manche!"

"Thanks," the Kid said, and clucked again.

" 'manche 'ware Smithy!" the mountain man howled after him, then leaned on his long rifle, still hatless, watching them go. The Kid waved once more as he led the blind man and Jos out of the glade.

After descending through thick growths of pine and fir they came out of the woods onto a rocky hill. The Indian camp was arrayed below in the narrow meadow called Greasy Grass, and the Kid gasped at the number of white lodges ranked on the green. Smoke rose from many of these, to float in a gauzy layer over the valley. There was a thin yapping of dogs.

They continued downward into cool shade again. A group of mounted braves awaited them as they debouched into the meadow. These seemed friendly, nodding and touching foreheads with their fingers. All wore eagle feathers in their hair. A tall, dark-skinned brave wearing a buffalo-horn headdress hailed them: "Welcome, brothers!"

The Kid raised a hand in greeting, and they rode on with their escort. Women in buckskins stood in the open flaps of teepees, and children hurried out to join the procession. The horses waded uneasily through a yapping pack of dogs.

The brave with the buffalo headdress rode close beside the Kid. He had a nose that looked as though somebody had stepped on it with a hobnail boot. The dogs continued to yap around the hoofs. A spotted one jumped up to nip at his stirrups, whereupon Buffalo-Horns raised his spear high, looking into the Kid's face. He put out a hand in restraint, Buffalo-Horns lowered his spear, and the spotted dog fled.

"That one Yellowfinger," Jos said out of the side of his mouth, as they rode on in a tight clump of horsemen. "War chief." They passed through the ranks of teepees with their astrological decorations, and the smiling faces of the squaws and children. At the foot of the valley rose a conical mountain, gray granite above wooded slopes, surmounted by a cap of snow.

The Kid noticed that the braves performed a curious ritual, each in turn jockeying close to Mr. Grace, to reach out and touch him on the arm or the shoulder while he rode seemingly oblivious of this, bandaged eyes raised as though to the conical peak.

Their guard halted before a lodge larger than the others and more brightly decorated, with lodgepoles poking up, and three vertical stakes planted in the ground before the tent flap. Women's faces appeared in the opening, and a stovepipe hat made its way slowly through the crowd of them. The guard dismounted, and the Kid and his companions followed suit. The chief with the stovepipe hat wore pure white buckskins with chest decorations of rainbow porcupine quills. His hands were tucked into his sleeves. He bowed from one to the other of them, his ancient face wreathed in wrinkles, while his squaws crowded around him.

"Welcome, my sons," he said in a deep voice.

He embraced Jos, holding him by the upper arms and pressing his cheek to the halfbreed's, one side and then the other. "My son, my son." Next he embraced Mr. Grace in the same way, saying, "The sightless one knows he is always welcome."

"We bring the true son of Two-Star," Jos said solemnly.

"So you are the one!" the chief said. He grasped the Kid's arms and pressed his cheek to his, one side and the other; he smelled like clean old leather gloves.

"Welcome, my son, welcome."

"Mighty glad to be here, sir!"

Jos jabbed him with a sharp elbow. "You got some little gift for the chief?"

Everything he owned had been lost when the stock had been scattered by the hubychoby and in the flash flood, except for the ring on its thong around his neck. He removed his hat to take the thong over his head, and presented it to Stonepecker.

The chief received the ring with its white carved stone into his two hands. He grunted as though he had been struck, raising one of his palms as against a too-bright sun. The women, who had been gathering around the blind man, each touching him in turn and murmuring what sounded like prayers, fell silent. Stonepecker bowed his head.

"Thank you, my son, but this must never leave your own breast." Reluctantly his arms rose and he looped the thong back over the Kid's head, his arms remaining raised for a time after he had let it fall back into place.

And he said, "For your generosity I will have a precious gift for you before you leave Greasy Grass."

The chief shuffled, turning, extending an arm. "Enter!" The lodge was huge and smoky, with a single slash of light falling from the peak to the circle of cooking stones. Buffalo-robe couches were banked around these. There was milling and whispering among the braves and the women while Stonepecker seated himself with the Kid on his right and Yellowfinger on his left. Mr. Grace and Jos took their places beside the Kid while the other braves were arrayed beyond the war chief, their eagle feathers glowing phosphorescently. One of the squaws filled a long pipe with tobacco, lit it with a coal from the fire, and, on her knees, presented it to Stonepecker. He inhaled smoke, groaning with satisfaction. Next the pipe was presented to the Kid, who sucked smoke and felt his head whirling. He remembered to groan appreciatively. The pipe was passed from man to man while the women watched in silence. A crying baby was shushed.

The war chief said in Kimanche, "This wapto is very young, great chief."

"But grows older every day," the Kid managed.

The blind man sat up straight as though galvanized, and Stonepecker cried out, *"Hah!* You speak Kimanche, my son?"

"But grows older every day" had been a kind of joke between him and Jimmy Tenponies, though Jimmy had told him it was a very important saying with the Kimanche. He had learned a bit of the language from Jimmy. He repeated the phrase.

"Hear the wisdom of this youth, my people!" Stonepecker said in his deep voice. He bent forward until his forehead was pressed to the buffalo robe on which he sat. Others did the same, except for the blind man. The Kid inhaled the sour, soapy smell of the fleece. There was a chanting murmuring all around.

"It is good!" Stonepecker went on, in a churchy voice. "See how each one understands one another here! Wapto and Kimanche. Young and old. For all are the People together in this place. We give thanks, Great Spirit!

"When I was a young man, strong in my arms, swift in my legs, everywhere was green," he continued. "Everywhere there were the buffalo, the antelope, the elk, the deer—they ran as the rivers ran, they grazed like great lakes! In the ancient wisdom it is said that when the sweet river returns, there will come also the deer, the elk, the antelope, the buffalo!"

The Kid's head went spinning off again from another suck of the cool smoke as the old chief's voice spun on and on, his subject the Kimanche grievances against the wapto, and his fears of Gopherman, who must be Big Mac. It was all a bit preachy for the Kid's taste. Then he realized that Stonepecker had begun talking about *him:* "—who speaks the tongue of the People, and knows the ancient words of wisdom!" Stonepecker stretched up his arms once more, then slumped in silence while the pipe was passed. At last he turned and beamed at the Kid.

"You are welcome here, my son."

"Mighty good to be here, sir!"

"You must call me Father, and I will call you Son."

"That's fine, Father."

"These companions of yours for the great task, they are not many. Gopherman has many warriors. Many."

"I expect I'll collect a few more fellows as we go along, sir. Father," he added. He'd been trying to keep both eyes open at once, but now he concentrated on squinting through one at a time at the wrinkled, anxious old face. The war chief also looked very worried.

"Turned one down already, didn't like his style," the Kid continued. "All we need's a few good fellows." He tapped his forehead, winking, nodding. "It's all in here."

"Do not underestimate Gopherman, my son. He also has much in here." Stonepecker tapped his own forehead with a finger like a dried-up bone. Yellowfinger leaned forward to listen to this conversation. His nostrils faced straight forward, like a pig's.

"Many braves will wish to accompany you, young wapto," Yellowfinger said in his rasp of a voice. "I suggest twelve braves, the number of the Faultless Ones."

The Kid shook his head, squinting through the smoke. The pipe was passing again, and it would be well if it skipped him this time. Yellowfinger's buffalo horns jerked with anger. "You disdain assistance, wapto!"

Stonepecker said placatingly, "Listen to the reasoning of the son of Two-Star, my son."

The Kid held up a forefinger, and spoke as the woman on her knees held out the pipe to him. "One," he said loudly. "Just one. The best one!"

He paused, and shook a finger at the pipe squaw, so that she carried the pipe along to Mr. Grace on his right. There was a great waiting silence in which he said, "You, Yellowfinger!"

Everyone around him broke into grins. He grinned back. Stonepecker had an arm raised for silence.

"And you shall have a thousand warriors when you need them, my son!"

He thanked Stonepecker. The pipe squaw was on her knees before him again. He sucked a little smoke and his head bobbed off into the smoky air like a captive balloon. His body lay back among the buffalo robes for a little nap, to a low murmuring of approbation from all around like the cooing of pigeons in the barn loft back home.

In the morning he waked to find himself cocooned in buffalo robes in the big lodge, which was even smokier than it had been last night, and stinking of too many people, who, from the look of it, had fallen asleep on the fly just as he had. Near the tent flap a warrior, his body gleaming with grease and vermilion paint, knelt straight-backed, holding his spear. Before him on a kind of shelf was a buffalo-horn helmet, and propped below that a feathered shield. It seemed a strange way for a guard to set himself.

The Kid sat up and immediately groaned and held his head. Now he could see that the kneeling warrior was Yellowfinger. He staggered outside to take a leak. There, tied to one of the upright posts, was a pale stallion, who curved his neck at him and whickered gently while all his hide seemed to flow and weave with motion like mercury, and his mane and tail to lift as though in some little breeze he kept about him.

"You are one beautiful fellow," he said in admiration. He heard a chanted muttering behind him, and looked back inside the lodge to see Stonepecker in his white buck-skins standing over the kneeling war chief, making gestures with a skeleton hand.

He stood politely by until Stonepecker had finished, to thank him for his hospitality and say it was time for them to be moving along. Stonepecker gripped his arm and swung him toward the silver stallion.

"My son, this is the mighty horse Muchoby, who can run like the wind and will be ever faithful to his master. He will carry you out of any danger. Or if you send him back to me a thousand warriors will come, as I have said. Muchoby, my lovely one, this man is your master now!"

The silver stallion whickered and tossed his head once, twice. The Kid thanked the old chief and went to stroke the stallion's velvet nose.

They rode out of Stonepecker's encampment on Greasy Grass with an escort of warriors with feathered lances and shields, barking dogs, running boys. The old chief waved from the flap of his lodge, with his women grouped about him and the stovepipe hat on his head. Again the blind man seemed oblivious of the horsemen and the boys who came to touch his clothing. Jos jounced pudgily on his pony. Yellowfinger, his broken-nosed face fierce as a hawk's beneath the buffalo headdress, was bare-chested and fantastically painted, with buckskin trousers on and armed with a rifle, a knife, and a hatchet. At the timberline there were more farewells, more hands outstretched to Mr. Grace, and to the Kid too now. Escort, boys, and dogs turned back except for the spotted mutt trotting beside the Kid in the shade of Muchoby, with a lolling tongue and self-satisfied air. The Kid deferred the lead to Yellowfinger, who disappeared into the shadow of the pines. The others followed in single file, the Kid stroking Muchoby's shoulder.

"Better go home, Duke," the Kid said, but the dog paid him no attention, trotting alongside as he fell into line.

The trail wound in and out of woods along the edge of a stream, which it crossed from time to time, the horses splashing through the water and clattering up the rocks on the far side. At noon they halted to eat jerked venison and cold sweet potatoes beside a rock-bound pool. Yellowfinger took from one of the pouches strung around his waist tinder, flint, and a bit of steel, and from another tobacco and a dried husk. He measured tobacco, twisted the husk, and held it between his teeth while he struck a spark into the tinder, waved a hand to bring this to a flame, and lit his cheroot. The blind man sniffed at the smoke, face raised to the sun. Jos squatted beside the pool. The spotted dog sat haunched down at the Kid's side, well away from the war chief.

In a moment of silence Yellowfinger rose, and, with a sweeping gesture as though shaping an umbrella that covered them all, said, "My brothers!" He passed the cigar from one to another, the Kid this time only pretending to swallow the green-tasting smoke, nodding and saying, "Good! Good!" in Kimanche. Yellowfinger was pleased. Soon after they had started on again, the trail joined another where there were horse turds trampled among innumerable hoof prints in the beaten earth. Yellowfinger dismounted to inspect broken twigs along the trail, and, squatting, poked a finger into one of the turds.

"Many horses," Jos said.

Yellowfinger chopped one hand across the palm of the other. "Half a day, no more."

"Headed which way?" the Kid asked, steadying Muchoby, who nervously curved his silver neck to one side and then the other.

Yellowfinger said, "First to the rising sun, later back same way, only not so many."

By mid-afternoon they had crossed a ridge of high country burnished red-brown in the late sun, terrain of sandstone and scattered boulders. Once they discovered the remains of a cookfire, stones arranged before a blackened boulder. Yellowfinger poked through the ashes, scowling. Here the trail wound steeply downward, and from the clearings enormous distances were visible. A thick bank of smoke or dust lay across the horizon, reddening as the red globe of the sun descended and sank into the haze.

"Gopherman!" Yellowfinger said, pointing. He looked challengingly at the Kid, who did not respond.

Presently they joined a wagon road, and at dark came upon a high-sided wagon with a canvas cover. In the glow of a fire words could be made out painted on the side of the wagon:

DOCTORS!

BALTHAZAR AND PEARL

MEDICINES, SURGERY, HERB CURES

TEETH PULLED $7

FASCINATING EXHIBITS!

Horses whinnied in greeting from a corral among the trees. The dog, Duke, kept close to Muchoby, tail curved between his legs. Against the firelight three men appeared as silhouettes, one tall and thin between his shorter companions. There was a gleam of rifle barrels. "Just in time for supper, am I right?" a voice called out.

"Please do come and join us, gentlemen," a second voice said. They dismounted to advance into the firelight past the charcoal shadows of the wagon. The tall figure proved to be a cadaverous man with a thatch of white hair. He wore a long gown, and he bowed and backed and beckoned, with an excessive waving of arms. With him was a knickered boy with a spoiled, freckled mug thatched with red hair. The third man was a dwarf. His short arms swaggered out from his sides as he approached. Shadows caught in the hook nose of his outsize face.

"Greetings, I'm Frank Pearl," he said. "So you're the Kid!" He shook hands with the Kid, Mr. Grace, and Jos, saying, "Greetings, greetings."

Yellowfinger held up a hand and said, "How, short one!"

"They're still trying to find all the pieces of the last fellow called me Shorty," Frank Pearl said, not unpleasantly. "This one is Doc Balthazar—"

"You don't look like much to me," the boy interrupted, staring at the Kid with green eyes hard as stones.

The dwarf swatted him with the back of his hand, and the boy staggered back.

"I'll fix your butt for you, you goddamn midget!" he shrieked.

The dwarf started after him, and the boy fled. They could hear him weeping and threatening from the outer dark.

"Have to apologize for that punk's manners," Frank Pearl said.

"Please come and make yourselves comfortable," Balthazar said. "The lad is very disturbed. Abandoned by his mother, fatherless. Still, he's a spunky little fellow."

"Going to get hairs growing out of the palms of his hands being so spunky," the dwarf muttered. They seated themselves around the fire, where there was a collapsible wooden table and camp chairs. The Kid breathed deeply of the delicious smells emanating from a black pot balanced over the coals.

"You won't mind potluck?" Balthazar said, rubbing his hands together. "We've lost our cook. Temperamental fellows, the celestials. However, welcome to our humble hearth!"

"Mighty fine to be here!" the Kid said. The blind man was standing over the fire, warming his hands. The dwarf passed a brown bottle and a tin cup.

"Best to fortify before tackling the doc's stew, am I right, Doc?"

The Kid passed bottle and cup along. "Never touch it, promise to my mum." Yellowfinger, with an expression of ferocious rejection, drew a finger back and forth in front of his face. With one eye squinted half shut he peered into the darkness from where the red-headed boy still occasionally shrilled curses. Duke lay shivering beside the Kid's boots.

"The little fellow is certainly upset tonight," Balthazar said to the dwarf. "I do believe it is simple jealousy."

"Thought you said it was spunk," Pearl said. He took the bottle and cup from Mr. Grace, poured and sipped. Balthazar rolled up his loose sleeves to dipper steaming meat, carrots, and potatoes onto tin plates. He passed these around, exclaiming at their heat and blowing on his fingers.

"You are heading toward Bright City?" the Kid inquired.

"Guess we are," Frank Pearl said. "Along with you."

"Such a depressing place now," Balthazar said. "Noisome air, a sense of hopelessness, and yet a kind of fever— Ah, I can remember when the Territory was a veritable Eden!"

"General's bad sick," the dwarf said.

"What's his trouble?" the Kid asked. Jos was pushing food into his mouth. Yellowfinger sat holding his plate, peering into the dark with eagle jerks of his head. The blind man sat high-headed and immobile as though paralyzed by the dwarf's words.

"Just sick," Pearl said. "He gets down sick and everything goes to pot, or else it's the other way around. Course, Big Mac racketing around tearing up the pea patch—anybody'd take to his bed. On your deathbed nobody expects you to do anything." He cackled coarsely.

From the darkness the boy screamed, "Motherbuggers! I'm out here starving to death while you feed your face, motherbuggers!"

"I don't know where that little twap learned to talk like that," the dwarf said. "Unless it was that mother of his."

"He must come back and eat his supper," Balthazar said. "He'll make himself sick crying out there like that."

"Come on in and have some chow, slimepot!" Frank Pearl called. In a moment the boy reappeared, sneering, face puffy with tears, hands in his pockets. Duke pressed closer to the Kid's boots.

"Don't just gimme one that's all potatoes," the boy said, as Balthazar heaped meat into a tin bowl, clucking placatingly.

Leaning forward, Yellowfinger caught the boy's hair in his hand, and, while the boy howled, twisted his head from side to side to examine the hairline intently. When the boy was released he aimed a kick at the Kimanche, which the dwarf neatly deflected.

"That peanut-nose nigger better keep his hands offen me!" the boy cried. Yellowfinger drew his knife and tested it on his thumb. He wiped the blade on his buckskin trouser leg, testing, honing, scowling, and retesting at intervals, while the boy wolfed his food and glared back at him.

From time to time the Kid smuggled a lump of meat to the dog at his feet. He was interested to note that the two doctors referred to Mr. Grace respectfully as "Lieutenant." He encountered the boy's green furious eyes.

"You're supposed to be so almighty good, are you?"

"Opinions differ," he said politely.

"Betcha you get laid out," the boy said.

"Kimanche boy not like this," Yellowfinger said, fingering his knife again.

Balthazar said, "He's a poor motherless child. Fatherless, also. An orphan, in fact."

"I'm the best shooter in the Territory right now, I betcha! You know how many cans I can knock off a fence post at fifty paces? I mean, without a *miss?*"

"How many is that?" the Kid said.

"Two hundred and fifty-seven, right, Doc?"

"I believe that is correct, little fellow."

"Whose paces?" the Kid inquired.

"Yours or mine either!" the boy said, staring at him with the bright green eyes. "Show you tomorrow. I can put you down at fifty paces, yours or mine!"

The blind man cleared his throat and pointed his bandaged eyes at the Kid.

"Don't hold with spraying lead all over the landscape," the Kid said, patting the shivering dog. "Bad for game. I may not be the best you'll ever see, but I am the careful-est."

"Huh!" the boy said. *"Carefulest!* I betcha they lay you out. I betcha I could do it!"

"Better get your growth first," the Kid said.

"I think that will not be," Yellowfinger said, testing his knife on his thumb.

In the morning the Kid was taken on a tour of the little museum. There was a dusty stuffed owl; a two-headed bobcat with both heads snarling, red mouths, white teeth, stiff whiskers; also a stuffed rattlesnake of impressive size. In a huge glass bottle that glowed from some light source the Kid could not make out, a tiny figure floated in pearly liquid, naked, less than a foot in length, a perfectly formed adult by the proportions of his body, tiny fingers with shiny flecks of nails. He seemed almost to be swimming in the liquid, rising or sinking slowly, head moving toward them, slit of pink mouth, minute closed eyes, wrinkled cheeks of an old face on a young body.

"Something, isn't he?" Pearl said.

The Kid asked what it was.

"Homunculus. You can tell when there's stormy weather coming by the way he'll sink to the bottom. Like he's doing right now."

"Not alive, is he?"

"Hard to tell. See how it looks like he's swimming? And sometimes you'd swear he's got his eyes open. Once I believe I caught him with a hard-on. That was when the brat's mother was still around. She changed her clothes in here, you see."

"He's right on the bottom now," the Kid observed. In-deed, the little man was almost prone on the bottom of his jar, chest a little raised and head raised further, long black hair drifting in some minuscule current.

"Stormy weather ahead," the dwarf said. "But he don't necessarily just mean *weather,* you know. See how it looks like he's shaking his head?"

The Kid moved along to examine displays of obsidian

and gold pyrites, where a handwritten card stated, "Reputed to come from the famous Lost Dutchman mine." Balthazar appeared in his long gown to beckon them into his study. The walls were lined with leatherbound books, and open on the desk was an enormous volume, one of the exposed pages filled from margin to margin with a tight hand as crisp and curly as the doctor's galvanized hair. The second page was two-thirds filled.

"Guess you were up writing last night," the Kid commented. "Saw your light burning late when I was tending my animal."

Balthazar looked pleased. There was a pair of wire-rimmed spectacles on the table with the book, an inkstand, and a collection of quill pens standing in a pewter cup. "Very, very late," he said.

"Every night, am I right?" the dwarf growled, and Balthazar nodded solemnly.

"Here I record *every*thing," he said. He pointed a finger at an entry in the open pages. "Your party arrives to join us. This is checked against what has already been written. He turned to blank pages, the creamy paper glowing. "Here will be recorded your progress and ultimate success.

"The work of a lifetime," he said, his eyelids drooping to reveal his exhaustion with his task. Then he perked up to indicate the shelves of leather books, battered journals, boxes containing sheaves of yellowing papers. "My sources." He pulled a volume half out of the shelf of books, only to jam it back. "Do I bore you?" he asked.

"Kind of interested, actually," the Kid said. "But what is it?"

"What is it?"

"What you are doing there."

Balthazar sighed, running the backs of his fingers along the spines of the books until his arm was stretched to its full length in an expressive and graceful gesture. "It is the history of the Territory," he said. "What has been, and what is to come as well."

"Comes out right prophesying about seventy-eight

percent of the time, we figure," the dwarf said, smothering a yawn. "Well, come on if you've heard enough. We'd better let the Doc get on with it."

Outside, clouds had gathered over the peaks of the Bucksaws, but sunlight brightened the little glade. The blind man sat beside the campfire with his face raised to the sun, and the red-headed boy lounged just outside the big wagon, seated on a stone with his hair gleaming like copper. He was whittling, a pile of pale shavings between his boots.

"Hidey!" he called to the Kid. "Been seeing all the book junk?" He grinned winsomely. In the sun his freckles looked like spots of mold.

"What do you want, wart?" the dwarf asked. "You want something, I know."

"I thought him and me'd go shoot cans off posts. I expect you can show me a thing or two at that," he said to the Kid, with a fraudulent grin. "I was just funning last night."

"Well, I wasn't," the Kid said, leaning his hands on his cartridge belt. "I hold against throwing lead all over the landscape when there's no necessity."

"It's practice, ain't it?" the boy whined.

"You scout up your shavings when you're through there, you hear me?" the dwarf said. "I'm tired of picking up after you."

The boy started to snarl, but wrenched the chipmunk grin onto his features again. The Kid asked if there was any place he could take a wash.

"Fine swimming hole down by the bend of the crick," the boy said, waving an arm. "That's where I always go to wash."

"Ever washed yourself, I never heard of it," Frank Pearl said.

The Kid strolled away in the direction the boy had indicated. Clear water purled over rocks that gleamed black and golden in the sun slanting through the pines. There were exposed roots along the cutbank like the limbs of buried men. The Kid disrobed, stuffed his rolled cartridge belt into one boot, which he hid in a snarl of roots, and left his revolver on top of his neatly folded clothing. He eased himself into the creek, splashing water up into his armpits and gasping. He marked the boy's approach by the flicking of the brush tops. The boy appeared on the bank beside the pile of clothing, watching him with arms folded. "Pretty good hung," he commented, "though I've seen better."

The Kid thanked him.

"I can tell you how most fellows is hung," the boy confided. "I come down here and watch." Grinning, he took the revolver and aimed it in an exaggerated way.

"Didn't anybody ever tell you not to aim a piece you didn't intend to fire?" the Kid said.

"No," the boy said. "Didn't anybody ever tell me that."

"I'm telling you now."

The hammer clicked.

"You have got a few things to learn, at that," the Kid said. "Apt to break a firing pin snapping dry."

"That so?" the boy said. He snapped the trigger again, aiming the revolver with both hands. Then he pushed the cylinder out on its crane, took a handful of cartridges from his pocket, and began inserting them in the cylinder. The Kid whistled.

There was a flash of black and white behind the boy. He screamed and leaped out into the water, the Kid leaning forward to catch the revolver as it fell from his hands. Duke stood on the bank with his teeth bared.

The Kid pulled the boy by the collar, spluttering and cursing, to where he could get his footing. *"Bit* me!" the boy screamed, holding his seat. Stinking mutt *bit* me! I'll—"

His mouth fell open. Standing shivering in his drenched clothing he stared at the Kid's chest.

"What's that?" he asked calmly.

"What's what?"

"Hanging on you there."

"It's a ring."

"That's my ring you've got on there, you know it?" the

boy said. He wiped his eyes on his soaked sleeve; then he screamed, "That's my mother's ring! You stole that ring from my mother!"

Duke slunk away as the dwarf appeared on the bank. The blind man's tall head approached through the brush. Pearl yelled, "You stop that yelling, hear! You'll deaf everybody within a mile, rotface."

"He's got my mother's ring!" the boy screamed. He jerked at his pants and a ridiculously long knife appeared in his hand. The Kid retreated into deeper water with the revolver. "You gimme my mother's ring!"

"Here!" the dwarf shouted.

The boy and the dwarf shouted in a kind of concert while Mr. Grace came out on the bank, flicking his long stick ahead of him. Finally the boy waded to the opposite bank and clambered up on it. Panting there he brandished his knife at the Kid.

"I got your number," he said in a calm voice. "You're a sham, that's what you are. Well, I'm heading out of here, but when they lay you low I'll be there!"

The dwarf flung a rock at him, which the boy coolly ducked. He spat, competently, and disappeared. There was snarling, a shout of pain, and the brush was violently disturbed, progressively receding. The dwarf bent to retrieve his hat, which had fallen when he flung the stone.

"Are you all right?" the blind man called out in an anxious voice, his bandaged face jerking from side to side, then bearing straight on the Kid in the water when the Kid replied that he was.

"That's a dangerous boy," Mr. Grace said.

"He's a nasty piece of work, that's for sure," the dwarf said. The Kid trudged out of the water with his revolver, to dress on the bank. He whistled. The dog appeared, to squat beside him, tongue lolling. The Kid sat down to pat and compliment him.

They returned to camp to find it in a turmoil. The boy had fled, running off all the stock from the corral. Yellowfinger paced like a caged cat before Jos and Dr. Balthazar.

"I will find him!" he jerked a finger along his hairline.

"Please don't think badly of the lad," Balthazar said, standing with his hands concealed in the long sleeves of his gown. "Surely we will recover the animals. The poor child has been badly treated. His mother—"

"You get that red hair," the dwarf said to the pacing war chief, "and I'll pay you ten dollars for it. But I don't want any boy underneath it."

"This rough joking makes me very uncomfortable, gentlemen!" Balthazar said.

"Not as uncomfortable as it's going to make squit-poop," Pearl said. "Am I right, Chief?"

There was a sound of hoofs and the silver stallion appeared, with an empty saddle. The Kid moved over to scratch Muchoby's pink nose while the stallion curved his neck from side to side and stamped a hoof.

Presently the other horses were to be seen, crossing the meadow toward them. Following them was a rider in a tall hat, in dark clothing, so that there was a moment of tension, Yellowfinger whispering, "Hubychoby!"

"No," Mr. Grace said, as the rider herded the stock closer. The horses plodded through the open gate of the little corral. The man accompanying them had a dark-brown complexion that looked as much whiskey as sun and wind. His eyes were bloodshot, and his graying mustache drooped on either side of his chin. "My name's Dockerty," he said.

The Kid reached up to shake his hand.

"So you finally come," Dockerty said. "Everybody's been waiting a time."

"Thank you for bringing back our stock," the Kid said.

"Horses are what I'm good at," the other said. He hooked a knee around his saddlehorn and sat looking from face to face, as though ticking each one off. "Some bunch," he said, and slipped from a pouch a flat pint bottle. He tipped this to his lips.

"Come to ride along," he said, wiping his mouth and recorking the bottle.

"You are welcome," the Kid said in a firm voice. "But you will have to take the pledge."

Dockerty shied the bottle off into the brush, swung down off his black mare, and began to shake hands all around.

3

At first light the Kid crawled out of his bedroll. Yawning and forking his fingers through his hair, he wandered around the side of the wagon, with its chorus of snores, to relieve himself. A big man in uniform stuck the muzzle of a carbine into his ribs.

"Get 'em up! Unbutton! I want to see what you wear on your belly."

"Can't do both."

"Unbutton!" the man snarled.

Wincing barefoot on the pebbly ground, the Kid twisted his fingers down the buttons of his long underwear. In a flash of black and white Duke shot out from under the wagon to fasten his teeth in the soldier's leg. The man swung the barrel of the carbine and Duke dodged and fled, yelping, the soldier cursing. Graying hair straggled from under his forage cap, and stacked yellow chevrons on his sleeve identified him as a sergeant. He was strung with harness, cartridge belt, holstered revolver, binoculars, and canteen. He grunted as he examined the ring on its thong, and bent to peer at the butterfly birthmark on the Kid's belly. Yawning, the Kid stretched to his tiptoes with his hands raised high and locked together.

He slammed these down on the back of the sergeant's neck and the big soldier went down like a dropped trunk. The Kid stepped on the carbine with both feet.

The sergeant rolled over on his back, grimacing, one hand pinned beneath the carbine and the other massaging the back of his neck. He had a beefy, red, pockmarked face.

"I'd take it kindly if you'd step off my hand," he said, and added, "General wants to see you, Kid."

"Whyn't you say so in the first place?" the Kid said, stepping aside so the sergeant could climb to his feet. "Just give me a minute to get my boots on and tell my friends where I'm gone to."

Early in the afternoon they rode through the fort's ruined gate into a weed-grown parade ground. A flag drooped from a central pole in the dusty heat. The sergeant dismounted before a doorway in an adobe wall, beating the dust and soot from his uniform with his cap. They stepped inside a dim anteroom, where there were a desk and a wall of empty pigeonholes. The sergeant detached his canteen from its strap and banged it down on the desk.

"Nip of whiskey for your dry throat?"

The Kid declined politely. Squinting at him, the sergeant drank deep. Then he lumbered over to tap on an inner door. There was a murmured summons.

They passed into total darkness, and a stink of eucalyptus oil. The sergeant lit a lamp and the room's contents took form out of flickering light. What looked like a headless dwarf proved to be a uniform hung on a clotheshorse, a gleam of gold buttons and stars. In a bed was a man so slight of frame he hardly disarrayed the coverlet. His mouth was open in a bristle of white beard, and he was snoring softly.

The snore broke off. "Thank you, Sergeant-Major," General Peach said in a small, hoarse voice. "If you would bring a chair—"

The sergeant-major hastened to comply, while the Kid gazed with interest at objects looming out of the darkness, a gleam of glass cabinet fronts, what appeared to be the varnished end of a coffin heaped with curios and mementos. On one wall was a shadowy painting of cavalry in action among Indian teepees, and on another one of a naked woman reclining on a red couch, her flesh as white as moonlight. The sergeant-major returned with a chair, which he placed beside the bed.

The Kid seated himself and the sergeant-major quit the room, leaving the communicating door open.

"Well, you've finally come," the general whispered.

"Soon's I could, sir!"

"Was your journey a difficult one, my boy?"

"There was a flash flood that was a pretty near thing. Other than that, nothing to complain of."

"Things have got very near here," the general said. A thin, liver-spotted hand appeared from beneath the coverlet, to rub across his forehead. "Can't make out what's happened, all of a sudden. Suddenly everything's beginning to give way."

"I don't know what you mean, sir," the Kid said uncomfortably.

"They've got land dredges on the old river bed!"

There was a silence while the Kid tried to understand this. The general continued:

"Oh, he's a devil for cunning! And those fellows of his—good men, once, probably. Remember that Lucifer himself was an angel once! They will simply destroy us all. They are like bank robbers on the verge of discovering the combination to the safe in which the veritable treasure of the world is hidden. The dial spins, the tumblers fall just so, perhaps one more quarter turn will swing the door open on that vast gleam—"

The general's lips blew in and out as he began to snore again. Through the open door the Kid could see the sergeant-major sitting at his desk, a cheek supported by a ham of a hand and the whiskey bottle before him.

"Take it another way," General Peach went on. "Let's say he has solved a different combination, one that has engaged the great economists throughout history. Dig and burn so no one can breathe for the dust and smoke, but dig and burn, dig and burn, and pay men for it, who are grateful to be earning a living. But of course the devil takes their earnings away from them again, selling them bright-painted gimcracks and whiskey to slake their throats, and women for their whiskey lusts. Gets it all back from them with a profit so he can buy bigger machines. Damn me if he hasn't found the right combination!''

The Kid laughed nervously. "Think you'd set the cavalry on him, sir!"

The general laughed, but bitterly, joined by a laugh from the anteroom. "There isn't any cavalry, my boy. Gone over to the enemy, all but one man." The frail hand gestured toward the other room. "One loyal fellow left," the general whispered.

"Maybe one day, if I had a bugler, and he blew a 'Boots and Saddles'—maybe old training would rally them back to me. By God I'd like to think it would!" He chuckled bitterly again. "Don't have a bugler, though."

There was a scrape of chair legs from the anteroom and the sergeant-major loomed in the doorway. "I've blown bugle in my time, General. I could blow a call that would rally a troop. If I had a horn."

"Thank you, Sergeant-Major," the general said. "That'll do, Eubanks." Tears glittered on his cheeks.

"Things sound in a pretty poor state, sir," the Kid said.

"Very poor, very poor," the general murmured. Then he said in a firm voice, "I'm afraid you are going to have to kill Henry Plummer, to begin with."

"Don't much like this talk of killing, sir!"

"They call him Holdfast," the general went on, ignoring his protest. "Well, he has held on too long. Knew his mother in the best Biblical sense," he said, chuckling fatly. "By Heaven, that was as fine a woman as the world has seen!" He strained his neck as though to gaze at the painting on the far wall, failing in the attempt. "A woman with some substance to her! A woman who couldn't sit down in a washtub! Bosom to smother a man!" The general listed gamier details the Kid found embarrassing.

"I believe I would come to attention still if she showed herself in that doorway right now!" the general said. "By God, there was a lady a man would throw away a fortune

for! Chuck a command! Forfeit an empire! My God!"
he cried. "Do you suppose the devil is doing it all for
her?"

He raised his head from his pillow, eyes open and blazing at the Kid. The sergeant-major loomed worriedly in the
doorway again. But the eyelids closed, and the gentle
snoring began once more. The Kid rose, hat in hand.

"I'll be heading back," he said to the sergeant-major,
in the anteroom.

"I'm to come with you," Eubanks said, staring at him
with hard little eyes set wide apart in his ugly face.
"Orders."

"Well, I guess that's all right," the Kid said, and so
they started back together.

After some miles Eubanks raised his canteen and
shook it. "Durn! Forgot to fill up!"

"You won't be needing any more whiskey," the Kid
said.

The sergeant-major grinned with one side of his mouth
only. "Teetotal, is it? Big Mac furnishes plenty of whiskey
for his fellows, like the general said. He'd promise any man
his heart's desire to throw in with him, and make good on
it too. Though you might come to wonder why you ever
wanted it."

"Think they'd back off from the pure mess of it all,"
the Kid said, and Eubanks laughed his harsh laugh once
more.

It was after dark when they returned to the caravan,
the others starting up from around the campfire, silhouet-
ted against the pale backdrop of the wagon cover. The Kid
introduced the sergeant-major to Mr. Grace, Dockerty, Jos,
Frank Pearl, Yellowfinger, and Dr. Balthazar, the dog
cowering and growling.

"This is all of us now except for Henry Plummer," the
Kid said. "We'll head through Bleeker tomorrow, then one
more day to Bright City."

"We had better be standing watches tonight, Lieutenant," the sergeant-major said.

197

"Yes," the blind man said. "We will be under surveillance soon, if we are not already."

4

The schoolhouse consisted of two one-room structures joined, one of logs, the other plastered-over adobe. The log half, Flora had been told, dated back to the earliest days of the Territory. There were two rows of pine desks, much scarred with initials, benches running the length of the room behind them, a slate blackboard, two shelves of books, and a desk for the teacher.

Facing her were eighteen dirty-faced children, the eldest of whom was twelve. She saw their eyes rolling toward the sound of hoofs and creaking wheels passing in the street, and she moved away from the blackboard, eraser in hand, to where she could watch the procession. A mustached, dark-faced desperado and a big soldier on a gray horse, sleeve hatched with yellow chevrons, rode in the lead. Following them were an aged halfbreed swaying dumpily in his saddle, a tall man of erect carriage with bandaged eyes like someone condemned to a firing squad, an ugly Indian with a buffalo-horn headdress, and a dwarf with a cigar between his teeth, like a big-headed child on a pony. Following these, on a white stallion, a spotted mongrel trotting alongside, came the young man she had known all her life. She retreated to lean weakly against the blackboard at the sight of him framed in the doorway. He passed from her view, to be replaced by a covered wagon with a medicine-show sign on the side. On the seat of the wagon was a thin, white-haired old man.

She watched the children's heads turning to follow the passage of the grim file, and, when it was out of sight, turning back to her with round eyes as though she might have wisdom, advice, or comfort to offer. In the faces of the younger children there was fear, but in the older only a kind of emotional blankness that caught at her heart the more painfully.

When the children had been dismissed, any attentiveness she might have commanded destroyed by the parade, she kept after school Willie Johnson, a thin, tow-headed boy of eleven, only one of the fearful children of the fearful parents of the Territory, but a special one. She leaned toward the boy with a finger close to her lips.

"Fah-ther," she said.

"Fod-der."

"Muh-ther."

"Mud-ther."

His face jerked around, and she glanced up to see the young man who had just ridden past standing in the doorway, hat in hand. She felt her cheeks burning as Willie turned toward her a face as empty as a pine board.

"Gotta go home, Miz Flora," he said. "My mudder'll bust my pants—" He fled, squeezing past the man in the doorway.

"Hello, Berry," she said.

"Hello, Florrie." He laid his dust-, soot-, and sweat-soiled hat on the desk nearest him. "Well, you are a schoolmarm now!"

"It is something I am good at," she responded. "That is what we try to do in our lives, is it not? What we can do well?"

"I guess I would like to do with mine what I *wanted* to, instead of people telling me what I *ought* to do."

"I am afraid I do not believe in High Destiny, Berry."

"Maybe it has just not come along and grabbed you by the neck yet." He grinned his disarming grin, which bloomed whitely for an instant before it was gone. His eyes regarded her gently, and with affection—she knew that—but they seemed to look in where polite eyes would not pry. Slapping dust from his shoulders and upper arms, with the late, smoky sun filling the doorway behind him, he appeared hazed in a golden glow.

She said, "What was that queer gang of men you were riding with just now?"

"Florrie, *you* know! It has started."

"Has it?" she said, leaning against the blackboard

once more. Of course she had known it had started as soon as she had seen him with his gang, felt it like a current that must sweep her along despite her pretense of ignorance, or of opposition to, High Destiny.

"We are headed for Bright City."

She knew that, too. "Dirty out," the Kid commented, brushing dust from his chest.

She looked down at her hands clasped together at her waist, with their white knuckles. She shook her head. "I am not on your side, Berry."

Sadness creased his face. For a moment he looked old, who was scarcely more than a boy. "No?" he said.

"I am on the side of that child who just left," she continued. "The side of the poor people of the Territory. The parents of the children I try to teach here, who have enough to eat for the first time in their lives, and are terrified it will vanish before their eyes. Be snatched away by you and that crew you ride with! I do not know what you are seeking! You may be men of the highest principles, but I wonder if you care anything for simple humanity!"

"Well, I *do*, Florrie!" he said, looking now like a hurt child. "But things have come to a pretty poor pass!"

"So you consider yourselves angels with swords!"

"This is fancy talk for a farm boy!"

"You will break my heart!" she whispered.

Swiftly his face loomed larger in her misted eyes. His arm circled her waist. She closed her eyes, and, weak as an infant, accepted his mouth. When she forced her face aside he retreated. The color of his cheeks matched the burning of her own.

"Well, I just stopped by for a look-in," he said, "since we were passing through."

She could only nod, holding her clasped hands against her beating heart. He moved back to the door, where he took up his hat, swinging around to face her, holding it arrested two inches above his matted fair hair.

"I believe you will wish me well, Florrie," he said, and she continued to nod.

*   *   *

That evening there was a confused milling of hoofs in the street outside her house, hurried footsteps approaching along her boardwalk, a knock. The door burst open. A man stamped in, a dirty-faced, lean, grinning man in black, others like him crowding close behind. When she tried to cry out, a stinking hand was clasped over her mouth, and she was swept outside in the midst of them, and flung astride a horse. They galloped out of town with her penned close in the midst of their blackness.

5

The figures were grouped two-dimensional and motionless against the firelight. In motion was the Kid, pacing, his hands braced on his cartridge belt, the spotted dog trotting alongside. Watching him were the dwarf, the breed, the sergeant-major, Dockerty, Balthazar, and Yellowfinger, with his buffalo headdress doffed to show a shiny, shaven head, glint of eye whites fixed on the Kid. The blind man sat beside the dog, bandaged eyes turned to the fire.

The old gypsy, in her many-layered skirts and orange turban, sat at the table in the white glow of the lantern suspended from the tree branch over her, dealing cards and studying their fall.

"Well, I don't like it," the Kid announced. "Who is it that's set all this up, anyhow? The Doc writing everything down as soon as it happens with one hand, and before it happens with the other. I just don't like it!"

No one spoke and he stopped behind the gypsy, watching as she shuffled the cards and laid them out one by one, black jack on red ace, black queen to red king, joker to the queen of diamonds. She pushed the cards together with quick brown hands, making a wheezing sound as she turned up the faces, black jack to black king this time, red king to black queen. The joker did not fall till last, while in the next shuffle it fell first. The gypsy paused to sip from her teacup. With a swift motion she turned the cup over onto the saucer, prodding the small tangles of tea leaves with a fingertip, muttering. The Kid watched this with his lower lip stuck out.

"Your hand, gentleman," she sighed at last.

The Kid reluctantly gave her his right hand, which she rejected for the left. She traced the curiously split life line, and the lines of the head, heart, and liver, the swollen mounds of Venus, Jupiter, and Saturn, and the shrunken ones of the Sun and Mercury. She pushed the hand away, to pack up her cards and tie a string around the deck, which took an interminable while.

"Well, old woman?" Balthazar said. "We did not bring you here to learn nothing."

Groping beneath the table, she set before her a wicker tea cozy with a brass handle and snaps, turned back the lid, and brought out her crystal ball, which gleamed in the firelight like a great opal. She polished it with her skirt, bending close to hawk, spit, and polish harder. Then she leaned toward the ball with her neck cocked like a striking snake.

"I see," she said immediately. She drew from the cozy a black velvet cloth, which she draped over the ball. From her throat issued a long keening sound. The dog howled dismally with her. From the darkness coyotes yipped, and horses stamped and snorted. A large bird flapped over.

"Jumping Jesus H. Johnson!" the dwarf said.

"Well, madam?" Balthazar said.

"All is double," she said. "Never have I seen two such lifelines before. Never have I seen the cards so troubled."

"You must tell us what this means," the blind man said.

"The ball shows," she said, holding up one finger, "a young man whistling. He is happy. He raises his face to the sun and wind. He passes through fields of grain where farmers are threshing. He joins them in their work. Yet once he glances back the way he has come, with an expression—how can I describe it?—perhaps of one who considers how different his life might have been if a different decision had been made. Yet there is no discontent in this expression, only wonder.

"And before my eyes he grows old. His hair becomes gray, he stoops, he has a limp, his joints are bad. Still he whistles, he enjoys the sun and air; though every so often he will look back with this expression I describe. He lives a long time, but he no longer has a face."

"What's that?" the dwarf rasped.

"No face," the gypsy said, brushing a hand before her face as though wiping away the features. "Where the face is, nothing. Does this have a meaning for you, gentleman?"

The Kid said, "No, it doesn't."

"But there is another path that branches, woman," Yellowfinger said.

"Get on with it, will you?" the sergeant-major said.

"Two paths!" she said. "And as the one way passes through fertile fields and friendly men, the other goes straight up the mountain!" Her voice had deepened. "There is thunder and lightning, and rushing waters. Dangers on every hand! There are beautiful women, and evil women, and evil men in numbers. Fire and flame and smoke! Rivers of blood!

"This way the face is clear always," she continued. "Though the way is short compared with the other, it is very full and not merely with those things I have mentioned already. If there is pain and grief, there is love and friendship; great struggles, but great victories. Great honor! The death of many but the redemption of many more—"

All were leaning toward her as she spoke, for it was as though another were speaking out of her throat in a rough, harsh, hypnotic voice, until the Kid broke the spell:

"Well, forget it!"

"This too is to be seen, gentleman," the gypsy said. "When one learns he has been chosen, always at first the spirit will rebel."

"I didn't ask to be chosen for anything, thank you!"

the Kid said. He began to pace again, boots scuffing in the dust. The halfbreed sneezed and stirred as though he had wakened from a nap, and Yellowfinger made a short explosive sound.

"One accepts one's duty," the blind man said in his serene voice.

"Easy for you to say," the Kid said. "That didn't get chosen."

"I have done my duty and will continue to do it," Mr. Grace said.

"All of us here's ready to help any way we can, Kid," Dockerty said.

"I'd just as soon go home and dig potatoes, if you want to know," the Kid said. "I'd rather shovel manure at Collins's stables than all this rivers-of-blood malarkey. If you want to know."

"Now, my dear fellow—" Dr. Balthazar started.

"I guess we want to know, all right," the dwarf interrupted grimly. Smoke from his cigar drifted in the firelight.

"There is only one issue," the blind man said. "Evil must be fought. You have not been chosen for that cause more than any other man. Or let me put that differently. There is only one choice any decent man can make, though some are more uniquely qualified than others. But there is no choice, really."

"What choice is that?" the Kid said. He sounded as though he had a cold in his head. "That's no choice, really?"

"To accept evil. Or to fight it," Mr. Grace said gently.

"I'm so simple-minded," the Kid said, pacing, swinging back, kicking his boot heels in the dust so that the halfbreed fanned a hand in front of his face. "I'm so simple I don't know what evil is. Just a bunch of hardcase fellows chasing around? Tearing up a little landscape?"

Yellowfinger leaned forward with a finger to the side of his nose, and blew one nostril, then the other, into the fire.

"I'm so simple," the Kid went on, "that I don't even know how I got badgered into coming into the Territory and all this rivers of blood and fire and the rest of it. All I'd like to do is get Jimmy Tenponies away from that big fellow." Muttering to himself he stalked off into the darkness with the spotted dog at his heels. The rattle of water on dry leaves could be heard.

Yellowfinger said, "In the end the young wapto will do what he must do."

"I have got my fingers crossed yet," the dwarf said, tapping the ash from his cigar.

"He is a good one," Jos said.

"Oh, he'll do it," the sergeant-major said.

"Him going to see that schoolmarm was a mistake," Frank Pearl said. "A woman will complicate a thing every time."

The Kid returned, scuffing his boots. "I don't want to hurt any feelings, but I'm not sure this is a bunch I'm wild to ride through rivers of blood with."

He took the lantern from the limb of the tree and climbed the steps to the wagon with it. Inside, in the lantern's light, the homunculus floated in his great glass bottle, slowly turning, hair washing in the pearly liquid. Immediately he began to sink to the bottom. Frank Pearl, Dr. Balthazar, and the gypsy crowded in behind the Kid to watch the tiny figure drifting downward, eyes tightly shut, mouth slitted in the ancient wrinkled face above the perfect young body. He lay almost on the bottom with his black hair floating out to one side. He appeared to be shaking his head.

Without a word the Kid thrust himself outside. At the periphery of the circle of firelight he stripped off his cartridge belt and dropped it. He spread out his bedroll and sat down on it to pry off his boots. Then he lay down on his side with his knees pulled up to his chest.

"I've got a headache you could roll downhill and wipe out half a county with it," he said after a while. "Besides, I got a sore leg—joint's gone bad already, probably."

The others, who had regrouped around the fire, stood with their backs to him, Dockerty kicking a boot against a rock, the sergeant-major with a distasteful set to his face.

"A woman will do it every time, am I right?" the dwarf said.

Yellowfinger hissed for silence.

There was a drumming of hoofs approaching, a voice shouting. The Kid only strained his legs tighter to his chest.

A horse was pulled to his haunches, halting in the circle of firelight, the rider's words torn to shards of sound by Duke's barking. They gathered around as the rider piled off his lathered horse, a bare-headed, town-suited man, crying, "They took her!"

"Took who, fellow?" Dockerty demanded.

"The schoolmarm!"

"Who took her? What do you mean, they took her?"

"Grabbed her right out of her house! Black riders!"

Dockerty groaned. The Kid had uncurled. He sat up, pulling on his boots. His face glistened in the firelight. He rose and crouched with his knees spread as he flung his cartridge belt around his hips, and buckled it fast.

"Where can we head them?"

"By the waterholes," the sergeant-major said. Yellowfinger had put on his buffalo horns.

"Let's go!" the Kid snapped.

Dockerty whistled, a low, urgent sound, and the horses began eagerly to stamp and whinny.

"Let's go!" the Kid said again, louder, and the blind man stretched out his hand toward the sound of his voice, as though in blessing.

At dawn they were riding hard through red sandstone country where reefs of rocks poked up gray snouts like beached sharks, and stunted trees threw westward shadows. In the lead the Kid and Dockerty raced flat out with the brims of their hats blown back, Muchoby flowing over the rusty land like quicksilver and Dockerty's black mare only a head behind. They were followed by the sergeant-major on his pounding gray, and Yellowfinger on his calico. Further back were Frank Pearl and Dr. Balthazar, white hair blown back in the wind of their passage, and, last of all, the breed and Mr. Grace, the blind man clinging to his saddle horn while Jos guided his horse along by the reins.

The red sun stood clear of the Bucksaws at last, bathing everything in a flat, hard light. Dust rose in a tilting cloud against the metal sky, perhaps closer as they raced onward, or perhaps only escaping before them like a dust devil whirling. Dockerty kept them to the gravelly bottoms flash floods had scoured in the red earth, so that they raised no warning dust of their own. All at once the cloud preceding them was closer. Then it was settling, and gone.

The Kid yelled urgently at the silver stallion, who laid back his ears as though he understood his rider's anxiety. Dockerty clucked and murmured to the black mare. The others strung out behind them. They wound along a stream bed with hoofs splashing through pools of brackish water. A line of treetops became visible, indicating more water still. They raced out of their defile into the open area of the waterholes, where a dozen dismounted men lounged and horses watered. The men started to their feet with warning shouts.

Crouched low on Muchoby's off stirrup, the Kid was in among them in an instant, with the black mare two steps behind, and the war chief on the calico pony not ten. The sergeant-major had dismounted to steady his carbine on the saddle of the big gray.

The Kid swung to the ground at a dead run, and plunged among the shouting men, swinging his rifle by its barrel. He clubbed one of the black riders, and, the rifle swinging faster than the eye could follow, smashed down a second and a third. Dockerty fanned off shots, border-shifting to toss aside the empty gun and fire the second. The sergeant-major fired more slowly. Yellowfinger, yipping in on his pony, caught one fellow who had managed to mount, and brought his hatchet down like a truncheon. The dwarf jumped from his horse to brace his rifle barrel against a rock, and, dead cigar jutting from his teeth, drew a bead on another fleeing man and dropped him. Next came Balthazar in his billowing robe, and finally the breed and Mr. Grace, just as, still in one seamless continuing motion, the Kid caught the last of the black riders and clubbed him to earth with a glinting sweep of the rifle against the risen sun.

They stood in the shambles of their victory among dead men and trembling horses trailing reins, while the Kid ran to one of the black riders crawling like a swatted fly, and caught him by the hair, twisting the head back and up until the man's eyes stared into his own.

"Where is she?"

"Grad," the man groaned. "Grad's got her." He motioned onward with his good arm.

The Kid let the man's head drop, while Yellowfinger stepped forward, honing his scalping knife on his buckskin trousers. The Kid vaulted into Muchoby's saddle. Without looking back, he set off at a gallop again.

They pounded onward, stringing out again in the same formation. And so they came to the great rim, and each one halted thunderstruck in his turn.

Before them the land was torn as though by a giant hand scratching at the earth in its death throes. Files and troops of men were to be seen stretching into the invisibility of distance beneath the blackish-brown cloud that shadowed the scene, the clanking machinery of power and complexity impossible even to estimate, stacks belching smoke, vast ponds of gleaming mud, and everywhere dust rising and dust devils spinning off across that blasted plain as though the place created its own hot winds along with its own thick atmosphere. Here and there the belch of flames lighted the murk, revealing clusters of laboring men with wheelbarrows, with mules and fresnos, carts, and round-bottomed wagons. Everywhere were the overseers in dusty black. From time to time the somber cloud would thin like curtains rising and parting, sometimes revealing the furthest reaches of the plain and the ants of men and watchworks of machinery milling there. The sandy coils and curves of the dry river bed extended into the distance, and at intervals along its course hulking monsters crouched, spitting smoke. Yellowfinger dismounted to fall to his knees, face covered with his two hands.

The Kid spurred down the twisting path from the rim, where, far below, two riders could be seen, one pulled along behind the other, the schoolteacher's pale face turned back. The Kid urged the silver horse down the steep trail, and Muchoby braced his hoofs, sliding, twisting, halting, and leaping forward again.

Peering behind him, Grad brought up his rifle and fired twice, small smoke rising against the great one. Dockerty had also started down the path, while the sergeant-major remained on the rim, trying to get a clear shot with his carbine. Yellowfinger had raised from his previous position to hold both arms outstretched to the sky. The sergeant-major cursed steadily, unable to fix his aim.

The dwarf and Balthazar came up and sat their horses in silence, staring out. The breed led the blind man to the rim.

"What's it like?" Mr. Grace cried, jutting his bandaged face. "Someone tell me what it's like!" No one spoke. "Frank!" he cried.

"I can't!" the dwarf said.

Balthazar said, "Hell is to be experienced and not described, my good friend!"

The sergeant-major fired, and cursed.

"What they do on the river?" the breed cried out.

"Looks like factories," Frank Pearl said, squinting.

"Land dredges," the sergeant-major said.

The dog limped up to the rim, and flopped down on his side.

Below, the silver stallion raced down the steep trail while Grad whipped his black onward, snarling back over his shoulder and jerking the girl's mare along behind. Tied in the saddle, the girl turned her face to peer over one shoulder or the other.

Dockerty put his fingers to his lips and whistled. Grad's black and the girl's mare halted, ears pricked, and both turned back while Grad squalled curses and beat his quirt down. When Dockerty whistled a second time, the two horses bumped together, jockeying a return up the narrow trail.

Grad swung out of his saddle and braced his rifle barrel to fire past the terrified girl. The Kid ducked, hanging on Muchoby's off side, while the stallion scrambled on downward. Then, as the black and the mare bolted to one side to avoid a collision, he launched himself from the stirrup, bounced once on Muchoby's saddle, again on the black's, and, with a yell, drove his boots into Grad's face. Grad fell away, screaming and rolling, to disappear over an eroded bank.

Slashing with his bowie, the Kid cut away the girl's bonds. She dropped out of the saddle and clung to him.

"Kid!" Dockerty called, from the trail above. Grad had reappeared over the bank, hatless, with a livid scraped face, to aim a revolver at the Kid. The Kid swung the girl from his right arm to his left, drew back his arm, and hurled his bowie. End over end it arched, glittering. Revolver grasped in his two hands, Grad fired, then pitched backward with the handle of the knife protruding from his throat.

Without haste the Kid helped the girl to remount, and mounted himself. Further down the plain a clot of dark horsemen could be seen approaching at a gallop. The Kid led the schoolmarm, again turning to gaze over her shoulder, back up the track, Dockerty falling in behind them.

The others awaited them on the rim. Jos cried out, "She hurt!" pointing to the blood on Flora's dress.

It was not the girl who was hurt. The Kid's shirt was gaudy with his blood, which had stained her dress, and his face was dead white. The sergeant-major caught him as he slipped from Muchoby's saddle in a faint. The dog began to howl.

6

When the Kid came to his senses it seemed he must be in the Livereater's cave again, for his ears were filled with a heavy buzzing, and there was a thick herbal stench in his nostrils. But it was a large room with red wallpaper, and a balloon ceiling draped from a central boss, with a glistening chandelier. The buzzing came from outside, as though many people were congregated there in conversation, and the stink was of some emollient emanating from the bandages that covered his chest. He slept, to dream of cigar smoke, a dog whining, a woman moving quietly around his bed. Once he opened his eyes to see Flora sitting at the window with sunlight golden in her hair.

He wakened again to Flora standing over him with a spoon. One of her hands held his chin while the other spooned hot broth into his mouth. He recalled desperately shaking in his fever, with a warm body pressed to his, arms holding him, a sweet voice murmuring in his ear. He smiled at her and she flushed deeply. "You must eat, Berry!" she said.

Next it was Frank Pearl and a very tall Dr. Balthazar looming above him as over a child in a cradle, while Duke whined and turned beneath the bed. He dropped his hand over the edge of the bed, where it was caressed by a wet tongue. Balthazar retired to sit at a little taboret across the room, writing, while the dwarf stripped off the bandages with gentle hands, halting once to tip the ash from his cigar. Then he stroked cool salve from a brown bottle onto the fevered flesh around the wound. The salve smelled like rotten turnips.

"Well, look who's come to the meeting," he said, grinning around his cigar. "How you feeling, Kid?"

"Better," he said.

"Had us plenty worried, am I right, Doc?" The dwarf held up the brown bottle. "But this here's the genuine gunshot special. Plenty potent!"

"Plenty potent smell!"

"There is color in your cheeks, my dear fellow!" Balthazar said. "For a week now you have appeared to be made of wax. A statue!"

"Where's Flora?"

"Ah, she will be here at any moment. She has been by

your side night and day. A guardian angel. An angel of mercy!"

He asked where he was.

"Why, Bright City!" Pearl said. "Best accommodation we could find. A bit noisy sometimes but that hasn't seemed to bother you much."

"No room at the inn," Balthazar beamed. "And no inn, in fact."

"How's your bowels?" Frank Pearl asked.

Flora, in a prim white shirtwaist, sat on the edge of the bed smiling at him, but with anxious eyes. She placed her two hands on his shoulders as he struggled to sit up, and he sank back.

"Got to get you out of this place," he panted.

She shook her fair head. "You must not worry about me. There is a back way to come and go that Lieutenant Grace has found. No one sees me." She indicated a door at the rear of the red room.

The dog growled, and could be heard seeking refuge under the bed. A man had appeared in the nearer doorway, the hum of voices louder with the door open on a show of mysterious lights. The man closed the door behind him.

He wore a black leather jacket and there were hol-stered revolvers on either thigh. His face was hard and contemptuous, with darkness like a shadow beneath the flesh. On the lapel of his jacket was a five-pointed town marshal's badge in silver tipped with gold. Flora had risen to stand facing him.

He said harshly, "I guess I always knew I'd finally find you here, Florrie. Being female."

"Surely you know better than that, Henry," she said.

The Kid was struggling to sit up again. "Apologize!" he muttered.

Henry Plummer glared at him; he looked vicious as a wolverine. "What's he say?" he demanded of Flora.

"He says 'Apologize'!" she said, forcing the Kid back on the bed. "Please help me! He will hurt himself!"

Plummer thrust the Kid down with his black-gloved

hands, the dog growling beneath the bed the while. Staring into Henry Plummer's eyes the Kid said through his teeth, *"I said 'Apologize'!"*

Plummer said in a rusty voice, "Maybe I spoke too soon."

The Kid relaxed, panting, and Henry Plummer stepped back to fold his arms.

"Feeling perkier, are you? Sorry shape when they brought you in here."

"Getting better every day," he said. "Thanks for taking me in."

"Wanted to see what you looked like," Henry Plummer said. He produced a cheroot and silver matchbox from his pocket, and a match from the box. He snapped this to flame with a thumbnail, applied it to the cheroot, and exhaled smoke and sulphur flames. Beneath the bed the dog turned, scratched, and growled. "Looked like you'd cash in sooner instead of later," the marshal said. "For that's the mortgage every man will pay."

"I am very sorry to find you so bitter, Henry," Flora said, standing with her hands clasped at her waist and her chin high.

"I would not call a man bitter just because he has come to think the worst of women out of his experience," Henry Plummer said.

The Kid began struggling to sit up again.

"Always excepting one," Henry Plummer said, with a sigh. With that the marshal of Bright City departed, and Flora covered her face with her hands.

"He is hanging by a thread," the Kid said.

Others came to visit, Mr. Grace with Jos, and again alone, seated tall-headed beside the bed with his black spectacles concealing his eyes.

"I can find my way about this establishment without trouble," he said with his serene smile. "I am at my best in dark passageways and tunnels, as perhaps you will have occasion to find out. Moreover, I know the secrets of this place."

"How's that, Mr. Grace?" the Kid asked politely. "Or I guess I ought to call you 'Lieutenant.' "

The blind man shrugged, his scarred forehead wrinkling. "It is inconsequential, except that you know that once I also came to the Territory with the highest aspirations."

"Well, I know that."

"To be betrayed by lusts of the body and an arrogance of attitude which I know are not part of your nature. And so when I give you counsel it is with the authority of failure. I am certain—all of us are certain—that you speak with the authority of success, which is of course the higher authority."

The Kid did not respond to this. The blind man adjusted the black-lensed eyeglasses on his nose.

"Dr. Pearl feels the authority of medical success in your case," he said. "He claims also to know a cure for defective vision. It is a medicine bitter as gall. He is uncertain whether the application should be internal or external, and so a little of both must be tried." He laughed gently. "Still, I cannot believe there is a specific for eyes that have lost their light."

Another silence followed this. Mr. Grace leaned forward conspiratorially. "Tell me this. There is a stairway just outside your door that ascends to a higher floor. Do you hear footsteps climbing those steps?" His face appeared pulled tight over the bone as he listened for an answer.

"Don't believe I have," the Kid said, and the other leaned back with a sigh.

"I understand you have encountered your enemy, Henry Plummer."

"I'm not so sure he's my enemy."

"He is certain you are his," Mr. Grace said. Soon he took his leave, crossing the room toward the door at the rear in that careful, never abrupt, but certain way of the blind.

* * *

When the Kid was considerably better, able to sit up with pillows braced behind his back, Yellowfinger came to visit, slitting his mouth wide, then bunching it up, and crossing his close-set eyes above his destroyed nose. The Kid realized that these grimaces indicated that the war chief was ill at ease.

"I do not understand the wapto, young wapto! These wapto squaws take men to their bodies not for pleasure, which the Great Spirit has granted, nor either for papooses who will grow up into strong sons, but for money merely. And when these men play games for money they have no eyes for these squaws, who paint their faces and show their breasts, and swing their backsides. I tell you, young wapto, it is not good for men and women to live in this fashion."

"That's probably true, Yellowfinger," the Kid said.

"There is one wapto in this place who does not care for the money on the tables, I observe," the war chief continued. "The eyes of this man do not glitter like the others."

"Which man is that?"

"One-Star. I observe that he does not care for the money, and these squaws push their chests at him in a different manner. It is said that he need not pay to take them upstairs. Though he goes with several at once, sometimes three but more often two. This is very strange to Yellowfinger, who prefers to enjoy his wives one at a time. Can you explain this two-at-once-ness of One-Star, young wapto?"

"I believe Henry Plummer is very bored with his life. Perhaps he seeks to dispel his boredom in ways that those who are not bored cannot understand."

Yellowfinger stared at him with his fierce black eyes, nodding. "Short-One seeks to cure Blind-One of his affliction. I have warned him that this is foolish, for Blind-One has great medicine, who otherwise would have none. Nevertheless he persists. He wishes rattlesnakes brought to him every day. For this he gives me money."

"Careful," the Kid said.

"Hah!" Yellowfinger said. "This hand is so swift it catches the snake even as it strikes!" He illustrated, "So!"

"Careful of the *money*," the Kid said.

Yellowfinger showed a mouthful of teeth as he grinned. "You are wise, young wapto. No, I will not buy any of the squaws of this place to take upstairs as do the others, for I have three wives of my own who smell better than these."

When the war chief had gone, Flora returned to sit by him, sometimes reading to him, helping him with an arm around his waist as he made his first halting steps, like a baby, on legs as weak as clabber. "That's enough," she said firmly, when he had crossed to the window and returned, almost falling when Duke curvetted around his feet.

"What will you do about Henry Plummer?" Flora said suddenly.

He plumped down on the bed with a grunt. "Don't have to do anything yet. He is more worried about me than I am about him. And I am bedbound still."

"He is such a sad man," Flora said.

That night he ate all his supper for the first time. Afterward Flora read to him from a dog-eared magazine. The story was called "Faded Blossoms" and concerned a beautiful girl whose skirts "swept electrically over the tiniest of black boots," and a young man with a "flourishing mustache." The young man proposed marriage, to be rejected for what seemed flimsy reasons.

Flora put the magazine down with a sigh. "She does seem terribly silly to me, Berry."

"Well, I was thinking the same thing about him."

She read on while he dozed, and, when he wakened to darkness dimly lit by a red-shaded lamp on a bureau across the room, she was gone. The racket downstairs was loud, and he sat up and dangled his legs over the edge of the bed, finally rising and steadying himself on the foot of the bedstead. Taking a deep breath he started for the window, shuffling so as not to trip over Duke. He parted the curtains to gaze out on Bright City.

Beneath him in the square were the dark shapes of horsemen passing, and men promenading along the boardwalks. At the end of the square was a medicine show, high, pale wagon cover, bleak lantern light, and an illuminated banner whose message he could not make out. Once, through the glass and distinct from the noise downstairs, he heard laughter, followed by applause. Beyond the rooftops were the black, blank shapes of mountains with a queer, smoky orange blush on the lower slopes. "Soon's I get my strength back," he muttered.

The dog brushed his legs as he crossed the room. He opened the door upon the complicated glitter of a great chandelier. Now the clamor below was very loud. Stairs descended in a graceful sweep into the crowd down there. He leaned on the railing and gazed upon the women who had puzzled Yellowfinger, as they moved among the men at the gambling tables and at the bar.

Above him the stairs continued their spiral to a higher balcony, where a dim light glowed. There was motion just at the periphery of his vision, and an after-image in his eyes of a pale face hanging like a lantern in the dark.

He staggered back to the bed to lie panting and exhausted. In the night he dreamed that he was smothering.

The sun was streaming in the open window and he had finished devouring his breakfast when J. D. Dockerty came in by the rear door, hat in hand. His mustachioed face was seamed with wrinkles. "Morning, Kid!"

"Morning, J. D.!"

Dockerty seated himself beside the bed, hat on his lap now. "Looks like they do all right for you here! Fancy a hospital room as a fellow could ask for!"

"A little too fancy for me."

"When'll you be up and around, do you think?"

"Took a couple of little strolls yesterday. Felt like I'd run up a mountain afterward."

Flora came in just then, and the horsebreaker rose quickly. Dockerty's eye jerked to the table beside the bed, and cords caught in his neck like wires as he stared at the white flower there, bruised petals, two green leaves, thrust of the pistil with its clustered yellow hairs.

In a voice like a rasp, he said, "Where'd that come from?"

The Kid said it had just showed up on the table. "Someone must have put it there in the night." Flora had moved closer to stare at the flower also, a knot of anxiety caught between her eyes.

Without another word Dockerty clapped his hat on his head and hurried out the rear door.

"What got into him?" he asked Flora.

She said she didn't know. The flower perfumed the room with its cloying odor. " 'Faded Blossoms,' " the Kid said, but Flora was not amused.

Three times he made the circuit from the bed to the window, to the door and back to the bed. Flora watched him worriedly. That night he slept like the dead, to waken to Duke growling.

A dim shape loomed between him and the window. There was no sound from the rooms below; it must be very late. The window was dark gray. A little breeze stirred the curtain, and a scent of smoke mixed with the redolence of the bruised blossom. He saw the ember of the cheroot. Duke continued to growl like a locomotive on a grade a long way off.

"Is that you, Henry Plummer?"

He heard a sigh as he sat up in bed to fumble for matches. He lit the lamp. The marshal stood straddle-legged, hands behind his back and cheroot jutting from his jaw, before the window with its billowing curtain.

"Wind's blowing up a little," Henry Plummer said.

"Is there some trouble?"

"That fellow Dockerty is drunk and on a rampage. I'll run him out of town if he doesn't settle down."

"We'll all be leaving soon."

Henry Plummer stared at him. His eyes were red and sunken. "Well, it is funny," he said after a time.

"What is that?"

"Seeing everything coming on as I have always known it would. I have been waiting for you a long time!" He laughed short and sharp. "Tell you what I hate, though. It is going out like it was nothing more than a dog run down in the street."

"It doesn't have to be that way," the Kid said.

Henry Plummer curled his lip, and shook his head. "I have kept the peace here for how many years now. And posted those Putaw fellows from town, and kept them out. But the people in this place would be pleased just fine to see Big Mac come in here with a bunch to lay me out." Again he was silent for a time before he said, "They will come to hate you, too, in your time."

The Kid took a deep breath. "I am not staying here any longer than I have to, Marshal."

"Polite young fellow to your elders, aren't you?" Henry Plummer said. "Well, I will give you one piece of advice. It is pie-easy to keep the peace in a place where every man is afraid of you."

"I am not afraid of you," the Kid said politely. He watched Henry Plummer pace three steps to the right, and turn. "I'm sorry for you," he said.

The marshal crouched as though to jerk his revolvers. His face looked made of wood.

"Sitting here for how long waiting for somebody to come and lay you out," the Kid went on. "Knowing all the time it was you should have gone after Big Mac."

Henry Plummer's teeth appeared at the corner of his mouth, but not in a smile. He straightened, to hook his thumbs in his cartridge belt. "Didn't care to go after them," he said. "None of my jurisdiction what devilment they were getting into over there."

"It is everybody's jurisdiction," the Kid said.

"You are telling me where I went wrong, are you?"

"Sat tight minding your precious jurisdiction, until things have almost gone past you. Almost! We will be moving against Big Mac when I get my strength back. Will you come with us?"

Henry Plummer passed a hand before his eyes as though brushing something sticky away. "Not interested."

"I will ask you one more time."

"Not interested in your side or the other either."

"Just singing sad songs to yourself," the Kid said, and sighed.

The other turned to face the window, smoke from his cheroot carried back into the room. A knife was thrust between the crossed cartridge belts at the small of his back. He stood gazing out the window into the dark.

"Looks like a medicine show out in the square," the Kid said.

"There's a fellow throws knives," the marshal said in a dead voice. "Girl that sings. Not much of a show."

"You have a reputation with a knife, I have heard."

"Yes," Henry Plummer said, and leaned forward to flick his cigar sparking out into the night.

"I have some skill that way myself."

The marshal said nothing, turning after a long time to pace slowly across the room, halting as though he had run into a glass wall at the sight of the browning flower in the little vase Flora had found for it. "Where'd you get that?"

"Somebody left it on the table there last night. Didn't even get a growl out of Duke." Duke growled faintly.

"You took it on yourself to give me some advice," Henry Plummer said in a deep voice. "I'll give you some back. Don't bother yourself about where that flower came from."

"Well, I don't. But everybody else seems to."

Henry Plummer stared at him with his swollen eyes. "I mean, don't go looking."

"Why, Marshal," he said as gently as he could, "I will do just what I have to do, you know that."

Henry Plummer nodded thoughtfully, his face tired, bitter, and dark around the eyes. "Surely," he said. "And so does every man. But you had better tell J. D. Dockerty to straighten up. While you are at it, the blind man had better stop prowling the back halls if he wants to keep his health. And that ugly dwarf is to stop scaring the girls with that boxful of snakes he has got, rattling and hissing." Henry Plummer went on out, a slim figure in black, pulling the door closed behind him.

7

The Kid climbed the stairs that curved upward to the higher balcony. It was the quiet time just before supper, and light was fading in the windows. Below him the faro layouts stood empty. The professor sat at the piano tinkling out a cheerful tune, and a girl dressed like a jockey watched him play. None of the other girls were in evidence, but four men, with whiskey glasses before them, had their heads together at the bar.

Halfway up the stairs he had to halt to rest his legs. When he tapped at the door a woman's voice called to him to enter.

At first glance the room he entered seemed filled with infinite riches. Dull gold frames enclosing muted colors gleamed from the walls, and deep red drapes closed off the window. Glowing lamps with intricate glass chimneys picked out the rich sheen of wood, the curve of vases from whose tops sprang frozen sprays of blossoms, a luster of brass, a divan corner with plump cushions. The scent of incense mingled with that of flowers, and the smoke of a cheroot.

"Rocks and shoals!" a coarse masculine voice said.

A woman was seated in a platform rocker, her face luminously pale, with soft pads of cheeks and smiling lips, a white flower gleaming in her dark hair. Her pale hand carried a cheroot to her lips. Near her, in a brass cage suspended from a chain, a green parrot sidled and peered.

"Right in the middle, now!" the parrot said in a feminine voice, and opened his beak to show a wad of gray tongue.

The woman's eyes glinted out of pools of shadow. He saw that she was no longer young. "I've been waiting such a long time! But I hadn't given up! Are you cold?"

"Legs letting me down. It is some climb!"

She laughed melodiously, rising from her chair, as tall as he and substantial fore and aft. She seemed to slide on tracks across the floor to dispose of her cheroot and take up a glass decanter. Wherever she was she concentrated the light.

"Will you join me in a liqueur?"

He thanked her, no, and watched her pour liquor into a thimble-sized glass.

"Success to your Quest!" she said. Head thrown back, throat on the strain, she drained the glass and set it down. "Now you must tell me how I can help you."

"Well, Henry Plummer is a problem."

She laughed again. The sound pleased him so much he found himself thinking of ways to amuse her. She shook her head and said, "I will see that Henry Plummer does not become a problem. It is all a matter of direction, isn't it? You must have a ring?"

"Watch out for—rocks and shoals!" the parrot said, in a coarse voice.

He unfastened a button of his shirt to produce the ring. The woman took it, turned it, pressed a spring he had never suspected existed; the flat white stone opened on an invisible spring. With the pin of the brooch from her breast she picked at the hole exposed. A bit of fabric appeared. She drew from the ring a pale scarf of such fineness it seemed to float. She offered this to him, and he stretched it between his hands. At first the curious markings on it seemed unintelligible. As the woman laughed and pointed to a particular pattern, the door burst open.

222

He crushed the scarf into a soft button, and crammed it into his pocket, turning to face the man crouched in the lighted opening, with the bright rainbow flicker of the great chandelier behind him.

Henry Plummer straightened. "You had to do it," he said.

"Yes," the Kid said. The parrot paced on his stand, regarding the marshal with one eye and then the other.

"He is not your enemy, Henry," the woman said, still smiling.

"You're not heeled," Henry Plummer said.

"Didn't want trouble."

"Go get yourself heeled."

"I will tell you who your enemy is," the woman said.

"Never mind it, Vinnie."

"It is yourself."

"Let's go, Kid."

Folding his arms so that his posture matched the marshal's, the Kid said, "Henry Plummer, I don't have any patience with this foolishness, or time for games either. I have got a proposition. You favor a knife, and I have told you I have got some skill that way myself. But I will pick the circumstances."

"No, you won't," Henry Plummer said.

"You have picked your jurisdiction, so I will pick the circumstances."

The woman laughed like pigeons in the eaves, and glided a few steps to stand before a pier glass, which held her murky reflection. Plummer glanced sideways at her.

"I don't know what you are talking about," he said harshly.

"Talking about a competition," the Kid said. "You and me, mainly. But there's the sergeant-major that I hear's got a pretty good hand. And that fellow from the medicine show. And probably others'll turn up, maybe even from as far off as the Putaw place."

"Right in the middle, now!" the parrot said. Henry Plummer was shaking his head, his face darkly twisted.

"You must do as he says, Henry," the woman said. She seated herself once more on the platform rocker, which creaked with movement.

"He is not going to lawyer himself out of what he has got himself into," Plummer said.

The Kid flipped his right arm back and forth on the pivot of his elbow, grimacing. "Believe I can throw a knife, all right," he said. He jerked his hand down for his hip, and shook his head. "But I would surely be slow going for my piece. No, *sir*," he said, continuing to shake his head.

"Get out of here now," the marshal said, and he got. Behind him he heard the woman's soft laughter.

8

For several weeks there had been performing in the square a medicine show consisting of a mangy bear pacing pigeon-toed in her cage, a red-faced barker, and a knife-throwing act. A consumptive girl, after singing a sentimental song, arranged herself before a backstop depicting a brick wall, formal gardens, and a distant mansion with porticoes and cupola. She gazed aloft with prayerful eyes while a sweating, squinting young man, billed as "Ned Beauchamp, Artiste de Knife," surrounded her body with a glittering fence of blades. This site was chosen for the competition, and adobe walls throughout the Territory blossomed with announcements: GRAND TERRITORIAL KNIFE TOURNAMENT!

The medicine show's backstop had been painted for the occasion with a bull's-eye concentrically ringed. A system of ropes strung across barrels, marching back from the dais at five-pace intervals, served to separate contestants from spectators.

By the smoky, dusty, rust-colored sunlight of early afternoon, contestants and spectators began gathering in the square. Flags, bunting, skirts, and coattails flapped in gusts of wind that also kicked up little dust devils. Carriages eased in to park along the margins of the square, horsemen secured their animals to the hitching rails, and men and women in Sunday best promenaded along the boardwalks. There was general speculation as to whether or not Big Mac's men would choose this occasion to dare Marshal Henry Plummer's edict posting them from Bright City.

The barker, in his straw boater with its red band, collected five dollars each from the fifteen contestants in the first round, winner take all. Six knives apiece were to be thrown from the ten-pace line, and, for qualification in the second round, three of these must stick within the bull's-eye or the red or blue circle surrounding it. Several of the contestants failed to make a knife stick at all, bowie handles banging against the splintery wood and blades ricocheting off so that the barker was kept jumping. Laughter from the crowd greeted some of the knives that had managed to stick, as they slowly angled down of their own weight and clattered to the dais. There were challenges on these knives that did not fall immediately, and the barker ruled that a knife must stick until the last of a set had been thrown. This resulted in less deliberate throwing.

Successful in passing on to the second round were Henry Plummer; the Kid, pale and thin from his convalescence; a fat cleric in black, with a reverse collar and a gingery beard; Ned Beauchamp, the "Artiste de Knife"; Sergeant-Major Eubanks, with his unorthodox, back-handed manner of throwing; and J. D. Dockerty, with his long, sad mustaches and liquor-darkened face.

By now the crowd had grown to hundreds, men in town suits and women in long dresses and bonnets, many with parasols. There were clusters of whores, halfbreeds with braided hair, town Indians in blankets, miners in their red sashes and heavy boots, and other roughly-dressed laboring men. Attending the blind man was the schoolmarm, wearing a blue bonnet, bending over his shoulder to inform him of the result of a series of throws. Nearby were the dwarf, General Peach, and Dr. Balthazar, who copied scores down on a tablet. Henry Plummer was observed frequently scanning the faces around him.

Bursts of applause greeted the six champions as they came up to the ten-pace line for a second round of throws, although it was a foregone conclusion that the contest must ultimately lie between Henry Plummer and the Kid. There was prolonged and enthusiastic applause for the latter, but only perfunctory handclaps for the former.

The barker announced that in this round five of the six knives must be placed in the bull's-eye or the red circle. Henry Plummer, who had won the draw for the first contestant, approached the rope barrier with his knives arranged up the leather sleeve of his left arm. He hurled them so rapidly that three were in flight at the same time. He centered five in the bull's-eye and had no need to throw his sixth knife. There followed the sergeant-major in his faded uniform. Two of his knives penetrated so close to the edge of the red that the barker made a great show of inspecting and measuring, finally disqualifying one so that Eubanks had to hurl his last knife, which he placed in the bull's-eye to cheers from all around, and bravos from the general. Ned Beauchamp was disqualified for a poor showing, to be comforted by the consumptive girl and ridiculed by the barker. Dockerty was also disqualified at this distance; it was whispered that he was too drunk to see the bull's-eye.

Next came the portly minister, who had a distinctive and very stylish manner. He held each knife poised haft high above his head for a moment, before sending it spinning and glittering toward its target, laughing so good-heartedly when one dropped and fell away that everyone laughed in sympathy with him, and someone shouted that if he could deliver a sermon like he could deliver a bowie the devil had better start running right now. To which the cleric laughed the more, and saluted his flatterer.

Last of all came the Kid, who threw his knives in a casual and almost offhand manner, and, like Henry Plummer, required only five throws to pass this test.

They moved back now to fifteen paces, Henry Plummer, the sergeant-major, the minister, and the Kid, four out of six knives to be placed in the bull's-eye. Eubanks failed at this distance, only three knives hitting, and stumped off discomfited. The Kid required five, one of his falling away, and an anxiety fell over the spectators that the Kid, not fully recovered from his wound, would find his strength lacking as the range increased.

By now it was clear that the good-humored cleric was also a master. Henry Plummer passed this test with just four knives while the minister required five, but his first knife was a questionable edge call, which he refused to dispute, waving the matter off with a flick of his hand to the growing enthusiasm of the crowd.

On the next round the Kid lost two of his knives from insufficient force, but managed to make up the deficiency, while Henry Plummer and the cleric both passed the test triumphantly. Next the three competitors moved back to the twenty-pace rope, where to depressed sighs and a few groans, the Kid failed. He bowed himself out cheerfully enough, slim and boyish and very pale of face, and men and women patted his shoulder and spoke to him comfortingly as he made his way through the press to join the schoolteacher and await the final competition.

There were two antagonists now, the minister with his sweat-streaming, reddish, bearded face and his clerical collar opened askew, and Henry Plummer, dark and deft and expressionless, always as swift with his throws as the other was deliberate. It was clear from the applause which of the two was the popular favorite, but in the betting taking place among the men Henry Plummer had the edge. The two tied at twenty-five paces.

The clergyman laughed and threw up his hands comically as he and his opponent trudged back to thirty paces. His lined face never smiling, Henry Plummer ranged his knives along his sleeve, squinted once, then plucked and threw as swiftly as the eye could follow, three knives spinning through their long arc to pierce the backstop whack-whack-whack, each in the center of the target. Three more followed also centered. The cleric took more time, and his knives were as accurately thrown, except for the next to last, which stood slightly off-center. He laughed his booming laugh as he strode down the aisle to where the barker was inspecting his marksmanship.

On the dais he stripped off his black sack jacket and stood in a loose dickey and voluminous trousers, arms spread before the splintered backstop with its bull's-eye painted over the distant mansion. In his rather high voice he called out, "Let's see what you can do with a *man* for a target, Henry Plummer!"

A mutter ran among the crowd at this disruption of the competition, and Henry Plummer hesitated for so long it seemed he might disdain the challenge. Then he began to range his knives along his leather sleeve, glancing once at the Kid standing with Flora close by the blind man's chair. The minister's ginger beard, beneath his broad grin, bristled in the smoky light.

With more deliberation than had been his wont, Henry Plummer hurled his ten knives to outline the other's body, above and below each hand, below each armpit, on either side of his neck, one above his head, and the last between his legs. The minister rolled his eyes at these last two vibrating blades, and, with a good deal of exaggerated movement, which delighted the spectators, pretended to be tugging his clothing loose from the blades.

"Your turn, Henry Plummer!" he called gaily. He gathered up his own knives, which the barker had collected, and, as the marshal strolled toward the dais, they passed en route, and Henry Plummer gave the clergyman's beard a jerk. It came away in his hand.

"Did you think you could hide behind that?" Henry Plummer said, to a general gasp. Revealed was Big Mac.

Big Mac raised an object to his lips. It was a metal penny whistle, and he blew a blast from it, shrill and long. Into the square in a cloud of dust raced a squadron of black riders, dismounting flourishing rifles and revolvers, to join their master. As Henry Plummer turned to face these, he looked a beaten man. The Kid had disappeared.

"We will continue this!" Big Mac said in his jovial voice. "*Your* turn, marshal!"

A man in a trance, Henry Plummer retreated to the

backstop. Big Mac had approached the twenty-foot rope, where he stood with his half-dozen knives, grinning, the clerical collar skewed out from his throat. The black riders were moving in amongst the crowd, knocking a man aside here, forcing their way through there.

"Assume the position, Henry Plummer!" Big Mac sang out. "And hold fast or I'll miss for certain!" One of the riders, whom Big Mac hailed as Tark, his rifle leveled, mounted the stage to approach the marshal, who now stood with his hands raised shoulder high.

Just then there was a disturbance amongst the spectators: women cried out, men jostled each other, and someone shouted, "The bear! The bear's loose!"

The black bear scampered among the spectators, who dodged, shouting or screaming. Tark took a step forward and brought the rifle to his cheek. He fired twice in rapid succession; instantly the bear lay stretched out dead, brought down in full flight. The shouts changed to a groan of despair. Henry Plummer stood facing his fate with his hands raised. Big Mac held a knife haft up. Then he flung it, the blade glittering in the dusty sunlight.

The knife nailed Henry Plummer's right palm to the backstop. There was a general gasp as the marshal sagged, half fainting. He managed to jerk the blade free. Blood streamed from his hand. Big Mac raised a second knife high.

Just then the Kid reappeared, staggering under the weight of a wooden box reinforced with black iron strips, augered holes in the lid forming the shape of a T. Panting, he set this down on the dais.

"Looks like you won the prize!" he called out, over the hubbub. The black riders trained their guns on him as he stood with hands on hips, gazing up at the flushed face of the outlaw.

"Open it up, Tark!" Big Mac said. Henry Plummer bent over his torn hand.

Tark strode to the wooden box. His rifle gripped under his arm, he tugged at the metal closures. He flung open the iron-bound lid with its T of holes, and screamed. Ten feet from him, the barker also screamed. Those nearby flung themselves back. Tark jerked away from the open chest, dropping his rifle. Earth-colored scarfs seemed to be twisting from his face. Rattlesnakes were hanging there, four, five, six of them, while dozens of others glided out of the box onto the dais. Tark flailed at the thick bodies. Finally he fell to the dais with a crash. The barker fled. Big Mac aimed his knife at the Kid, who ducked into the crowd. In a moment the square had turned into pandemonium, with spectators, black riders, and presently Big Mac himself fleeing on every side. The Kid, very cool, ran to Henry Plummer, and, supporting him and shouting for help, hurried toward the French Palace.

9

From the windows they could occasionally see their besiegers, one or another of the rusty-black-clad men running swift and low to the ground as black cats. The fusillade of firing increased again, like strings of firecrackers set off, slap of lead into wood, shrilling of ricochets, splintering pops of lamp chimneys smashed, and continual brittle toll of the crystal chandelier.

The Kid had had the faro tables tipped on their sides to shield the lower halves of the ground-floor windows. These were padded with mattresses from upstairs. All the girls had fled when the firing began, and now in the great room were the Kid, nearer the door, Frank Pearl, with his rifle stock pressed to his cheek, and, beyond him, Josiah. Seated behind the protection of the piano, Lieutenant Grace loaded cartridge belts and bandoliers with ammunition. These were stacked into a pack-saddle arrangement constructed from a pair of pink silk bloomers fastened to the dog's back. Duke then raced across what they had taken to calling "the shooting gallery," where bullets snapped past, and, yelping with excitement, up the stairs to where the sergeant-major, Dockerty, and Yellowfinger were sniping from the second story. During lulls in the firing, the blind man leaned against the piano, staring at nothing through his black glasses. Beyond him, against the wall, Henry Plummer sat with his hand bandaged and his eyes closed. He seemed to be dozing, or half unconscious, only occasionally raising one knee or the other in his agony.

Dockerty appeared on the landing. "They are building something out there, Kid."

The Kid snatched up several filled cartridge belts and sprinted for the stairs, with the pink-silk-shrouded dog scrambling after him. Yellowfinger pointed out one of the second-story windows. Past the bank corner something was being constructed on the running gear of a wagon. Bales of hay were stacked there, hammering sounded in the lull of firing, and black-clad men dodged purposefully. Dockerty braced his rifle barrel against the window frame, aimed and fired. "Got one!" he said, and jerked on a mustache end as though it was a billiard marker. The sergeant-major was firing from the next window, yellow-chevroned sleeve raised and braced.

"What is it these evil ones do there?" Yellowfinger growled.

"Building a go-devil," the Kid said.

"Likely," Dockerty said, nodding.

"What is this thing?" Yellowfinger asked.

"Rig they can hide behind while they push it close enough."

Yellowfinger scowled cross-eyed. "With fire?"

The Kid nodded.

Dockerty aimed and fired again, this time without success. The riflemen below began firing at a faster clip.

"Hold off!" the Kid said.

Across the square came the whores, mounted, closely packed in their bedraggled gowns. A couple of the black riders rode among them. Some of the girls wore hats, most had tangled and windblown hair, the dresses of several of them were torn so they must cover bare flesh with their arms or swatches of skirt. Fearful white faces turned toward the French Palace.

The sergeant-major chanted curses. Last of all came the general. He was mounted backward in the saddle, maintaining his balance and a modicum of dignity with great difficulty. His hat and tunic were missing. The horse with its derided rider traversed the square, following the company of whores, and disappeared beyond the go-devil.

"*Where is Flora?*" the Kid said hoarsely. There was no reply to his question. He ran downstairs to squat beside the halfbreed.

"Muchoby's in that corral behind Swenson's place," he panted. "Ride for Stonepecker."

With his rifle, crouching, Jos made his way toward the rear of the house. The Kid raced up the stairs again, this time continuing on past the balcony. Behind him the firing increased again.

The bales of hay that had been stacked on the go-devil were moving slowly out from the corner past the bank. Booted feet showed beneath the wheels as the machine executed a slow turn to face the brothel. All fire was now directed at this lurching fortress, and from the clang of metal it was clear that there were iron plates behind the hay. Progress was slow, with frequent rests, but always the go-devil lurched forward again.

The lieutenant continued to load cartridge belts, from time to time raising his head to listen to the volume of the fire. Henry Plummer sat up a little straighter, holding his bandaged hand before him.

The go-devil rolled closer, halted, and proceeded again, finally coming to rest jammed against the boardwalk outside at point-blank range. There was a flicker of flame. Orange fire licked up through the straw toward the dry planking of the boardwalk. Frank Pearl backed away from his window, swabbing at his sweating forehead with a handkerchief. The blind man rose, one hand smashing down on the piano keyboard with a clash of discords. He hooked a hand under Henry Plummer's armpit to hoist him to his feet. "Come on. There are ways out of here that you and I know."

The three from the second story came down the stairs

at a run, Yellowfinger, Dockerty, and the sergeant-major festooned with cartridge belts, Duke yelping furiously. The Kid had reappeared. He carried a metal cage with a green parrot inside. Following him was a woman all in black, gliding down the stairs as though to a reception, a hand sliding along the bannister. She wore a black hat covered with shiny black cherries, a veil shrouding her face.

At the foot of the stairs the Kid set down the parrot cage, whose occupant squawked once, while the woman bent to inspect the floor, moving a few steps this way and that, finally pointing. The sergeant-major shoved aside the heavy lookout stand, and tugged on a handle. A trapdoor rose, uncovering darkness.

The woman lit a candle, and, shielding it with her hand, descended into the passageway. Flames licked in the window.

The lieutenant crossed to the trapdoor, flicking his stick before him, and squatted to enter. Henry Plummer followed him, wooden-faced, his bandaged hand tucked in his left armpit. The others in turn descended into the hole, carrying rifles and cartridge belts, the sergeant-major with a lamp, Dockerty a coil of rope. In the pit darkness beneath them was visible only the tiny glowing spike of the woman's candle.

Last of all the Kid captured the yelping dog and tossed him into the hole. Carrying the parrot cage, he ducked in himself and pulled the trapdoor closed over his head with a hollow clap.

The tunnel in which they found themselves descended at a gentle angle. In the white bath of lamplight, it could be seen that the rock had been smoothly cut by expert craftsmen, long curves of the wall laid up in gray-brown stone with mortar joints no thicker than pencil lines. Other passages intersected, impenetrable to the lamp's rays, some with a cool breath that made the flame of the candle leap. Shadowy figures hurried along, a moving frieze upon the wall. Few words were spoken; there was only the scrape of boots on stone, rattle of the dog's claws, clink of metal, once a muffled squawk from the parrot. There was a halt before a rusty iron grillwork blocking the passage, a locked gate centered in it. The sergeant-major handed the lamp to Dockerty, set his shoulder to the gate, and with one grunt shoved it from its hinges with a shriek of metal.

They heard a patter of rodent feet. Duke raced in pursuit, to return panting. A little further on Dockerty shone his light into a side passage half blocked by rubble, to a multitudinous buzzing. It was a nest of snakes, a hundred it seemed, evil flat heads on their stalks pointing toward the light. Milady made a hoarse sound like a whispered scream, and all carefully skirted the place.

They continued at a slower pace, with Dockerty holding the lamp aloft to illuminate the passage. A sound had swollen to fill the silence, rising in volume like liquid filling a jug, first only a part of the silence but presently felt along the nerves and through the soles of the feet, louder and louder in its vast quiet rush.

"Rocks and shoals!" the parrot squawked.

Another halt was necessary where the passage was blocked by a fall of rock, with water trickling nearby. The party leaned or squatted along the wall while Frank Pearl squeezed in among the fallen rocks. For a time only the soles of his boots could be seen. He backed out, grimly shaking his head. Yellowfinger was holding up a finger.

"Wapto!" he whispered. "Listen! It is the lost river! Very near!" He scrambled in the rubble to scoop water into his mouth. "It is *sweet!*"

The sergeant-major hissed. Voices could be heard echoing behind them in the passage. Rifles were cocked. "The map!" Milady said. The Kid jerked the flimsy scarf from his pocket. Its complex pattern was indeed a map. He spread it on the passage floor and traced its lines, a maze slashed through by the oblique double line of the river. Rising, with a hand up from Dockerty, he boosted himself into the jagged opening from which the rubble had fallen. He disappeared with the candle. A succession of small stones rattling down marked his progress.

"If I can just get this one moved—" he muttered. The voices approaching along the passageway were louder, then all at once a vast sound of rushing water drowned them. "The rope!" the Kid called down.

The rope was tossed to him, and Dockerty swung up into the opening. Next a loop was tied for Milady to brace her feet in, and she was pulled upward, bearing the parrot's cage. Henry Plummer was lifted in the same manner, gripping the rope in his arms that were crossed on his chest. He had not spoken since his wound had been bound by the dwarf.

The others followed, the sergeant-major giving each one a push up, while the dog ran in frantic circles. Last of all Eubanks, Duke wriggling under his arm, was drawn upward, and, with Yellowfinger's and Dockerty's help, slid a broad rock over the hole through which they had passed. All sat panting with exertion and relief on a damp ledge. By the light of his candle the Kid pored over the map marked on the almost transparent scarf.

Held high, the lamp showed an enormous cavern of black rock gleaming with moisture. Held low, nothing but darkness was revealed. The rushing shook the rock they sat on. Dockerty tied an end of rope around his waist, gave the other to the sergeant-major to hold, and clambered down from the ledge, holding the lamp out. At first the spreading light seemed to show only black, slick, tumbled rock. But it was water, sweeping past like black glass in motion. The sound of that terrific motion had already become the sound of silence.

"It is the *Sweetwater*," Dockerty said, in a voice so thick that at first no one understood the word. "The *river!*"

"I can remember when it made the Territory a garden," Milady said. "Then one day it was gone."

"Because of sins of wapto!" Yellowfinger growled.

"It was an earthquake," Dockerty said. "I remember it."

The blind man said, "There is a saying that faith moves mountains."

"Let's just not have anybody's faith moving this

235

mountain while we're in it," Frank Pearl said. He had lighted a cigar, and he blew a cloud of smoke. "Am I right?"

The sergeant-major climbed down to grip the Kid's belt while the Kid stretched out with the light. The far bank came into momentary view, a gravelly slope turning black again.

"Somebody'll have to get across with the rope," the Kid said.

Yellowfinger crossed his arms on his chest and appeared to stare at the end of his nose. Dockerty chewed on a mustache tip. The sergeant-major cleared his throat: "Anybody here a swimmer?"

Lieutenant Grace rose. While he stripped the clothes from his bone-thin, milk-pale body, the Kid found more secure footing at the water's edge. Dockerty clambered down to help him and Sergeant-Major Eubanks hold the end of the rope. Milady stood gazing down on the scene below her.

"In the middle, now!" the parrot said. Duke patrolled the ledge, whining, as the blind man was assisted to the rocks below.

He sat with legs dangling into the water while an end of the rope was made fast around his waist. The lamplight illuminated the ugly centipede of a scar at the hairline of his forehead, and made deep shadows in his eye sockets. He slipped into the water.

The Kid, Dockerty, and the sergeant-major braced themselves as he was borne downstream, Yellowfinger kneeling on the ledge above them with a hand shading his eyes from the lamp's rays. Lieutenant Grace could be seen fighting to keep his head above the waves, making progress across the current. He disappeared into the darkness. The jerk on the rope, when it came, almost hurled the Kid into the river, but the other two held firm. There was a slackening, another tension, another slackening, followed by two tugs of a signal. A skeletal figure appeared in the gloom of the opposite bank, cupping a hand to his mouth to shout something lost in the roar of the water.

The curve of the rope cut the waves in a taut bow. The dwarf was taking off his clothes, his cigar propped jauntily between his teeth.

"Lightest goes first!"

Yellowfinger handed him down to Dockerty, a belt was buckled around the rope, and he was instructed to hold on to this. His clothing was strapped into a bundle for his back. With a gasp at the cold he slid into the stream. Quickly he was carried halfway across, the belt sliding on the rope, but there the rope sagged downstream under his weight. On the far shore the blind man braced his legs and leaned on the rope, and Frank Pearl coasted on across. There was a shout of triumph.

Milady set down the lamp while she disrobed, piling her petticoats beside her, her loosened black hair sliding over shadowy, abundant flesh. She rode Dockerty's back across, holding the lamp, while the Kid laid a bight of rope around a rock to take the strain. On the far shore she disappeared into the shadows, to reappear fully clothed, with hat and veil in place.

While the crossing was completed—Henry Plummer, his face taut with humiliation and pain, rigged upon the sergeant-major's broad back; Yellowfinger with the parrot cage and a brace of rifles; the Kid pulling Duke through the current—Dockerty and Frank Pearl explored with the lamp back from the stretch of gravelly beach. There was another shout as an opening was discovered, high on the sheer rock wall, and all gathered beneath it. Eubanks braced his hands against the rock, beckoning to the Kid, who climbed onto his shoulders in his stocking feet. His outstretched hands still fell short.

"Good thing there's a little fellow around," Frank Pearl said, and swarmed up the sergeant-major and the kid as though they were a palm tree. He boosted himself from the Kid's shoulders into the hole, where he squatted grinning down. Dockerty tossed him a rope end, and the others were helped up the wall, one by one. On the far side was a drop even deeper, and the rope had to be shifted from side to side, for there was room for only two at a time in the hole. The blind man stood with his ear against the rock wall, which vibrated like a diaphragm with the force of the river behind it.

"How thick is it here?" he asked.

"Sounds like about an inch," Dockerty said.

"Let's get out of here before she lets go," Frank Pearl said, and with Yellowfinger holding the lamp they started on along a sandy, widening passage.

"Back on track," the Kid observed with satisfaction, and indeed they were passing along a masonry wall again.

"Spanish, huh?" Frank Pearl said.

"Dutch," Henry Plummer said. There was a silence. Dockerty began to laugh. "The Lost Dutchman!"

They descended at a shallow angle along the masonry wall, which made a broad curve to the right. The ceiling reappeared in the lamp's illumination, virgin rock dropping close overhead. Stone columns supported it, and cross walls were revealed, forming long galleries. The distant rush of the river was barely audible now, but it could be felt like a faint quaking of the earth.

"Jumping H. Johnson!" Frank Pearl said. "We have *found* it!"

Yellowfinger halted, holding the lamp high. Behind him, the Kid set down the parrot's cage. The transverse walls formed storerooms, rows of them extending away into darkness. Wooden walls had collapsed into dust, but stationed at intervals were stone coffins glinting with vermilion paint. The side of one of these had crumbled to reveal a mummified body, blackened buckskins, eagle feathers like birds' nests. Beyond these, chests of rotting wood and rusted iron were stacked, hundreds it seemed, in each of the repositories. Several had collapsed to spill glittering contents. The war chief stepped close to the crumbled coffin.

"See the Twelve Faultless Ones in their caskets!" he said. "It is the treasure of the People!"

"Shame the doc isn't here to see this," Frank Pearl said hoarsely. He ran on his short legs to fall on his knees before one of the broken chests, scoop up gold coins, and pour them over his head.

"Beware, Short-One!" Yellowfinger said. "You will offend the spirits with your avarice!"

"Get back from there, Frank!" the Kid called. The dwarf rose and retreated, sheepishly brushing coins from his shoulders.

"We have beat Big Mac to it," Dockerty said.

"There is a curse on it," Milady said, hand to her throat.

The sergeant-major cried, "Watch out there!"

The rattle was audible over the distant rush of the river. The long brown body with its pale rattle vibrating sprawled in curves across the floor. With a snarl Duke flung himself upon the snake. He caught it by the throat, shook it, shook it again. They hurried away from the scene, leaving the dog growling behind them. The glittering coins, the stacked chests, the stone caskets with their mummies faded from the swaying circle of light. Behind there was another growl and scraping as Duke pounced on another rattlesnake. As they hastened on, the lamp's light began to fade, the tongue of flame shrinking, flickering up once, then gone. Again they heard Duke in action. Milady sobbed with terror.

"No more light here, waptoes!" Yellowfinger said, and flung the lamp from him with a splintering crash. A sigh of exasperation escaped Frank Pearl. The darkness had weight.

"Who's got the candle?" the Kid asked.

"Save the candle," Lieutenant Grace said. "I can lead you."

They formed a line along the rope, the lieutenant taking the lead. They could hear the tapping of his stick ahead. Once more Duke growled. Grasping the rope, sometimes touching the stonework wall on their right, they followed their blind leader. There was no longer any sense of ascending or descending, of turning right or left, or of the duration of time either, so that the slow hours seemed to pass in a moment, although their steps lagged in weariness and more frequently Milady called for a rest. Once when she had halted wilting against the wall, there was a scraping sound ahead, and the rope jerked, then went slack.

The blind man's voice came from below them. "Careful. There's a hole here."

A match flickered, a candle flame swelled, dancing in a cool breeze that blew into their faces. Dockerty held the candle over a hole, where the lieutenant's shadowed face could be seen. He was surrounded by stacks of wooden boxes. The sergeant-major scrambled down to join him.

"It's a kind of dynamite locker down here!"

"Air's moving," Dockerty said, shielding his candle flame.

Eubanks began stacking the boxes to form a stair. The current of air flowed sweet and strong into their faces as they stepped down the cases, which had black printing and red devils stenciled on them. The Kid set down the parrot's cage, and assisted Milady's descent.

The dynamite locker opened onto a tunnel where they all halted to breathe deep of the fresh air. This passage was supported by heavy wooden timbering; there was no stonework. The blind man's face was tense and pale in the candlelight as he asked for a knife. He prized the lid from one of the boxes, and turned back heavy waxed paper to reveal the red dynamite sticks connected by their gray fuses like firecrackers. He drew some of these from the paper and hung them around his neck.

He said, "I will be leaving you here."

The Kid gazed at him in dismay. Others swung around toward him.

"A while back I said there used to be faith that could move mountains," Lieutenant Grace said. "Well, as a green young officer coming out West I did believe a way could be found to bring the waters back to the Territory.

"Once I was told something I didn't understand," he went on. As he spoke his fingers continued to free the heavy paper tubes, twisting the fuses together and hanging the dynamite sticks around his neck, where they formed a stiff red wreath. "That it was the destiny of the blind to free the waters." He managed a laugh. "So you see your efforts in my behalf were bound to be fruitless, Frank. Though I thank you for them."

"I just think we had the wrong brand of diamondback, was all," the dwarf growled.

"Wait, now!" the Kid said. "Maybe we can figure some other way—"

"No one else could find his way back there," the lieutenant said proudly. "Even with that map. Even with eyes! No, there is no other way."

"No!" Milady whispered.

"Those durn rattlers," Dockerty said.

Smiling, the lieutenant adjusted his wreath of red dynamite sticks. "I believe I have imbibed enough viper gall to be well immunized."

"Well, I knew we were all bound to get called on sooner or later," the Kid said.

"May each of you find your call as perfectly suited as mine," the blind man said, and began shaking hands all around.

"Good luck, there, Lieutenant," the sergeant-major said gruffly.

The Kid thought to drop a box of matches into the blind man's pocket, while Lieutenant Grace gently disengaged himself from the sobbing Milady. Flicking his stick he mounted the stair of dynamite boxes, shrugging his shoulders to settle his load. He disappeared into the darkness above. For a while longer they could hear the tap and scrape of his stick.

In silence the remainder of the party started on, falling in behind Dockerty with the candle. Frank Pearl had found a miner's cap with a stub of candle hanging on a nail in the dynamite locker, and he brought up the rear with this illumination. Ahead of him Henry Plummer plodded along, wounded hand clasped in his armpit, head down. Yellowfinger began singing a lament that rose at intervals to a kind of yip. This caused Duke to whine in sympathy, and the parrot to call out, "Right in the middle, now!"

With a crumbling crash, the entire right-hand wall of the ancient tunnel disappeared in a smoke of dust. The sergeant-major, Yellowfinger, and Dockerty, who were in the lead, vanished in a rattling, sliding fall that diminished to silence. Far below, the sound began again, and ceased again. The open side of the tunnel now revealed, through clearing dust, a distant glitter of stars like specks of ice. Nearer and lower hung a rotten half moon. Thousands of feet below were scattered tiny lights and, far off, a glow of banked fires.

The Kid shouted down the precipice that had opened at their feet. In answer came another whisper of sliding earth. The dwarf's candle flickered, then burned steadily.

"Three poor fellows snuffed out like you'd snap your fingers," Frank Pearl said in an awed voice, crouching to peer into the abyss. Henry Plummer, who had been next in line, leaned weakly against the remaining wall, while Milady stood as if turned to stone.

A ledge of floor still held, and the Kid, with the coiled rope over his shoulder, edged across this to the far side of the bottomless hole. He tossed back an end of rope, which the dwarf held while Henry Plummer and Milady passed to safety. Frank Pearl sidled across with the parrot's cage. The dog yipped and danced until the Kid whistled, whereupon he raced sure-footed to the other side, where the tunnel began again.

Below, the tiny red lights of the plain seemed as distant as the frigid stars. The moon tipped with gold the peaks of the Bucksaws. Dawn was close. From the far side of the hole that had swallowed their companions, more lights were visible, nearer ones.

"Putaw Crossing, am I right?" Frank Pearl said. "Big Mac's palace ought to be right on top of us."

Wearily they trudged on, until they encountered steps hacked out of stone that rose to an iron-bound door. Just beyond this turning, the main passage was blocked by a fall of rock and splintered cribbing.

With the miner's candle the dwarf explored the tumbled rock. He squeezed between a V of timbers and disappeared. His voice came back: "Sure helps to be a little fellow sometimes." He reappeared, and handed the candle to the Kid. "I can get through. Sunshine up ahead, too."

"Sure be a help if Stonepecker and his bunch got headed out this way," the Kid said to him. "The map takes the rest of us up those steps there."

Pearl saluted the Kid, Milady, and Henry Plummer, crawled into the hole, and vanished. His voice came back again: "Depend on Frank Pearl!"

The Kid climbed the steps to the heavy door and tried to shake it. It stood as solid as the walls. He bent to hold the candle flame close to the keyhole. Then he drew his revolver.

"Try this first," the woman said, and produced a heavy iron key. The Kid inserted this in the lock and tried to turn it. The lock was frozen with rust. He grasped the key with both hands and strained, to no effect, until Henry Plummer added the strength of his left hand to the Kid's. Reluctantly the key turned, the tumblers released, the door creaked open.

10

Hands bound to the pommel, she galloped with her escort along the edge of the teeming plain, following their furious leader with his buckskin fringes streaming, and the brim of his hat blown back against the crown. Close around her were ten men with intent, grime-ingrained, gargoyle faces, black-clad gunmen with a sense of terrible urgency about them as they quirted their animals to keep pace with Big Mac on his black stallion. Far behind, leading a long drift of dust, was the main body of riders. She was certain from the outlaw chief's fury that the Kid had escaped.

Her escort strung out on the road that curved along the base of stony hills past the diggings. The great cloud crouched on the horizon, illuminated by the glow of many fires, and there was a seasoning of dust and smoke in the air, like smoldering ashes. In the middle distance were men on horseback, men with mules and scrapers, wagon-loads of earth lurching toward the dumps, and the copper gleam of muddy ponds. Cumbersome contraptions crawled listing here and there.

She was fainting with exhaustion trying to keep her balance on her jolting-gaited horse, thighs rubbed raw trying to grip, when Putaw Crossing came into view, the ugly butte rearing above it lichened with the profiles of build-ings and topped by the carbuncle of the Castle. Big Mac glanced back at her, his face covered by a dusty bandana so that it appeared animal-snouted. The other riders had also pulled bandanas over their noses in facsimile of their leader. Their hat brims seemed to slant at the same angle, their quirts to flash in unison. None seemed to speak unless absolutely necessary, as though each knew his fellows' minds perfectly. Despite herself, she moaned in fear.

They passed heaps of broken earth and stones, and the gaping holes between. In some of these laborers were visi-ble tossing up shovelfuls of earth that hung in the air be-fore falling on the piles. Some of these sprays of earth rose from invisible sources, the holes were so deep. Here more of the black riders were congregated, riding between the hummocks of earth and the holes, one standing in his stir-rups to swing his whip.

On panting, lathered animals they skirted the cactus-covered dry hills, past one of the machines with its clank-ing buckets revolving like a treadmill. Across the plain more of these crawled, belching smoke that rose to blot out mountains and sky. Nearer now was the dark hill. The windows of the structure at the top winked in the little morning sun that came through the smoke. It must be their destination—Big Mac's stronghold.

In their cocoon of dust, far behind their leader now, on panting horses with no longer a pretense of even a trot, whips slashed to maintain a walk even, they came to a road juncture, where there was a little bridge and weathered buildings with wooden awnings above the boardwalks. They turned over the bridge and uphill, to fall into a double file through a narrowing way where the second stories of the buildings hung over from either side. Between two of these Big Mac sat motionless on the black, his bandana pulled down to reveal his red ugly face.

Up the rutted track they mounted, the hundred rising columns of smoke seeming to lean over them, congealing like thick black liquid defying gravity to flow upward into the filthy atmosphere.

Winding upward under vacant balconies and shuttered windows, they passed a dump, where tin cans, bottles, ripped mattresses, and broken furniture were scattered in astonishing quantity, the sweet-sour stink of garbage stronger for a time than the bitter redolence of smoke and sewer. Papers were plastered against bedsteads, broken chairs, dry branches, bloated dead animals, spirals of rusted wire fencing: all the vast and mean clutter of the talus extending down to merge with the ruin of the plain.

Into view came the stone walls of the Castle, skinny staring windows and slate-roofed cupola towering beyond a yard cluttered with junk and refuse centered on an abandoned fountain like a cement tulip. Past this was a broad veranda.

They halted. Men dismounted to untie her with their hard fingers. Exhausted legs almost betrayed her. Hands like pliers gripped her, mean, narrow faces were thrust at her. Big Mac strode up to catch hold of her arm as the others backed away from him. They stood waiting before the steps for the main body to come up, and, as soon as they were in sight, Big Mac jerked her around, up the steps, and across the veranda's creaking planks.

His grip forced her forward. Other hands thrust the doors aside. Inside was a kind of ballroom, stairs sweeping to a balcony, and up to a higher landing. Windows threw down parallelograms of rusty sunlight, and a six-armed chandelier glittered with diamond rays. The higher walls were paneled, those below papered in red plush sporting foulard designs. The floor gleamed with wax, and mirrors reflected light and dark from behind a monumental bar. The place looked newly-finished, veneered, plated, shined, decorated. A black piano, its player invisible behind a raised lid, struck up a bouncing tune as she entered. Before the bar was a dais, two steps up with a tail of red carpet leading to them. A curved green trellis stood there, enclosing a space broad enough to hold two people. Paper leaves and flowers had been plastered over the structure.

Again they waited, on the bit of carpet, facing the queer garden arch. The black riders of the advance guard filed inside, hard faces and reddened eyes examining her where she stood with their chief. A big, sandy-haired man forged through the rest, holding a circlet of imitation red blossoms. Another bore in his arms a red robe lined with white fur. Big Mac took the coronet and placed it firmly on her head.

"Get your robe on," he said, grimacing at her to show yellow teeth. His breath was a pestilence.

Just then a sound caused all eyes to jerk toward the door, the brassy notes of a bugle swelling and strangely turning into a prolonged whistle, so penetrating she saw some men flinch and slap at their ears.

"Hurry it up, hurry it up!" Big Mac bellowed in his shrill voice. "No time for any more botches now!"

The sounds had galvanized him into haste. He relinquished her arm to the sandy-haired man, barged off through his men and lumbered up the stairs, to disappear through red curtains on the first balcony. Two men carried in a heavy box from which a third took candles, placing them in holders and lighting them. Flames swelled and floated with a smell of wax.

Behind the bar, mirrors winked with the little flames. The second contingent of riders drifted inside, herding the exhausted, terrified women from the French Palace. These were stationed off to her right as some kind of attendants.

The sandy-haired man thrust the robe at her. "Hurry up and get your bridey duds on, little lady," he said.

11

Dockerty thought he must be dead. He had fallen end-
lessly through blackness shimmering with lights, struck
on his back on a soft slope, rolled and tumbled loose-
limbed as a rag doll, to fall again through plain air with a
yelp of fright that didn't even seem to have come from his
own throat, to bounce with a shock that knocked all the
wind out of him, and to slide again. Finally he had come to
rest with his face pressed into the loose dirt. It had seemed
to him that since he must be dead, maybe buried, he
might as well get some sleep.

When he wakened the sun was just up. Smoke and
dust were rising to obscure the Bucksaws. Before his eyes
was a brown blade of grass with a drop of dew shining on
it. As he inched his aching body forward, nothing seemed
broken. With great care, eyes crossing with the effort, he
licked the drop of dew from the grass.

There was a stink of garbage. He turned on his side to
gaze out over a swamp of refuse, rusted cans, broken beds,
mattresses with horsehair bleeding out, planks, bricks,
springs, empty boxes, bottles gleaming in the sun, a broken shovel handle standing upright, a buggy wheel with
missing spokes, a section of picket fence with papers plastered against it, rusted pipes. To his right was the cliff
from which this refuse had been thrown. Above it he recognized Helix Hill, with its buildings profiled as they
mounted the back side. The Castle was invisible from
here.

He rolled on his back. Above him a dozen vertical ra-
vines slanted toward where he lay. The sun made his eyes
water. He heard a grunt.

Yellowfinger squatted on his heels nearby, his buckskins torn and abraded with dirt, shaven head shining. A
ferocious scowl was centered on his mashed nose. He nodded to Dockerty.

"Where's everybody else?"

Yellowfinger jerked a thumb and Dockerty sat up. On
the far side of the dump the sergeant-major poked through

the trash. He straightened, holding up something that shone brassily.

"Nobody else?"

Yellowfinger shook his head. He had taken a snarl of rawhide thongs from a pouch in his buckskins and sorted through them. Dockerty managed to rise, and stood swatting the dirt from his shirt and trousers. There was not much left of one trouser leg, and his cartridge belt and revolver were missing. His boots were packed full of dirt and he sat down again to empty them. There was a broken-off horn call. It must have been a bugle the sergeant-major had found; he was beckoning.

The footing was treacherous as he and Yellowfinger toiled across the dump. Yellowfinger caught the nub of his nose between thumb and forefinger, expressively.

"Bad smell."

"Bad."

"Wapto too many thing!" Yellowfinger said.

"Appears so," Dockerty said. The tangle of refuse extended away to join the ruined plain below. "That is one hell of a mess they are making down there, too."

"Great Spirit not forgive wapto," Yellowfinger growled.

Dockerty could still taste that sweet drop of dew on his tongue, and he tried a tentative whistle. It came out pretty well. The war chief looked at him curiously with his black button eyes. Eubanks was gesturing with his hand holding the bugle.

"Coming as fast as we can!" Dockerty called to him. "The Kid and them didn't get dropped, then?" he said to Yellowfinger.

The Kimanche shook his head. His moccasin was stuck in a bedspring and he grumbled and muttered, hitting at the rusted coils with a little carved stick he had produced from somewhere.

"Look at this!" the sergeant-major said happily, holding up the dented, green-tarnished bugle, still with a bit of red cord hanging from it. "I swear it's mine! My old bugle. What in hell's it doing here, I'd like to know?" He swiped at his sweating face with his shirt sleeve. Yellowfinger seated himself to strip off his buckskin trousers and knot the rawhide thongs around his calves.

"Waiting for you to find it, that's what, friend," Dockerty said. "You remember how to blow on it?"

"Huh!" Eubanks wet his lips. "I can blow a 'Boots and Saddles' that'll bring every trooper in earshot running, lessen he's tied down."

Yellowfinger wound the thongs around his legs, and jerked them tight.

"They'll come if they got one speck of trooper left in them, and I never knew a solger sunk so low he didn't!"

Both of them stood watching the war chief tightening the thongs over his limbs and body until his flesh looked like chocolate quilting. Then they made their way together across the dump, cursing at the difficulty of the way, stumbling. The sergeant-major gripped his bugle like a long-lost sweetheart. Yellowfinger had a hatchet and scalping knife tucked in his breech clout, and carried the little stick.

Where the dump narrowed into a ravine, Dockerty said, "Hold up a minute. I don't like walking."

He put his fingers to his damp lips and gave a low-grade whistle, which caused Eubanks and Yellowfinger to grimace.

Within minutes a spotted mare appeared. Dockerty stroked her velvet nose and murmured reminiscences and endearments. Soon three more horses came over the ridge, then five or six in a clump. One of these was a magnificent stallion with a saddle on. Yellowfinger vaulted into the saddle, crying out, "Hoo-hey!"

The sergeant-major chose for himself a cavalry gray, with a saddle and scabbarded rifle. He mounted and sat with a ramrod back and the bell of his bugle braced against his thigh.

Two black riders hurtled into view, shouting and waving their hats. Dockerty jerked the rifle from the sergeant-major's scabbard and shot one out of his saddle. The other disappeared. Dockerty mounted a mare named Betsy.

With difficulty the three of them made their way through the continuing current of horses coming over the ridge from Putaw Crossing. These now began to mill in order to follow behind them. The rutted winding street that climbed to Helix Castle was deserted except for two dogs tearing down it at a dead run, a big black hound chasing an ugly spotted dog running flat out in terror, tongue lolling and ears blown back.

Dockerty scratched his chin and said, "That one sure did look like the Kid's mutt, didn't it?" A clatter of hoofs approached.

Riding hell for leather, quirt slashing, a small man on a big horse bore down on them so fast they had to rein back away. It was a boy on the horse, Dockerty realized, a shock of bright red hair and a frantic freckled face with an open O of a mouth, shouting at the sight of them. The boy produced a revolver and fanned off five shots in all directions, hurling the empty revolver at Yellowfinger as he galloped on.

"Hoo-*hey!*" Yellowfinger cried. *"That* one!"* With a whoop he urged his stallion after the boy. The two of them disappeared from view, reappearing through gaps in the buildings, Yellowfinger bent low over the neck of his stallion. The two dogs were also visible, very small now.

Dockerty and the sergeant-major rode on down between the close-set buildings at a more leisurely pace. When they came to the crossroads and the bridge, out on the plain they could see the two racing horsemen, with a cloud of dust rising behind them. Dockerty pointed to a stony hill nearby.

"You might get some steam up from that rise over there," he said. The sergeant-major swung his gray, close curbed, to trot toward it.

Grinning as though his lips would split, Dockerty watched his friend climb the hill, and, profiled there against the dragon cloud, raise his bugle to his lips. The sun struck sparks from it.

The first notes sounded, loud enough. He let them

soar clear and true for a moment before he stuck his fingers between his lips and, with a deep breath, blew such a whistle as he had never blown before.

12

When the door swung inward the Kid, Milady, and Henry Plummer found themselves again in a musty darkness, which the bright blade of the candle flame seemed scarcely to touch. Spider webs brushed their faces. Many doorways led off the dark main passage, each with its lintel of a single beam of rock. At least one of these had been blocked by a cave-in. The Kid spread out the scarf with its map on the stone floor, and the three bent over it, Milady with her veil drawn back, pale planes of faces gathering the light and eye sockets the darkness. The Kid traced a route with his forefinger. "See, that's where we came through just now—"

"Now we're on that corkscrew there?" Henry Plummer asked.

Milady leaned back with a sigh. "We must turn to the right soon."

A hundred feet further along the passageway a narrow, low-linteled doorway seemed to be the route. Duke kept close to the Kid's legs, almost tripping him, as the Kid, holding the candle out before him, revealed stone steps curving to the left. Carrying the parrot's cage, he started up these, the others following. Soon the steps changed to wood, their footfalls resounding and the candle flame flickering in drafts of air. Once the dog whined and scratched the wall.

At last the Kid halted, crouching, to set the cage down on a step. Above his head the flame revealed a trapdoor of heavy planks strapped with iron. He set his shoulder against this, and, grunting with effort, budged it slightly. Henry Plummer joined him; together they raised the trap six inches, only to let it fall again. The woman added her strength, the Kid counting, "One, two, *three!*" They threw the trapdoor up with one great heave. There was a complicated crash as it toppled open, and a scream.

The Kid leaped up into a room filled with sunlight so brilliant he was blinded. Henry Plummer joined him. The dog was snarling. Facing them in the painful light was a woman in a black gown, a black mask on her face with a fringe that trembled on pale cheeks. She held a cocked shotgun trained on the Kid's belly.

"Shut up, Duke," the Kid said, raising his hands. The walls of the room formed an octagon of windows that surveyed the plain with its towers of smoke rising to join the great cloud that obscured the mountains. This must be the cupola of Big Mac's palace, with steep roofs slanting away on every side. Mirrors, oleos, photographs, and framed embroidered mottoes decorated the spaces between the windows. An easel with a picture had toppled with the trapdoor to lie sprawled, pointing toward a closed door that filled one of the interstices.

Milady mounted into the cupola and stood with her hands at her sides, gazing at the masked woman, who shifted the muzzles of her weapon from one to another nervously. White teeth were revealed between blood-red lips.

She shifted the angle of her shotgun barrels, training them on Milady, the Kid, and Henry Plummer in turn. The dog lay belly down, growling faintly.

"Give me the map!" she said through clenched teeth. "*I want that map!*" Her finger whitened on the trigger.

Just then from the open trapdoor came a coarse, masculine voice: "Watch out for—rocks and shoals!"

The masked woman gasped. She aimed the shotgun at Henry Plummer, whose hands were raised shoulder high, the right one with finger protruding from the soiled bandage.

"Tell him to come out of there with his hands up!" she panted. She sidled toward the door, where she had a closer vantage of the hole in the floor.

The cupola door burst open and slammed into her. The

shotgun roared harmlessly in an invisible smash of glass. A whirlwind with a mop of red hair raced into the room, with him a great black hound, who was instantly locked with Duke in a snarling, yelping fury. The red-headed boy stabbed his long knife blade into the Kid's belly with a shout of triumph, ducked under Henry Plummer's arm, and leaped into the trapdoor hole. The tangle of roaring dogs fell in behind him, where they could be heard noisily descending.

Behind the open cupola door there was a sliding, screaming scrambling on the steep roof, and a despairing cry.

Milady and Henry Plummer stood frozen staring at the Kid, who was bent over with his hands to his belly. He straightened, working the tip of the knife loose from his belt, where it had been embedded. He blew out his breath with force. Henry Plummer took the knife from him with his good hand. The tinkling notes of a piano could be heard, coming up the stairwell, the melody strengthening into a slow march. Milady stepped past them to close the door. Behind it the glass and mullions were burst out. She stared down the steep slant of the slate roof with a hand to her throat.

"Duke!" the Kid called down the trapdoor opening, to no response. From below there was a shuffling of feet, and coughing, audible over the piano chords, as though a congregation was assembling there. The Kid turned to face the door.

He jerked it open, and in a swelling of music stepped out on the high landing. Stairs curved downward past a chandelier sparking with reflected sunlight from the clerestory windows, and hundreds of candles set upon every horizontal space two floors below. The candles flickered luridly, and there was a musty stink of soot and sweat. The room was half-filled with a dark company of men, and a dozen women huddled together at one side. They faced a girl who stood on a dais before a kind of garden arch decorated with leaves and flowers. She wore a crown of red blossoms, a red domino, a red robe faced with white fur.

Her face was as white as the fur of her gown, and it was Flora.

The Kid skipped a step back, loosening his lariat from his belt. He tossed the loop to catch an arm of the chandelier with a brittle smash of glass petals, hurried a slipknot into the other end of the rope, fitted a boot into the smaller loop, and flung himself from the balcony, paying out rope. The chandelier swung and creaked with his weight. He glided over the ducking heads of the black riders crowded around the dais, the piano ceasing its music in a crash of discords. Flora's pale face turned up toward him, her arm held by a tall sandy-haired man, who switched his neck around to gape upward. The Kid flew over them like a furious bird, lowering himself with his slipknot, the men shouting as he passed over. He kicked off the far wall and swung back, knocking down a quartet of candles, and driving a boot into the face of the sandy-haired man. He plucked up Flora, and, with her, swung back to the stairs. They came to rest on the lower landing, where he waved her on up the steps. In an instant he had kicked loose one of the balusters.

He swung this around his head, bellowing, "Come on! Come up and take your medicine!"

The black gang swarmed up toward him and he hurled himself to meet them, swinging his club. Surely, Henry Plummer thought, holding the knife that had failed even to wound the Kid, the youngster moved with more speed than mortal man was capable of. The baluster flashed like white lightning, smash of wood on bone, screams, shouted curses, the black tide retreating before his charge. The Kid disappeared inside it, but the chaos of his progress was clear. Men scattered before him, and fought to get out the door.

Someone shouted from outside, "The *horses*—gone!"

The last of the black mob shoved their way out, a half dozen remaining sprawled or huddled on the floor. The Kid stopped to bash one crawling after the others, then, revolver in one hand and the baluster in the other, stepped into the doorway.

Flora had halted halfway up the second flight. She turned her face up to Henry Plummer, where he leaned on the rail above her. *"Henry!"*

He saw the rifle barrel poking out between the red folds of the curtains on the balcony. Big Mac, in pure white buckskins, eased out behind the rifle. His hair was slicked down; there was a flower in his lapel. The buckskin fringes rippled like wind on water as he raised the rifle to his cheek, aimed at the Kid's back, framed in the doorway.

Henry Plummer stripped the dirty bandage from his torn hand, flipped the knife once to test its balance, and called, *"Mac!"*

The rifle muzzle swung up toward him, red whiskered face clamped to the stock, one eye squinting, teeth bared. As Plummer flung the knife, smoke spurted from the muzzle. He was slammed back against the wall. Staggering forward to grip the rail again, he saw the buckskin bulk lurching back. Big Mac pulled down one of the red curtains as he fell. "Got you!" Henry Plummer whispered.

He let himself slip to his knees. How easy it was then to slide on down and onto his side. So this was how it was to be. Always he had thought he would be shot down by some young fellow come to the Territory with courage honed to a bright edge, and an ambition like a locomotive, but Heaven had kept a surprise for him. It was queer there was no pain, only a slow dreaminess, and angel faces bending over him, one dark, one fair. They whispered his name.

The Kid raced up the steps and ducked past the curtain. Big Mac was not in sight. The rifle lay on the floor with a small bouquet of roses, a knife, a still-smoldering cigar, a tangle of red curtain, a puddle of blood. He slipped into a small room, on the far side of which a door stood open on darkness, creaking still. In the room was a narrow cot and a high shelf from which ten or a dozen seated dolls gazed down. Near the far door was another streak of blood, as from someone moving swiftly. He halted before the black opening.

"Berry!" a voice shouted behind him. Jimmy Tenponies burst into the room in his shirt sleeves and striped vest.

"Jimmy!"

"Don't you go in there!" Jimmy snatched up a chair, and advanced, thrusting it ahead of him into the doorway. A shotgun blast tore the chair legs into splinters. Jimmy tossed the remnant of the chair into the opening.

"I'm going after him," the Kid said.

Jimmy Tenponies blocked his way. "No knowing how many other deadfalls he's set!"

The Kid turned, sprinted out of the room and up the steps, past the two women kneeling beside Henry Plummer. He burst into the cupola, and flung himself through the trapdoor and down into darkness.

Some minutes later the palace heaved and shook, the glass leaves of the chandelier setting up a melodious tinkling, window glass rattling, a shutter slamming.

"It is an earthquake!" Flora cried, looking into Milady's grieving face, where she knelt on the other side of Henry Plummer's body. Distantly came the dull boom of an explosion.

"No, that is not what it was," Milady said sadly.

More than half the black riders rushed on foot down the hill in pursuit of the horses, which had apparently spooked and burst free of their harness. Thirty or forty men remained in the area before the veranda, where there were piles of rusty junk and the spokes of cluttered, whitewashed-boulder-bordered paths led to the hub of a concrete fountain, whose murky waters were drowned in sodden trash. Revolvers drawn, they faced the doorway from which the Kid had disappeared.

"It's a trick!" one blustered. "Watch out for him!"

"Where's the big fellow, I'd like to know?"

"Went upstairs somewheres!"

"Where's Red?"

"Laid out!"

Suddenly two mounted Kimanche hurtled around the side of the palace, and drew up facing them. Revolvers shifted around. The warriors were bound all over with tight thongs cutting into their dark flesh. The tails of their gaudy ponies had been braided. They brandished hatchets.

"*Hueycoha!*" a man shrilled in panic.

"Stand steady!" another yelled, as two more hueycoha appeared, then half a dozen more, the pack of them jammed together, horses rearing, feathers blowing. For a frozen moment the two groups faced each other in a stand-off, the first hueycoha pointing to certain ones among Big Mac's men like housewives picking out apples and peaches in a fruit stall.

Then the ground convulsed beneath them. The windows of the palace rattled furiously. Men and horses staggered, the Kimanche mounts rearing in fright, a few of Big Mac's gang squalling hysterically as loose slates clattered down on them from the roof. A trio suddenly broke and sprinted for the street that led down into the town. Others followed, one tripping to fall flat, his comrades racing around him as he struggled to his feet. Immediately all were in flight, pale blobs of faces peering back. The hueycoha called out, "Hoo *hey!*" and urged their ponies in pursuit.

At that moment Stonepecker's main force thundered onto the hilltop, the troops of warriors armed with feather shields and repeating rifles. Bodies gleamed with oil and vermilion paint. The minor chiefs were arrayed in full hundred-feather headdresses, the ancient high chief in his stovepipe hat. He pointed ahead with a coup stick like a marshal's baton. Accompanying the Kimanche were Dr. Bathazar, like some tall, white-crested bird on his Indian pony; Josiah mounted on Muchoby; and Frank Pearl with his short legs thrust straight out from his saddle.

On the blasted plain the vast horse herd was visible, bent into a long, interrogatory curve following a single mounted man. Elsewhere, a fast-moving dot was pursued by a larger one, in whose wake bounded some still larger animal.

With Josiah's help, the frail old chief dismounted and toiled up the steps to the veranda. In a solemn, deep voice he called out, "*See!* The sweet river comes again!"

"Holy Jumping H. Johnson!" Frank Pearl said in awe, and a gasp and sigh like a rustle of wind rose from the warrior host, for the Sweetwater had indeed been freed from her long bondage, a bore of water like fifty burst water mains arcing out of the mountainside.

Facing his warriors in their crowded ranks, their bodies gleaming and feathers fluttering, Stonepecker raised his coup stick high and cried out, "Zigosti! Dah-koo-gah! Dju-klinney! *Tze-go!*"

The Bright City women had edged fearfully out onto the veranda, pointing and exclaiming at the leap of water and the rainbow clouds rising from it, and at the motionless figure of the Kimanche chieftain. Their bright gowns were in disarray, their hair windblown and dusty. They began to tend to one another, arranging, brushing and primping. There were giggles and side glances as Dr. Balthazar brought a table from inside, and sat at it to write in his journal.

Also from inside appeared a Chinese cook in a stained white apron and engineer's cap, his queue dangling behind. With him was a young girl of his race in a smock and black bloomers, her pretty Oriental features marred by severely crossed eyes. Bounding out behind them came the young Indian butler, calling to Frank Pearl, "Flora says you must come! Henry Plummer is bad hurt!"

As Frank Pearl hurried inside on his short legs, Jimmy Tenponies halted, almost vibrating, as he stared first at the outpouring of water, then at Stonepecker declaiming to the Kimanche.

There were exclamations of alarm from the French Palace women as the chief shouted, "Dah-tze-*choby!*" and the warriors were galvanized into motion. Horses rearing, rifles brandished, they let out a great whoop and swept down the hill in pursuit of the black legion.

Head down, Jimmy Tenponies approached Stone-pecker, who turned to clasp him to his breast, murmuring, "My son!"

On the plain the water was swelling into a clear lake, and rushing along its old course, threatening the first of the machines crouched like leeches on the bends and sandy ox-bows. Stonepecker stood with an arm around Jimmy Tenponies' shoulders, his face raised heavenward in thanks to the Great Spirit.

Sergeant-Major Eubanks gathered his little troop behind a low ridge that ran out beyond the slurry pits within carbine range of the bridge and Putaw Crossing. His dozen, considerably fewer than he had bragged he could call up, lay watching Big Mac's men scurrying down between the adobe buildings and tarpaper shacks of the Crossing. It was clear they were running from something.

With Eubanks was a pair of sergeants who had enlisted with the outlaws, but, sniffing the wind, had come at a run at his bugle call, and ten muckers from the digs, nine privates and a corporal. Among the lot of them they had two carbines and three handguns. He'd set the corporal to guarding the picket line of cavalry remounts from Dockerty's remuda.

"They are all afoot, Sergeant-Major!" one of the privates sang out.

"Every man jack," he said with satisfaction.

"Where is the Big Fellow, I wonder?" another said.

"I just wish he would show up in that white suit. I'm laid in to knock some spots in it."

The men stretched out beside him on the ridge laughed nervously, not yet convinced that Big Mac had run out his string. The muckers all had filthy faces, layers of dust on mud on top of plain dirt. The two sergeants had goggles pushed up on their foreheads, and their eye sockets looked pale and queer.

A muffled long thump shook the ground beneath them. It was a second before Eubanks realized what it was. The first of the Big Mac's men boot-clattered across the bridge just as the side of the mountain exploded. Water spewed in a giant arc, flashing in the sun, and smashing down on the pulver mill directly below. His troop yelled at each other, "What was that?" "What happened?" "Looks like the ammo dump blew up!" "The side of the mountain just—*gone!*" "Look at the *water!*" Sergeant-Major Eubanks touched the brim of his cap in salute.

More of Big Mac's fellows streamed over the bridge, running in panic. There were horses up the hill behind them; he could see their movement among the buildings, and paint and feathers—Kimanche! There were some to say that Injun was the finest light cavalry in the world, and if there was anything that played straight to cavalry it was infantry on the run. Eubanks told the skinny sergeant to take a couple of men and relieve some of those skedaddlers of the weapons weighting them down, find out what was going on while he was about it.

He squinted at the fine gleam of water in the sun; not often you had a view of a river flowing through air like that. The black bunch had pulled themselves together to form a defensive line, hunching down behind earthworks that had been thrown up by the diggers. The sergeant's detail had sneaked around toward the bridge, to surprise a straggle of blackies busting through there.

The sergeant brought back enough rifles and sidearms to outfit everybody; he had the makings of a soldier to him. "They say there's a thousand Injun up there," he panted. "Hacking and scalping the slow ones."

"What else did these fast ones say?"

"Bunch more of them up in some canyon. These're going to join them, make a stand there."

Eubanks wiped off the mouthpiece of his bugle and blew a "Boots and Saddles," not loud, just serviceable. The troop hurried to mount up. Armed and aboard horse they looked a good bit more like soldiers.

He told them, "The Injun chasing this lot is our friends. Anybody that takes a shot at one I'll fricassee his heart for supper. We are going to work this bunch together, hear?"

They heard. It didn't matter if they understood what it was all about, just so they obeyed orders.

"Look at *that!*" one of the privates said. Injun had arrived at the bridge, about a hundred of them, vermilion paint on paint ponies, eagle feathers, tossing manes. They drew up there, milling a bit at the first rifle shots.

Eubanks raised his fist for the advance, gave the skinny sergeant a long squint, and started out. He didn't look back right away to see if anybody was following him, just giving a little right rein so as to check out of the corner of his eye. The two sergeants were coming along, and a couple of privates, the corporal; they *all* fell into line. He spurred from a walk to a good trot, heading for the rear of the forted-up bunch, see if they'd run. Trained soldiers could stand against a rear assault sometimes, but he would bet these ones wouldn't hold two minutes.

The general had found time to stop off at the fort and don full dress uniform before proceeding to Helix Hill. Descending from his cavalry gray, hale and straight-backed he stamped up the steps and encountered his old friend and antagonist, Stonepecker, to engage in a formal program of nods and smiles, raised hands, hands clasped to chests, shaken hands, before he strolled along the railing, halting to beam at the spectacle of mounted soldiers and Indians pursuing men afoot.

A dozen riders from Bright City had also arrived to join the fight, grim-faced and heavily armed. Two of these dallied after the others had ridden on, standing with their arms around the waists of the French Palace girls. They pointed out aspects of the action on the plain, where it was clear they were not needed, and cheered the flood lapping around the nearest of the digging machines.

There was a hush and people gathered silently as Henry Plummer was borne outside on a litter by the cook and Jimmy Tenponies, with Frank Pearl trotting alongside. The marshal was propped up so he could witness the scene below. He stank of the dwarf's embrocations, and he was pale as wax from loss of blood. Whenever he turned away from his patient, Dr. Pearl's face was grimly worried.

Milady came to stand beside Henry Plummer, her hand on his shoulder and his bandaged hand weakly rising to rest on hers.

"Where is the Kid?" he whispered.

"He went after Big Mac." She tapped a warning with her fingers as Flora joined them. The girl had removed her robe and coronet of blossoms, and now was dressed in her schoolmarm black skirt and soiled white blouse.

"The air is clearing! See!" she said, and indeed, as the combers flooded out over the plain, the dark cloud that had been the bane of the Territory for so long had begun to disperse, thinning and torn into patches by cool winds. The sun had lost its copper glare. It was though the land, which had been parched and poisoned, smothering in grime and smoke, could be seen springing green.

There was rejoicing as water swamped the first of the ugly machines, and surged toward the second. Clusters of tiny figures were shifting and dispersing like the cloud that shadowed them. From time to time, faintly, a bugle call sounded, and the sergeant-major's little troop charged anew. The hueycoha were in dreadful action also, and now the main body of Stonepecker's Kimanche could be seen, fanning out on the plain, star-shaped on their galloping ponies. The horse herd with its leader had disappeared from view.

Frank Pearl turned from his half-conscious patient to ask advice of the cook, and McQueue snapped at his niece to run inside for his bundle of medicines. Milady worriedly answered the questions of the French Palace girls. Yellow-finger appeared, with his creased limbs and gleaming shaven head, to tether his stallion and seat himself on the steps. He unknotted his war thongs with sighs of relief, and flourished his string of scalps for Stonepecker's congratulations. Then he strode along the veranda, the women fluttering away from him with exclamations of disgust, to haggle with Frank Pearl over one of the bloody trophies.

"See the birds!" Flora cried, for the first ragged Vs of birds were winging in over the lake, where none but turkey buzzards had flown for so long.

The Kid had never had much trouble finding his way in the dark; good eyes from plenty of fresh farm provender and reading late by candlelight. He was on the reverse track of the map, clambering up the stacked boxes of the dynamite locker into the long corridor with its stone walls cold to the touch and slick with damp. Up ahead was a brightening haze of sunlight, where the side of the passage had fallen away, to toss Dockerty, Yellowfinger, and the sergeant-major down the mountainside. He edged past the place, squinting in the glare. Another streak of blood on a stone indicated that Big Mac was still ahead.

He was trotting in darkness again when the mountain shook as though it had been jostled by a giant hand. A blast of sound boomed down the passageway, strong enough to send him staggering. He turned to run as another and different roar began building.

The water caught him like an express train, sending him gasping and tumbling down the passageway in the direction from which he had come, jamming him straight ahead like a bullet in a gunbarrel. The intolerable roaring in his ears was the whole yell of the Sweetwater trying to break out of the mountain. When he had to breathe, couldn't *not*, there seemed to be some air around him in the whirling surge. Big Mac must be shooting along this way at about the same rate.

Then there was liquid brightness and he was sailing through space, nothing for it now but to be smashed to smithers on the rocks below. He tried to roll into a ball, maybe bounce when he hit—He slammed to earth so hard all the bright turned to darkness, but still there was that sensation once again of being pulled from the water by something grunting with effort, and with sharp teeth.

Dockerty's mare plodded up the hill from the plain below the town, a prisoner apparently seated behind his

263

saddle. When he dismounted to help the bedraggled fellow down, Milady cried out in joyful recognition, for it was Lieutenant Grace. The blind man, with a sure step, mounted to the veranda, arms outstretched to the embraces of unexpected reunion. Even Henry Plummer, eyes closed, made a half gesture of greeting, smiling faintly.

The general remained staring out at the river, arms folded on his chest. "River's on fire," he commented, just as the chief cried in his deep voice, "The great river *burns!*"

There was a chorus of exclamations. Flames licked up from the rushing waters, and sailed in airy orange clumps along with the current. One had collided with the stern of the second land dredge, which was almost submerged now, and darker, denser flames climbed the superstructure. A lace of smoke drifted over the river.

"What is it, Doc?" Frank Pearl cried.

"The boilers of the dredge have exploded," Balthazar said, looking up from his writing. "Igniting the petroleum ether from the slurry pits."

"It is strangely beautiful, " Milady said, and shivered. "But it looks very dangerous!"

Just then the dog Duke appeared, moving slowly, to flop down at Flora's feet with an exhausted grunt. Bending to rub his ears, she whispered, *"Where is your master?"*

The Kid came to his senses lying spread-eagled with the sun full in his face and the water roar still filling his head. He sat up, to cry out, "Oh! *My!*" The Sweetwater cascaded like braided diamonds, out of the mountainside, and water lapped at the incline upon which he lay. The pulver mill had been flattened, and one of the dredges turned over on its side, only a patch of darkened wood showing between the waves. A second one, half a mile further along, was already surrounded, water up over the deck and threatening the bucket boom that slanted out ahead like the bowsprit of a ship.

There was a sharper roar as the first dredge blew up, in a hump of white water. Timbers rose and seemed to hang in the air before they lazily fell. With popping sounds, clumps of flame leaped up around the falling timbers, each with a little crown of greasy smoke. Some of these flame patches were the size of bushel baskets, but others grew, and combined, until they were as large as Concord coaches, all sailing downstream with their tints of orange and yellow, and licking, climbing motion. They sped past the Kid's perch like fairy ships, so pleasing to the eye that he cried out in pleasure. One jammed against the second dredge, and flames climbed and spread forward.

Between the flame boats he saw a slash of white trailing from the bucket boom of the burning dredge, a black ball bobbing beneath it. He scrambled to his feet as a white mass surged out of the water. A fat man hung from the chain, one leg kicking up and falling back, kicking and falling back. The third time a foothold was gained, and Big Mac pulled himself up onto the boom of the burning dredge. Surf already broke over the dangling buckets.

The Kid skipped down to the water's edge and back again. A fleet of fiery boats floated past, then none for a space. Far off he could hear shots, a volley and some singles spaced out, but he couldn't see much of anything from where he was, except for the half dozen dredges that looked like big toys adzed out of hardwood, all with their bucket booms heading in the same direction. The river whooped down the channel, drowning the mess of gravel piles along the way.

Lumber floated past him from the smash of the pulver mill and the exploding dredge, and he pulled ashore a big timber that was untidily snared to another with a tangle of watersoaked rope. His knife in its scabbard was still nestled into the small of his back, and he cut the timbers free and then lashed them tight together into a kind of raft. He salvaged a flat board for an oar. Another fire fleet raced past.

Big Mac had clambered up on the boom, thick white legs braced apart, waving one arm; maybe he was waving for help. The waves lashed up at his legs like teeth, and the whole superstructure of the dredge was blazing.

Straddling the timbers of his little craft, the Kid set out paddling in the next interval betwen the flaming patches. "Rivers of fire!" he yelled, to keep himself company. The current spun him along, too fast, toward the dredge where Big Mac couldn't last much longer. A barrel of fire floated along with him. When he slashed at it with the paddle it broke into bits. He splashed water on one of these that lit on his trouser leg.

He glanced up to see a flight of birds slanting over him, and there, on a height of land, the bear stood watching him, head tilted alertly, front paws dangling. He freed a hand from his paddle for a second to wave.

He sped toward where Big Mac teetered on the high end of the boom. Big Mac was bellowing over the bellow of water, though the Kid couldn't make out a word; what he was doing with his arm was shaking a fist. His soaked hair was fringed down around his head, and his white buckskins were draggled and dripping.

The Kid dodged another fire boat and banged up against the chain that dipped below the boom, about as close to Big Mac as he wanted to come. Big Mac stared down at him goggle-eyed. The rag tied around his right hand was stained pink.

He beckoned Big Mac to climb aboard his raft. The other retreated a step instead. He couldn't do that again, end of the line; he tottered there with nothing to hold on to. The Kid had to busy himself slashing another clump of fire apart, like killing snakes.

"Come on!" he yelled. He took a loop of the soaked rope around the chain, which let him free both hands. Now he could feel the heat of the dredge timbers burning.

In a kind of staggering convulsion Big Mac pulled the blacksnake whip from the sleeve of his shirt, swung his arm back and started it forward. But the Kid had been here before. He jerked his knife free and slashed it toward the whip, which parted neatly with his stroke. Big Mac bowed and buckled, trying to regain his balance; then he toppled into the teeth of the river, which seemed to rise to accept him. His head popped up once, face swinging toward the Kid. It looked as though he was grinning in victory, red gums and yellow teeth strained open. Then the stuffed-bobcat snarl was gone, and his head with its plastered-down black hair gone, and just the bloody-bandaged hand held up in a fist; then that gone too.

When the Kid cut himself loose from the chain, his craft was caught in the same current that had swept Big Mac away. Astride his timbers, digging hard with his oar, he eased out of the river rush. A clump of fire bore down on him, and he was too tired even to try to whack at it. It swept by him with a hot breath in his face. He coasted into calmer water, his toes touched bottom, and the timber ends pushed up onto dry ground. He dismounted and staggered up the bank, to fling himself down, panting as though his lungs would burst.

At first glance it looked like a bear on horseback, with two led animals trailing, a man swaddled in a fur garment despite the warmth of the day, and a wool hat pulled down to his ears. It was Livereating Smith riding around the corner of the palace and picking his way toward the veranda.

The spectators there fell silent, the old chief folding his arms and drawing himself up tall. Yellowfinger and Jimmy Tenponies stepped quickly to his side, the three Kimanche staring with a vibrating intensity as the mountain man's animals plodded past where they stood. The general raised a hand in a greeting Smith ignored. Dockerty and Josiah moved closer to the railing as the French Palace girls ceased their chatter, and retreated.

The Livereater's feral eyes glanced at each face in turn. With a jerk of his reins he drew up close by where Henry Plummer lay on his litter, attended by Frank Pearl, Milady and Flora. Flora straightened quickly, with one backward step. The dwarf chewed worriedly on the butt of an unlit cigar.

"Loadim onere," the Livereater said, with a flip of his hand toward the pack animals.

"No!" Milady whispered. Behind her Mr. McQueue held up a palm as though to prevent his niece from seeing the mountain man. Dr. Balthazar had risen from his writing table, a little wind riffling his white hair.

"I guess it is last resorts, then," Frank Pearl said. "Am I right, Doc?"

"Loadim onere!" the Livereater repeated.

"Bring rope," Josiah said to the cook, who disappeared inside, pulling the girl after him. The women also retreated as Livereating Smith swung down from his horse.

"It is his only chance," Lieutenant Grace said, laying a hand on Milady's arm. Mr. McQueue reappeared with a hank of rope, which he tossed to Josiah. A flight of birds passed over, low, with piping cries. Henry Plummer's eyelids trembled, but did not open.

Dockerty and Josiah carefully lifted the litter, and, with Frank Pearl helping to steady it, bore it down the steps, Dockerty backing and holding his end high.

"Just go easy here, fellows!" the dwarf said.

The stink of the Livereater's badly tanned bear hide mingled with that of Frank Pearl's gunshot medication as the four of them made the ends of the litter fast to the pack frames of the two animals, which had been lined up head to tail. Frank Pearl scowlingly examined the lashings, and Dr. Balthazar joined them to help rig a cloth sunshade, stretched over the marshal's face on a curve of rusty wire.

The Livereater laboriously remounted. He squinted at the general and muttered something unintelligible.

"Yes, we will be grateful for anything you can do, Smithy!" Peach said, who seemed to have understood.

The three Kimanche had not moved a muscle since the Livereater's arrival. Now their eyes turned to watch him swing his little procession away over the whitewashed boulders that marked the converging paths, between the piles of refuse. Milady was sobbing quietly, Flora with an arm around her trying to comfort her. Dr. Balthazar had reseated himself and was scribbling.

One of the whores cried out in dismay as the Livereater raised his wool hat in a farewell salute. There was no sound but his harsh laughter as he disappeared around the corner, bearing Henry Plummer back to his cave in the mountains.

The Kid lay on his back watching another flight of birds pass over, high up. He heard a clop of hoofs coming toward him, over the rush of waters. He gazed up at a horse's legs, gray barrel of body, cinch, stirrups, a man's boots. He collected himself to stagger to his feet and confront the sergeant-major, in his torn and grimed uniform and tipped-forward cap.

"I guess that's the end of him," Eubanks said, when the Kid had told him what had happened.

"Looked like it."

Eubanks extended a hand. "Come on up, Kid. A lot of folks been worrying about you."

He skinned up behind the saddle. "If I could've just talked turkey with him," he said.

The sergeant-major clucked to the big cavalry gray, turning away from the river.

"You can't talk turkey to a fellow like that, Kid," he said.

L'Envoi

It was me accompanied the newlyweds out of the Territory, them in the buggy and me on the fancy horse. To my mind a horse like that is a fine thing in certain circumstances, but on a regular basis I will take a livery-stable hack or a mule even, which does not require a bunch of fancy feeding and grooming, and you don't have to get out of your bedroll to throw a blanket over him on a chilly night. Not only was it no treat riding the Kid's horse, but it was not a pure blessing either being along with new-marrieds, for when the Kid was not holding her hand, she was holding his, with a considerable amount of giggling, and of "Sweethearts" and "Miss Pets", which is what they had taken to calling each other.

In fair time we left the Territory behind, with its snowy mountains and waterfalls glistening in the sun. The Kid claimed to have spotted the bear watching us from a crag, but I didn't see her myself. There are more bears than the one to be seen in the mountains if you look sharp, and there is such a thing as looking too sharp, too. The buggy, with me riding drag, rolled through fields where domestic stock grazed, and fresh-cut hay was stacked. Duke trotted in the shadow of the buggy. That is one spoiled, useless mutt, if anybody asks my opinion.

I heard Flora say, "Oh, Berry, everything would be perfect if only Henry will recover!"

I said that Doc Balthazar had claimed the Livereater would nurse him back to health, and the doc was right about seventy-eight percent of the time.

"At least he won't be feeding on rattlesnake glands," the Kid said, with a grin at me.

"Well, I won't speculate on how Henry Plummer is enjoying his victuals," I said. "But I believe the lieutenant would've been a sight better off if he'd kept after those glands."

The Kid shot me a complicated look, and hooked his arm around Flora's waist. They fell to hugging and whispering. Three years of fire and thirty of ashes, that is marriage for you.

"Will you be content, Miss Pet, to be just a fellow's wife?" the Kid asked. "After all the excitement?"

"If you will be content to be just a girl's husband."

They fell silent, no doubt thinking of the dangers they had passed, and Big Mac drowned in the river. The Kid took some blame on himself there, saying that if he'd had his lariat he might've got Big Mac out of that fix, as he had done with Jimmy Tenponies once. "For what?" I asked him. There wasn't a jail built that would hold Big Mac, and it would've all been just to do over again.

Of course the Kid said, "You can't let a man drown when it is in you to help him, Frank!" Of course the Kid, being the Kid, has got to think that way, which is why he needs sidekicks like me by him, so he don't snare himself up in his own rightfulness.

And I had to think of him becoming just a girl's husband, and what I figured out then was that a nonpareil like the Kid must have his own Big Mac to pile up against and show his worth, or else he is no more than just a husband, and a farmer or pharmacist or shoeclerk, or whatever it is a man does in his life for what is called a living.

We topped a rise. The old town was spread out over across the valley. It had grown a good bit, as towns will do since you saw them last. New houses were set cheek by jowl fronting on raw new streets that had been brushed out up the hill, and Flora pulled her duster tighter around her as she pointed out what must be a factory, a low gray building with a tall stack leaking a wisp of smoke, that climbed to spread in a thin layer higher in the sky.

The Kid sat up straight, and I felt a queer little chill myself, like sometimes when you come into a patch of cooler air, as we started down into the valley on the road that stretched straight as a string to the far side.